THAT
# Churchill Woman

**BALLANTINE BOOKS**

**NEW YORK**

THAT

# Churchill Woman

*A Novel*

**STEPHANIE BARRON**

Copyright © 2019 by Francine Mathews

All rights reserved.

Published in the United States by Ballantine Books, an imprint of Random House, a division of Penguin Random House LLC, New York.

BALLANTINE and the HOUSE colophon are registered trademarks of Penguin Random House LLC.

Grateful acknowledgment is made to Curtis Brown, London on behalf of The Master, Fellows and Scholars of Churchill College, Cambridge for permission to reprint 403 words from the Churchill College archive consisting of 276 words from the writings of Lord Randolph Churchill and 127 words from the writings of Robson Roose, copyright © Master, Fellows and Scholars of Churchill College, Cambridge. Reproduced with permission of Curtis Brown, London on behalf of the Master, Fellows and Scholars of Churchill College, Cambridge.

LIBRARY OF CONGRESS CATALOGING-IN-PUBLICATION DATA
Names: Barron, Stephanie, author.
Title: That churchill woman: a novel / Stephanie Barron.
Description: New York: Ballantine Books, 2019.
Identifiers: LCCN 2018038263 | ISBN 9781524799564 (hardback) |
ISBN 9781524799571 (Ebook)
Subjects: | BISAC: FICTION / Historical. | FICTION / Biographical. |
FICTION / Contemporary Women.
Classification: LCC PS3563.A8357 T48 2019 | DDC 813/.54—dc23
LC record available at https://lccn.loc.gov/2018038263

Printed in the United States of America on acid-free paper

randomhousebooks.com

24689753

Title-page and part-title images: © iStockphoto.com

*Book design by Dana Leigh Blanchette*

*Dedicated to the memory of*
*Gwendolyn Ashbaugh Mooney,*
*who did so much with her one wild and precious life*

THAT
# Churchill Woman

# PROLOGUE

## July 2, 1921

Sunlight streamed like wings through the chapel's clerestory windows. Margot Asquith raised her face to the feathered radiance. For all it belonged to the House of Commons, St. Margaret's was a feminine church. Lifting the black veil of the ceiling, the cream-colored pillars were as girlish as a debutante's arms. It was the perfect place for weddings—indeed, Winston had chosen to be married here, and his mother had stunned them all that morning years ago, looking as rare and precious as a Russian icon in a frock of antique gold satin.

Strange how flat the chapel seemed today without her.

Margot waited for a flash of movement somewhere near the rafters, the echo of a throaty laugh. Jennie always hated to miss a party, particularly one in her honor. But not even Mozart's Requiem could summon her today. When the treble choristers' voices died away, Margot stepped out with the rest of the mourners into the heat of the London afternoon. There was no casket to follow, no rose to cast into a grave. That would all be done privately by the family at Blenheim.

The light on the street was colorless, the humidity dense. Cabs would be impossible to hail in such a crush. People would linger on the paving stones, flutter gloved fingers at Margot, demand her opinion of sudden death. *Tripping down the stairs in Italian high heels! Far too old for such a thing. Naturally she fractured her ankle. And then the hemorrhage . . .*

Margot turned her back and strode away from them all. There

would be cabs near London Bridge. She would dine at her club and then meet her stepdaughter at King's Cross for the night train to Aberdeen. Suddenly, there was nothing she longed for more than the cold Scottish wind off the North Sea.

"Good turnout?" Violet asked.

The attendant had brought cocoa to their sleeper carriage. They were seated at opposite ends of the lower berth—accorded to Margot by age and precedence. Mother and stepdaughter wore silk wrappers. They swayed rhythmically with the train. Margot had braided her gray hair in a single plait, and Violet's bob was pinned up in black net. They held their cups delicately at the level of their breasts. Blowing on the boiling stuff. Cocoa in July. But Margot would never sleep tonight without it.

"Easily four or five hundred people," she answered.

"And gawkers pressed against the railings. Watching the nobs do their duty by *Lady Randy*." Violet set down her cup with delicate violence. "That's some solace at least—no more sickening black-bordered columns about how brilliant and good and sincere Jennie was, the brightest ornament of a vanished age. *Such* tosh. The woman was nothing but a high-class tart."

Margot's cup paused halfway to her lips. "Unnecessarily harsh, my dear. Not to mention vulgar."

Violet snorted. "Jennie was never remotely faithful to her husband."

"No," Margot agreed. "But she was immensely *loyal* to him. The older I get, the more I believe it's loyalty that counts. I suppose that's something you modern girls wouldn't understand."

"Our parents' hypocrisy? No, Mummie, I'm happy to say we don't comprehend it in the slightest." Violet's nose, too long and broad for real beauty, twitched in contempt. "The war changed all that. Men and women deal frankly with each other now. If the marriage doesn't work—get out of it. That's where honor lies."

"Divorce was thought *dis*honorable in my day."

"Because you were too afraid to challenge Society!"

"No, no, my dear. That's where you're wrong. Jennie challenged Society just by breathing. She wasn't one of us, remember. The American bride. How we envied her freedom——"

"To sleep with anybody who asked?"

"You make her seem so *sordid*. And Jennie was never that! The *very last* thing!"

"We needn't quarrel over the bones," Violet said impatiently. "This is all down to your bloody class consciousness. If Jennie were a fishwife in the East End, you'd call her a tart and be done. But you can't bear to have a *lady* thought cheap, can you?"

For an instant, Margot doubted herself. Was she merely a snob? Or was there something more important her stepdaughter ought to understand?

"Jennie was a friend of mine," she attempted. "And more important to you, I should have thought, Winston's mother."

"She'd much rather have been taken for his sister!"

"She very often was."

Violet was still close to Winston; almost too close, Margot thought. Still in love with him, despite both their marriages. Still determined to defend him against all comers. A week after his wedding, desperately unhappy, Violet had tried to dash herself off a Scottish cliff.

"Don't you *see*," Margot demanded, "that Winston would never be *Winston* without Jennie? The way she snapped her fingers at convention, Violet! And her wit! We all queued at Hatchards when she published her memoirs, you know—and not just for the racy bits. Jennie was *clever*. They say she wrote Randy's best speeches for him."

"Cleverness is no substitute for love," Violet retorted. "Jennie barely spared Winston a thought when he was a boy. Only when he was old enough to be *interesting*—to worship her as she liked— did she bother to take him up. Poor chap might have been raised by wolves."

"That was as much Randolph's fault," Margot protested. "One almost suspected he *disliked* Winston."

"It was Jennie's job to bring them together. Instead, she packed Win off to school at the age of six! But I suppose it suited her to have him out of the way. More time for her *men,* Mummie."

"Nonsense! We all reared our young exactly the same way. You don't understand how it was, Violet, before the Vote and women's colleges and having one's own clubs. So much emphasis on *birth* and *dress,* all of us martyrs to our husbands' careers. Particularly in public life. Entertaining callers every day of the week—and hosting endless dinners. Sitting in the Ladies' Gallery at Commons until the middle of the night. In *bustles,* Violet! We sent you children off to the nursery because we had no choice. And much better you were for it, too."

"How would you possibly know?" Violet rose and gathered the cups. Her wide mouth had turned down bitterly at the corners. "Anyway—I didn't think *you'd* spout such stuff, Mummie. You never *really* admired Jennie. All these fine words of friendship are due to her being *dead.* You weren't always her champion. I remember you saying to Papa once, when I was small, 'If Lady Randolph had been like her face, she could have governed the world.'"

"Oh, my dear," Margot said faintly, and sank back against her pillow. "*Did* I say that? How brutal of me. I must have been jealous. I think I resented her supreme social ease. And your father admired her immensely, you know."

"Papa was a martyr to a pair of pretty eyes." Thus did Violet dismiss former Prime Minister Asquith. "You know Jennie had no more principle than a mercenary or Gypsy. Cross her palm with silver, and she'd promise you the earth."

"She kept her promises. If you had known her in her prime, Violet—she had the face of a Valkyrie. A commanding sort of beauty, with a frightening power."

"And nothing behind it, really, but selfishness."

"Perhaps," Margot agreed. "But what I liked most, if you must know, was Jennie's *restraint*."

Her stepdaughter laughed. "You can't be serious!"

"She could have ruled the world, as I said," Margot insisted, "if she had been half as *ruthless* as her beauty."

"Mummie—"

"With a face like hers, Jennie could have trampled all over the people who loved her. Including her son. But she didn't. Unlike many women with her power—unlike *you*, darling—Jennie was *kind*. She understood pain and how to endure it. That's why other women adored her. Even when she stole their men."

"Am I unkind?" Violet shrilled. "Or merely *honest*?"

"A great deal of hurt has been done in the name of honesty," Margot said gently. "And now, if you please, I would like to turn out the light."

The cocoa failed to do its job. Margot did not sleep. Violet never stirred in the berth above her; she was unmoved by doubt. It was Margot who mourned. Was she hopelessly out of date? Was Violet right to dismiss them all? Had they been an entire generation of useless women?

Jennie was a contradiction and a puzzle—but weren't most complex people? At least she had been true to herself, Margot thought. Wasn't there an enviable freedom in that?

Violet wouldn't agree, of course. Scarred by the Great War, her generation considered their parents shallow. But Jennie had known tragedy. She had suffered loss. Chosen it, time and again, over simple happiness, in fact. How had she managed her grief? Gotten out of bed each morning to charm the world? Kept her secrets safe? Margot had no idea. But without a Jennie Churchill, would a Violet Asquith ever have been possible?

Margot's berth swayed. Images flickered through her mind. Jennie on horseback at Sandringham. Arguing politics with Ar-

thur Balfour, in the dining room at Connaught Place. Chopin un-
reeling from her disciplined fingers. Leaning forward in the
Speaker's Gallery, her gaze fixed on Randolph as he rose to speak.

Jennie spiraling through a ballroom with Kinsky.

God, *Kinsky*.

He was the only one, Margot thought, who'd ever really known
her.

*Tell me, Count,* Margot demanded. *Was it worth all the love and
anguish? Give me the answers, for myself as much as Violet.*

Where would Kinsky come down, on the value of Jennie's life?

Was Lady Randolph Churchill, née Jennie Jerome of New
York, one of the world's most brilliant creatures—or merely frivo-
lous?

Tragic—or indomitable?

An inspired mother, or an indifferent one?

A creature of genius and purpose, or a butterfly who squan-
dered her talent?

Courageous? Unique? Or nothing more than a follower?

An equal of the men she seduced?

Or . . . simply a whore?

Margot lay sleepless in her swaying berth. The answers mattered as much to her peace as they might to history. While the train
shunted north and her memories unreeled, she urgently sifted the
evidence.

*Singapore, 1894*

*She found the Malay tattoo artist with his ivory and steel knives, his ink
intended to brand the skin, set up under an awning near the entrance to
the docks. She watched him, fascinated, as he bent over the arm of a
British sailor. But it was impolite to stare, even here, on the far side of
the world. She walked on. She had so little time for exercise.*

*Late that afternoon, the Malay met her gaze unsmilingly as she strolled past, returning to the ship. He was alone now, his customers drinking in the sailors' bars. There was no one to see her if she stepped into his tent.*

*Was it an affront to such a man, for a woman to ask for his art?*

*Impulsively, she held out her left forearm. "How much?"*

*He shook his head. "The lady will swoon."*

*"I have borne two children. I will not swoon."*

*He hesitated, glanced beyond her as though searching for the man who must have her in his keeping. There was no one. The artist lifted his shoulders slightly.*

*"These do not wash off. You understand?"*

*"I understand." She slipped under the silk awning and seated herself on his leather stool. "I am embarked on a very long journey. Of the soul, as much as the body. There has been too much pain—inside of me, if you understand."*

*She rejected crosses and hearts, flowers and wings. He showed her drawings of snakes, in rings and figure eights, the serpents' mouths devouring their tails—sinister, capricious, exquisite. Why did these images enthrall her?*

*"This one," she decided, and gave him her wrist.*

# PART ONE

# The Dark One

*1883*

# CHAPTER ONE

She was the last woman to enter the drawing room at Sandringham that Thursday night, hurrying down the stairs in her black satin slippers, one slim hand adjusting a glove. She'd kept the Prince of Wales's guests waiting a full quarter hour while her maid, Gentry, finished dressing her hair. The cream-and-gold room was filled with the chatter of her most intriguing enemies and friends. The men were elegant in black evening dress and the ladies like a bouquet of tulips in their draped pastel gowns. Every head turned as Jennie Churchill swept through the doorway. The genteel chatter ceased. More than one gentleman ran his eyes the length of her figure; a few women gasped. Was her appearance *that* spectacular?

She glanced at her reflection in the towering looking glass over the mantel. She had ordered the blood-red damask from Worth in Paris, and it was the very latest fashion: skirt gathered flat against her pelvis and flared at the rear in a half bustle, with a demi-train that flirted across Sandringham's Aubusson carpets. Falls of black lace and jet graced the plunging neckline. Gentry had piled her thick black hair high on her head and left a few curls trailing at the nape. A seven-pointed Cartier star glittered with diamonds on her brow. It was the only jewel Jennie owned, but she was famous for it.

Yes. *That spectacular.*

She smiled secretly at her reflection and sank into a curtsey deep enough to encompass the entire room.

Consuelo, Viscountess Mandeville, winked back at her. Minnie Paget, another old friend, turned away and redoubled her efforts to charm Harry Cust. But it was Jennie he was staring at over Minnie's shoulder.

"You're looking well, Jane." The Marquess of Hartington came toward her with a glass of sherry. "That color suits you. Matches the flush in your cheek."

Hart always called her Jane; it was a mark of affection. As he was old enough to be her father and in love with another woman, she laughed at him and said, "I've been squabbling with my maid. She made me scandalously late. How was the shoot today, Hart?"

"Damnably wet." He handed her the glass. "You should have come out with us. Fresh air and mud would do you good."

Spring storms had deluged Sandringham all week. The gentlemen played billiards and potted rabbits when the weather was bad. The ladies gathered in the library and the morning room, writing letters and trading gossip and making faint gestures at needlework none of them gave a fig about. Jennie was used to riding in London nearly every morning and she longed to tear through the Norfolk fields. Her body ached tonight with restlessness.

"Nothing will keep me indoors tomorrow," she confided, smiling up at Hart, "if I have to scrape the mud from my boots with a chisel. Are you taking me into dinner?"

"I believe that honor is mine," Harry Cust broke in.

"You bounder!" George Curzon protested, with a hand on Harry's shoulder. "You *know* we tossed for the privilege, and I won!"

"Gentlemen," Hartington said warningly. "It does not do to make a prize of the lady. Particularly when your Prince is present."

Jennie glanced swiftly toward the fire, where Bertie, the Prince of Wales, surveyed her with heavy-lidded eyes and thumbs thrust in his waistcoat pockets. In most English households, guests entered the dining room by order of social precedence. Not at Sandringham. Bertie liked to buck convention, and he loved women in Worth gowns. They were unabashedly feminine—one reason Jennie had ordered the red damask. Bertie's wife, Princess Alix, wasn't allowed to patronize French dressmakers. Her mother-inlaw, Queen Victoria, thought it unpatriotic.

"We shall draw lots for Lady Randolph," Bertie said deliberately.

A titter of interest followed his words. The cluster of men around Jennie fell back. The Prince summoned a footman. A pen. A pad of paper. He jotted down the names of his male guests and dropped the twisted squibs into a silver ewer. Then he offered it to Jennie with a slight bow.

She reached into the ewer's depths, twirling her fingertips among the possibilities. Her lips were parted, her long-lashed eyes swooped lazily at half-mast. Minnie Paget, her thin brows soaring to her hairline, was muttering behind her fan to the Duchess of Manchester. Jennie was pleased to note that Louise Manchester looked merely bored.

She withdrew a slip of paper and offered it triumphantly to the Prince.

He grunted, and passed it to Hartington.

*"Count Charles Kinsky,"* the Marquess read aloud, and turned his head to the far end of the double drawing room.

Jennie followed his gaze.

A dark-haired young man whose face tugged at her memory was studying her in a way she recognized: both assessing and caressing at once. He had not been present at breakfast or tea.

"A new arrival," she said, ignoring the leaping flame at her heart.

"He won the Grand National last month," Hart told her. "I'll take you over to him."

Jennie had heard a good deal about Charles Kinsky—or more accurately, about Count Karl Rudolf Ferdinand Andreas Fürst

Kinsky von Wchinitz und Tettau, as the Austrian peerage called him. He was the eldest son of Prince Ferdinand Kinsky, a knight of the Holy Roman Empire. Charles held a minor post at the Austrian embassy, but his job was far less important than his family pedigree, or his father's palaces in Vienna and Prague, or the stud farms his dynasty cultivated in the pastures of Bohemia. The *Equus Kinsky*—the Kinsky Horse breed—supplied the Austro-Hungarian imperial cavalry, and all of Europe knew it. Blue blood had run in Kinsky veins since the twelfth century.

He stood carelessly in the Prince's drawing room as though it were the platform of a railway station and he had somewhere else to be. Kinsky was blue-eyed and tall, with a straight nose and a dashing hussar mustache. His perfectly fitted evening clothes, Jennie guessed, had come from Henry Poole, the Prince's Savile Row tailor. She found the contrast between him and Bertie almost painful. Queen Victoria's son was forty-two years old, bloated with self-indulgence and incipient coronary disease. Kinsky was just twenty-five: elegant, athletic, and whipcord-lean. He had won the premier English steeplechase a few weeks before at Aintree on his own horse, Zoedone, jumping her viciously round a field so muddy that it brought all but three contenders to their knees.

No amateur had ever won the Grand National. When Kinsky triumphed at Aintree, Jennie saw his face suddenly in all the sporting magazines and some of the ladies' weeklies as well. Clubs concocted drinks they called "the Kinsky" and toasted him whenever he passed through their doors. Jennie's friends begged for his presence at their balls and round their dining tables and, it was rumored, in their beds. He was chary with his time and attention. It had taken weeks for Alix, Princess of Wales, to lure him to Sandringham.

Jennie's pulse quickened as the Marquess of Hartington led her to the Count. She had been a guest at Sandringham for three days already. She knew every single person wandering through the great house and had nearly exhausted her fund of trivial conversation. That must be why her heart leapt at the sight of Kinsky, she decided; he was a welcome diversion. He couldn't be worse than the tedious spring weather. She dropped him the curtsey due to a minor royal.

"But we've met before," Kinsky protested.

"Have we?"

"Ireland, County Meath," he said immediately. "Lord Langford's estate, Summerhill. Four years ago. Your husband's family hosted the Empress Elisabeth. I was in her party."

"I'm surprised you remember." Jennie lifted her brows.

"How could I forget? You were the only woman in that wild country wearing a riding habit by Redfern."

"Good Lord, how could you tell?" She had discovered the sporting tailor years before, in Cowes; now no lady in England would hunt in anything else.

"Like you, my mother is a magnificent horsewoman. She taught me to recognize quality and elegance—wherever I find it."

Did he intend the compliment? Delighted, Jennie laughed at the Count and allowed him to carry her into the dining room.

It was an intimate space for a royal household, the walls lined with Madrid tapestries after the style of Goya, dark and vivid. A fire crackled at one end. Kinsky led Jennie around the long table, set for twenty, assessing the place cards. He found hers and without hesitation picked it up. "Do you know what I remember most from that time in Ireland?" he asked.

"The Empress's leather riding habit? Or the fact that she was sewn into it each morning?"

"The sapphire-blue gown you wore the night we danced together. You looked glorious. More like a panther than a woman."

"A *wild beast,* Count? Should I be flattered or insulted?"

"Neither. I'm simply telling the truth." He exchanged her place card for the one next to his own. "Indulge me, Lady Randolph. It's long past time we got to know each other."

———

Dinner at Sandringham never lasted more than an hour. That night Jennie found it far too short. The soup and fish and saddle of mutton passed in a blur; her wineglass was effortlessly refilled; she turned with regret from Kinsky on her right to the Earl on her left; and when the ladies rose to follow Princess Alix, leaving the men to their port, she paced alone before the great fireplace in Bertie's saloon as the other women talked indolently among the velvet sofa cushions. She was frustrated with herself. What was so instantly dazzling, so absorbing and consuming, about Count Kinsky? She knew hundreds of men—men of power, intelligence, fashion. Some of them had gone down on their knees, begging her to be their mistress. So why, suddenly, had this man caught her interest?

"I'm told you're an American," Kinsky had said over dessert, "but no one with your command of French grew up in New York. When did you live in Paris?"

"Mamma settled us there for her health when I was thirteen." It was the standard explanation for her parents' separation, but Mamma had never been ill a day in her life. She'd been sick of Papa's opera singers.

"And suffered at the hands of a governess?" Kinsky guessed.

"I was sent to a convent school." When she'd rather have gone riding each day with Papa back at Jerome Park. "I caused endless trouble for the nuns."

"Of course you did." His warm blue gaze met Jennie's. Disconcerting; most dinner partners kept their eyes firmly on their plates. "That explains the French. You were young, and the young pick up languages effortlessly."

"Your English is just as good," she countered.

"Thank you. My father was a diplomat before me. I was raised as much in London and Paris as on my own estates."

*My own estates.* That was part of what made Charles fascinating—he was one of those men who ruled the earth, or at least a good swath of it. He expected to have whatever he wanted. Her husband, Randolph, was similar—a duke's son, in the habit of ordering people around. But younger sons owned nothing.

"That's when I first met Sisi—your Empress Elizabeth," Jennie observed. "I was fifteen, and we hunted together at Compiègne. She treated me like a daughter."

"Don't tell me you were in France during the Prussian invasion?" Kinsky asked suddenly, frowning. He must have hazarded her age and done a few sums. The invasion, a dozen years ago.

"Not quite. We caught the last train out of Paris," Jennie supplied, "ahead of the cavalry. Our maid was supposed to follow. She never did." Marie had simply pocketed the train fare and lived on in the empty house, selling the Jerome family's belongings piece by piece to survive. "We managed to cross to Dover and install ourselves at Brown's Hotel, like the other refugees."

"So much for the convent."

"Well . . ." Jennie flashed him a smile. "I was seventeen by that time, and straining at the leash. But poor Paris! The Prussian Siege was bad enough. The Commune that followed . . ."

"You saw that, too?"

"Mamma insisted on returning to France once the war was over."

"For her *health*," Kinsky suggested, amused.

"A mistake, Count, from which Mamma eventually recovered."

The enchanting city in ruins. Sixty-five thousand people buried in mass lime pits on the outskirts. The Bois de Boulogne, through which Jennie had galloped almost every day, cut to the ground for firewood. The Tuileries Palace a heap of smoking rubble.

"You have a gift for survival, Lady Randolph."

She shrugged. "Americans are hard to kill."

"And eventually you settled in England?"

She'd met Randolph Churchill when she was nineteen, two years after the Commune. It seemed an eternity ago. "Barring a few visits to Paris dressmakers? Yes."

Charles touched his glass to hers. "Then France's loss is England's gain, my lady."

Minnie Paget was studiously shunning Jennie as a result of the lot-drawing before dinner, but Consuelo Mandeville joined her in front of the fire. She was petite and plump and had masses of dark bronze hair, secured to her head by ebony combs riddled with emeralds. Consuelo's father was Cuban but she had been born on her mother's cotton plantation in Louisiana before the Civil War. She was one of Jennie's oldest friends, along with a girl named Alva Erskine Smith, who had recently become Alva Vanderbilt back in New York. The girls had met at Delmonico's dancing class when they were nine, then gone on to the same French boarding school a few years later. Alva had named her first child Consuelo in honor of Viscountess Mandeville. The three of them did not really trust Minnie Paget, the fourth member of their American set. Minnie had carried tales as a girl, and Jennie knew she was still doing it now, when the cost was so much higher.

"You look like a caged lion, my love." Consuelo parted her rosy lips and blew an admirable set of smoke rings; she made a point of waving Cuban cigars around the Prince of Wales. It was not enough for Connie to be called her ladyship; she wanted to be called *exotic*.

"I look like a panther, Connie. Or so I've been told."

"Was that meant as a compliment?"

"A challenge, I think."

Consuelo sank down on a loveseat ranged below the Prince's Spanish tapestries. She was a lazy creature and Jennie's energy always exhausted her. "From the dashing Kinsky? He's brought up your color. You look more ravishing tonight than I've ever seen you."

"Nonsense! I'm always ravishing," Jennie retorted tartly. With just a courtesy title and a modest fortune to her name, she had no choice but to look her best. Her face and wit needed to open all the right doors.

"It's good Freddie's not invited this week," Consuelo murmured. "He'd force Kinsky to a duel."

Colonel Freddie Burnaby of the Horse Guards was Jennie's latest flirt.

"I'm growing rather tired of Freddie," she mused. "He has so little conversation."

"But such massive shoulders." Consuelo patted the silk cushion beside her. "Come and have a cigar, darling. You can tell me all about your new Austrian conquest."

Jennie did not see Kinsky again that night; he was recruited to play whist with the Prince, and no one refused that invitation. The men would be at cards until dawn. At eleven o'clock, with the rest of the ladies, each holding a lighted candle, Jennie ascended Sandringham's wide paneled staircase, which was lined with prints of Bertie's favorite horses. She did not look for Count Kinsky's name on one of Alix's engraved cards pinned to the bedchamber doors along the carpeted passages. The Count had arrived too late in the week; he would be placed in one of the outer wings with lesser mortals. And he would sleep until noon.

She was astonished, therefore, to find him in the stables the next morning as she prepared to mount the little mare Alix had set aside for her use—Candida was her name, a silver-gray sprite with a soft mouth and a dancing gait. The rain had stopped, a fragile sun shone on the wet spring grass, and Jennie meant to ride with two of Bertie and Alix's daughters: Princess Louise, who was sixteen, and Princess Maud, two years younger. Their grooms would accompany them through the Wild Wood—part of Sandringham's six-hundred-acre park.

Charles Kinsky wore a dark field jacket, a low-crowned derby, and tight pantaloons tucked into black leather boots. He was shaking his head at the roan gelding a groom had led out for his use. "Be a good fellow and find me a mount that can gallop. That black devil over there will do."

The groom eyed Kinsky. The Count's racing reputation had run like fire through the stables.

"Devil is right, sir," the groom muttered as he led the roan back to its stall and turned out the black. The horse rippled with violent energy. "Barely two years old and not fit to saddle. HRH intends him for the next National."

"Then let me school him for you. What is he called?"

"The Scot. My master will have my head if you break his neck—or your own, sir."

"Tell the Prince I had a death wish," Kinsky said easily. "It's true enough, most days." He walked up to the horse with his palm extended, and the flaring nostrils blew briefly at his hand. He slid his fingers over the velvet nose and The Scot thrust his head into Kinsky's chest in a gesture of acceptance Jennie recognized immediately. Hadn't she wanted to do the same thing last night?

She mounted hurriedly. The two princesses wore matching dark blue riding habits, thoroughly sensible. Maud resembled her mother, Alix, though without her ethereal beauty; Louise, poor thing, looked like Bertie.

Kinsky edged his stamping, nervy horse near Jennie's Candida, who tossed her head and danced sideways.

"Your stallion's as fresh as paint," Jennie told the Count. "Please keep your distance from my charges, sir; I should hate to have to answer to their mother."

"*Are* they your charges?" Kinsky murmured. "I thought their grooms looked after them. You must be longing for a gallop."

"Of course," Jennie said, "but—"

With a casual flick of his riding crop, Kinsky grazed Candida's flank. The mare snorted, then wheeled for the arched entrance to the stable yard, Jennie's thigh braced against the pommel of her sidesaddle. Kinsky was right on her heels. Even if she had wanted to stop the mare, she could not safely have done so; The Scot would have run her down.

The open ride to the Wild Wood was graded and beautifully turfed, an invitation to race.

She gave Candida her head and did not look back.

# CHAPTER TWO

## *Isle of Wight, 1873*

Jennie Jerome felt a flush of warmth in her cheeks as she mounted the *Ariadne*'s gangway, her elbow-length satin gloves wilting with humidity. It was hot and sticky this August in Cowes. Most people watched the Regatta Week races in cool linen sailor dresses. But *this* was a royal tea dance, and demanded evening dress at three o'clock in the afternoon. Jennie quelled a spasm of irritation, and stepped aboard with all the grace of a girl raised on her father's yacht.

She wore a cream silk robe overlaid with lashings of bronze lace and gold spangles; unusual and arresting for a nineteen-year-old. The *Ariadne* was full of virgins in white, shining faintly with perspiration and ambition. Jennie drew a deep breath to steady her racing pulse and glanced around. The Prince and Princess of Wales were posed beneath a white canopy on the *Ariadne*'s foredeck, receiving their guests. Princess Alix's sister and her husband—the Czarevna and Czarevitch of Russia—stood beside them. The Russian royals were visiting England for the yacht races, so of course a ball was in order. The Jerome ladies—Jennie, her mother, and her sister Clarita—were among the few American guests. Jennie's father, Leonard Jerome, was an honorary member of Cowes's Royal Yacht Squadron.

Prince Edward Albert of Wales was chatting with Sir Ivor Rules, an aging sportsman just down from London. Rules stopped short, raised his monocle, and swept his gaze the length of Jennie's figure. She lifted her brows at him satirically—did he think she was a filly at auction?—and let her attention wander to an impeccably dressed young lord with a walrus mustache and a rose in his buttonhole. He was leaning against a mast.

Randolph Spencer-Churchill. She'd noticed his sketch in the Society columns.

Lord Randolph's father was the Seventh Duke of Marlborough. His elder brother, the Marquess of Blandford, was heir to the dukedom and a notorious rake. The family ruled the Cotswolds from the immense and chilly splendor of Blenheim Palace, one of the greatest treasure houses in England. Jennie felt Lord Randolph studying her as she curtseyed to the Czarevna.

*Definitely a filly at auction,* she thought wryly.

Within minutes of her exit from the receiving line, the Duke's son was at her side.


"You waltz divinely," Randolph observed as they turned to something by Strauss, "but I'm treading all over your gold sandals, Miss Jerome, and you're far too kind to kick me. Shall we drink champagne instead?"

"I'd love to." The crush was dreadful and Jennie hadn't eaten in hours. She let Randolph lead her to the *Ariadne*'s rail and summon a footman. There was salmon and pâté and grapes as well as champagne.

She accepted a plate. "I understand you've recently been in Paris." A few lines beneath his face in the Society column had told her that. *Duke's son returns from Grand Tour.*

"The charnel house of Europe." Lord Randolph raised his glass. "Or at least of its hopes. There's nobody left to execute and nothing left to destroy."

"But the Commune's long since over," she objected. "Indeed, Mamma is carrying us all back to France next month."

"Then you've more courage than is good for you."

"You don't think it's safe?"

"I'd be inclined to wait at least until Christmas." His brown eyes swept over her coolly. "But I forget—you're American. Americans never heed anything I say."

She laughed delightedly. "So you think we're fools, of course?"

"On the contrary, I think you're invincible. I've yet to visit America, Miss Jerome, but with qualities like yours, I'm persuaded it's the future."

"Now you're teasing me, my lord. Every Englishman regards London as the center of the world."

"Not if they've read Gibbon as many times as I have. *'The ascent to greatness, however steep and dangerous, may entertain an active spirit with the consciousness and exercise of its own power,'* " Randolph quoted, " *'but the possession of a throne could never yet afford a lasting satisfaction to an ambitious mind.'* That's Gibbon for you."

*"The Decline and Fall of the Roman Empire,"* Jennie guessed.

Randolph inclined his head. "I've read the entire work at least five times. Thrones like ours are out, Miss Jerome. It's power that's all the rage—the power of money. Which your countrymen command in revoltingly prodigious quantities."

Was that an insult, or envy? "I shall have to read Gibbon."

"Nothing easier. I'll drop the volumes at your door by breakfast."

"Is history your passion, then, Lord Randolph? What do you mean to do with it?"

"Stand for Parliament," he said immediately. "I should go mad on a steady diet of grouse shooting and fox hunting."

"Are those the only alternatives?"

"For a man of my class? Tragically, yes. But politics is the greatest blood sport of all, Miss Jerome. Beats bagging tigers all hollow. Have you visited Commons yet?"

"No, I . . ." A sense of insecurity and confusion swept over her. She knew nothing about British politics. Mamma did not even take a daily paper in England; ladies were not supposed to read much beyond fashion magazines. Jennie thought fleetingly of Papa, far away in New York—without his influence, the Jerome household was entirely female and firmly superficial. She felt a stab of impatience at the depth of her own ignorance. "I should *adore* to see Parliament, Lord Randolph."

"Come up to London during the session and I'll secure you a ticket." His gaze moved past her. "Good God. Are we about to be rammed by a ship under full sail?"

Jennie glanced around. He was staring at *Mamma,* who was magnificent but perhaps too substantial in a silk evening gown of old rose satin, massively hooped behind, the entire hem and train draped in garlands of beaded vines and chrysanthemums eight inches wide. She was hurrying toward them as fast as her delicate slippers and the pitch of the *Ariadne*'s deck allowed. Her expression was forbidding. The three plumes in her dark hair quivered with indignation. Jennie had been too exclusive, speaking to Lord Randolph alone for nearly half an hour.

With a pang of regret—it had been the most interesting conversation she'd enjoyed all week—Jennie rose hurriedly to her feet. "I must go."

Lord Randolph grasped her wrist. "Tell me your name."

"We've already been introduced!"

"Your *first* name. I'll mutter it like an incantation after you've left me."

His cool eyes had darkened suddenly. She felt slightly unsteady—had the boat breasted a wave?—and smiled at him.

"Jeanette. But call me Jennie."

"And how will I find you again, Jennie?"

"We're on an island, sir. You'll be sick of the sight of me before the week is out."

The next morning at the Villa Rosetta, the Jeromes' rented cottage, she wandered restlessly among the sunlit rooms. No set of Gibbon had arrived with her morning coffee. Jennie tried to shake the specter of Lord Randolph Spencer-Churchill, but he persisted in her mind. The quicksilver emotions flitting across his face; the alertness of his brain; the way he dealt words as deftly as some men dealt cards. The unexpectedness of that parting grasp on her wrist. *I have never visited the House of Commons.* Did he find her gauche? Naïve? Heaven forbid—*unintelligent?* The wind off the sea gusted through the open casements and tugged at her black hair. And that suddenly, she was nine years old, back in Newport: a pair of donkeys and a dogcart, herself whipping the team up Bellevue Avenue. Children shrieking. She had dirtied her dress. Mamma was extremely cross and she was not allowed down for dinner.

She stared out at the August daisies, starlike in the Cowes garden, and wished for speed. A dogcart, a team, a whip in her hand. Something reckless that might carry her off.

"So *tiresome.*" Her mother's voice drifted through the open window. "Colonel Edgecombe wants to bring a friend this evening. Which means we'll have to ask a third, Clarita, or be uneven at table."

A murmur from her sister, indistinguishable.

"Lord Randolph Churchill!" her mother retorted indignantly. "The ugly little man with the courtesy title, who cornered poor Jennie last night. I don't know when I've witnessed such deplorable manners. . . ."

Jennie flushed and almost called out in protest, then bit back the words. So that was how Mamma thought of him. *Deplorable* and *ugly.* It was true that Lord Randolph's eyes were a bit prominent, arresting above his walrus mustache, but he was of average height and reasonably fit. And when he talked—when his mind was engaged . . . She'd stayed near him too long just to watch him gesture with his hands.

She turned irritably from the window. She'd met any number of men that summer in England, aristocrats and rogues alike. Most of them threw out lures to her on a daily basis. That's what they called improper proposals in England—*lures.* As though she were a trout waiting to be reeled in to some cad's bed. Sir Ivor Rules, for instance—a man her father's age. His constant flirtation relieved the boredom of so many Society parties—Jennie supposed she en-joyed sparring with him—but she was shrewd enough to stop short of disaster. Sir Ivor was married. If she consented to become his mistress, he was perfectly willing to stand her a Mayfair ad-dress and all the horses she could possibly ride—but nothing more. Was it because she was American? Or appeared to be fatherless? With no title to bolster her name? It was astounding how many propositions she'd received this summer. And Mamma was oblivi-ous. Determined to regard everyone they met as *so terribly kind.*

Lord Randolph Churchill was the first Englishman who'd treated her as though she had a mind as well as a body. As though she were more than a man's plaything.

And he was coming to dinner tonight.

Suddenly breathless, Jennie sat down at the piano and belted out a piece by Beethoven. Crashing and furious and exhilarating at once.

Colonel Edgecombe was Clara Jerome's latest beau: a bearded and bronzed soldier who'd served in the Eighth Bengal Cavalry and was only recently "home" from India. He was forty-five to her forty-eight and treated her with a blend of dash and deference. He led Randolph Churchill through the cobbled streets of Cowes to the Villa Rosetta that evening along with Tommie Trafford, a friend of Churchill's who'd been invited to balance the table.

"You'll find that the ladies smuggled their cook out of France along with their trunks," the Colonel confided to the younger men as they waited on the villa's doorstep. "The Jerome grub is un-equaled."

The meal, as he predicted, was excellent. It ran to seven courses, the wines well matched. The dining room doors were thrown open to the cool sea night. Edgecombe allowed himself to remi-nisce about Simla without becoming, he hoped, a Colonial Bore. The two girls listened to him with a pretty air of interest. When the last bite had been savored and Clara rose from her chair, they followed their mother meekly enough—as though, Edgecombe thought, they'd actually been raised properly.

The port was before him. Edgecombe poured a glass and passed the decanter to his left. "Well, gentlemen—what's your opinion of our lovely hostesses?"

Trafford's lips quirked. "Miss Clarita should be modeled in porcelain. Her resemblance to a doll is remarkable. I gather you've been acquainted with the Jeromes for some time, Colonel?"

"Since last summer. Delightful creatures, and very easy in their acquaintance." Edgecombe pushed back his chair, one hand thrust into his coat. "I imagine we'll be treated to the girls' performance on the pianoforte this evening—the Dark One is very adept, almost a *professional*." He gave the word a certain taint. "She lets the Fair One play duets with her sometimes."

"Is that what you call them?" Lord Randolph interjected. "Dark and Fair?"

"Like a story from the Brothers Grimm," Trafford mused. "Rose White and Rose Red. Surely Miss Clarita should be married by now? She's been finished to a fare-thee-well in Paris and New York. Speaks Italian and French. Has enough money to figure as an heiress . . ."

"And can mount anything on four legs," Churchill said.

"Why mount four when you can mount two?" Edgecombe murmured slyly. "But as to that . . . there's no birth to speak of, being American. Which may be why the girls don't take. They say dear Clara is part Iroquois."

"Negro, I've heard," Trafford countered. "The Fair One escaped the blemish, of course, but our Jeanette has a lovely color to her skin. I'll wager she's a tigress between the sheets."

"Careful," Edgecombe warned. "The Dark One is spoken for."

"What do you mean?" Lord Randolph broke in suddenly. His prominent eyes had an ugly look in them. "What are you talking about?"

"Sir Ivor Rules." Edgecombe savored the wine and his superior knowledge; it was not often he had a chance to school a duke's son. "Rules has his eye on the girl. Means to set her up as his mistress. Can't say I blame him. Jeanette encourages his attentions, and we can all see she's a ripe one. And not too particular as to morals, I daresay—these half-castes never are. Kept a number of 'em myself in India—"

There was a tinkle of broken crystal and a blot of wine spread slowly across the tablecloth. Lord Randolph's glass had shattered in his fingers.

"My dear fellow!" Trafford cried.

"It's nothing," he muttered, wrapping a napkin tightly around his palm. "Shall we join the ladies?"

Moonlight washed the Solent and the far shore of England; washed the Royal Yacht Squadron as it lay at anchor; washed the towers of Victoria's beloved Osborne, where the ghost of Albert wandered the halls. Jennie's music drifted through Randolph's mind—when he'd joined her in the drawing room, she had played, appropriately, Beethoven's "Moonlight" Sonata. *Professional* did not begin to describe her talent. Randolph might be a dreadful dancer but he understood music. He recognized that Jennie was an artist. He had barely known how to take his leave of her when the last notes died away.

She had touched his hand with her cool one.

*Tomorrow,* she breathed. *I walk the Parade before breakfast.*

"Tedious evening," Trafford complained as the two men strolled through the quiet streets. Orchestral music wafted to their ears; the Prince, no doubt, was entertaining. "Old Edgecombe is a fright, isn't he?"

"He should be flogged," Randolph snapped. "It was all I could do not to slap him with my glove." *I walk the Parade.* What time was her breakfast? What time would she wake?

"Duels have rather gone out, old chap."

"But horsewhipping, thank God, has not." His brother Blandford had flogged a man only last year. It was an act of contempt. Duels, being affairs of honor, implied a gentleman's respect. Randolph refused to give Edgecombe that.

Trafford stopped short on the paving and stared at him. "This cannot be about those women?"

"Can it not?"

"You're mad. *Ivor Rules,* Randy! The betting's running all his way at White's, I assure you."

"Immaterial. Ivor's wagered on a mistress."

"And?"

"I intend to make the Dark One my wife."

"Bloody *hell*." Trafford glanced swiftly at the genteel houses looming around them, as if afraid he'd been overheard. They were standing beneath a ginkgo. The paving was littered with fanlike leaves wet from a recent shower. The scent of decay rose to their nostrils.

"Even if she weren't American—even if those rumors are pure tosh—you can't be serious, Randy!"

"I believe marriage is usual for a man my age." He was twenty-four to Jennie's nineteen. Time to be setting up his nursery.

"You loathe blushing young girls."

"This one interests me."

"She won't for long. And then what will you do, when she invites all and sundry into her bed?"

"Jealous, Tommie?" he taunted.

"Don't be a brute. I'm trying to save you from yourself." Trafford drew out his matches and a cigar flared between his lips. The odor of tobacco—familiar from a thousand shared nights at Eton and Oxford and Blenheim—wrapped them in memory.

"You don't believe I've changed," Randolph said.

"In some ways, perhaps." Trafford extinguished his match. "But in others? Never."

———

He met Jennie on the Parade the next morning as if by accident, a set of Gibbon under his arm. She wore a navy- and white-striped sailor dress and her bonnet was tied coquettishly with a deep raspberry ribbon under her left ear. She strode at an impatient pace along the Parade, a furled parasol swinging from one wrist, and Randolph finally found words for his attraction—this girl was arrestingly beautiful, yes, but she was also as free and athletic as a boy. Beneath the voluminous skirts her hips were narrow and her legs were long. Randolph's sisters—he had six—were frail creatures, much given to languishing on sofas and fainting in excessive heat. But this American was an Amazon. She radiated life; he found her vitality mesmerizing.

He secured another invitation to dinner at the Villa Rosetta that night. Without Tommie Trafford this time.

"What can you possibly see in those people, Randy?" Trafford demanded.

"The future," he answered.

Clarita hated his mustache and found him a bore. But Jennie had never felt more alive. Her gorgeous skin was flushed and her amber eyes unnaturally brilliant, as though she suffered from fever. Randolph tossed her sentences like a volley of colored balls, and to her delight she served them back, spinning with laughter. Her mother noticed their sudden intimacy, the crackle of energy linking them, and was alert with worry. *If Lord Randolph has come in search of a fortune—younger sons are often so desperate as to lack all principle—*

"I leave the Isle of Wight tomorrow," he told her as he bowed over her hand at dinner's end. "But you have my deepest gratitude, Mrs. Jerome, for making Cowes Week memorable."

"The pleasure was entirely ours, my lord," she said with relief. And gave him her first smile.

When the villa door closed behind him, Clarita heaved a dramatic sigh. Her golden curls were limp with humidity—the day had been oppressive—and her cupid's-bow mouth drooped tragically at the corners. There had been no one to pay her compliments or attention all evening, though she had worn her most cherished cornflower silk and a sapphire brooch in her hair. She was three years older than Jennie and ought to have been treated with deference, but Jennie and that ugly Lord Randolph had talked of books and music and *politics* until Clarita feared she would scream.

"I have *such* a headache," she mourned. "How that man chatters! Like an organ-grinder's monkey."

"I must write to your father," Clara said worriedly. "Are you coming, Jeanette?"

"In a moment, Mamma," Jennie replied. "It's such a beautiful night. I want a glimpse of the stars."

"Take care you do not catch your death."

Clara Jerome hurried upstairs. Lord Randolph might be leaving Cowes, but she felt his danger all the same. Jennie was precious to Leonard; he must be warned. If only her husband were not across the Atlantic . . .

At the wide French windows, Jennie glanced over her shoulder; then, her breath in her throat, she hurried down the steps to the garden. Dew spattered the hem of her gown and her bare ankles.

Randolph waited at the far gate that led to the sea.

Neither of them spoke. They stood in the well of shadow cast by a towering yew hedge. Jasmine scented the darkness. They were nearly the same height; Jennie perhaps half an inch taller. Randolph reached for her shoulders—white and rounded as a Michelangelo in her pale evening gown. She had felt the headiness of their connection all night, but suddenly she wanted more—she wanted to feel his skin on hers. On impulse, heart racing, she took his left hand and slipped it inside her bodice.

Randolph froze.

She breathed his name and leaned toward him, her mouth parting under his.

He felt the softness of her lips, her tongue, and broke from her quickly. His lips grazed her collarbone.

Did he even think the phrase *Marry me* before he spoke it out loud?

*Pray take care, my own one,* Jennie's father wrote to her when he learned the news a week later. *I fear if anything goes wrong, you will make a dreadful shipwreck of your affections. You were never born to love lightly.*

# CHAPTER THREE

"You ride as well as I remember," Kinsky remarked as he and Jennie halted in a clearing at the heart of the Sandringham woods.

His voice was intimate, without the slightest reserve of a stranger. They might have known each other for years. Perhaps they had. Jennie felt herself lean mentally into Kinsky's warmth. She was in the presence of a friend. She had learned with time and experience to distinguish them quickly from her subtle enemies.

"My father threw me up on my first pony when I was two," she said, with a hint of challenge.

"So did mine." Were his blue eyes laughing at her? "Forgive me for cropping your horse. It was unpardonable."

"But too tempting. I shall have to return the favor one day when you're not looking, Count, and make a fool of you in Hyde Park."

"Will you ride with me, then, in London?"

"If you happen to ask," she said equably. "I try to get out every day, regardless of weather."

"And rarely alone. You're very much in request, Lady Randolph."

"Which is why you find me bewitching." She glanced at him knowingly. "Confess! If I were not in fashion, Count, we shouldn't be ambling through the woods together. Isn't notoriety its own reward?"

"Nonsense. I've admired you for years. I looked for you everywhere after that ball in Ireland, but you were not to be found."

*Had* he? Surprising.

"That's because the Government fell," Jennie explained, "and my father-in-law, the Duke of Marlborough, was no longer Lord Lieutenant of Ireland. We returned to England three years ago."

Kinsky urged The Scot into a walk to cool him. Jennie kept Candida at a slight distance; she did not want the little mare nipped or kicked.

"Three years, Lady Randolph. But only just invited to Sandringham. Why?"

"You're curious about our exile?" Jennie managed an easy laugh. "How vulgar of you!" She could treat her humiliation as an absurdity now, but for months—years, even—Bertie's rejection had stung. She had been very young when social disaster broke over her head. Proud enough, however, to show the world a smiling face.

"*Exile* is a harsh word."

"An exaggeration, too. I shouldn't complain about my time in Ireland—the countryside is lovely, and the hunting like nothing on this earth—as you know, of course, having been in the field with Sisi." Jennie paused for an instant, weighing how much to tell him. "There are benefits to losing the Prince of Wales's favor, Count. We lived *very* quietly. I hardly taxed my dress allowance, and my husband was *much* less idle than he might have preferred." Jennie glanced at Kinsky in amusement. "Lord Randolph threw himself into politics and made a name for himself. Something Bertie never expected."

"And you?"

"Supported my husband, naturally." She must not betray the slightest chink in her armor. "We have new friends to replace the old. And some people, like Connie Mandeville, never deserted us."

"Why should she? I refuse to believe *you* could possibly offend anyone."

"I never said I did." Jennie flashed Kinsky a smile, took up Candida's reins, and urged the mare forward. "Come, Count. It's too glorious a morning for gossip."

She broke into a canter beneath the canopy of trees, the mare's hooves muffled by springy turf. This part of Norfolk was not far from the coast, and the ground underfoot was sandy in places and covered in others with dense falls of conifer needles. Jennie felt as though the tight band constricting her chest was finally loosening. She had been cooped up indoors too long; now she could breathe again. Bluebells were awakening everywhere in the wood—great drifts of vibrant color unfurling with the wet spring. It was enough for her to feel a kind of communion with Charles Kinsky that had everything to do with the horses surging beneath them and the morning slipping by in splotches of branch-riven sunlight. She had completely forgotten the young princesses she'd left behind.

She reined in at the edge of the wood, overlooking broad pastureland and rising downs. Kinsky clattered to a halt beside her, his mount blowing.

"You've finally tired The Scot," she remarked. "Throw him over a few hedges, and he'll be tame as a lamb all the way back to the stables."

"I'm not simply prying, you know." Kinsky studied her profile. "I'm asking about your past out of self-preservation. Last night in Bertie's card room, I mentioned our meeting in Ireland, and the most appalling silence fell. No one would look at me."

"Poor Count," Jennie murmured. "It is *hard* to be a stranger among friends."

"As you know too well, Lady Randolph. You're no more English than I am."

*Bastard.* He pulled no punches.

"Ah, but I have my compensations," she returned mildly. "A remarkable degree of freedom is accorded American women in this country. More, perhaps, than in our own. And Bertie loves us so!"

"Is that why you're staying with the Prince—and your husband is not? Because you're an American? Or is there some deeper mystery I've blundered into?"

Jennie's eyes narrowed. Kinsky was asking if she was Bertie's mistress. Perhaps his desire to know had been the point of this conversation all along. The Prince of Wales collected around him the women he hoped to bed—and he'd spurred that odd ritual the previous evening, drawing lots for Jennie's favor.

Kinsky waited for her answer, his hand smoothing his horse's black mane. His fingers were long and unexpectedly sensitive. Jennie could let him think she was spoken for. Or she could tell him the truth. Watching his hand on the horse's neck, she felt a faint shudder at the base of her spine; to hide it, she rushed into speech. "The bad blood between the Prince and my husband is *ridiculous,* really. Lord Randolph's older brother George—"

"The Marquess of Blandford. We've met."

"—had a tawdry little affair with the Countess of Aylesford, while her husband was away in India with the Prince of Wales some years ago."

"*Tawdry* because the Countess was married?"

"*Tawdry* because, instead of conducting his *amours* in private, my brother-in-law chose to throw them in the world's face. He eloped with Edith to Paris," Jennie returned impatiently. "She was delivered of a child there. Lord Aylesford obtained a legal separation, and Goosie—George's wife—is divorcing *him,* to compound the scandal. But George can't marry Edith until her husband dies. Which is just as George likes it. He says Edith's good enough for a mistress, but not for a future Duchess of Marlborough."

"So your brother-in-law is a scrub and a cad." Kinsky frowned. "Why should that affect *your* place in Society?"

"Because Edith Aylesford was Bertie's mistress before she was George's."

He whistled softly under his breath. "The Prince punished the entire Churchill family out of jealousy over a woman?"

"Oh, no. HRH never cared that much for Edith. No one can, poor thing." Jennie slackened her reins and let Candida's head drop so the mare could tear at the spring grass. "Bertie punished us because Randolph made Princess Alix cry."

"I don't understand."

"My husband chose to take up his brother's cause, you see. Which was extremely foolish." How to explain that Randolph could be suicidally impulsive? "Edith Aylesford had a packet of love letters. Randolph thought he could use them."

"Letters from Blandford?"

"From *Bertie*. Randolph carried the Prince's letters straight to Alix at Buckingham Palace. He threatened to publish them—expose her husband as an adulterer—if HRH did not order Aylesford to take Edith back."

"Poor Alix," Kinsky said softly. "Your husband is ruthless, Lady Randolph."

"When it suits his ends. *Yes*."

"But why in God's name should Aylesford kill the rumors? He seems to me the only honorable person in the entire affair!"

"No, no," Jennie protested, amused. Fresh color rose in her cheeks. This was no gossip; Kinsky was trying sincerely to understand. "By separating from Edith, Aylesford brought scandal on everyone involved."

"You're joking."

"Not at all. Had he behaved like a gentleman and settled his differences with his wife in private, so much misery might have been avoided! But he refused. He left Edith no choice. She had to throw herself under Blandford's protection and live notoriously in Paris."

Kinsky threw back his head and laughed.

"*Aylesford* was the scrub and the cad, Count," Jennie concluded furiously.

"When I thought he was simply a cuckold, poor fellow. And Lord Randolph? What happened to him?"

*Disaster.*

Jennie flinched, recalling those months. The uncertainty of whether they'd receive an invitation; the suspense when they accepted, only to be hustled through their hosts' back service entrance when the Prince unexpectedly arrived . . .

"You know how priggish the Public is. Publishing Bertie's love letters would have disgraced the monarchy. So Alix went to the Queen. Her Majesty has never approved of her son, but to avoid a scandal for the Crown . . ."

"Victoria supported Bertie."

"Naturally. She summoned Randolph's parents. She told them how he'd blackmailed the Princess. The Duke of Marlborough was mortified, of course. He offered to take us all out of England. The post of Lord Lieutenant in Dublin was open, so that's where we fled."

To a house called White's Lodge, in Phoenix Park, down the carriage sweep from the Viceroy's residence. Jennie found the house comforting, a refuge after all the anxiety and distress of that hideous long winter. The Duke appointed Randolph his secretary to secure him a salary. A few of their friends crossed the North Sea from time to time. And Kinsky himself had come, to dance with her at Summerhill. . . .

"My poor father-in-law ordered my husband to write a letter of apology to Bertie," Jennie added, "which Lord Randolph did. Bertie challenged him to a duel anyway."

"Good God," Kinsky muttered. "They *can't* have met at dawn."

"No," she agreed. "To point a pistol at the Prince of Wales's heart is high treason. Randolph refused the challenge, of course. And that actually made Bertie feel better—as though he'd proved Randy a coward without firing a shot! Banishing us from Society after that was just so much cream on his royal whiskers."

"And yet, here you are at Sandringham, Lady Randolph." His gaze was disturbingly warm.

"Here I am." She inclined her head. "From *persona non grata* to valued guest. My style is too good and my husband too much of a political star for either of us to be ignored. Bertie has made peace. Randy remains in London, but he sends me as hostage."

"Farcical," Kinsky snorted. "And the source of all the trouble, your brother-in-law Lord Blandford . . ."

"Carries on happily to this day. George never quarreled with the Prince, you see." Jennie gripped the reins. "There you have it, Count. The chief rule of British Society: Sleep where you like, but be in your own bed by morning."

The air between them was suddenly charged. Jennie felt her heart thud erratically.

"If that's an invitation," Kinsky muttered, his eyes darkening, "I'll have to call you Jennie."

Reckless, to reach for her with The Scot snorting beneath him. He ought to have been thrown from the saddle and taken Jennie with him. But the kiss flared in her like a match and she leaned in, wanting more, her hand on his coat collar. Charles groaned deep in his throat and his fingers tightened on her chin, her hair. For an instant the world swung dizzyingly—then she broke away.

"I prefer Lady Randolph to Jennie," she said breathlessly. "I worked too hard for my courtesy title, Count, to abandon it for *you*."

"As you like. *My lady*." He was staring at her, deadly serious. "It won't change this bond between us. I've felt it ever since Ireland."

Jennie caught the raw throb in his voice and wondered, Was he simply aroused? Or . . . oddly moved? She refused to ask that question of herself. Instead, she wheeled the mare and broke into a trot. It was pleasant enough to dally in the woods, but not when her response to Kinsky was so uncontrolled. She could not give him power over her. She gave no man that.

"I don't deal in bonds, sir," she called back over her shoulder as she fled for the stables. "They're too much like chains."

# CHAPTER FOUR

The young princesses, Maud and Louise, greeted Jennie with frantic relief when she clopped into Sandringham's stable yard half an hour later. They were sure she had been thrown, and were only waiting for the mare to return without a rider before sending out a search party.

"But of course, you were with the Count," Louise sighed as Kinsky appeared in the arched gateway behind Jennie. "And with such an escort—so capable in the saddle—you must always have been safe."

"Goose! If I could not manage your mamma's precious mare, I deserved to walk home! Never mount an animal you can't handle."

If her words had a deeper meaning, only Kinsky caught it. His lips twitched as Jennie shooed the chattering princesses toward the castle, but he was enough of a gentleman not to laugh in her face.

Jennie changed her forest-green riding habit for a suitable day dress of mushroom-colored silk, picked out with ravishing copper fringe. When she glimpsed her face in her bedroom mirror, she was startled by the feral light in her eyes, the high color in her cheeks. That could be due to the gallop through the awakening woods, but Jennie knew it was Charles Kinsky's fault. His boldness intrigued her. And excited her. And, damn him, he would know that now—having felt her desire in his kiss. Jennie felt a flicker of annoyance and turned away from the mirror. Kinsky thought he could seduce her! When it was always *she* who determined the pace of her affairs, *she* who snapped her fingers for the next suitor! *I shall have to punish him,* she thought. Disappear for the rest of the day—but charm every other man within reach.

Had he been aroused? Or moved?

*Aroused,* she decided dismissively. Nothing but vanity really moved a man.

"All by your lonesome, Jennie?" Minnie Paget inquired as Jennie stepped into the passage and pulled her bedchamber door closed behind her. "How singular! I cannot remember when I last saw you without some fellow on your arm."

Minnie was wearing last year's gown this morning, blatantly dressed up with this year's lace.

"Now that you mention it," Jennie returned thoughtfully, "neither can I! Particularly when leaving my bedroom. How *are* you enjoying your stay at Sandringham, Minnie? We've barely had a moment to talk."

She smiled pleasantly, aware of the hardness in her old friend's eyes. Minnie surveyed Jennie's mushroom silk, and her thin lips compressed. Arthur Paget was known to have married her in expectation of a staggering fortune—ten million dollars was bequeathed Minnie in her father's will—but the estate was hopelessly tangled in litigation in the New York courts. Minnie viewed the world solely in terms of gains and losses. If Jennie gained—in happiness, influence, or social esteem—Minnie somehow lost. Although she would proclaim the depth of their attachment and mutual devotion to anyone who'd listen, Minnie would only be truly satisfied when Jennie was ruined, or died. And they both knew it.

"Is it possible you made only a *slight* impression on Count Kinsky?" Minnie marveled. "Though I must suppose he is accustomed to the very *best* circles in Europe. Dallying with the mother of two schoolboys can hardly be to such a man's taste—he is barely out of the schoolroom himself."

"We didn't talk of my boys when we rode this morning." Jennie slipped her arm through Minnie's with a roguish smile. "Count Kinsky is a bruising enough rider, of course, but found it hard to keep up with me. I daresay he saved his breath for the chase, Minnie."

Jennie practiced duets with Princess Alix in the comfortable sitting room Her Royal Highness kept for the purpose, filled with pale Swedish chairs and a vicious gray parrot who ruled everyone in Alix's orbit. It was a sign of Jennie's intimacy that she was admitted to the secret of the Princess's deafness, a progressive condition Alix fought with increasing despair. There were matching pianos, side by side, so that Alix could feel the percussive beat of the keys and attempt to keep time. Jennie found it restful to spend a few hours this way, freed of the necessity of social chatter, in the presence of a woman who felt Chopin in her veins. When they played the last trilling notes, Alix sighed deeply, and kissed Jennie on the cheek.

"I shall rest now," she murmured, as Jennie went in search of Consuelo Mandeville.

She found Connie in the billiards room. It was a dusky and intimate space overlooking the garden, lined with gingerbread carstone that gave it warmth on wet days. Bertie had built a bowling alley next door in the same style—*for the amusement of my American guests,* he said. Minnie played at ninepins occasionally to gratify the Prince, but Jennie and Consuelo preferred pool.

The Viscountess liked to sharpen her game while the men were out shooting. Her mother-in-law, Louise, Duchess of Manchester, sat perched on the edge of a deep leather chesterfield that ran along one wall. Hunting prints were framed on the wall above the sofa, and higher still was a row of antlered heads, shot by Bertie and his guests.

The Marquess of Hartington lounged next to Louise, whom everyone called Lottie; he'd been in love with her for years, although she was another man's duchess. Like Consuelo, Louise and Hart were smoking cigars.

"Take a cue, Jennie," Connie suggested.

They had learned to shoot pool together in Jennie's vast home on Madison Square during the winter of 1866, when both girls were twelve. Jennie's father had challenged them to penny points while the snow fell outside the windows and cigar smoke curled above his head. Afterward Leonard Jerome had driven the two giddy girls in his horse-drawn sleigh to a confectioner's and allowed them to spend their winnings. Whenever she smelled tobacco smoke, Jennie remembered the firelight in that beloved room and her father's voice.

"Stripes or solids, Connie?"

"You're stripes."

Jennie surveyed the table. Called her pocket and ball. It dropped with a satisfying sound.

"We missed you at breakfast, Jane," Hart remarked. "Where have you been?"

"Out in the fresh air and mud. As you suggested."

"That explains Kinsky's absence from breakfast, too," Connie murmured. "Did he show you his paces?"

Jennie ignored her and dropped a second striped ball.

"He is a distant cousin of mine," Lottie observed. She had been born in Hanover, a Countess von Alten. "As no doubt you discerned from his remarkable good looks."

"Fellow making a nuisance of himself?" Hart asked.

Jennie smiled. "Not yet, thank you."

"But she has hopes," Connie added.

"You wretch." Jennie missed the third pocket and rested her cue. "When I've hidden myself away on purpose!"

"Hiding has never been one of your talents." Connie bent low over the green baize surface. A tall figure had appeared in the doorway, leaning against the lintel, blue eyes intent and focused. Following the players and the game.

Jennie kept her back to the door, cue upright, as she waited on Connie's shot. But her heart caught in her throat and she knew that it would be like this now, from this day forward. She would sense instinctively whenever Kinsky breathed her air.

By the time she had exchanged the mushroom silk for a tea dress the color of wood violets, and still later for a silver evening gown and high-heeled slippers, Jennie was forced to admit that the only thing more frustrating than being alone with Charles Kinsky was to be separated from him by a crowd. Dinner, usually so swift at Sandringham, was endless torment. She was seated near the Prince of Wales, at the head of the table. Despite her drollest attempts at conversation, Bertie's heavy-lidded gaze never lifted from her heart-shaped neckline and the seven-pointed diamond star she'd set tonight in her cleavage. The length of the table separated her from Kinsky, at Princess Alix's left hand. Alix was prim perfection in lavender silk overlaid with Nottingham lace. An opulent five-stranded dog collar of pearls circled her neck. It hid a disfiguring burn or scar; nobody but Bertie knew which. The Princess's wide and lovely eyes were trained on Kinsky's mouth; he leaned close when he spoke to her, intimate as a lover. Jennie guessed this was nothing more than the Count's accommodation of Alix's deafness and her attempt to lip-read. But Jennie's distracted gaze strayed far too often to the foot of the table.

Minnie Paget was seated at Kinsky's left, waiting impatiently for the change in courses, when she might claim him from the Princess.

George Curzon, the MP who'd clamored for her arm the previous evening, sat beside Jennie. He idolized her husband, Randolph; the two men had Eton and Oxford in common, but George was barely down from school, ivory-skinned and blond-haired, with cheeks that burned bright red when he argued.

"Randy *must* be in the Cabinet when Gladstone falls," he assured Jennie rather too loudly. "The party leadership owe him that! He's the reason we'll be swept into power. The common man loves Randy."

She sensed the genteel conversations all around them falter. Minnie Paget's head turned sharply, her red lips parted on a suspended word. Even Kinsky had torn his attention away from Princess Alix. Jennie could feel the weight of his stare, like a warm hand on her neck. She continued to smile faintly, as though Curzon had not just suggested her black sheep of a husband was likely to overthrow Bertie's favorite Prime Minister.

Hartington, the most senior Cabinet member at Sandringham, shifted in his chair directly across from Jennie, dark head lifted to the elaborate plasterwork ceiling. "Gladstone is as safe as houses," he muttered, with undisguised contempt. "Particularly from Little Lord Random."

Curzon, too junior to challenge the Minister for War, flushed scarlet.

"Gladstone may be safe tonight," Jennie murmured. Was it a spark of loyalty to her outrageous husband—or because Kinsky was watching her? "But next week, my dear Marquess? Next *month*? Who can say? Lord Randolph always confounds expectation."

"Just as you *defy* it, my dear," Hart retorted dryly.

"Hear, hear," Curzon said in Jennie's ear. And drained his claret glass.

After dinner, Princess Alix begged Jennie to play Chopin. Her heart surged toward the Princess, who asked so little of her guests and whose kindness never permitted her to gossip or misjudge. Alix was one of the few transparently *good* people Jennie knew, utterly free of guile or malice. "I should be delighted," she replied. "In the privacy of your rooms, Your Highness?"

"No, no," Alix rejoined. "I could not be so selfish. A talent such as yours, dear Lady Randolph, was meant to be shared."

In groups of twos and threes the house party drifted toward the music room, a high-ceilinged space lined in pale gold damask. The piano was set at one end, the only dark piece in the room; a perfect foil for Jennie's black hair and silver gown. She would scintillate over the keys like a flash of moonlight. As she arranged her skirts, three men hurried to turn the sheet music for her. But Kinsky reached the piano first.

"Normally I play from memory." She kept her eyes serenely on the music, avoiding the clean line of his jaw. He had shaved again before dinner; the dark bloom on chin and cheekbone she'd glimpsed during tea in the Small Drawing Room was gone. What would it feel like, to sweep the back of her hand along that curve of bone? "This particular piece is a favorite of the Princess's, but I haven't mastered it yet."

It was no. 19, in E-flat Major, one of the most difficult of Chopin's twenty-four preludes. The tempo was *vivace,* with continuous, triplet-quaver movements in both hands, spanning at times fourteen notes. A joyous and yet yearning piece—exactly the romantic mood Alix preferred. The Princess had placed her chair quite near the piano to catch as much of the music as her deafness allowed.

Jennie glanced sidelong at Kinsky, her fingers poised over the keys, and nodded her head to begin.

He was silent and concentrated as he followed her glinting progress through the piece. The Count could read music, Jennie realized; he turned the pages with precision. She made two errors in fingering and noted them in a corner of her disciplined mind. No one but Kinsky would notice. Still, she must practice the prelude again in the morning.

"*Brava,*" he said as she struck the final chords, and applause rippled across the room. "I had no idea you were so accomplished."

Jennie wrinkled her nose at him. She loathed the word. *Accomplished* was for women who netted purses and embroidered screens. Not for virtuosos impassioned with music.

"Indeed, and I'm not," she retorted.

"Indeed, and she is," Consuelo interjected as she joined them. She had traded her emerald combs for rubies this evening. They flashed from platinum branches woven through her hair. Connie's velvet gown was a deep claret, Jennie noticed, molded to her body. Exquisitely touchable. "Lady Randolph studied with one of Chopin's disciples, Count, when we were girls together in Paris. Four hours a day. We trot her out whenever there's a charity concert, as our particular trained bear."

"Panther," Jennie murmured wickedly.

"Beast," Consuelo retorted, smiling.

Princess Alix bid her friends good night, releasing them all. The gentlemen quitted the music room for cards. But Charles Kinsky lingered.

He took Jennie's place at the piano, hands raised.

"Do you play?" she asked, surprised. Few gentlemen did.

By way of answer, he launched into his own bit of Chopin, from memory.

It was no. 8, the prelude in F-sharp Minor. Another difficult piece, but one that tore at Jennie's soul. One of Chopin's admirers had called it "Desperation." To Jennie it sounded like a woman racing headlong down a flight of stairs—a terrified woman, fleeing what she most feared. Only to come face-to-face with it on the final step.

*What do I fear?* Jennie demanded of herself.

*The loss of self-control. The loss of my freedom, to live as I choose. Live as I must.*

Kinsky played the prelude unerringly. His dark head was bent to the keys, oblivious of his audience; his torso swayed with the swell of sound.

*Emotion so deep and wide it drowns me.*

She would always be terrified of that.

Jennie sank onto a settee beside Consuelo and closed her eyes. The notes multiplied around them, heartrending and unconsoled. As they rippled over her, Jennie could almost feel Kinsky's fingers on her skin. She ought to leave the room, she knew—walk out alone into the dark April night—but she stayed where she was. Her hands balled into fists in her lap.

Charles Kinsky was determined to seduce her. He could not be ignored; he would have to be beaten. Jennie knew suddenly how to shatter his particular power. Make it commonplace. She would treat him like any other man who had ever wanted her.

Just snap her fingers. And be the one to *choose*.

The last phrase of music died away. Kinsky's hands drifted to his thighs and rested there an instant, as though he were gathering himself. Then he rose from the bench and bent over Jennie's palm.

"Come to me tonight," she whispered, low enough that Consuelo could not hear. "Or never come to me again."

# CHAPTER FIVE

That was how it began: with a battle royal in the wee hours of an April morning, Jennie lying on her chaise longue in the Prince of Wales's country house by a dying fire, no other light in the room. Her body free of its stays and confining layers beneath a peignoir of silk chiffon and lace. Her thick black hair unbound. Her maid asleep. Her thoughts fixed firmly on the man who was about to enter her room in a fever of desire.

She had taken lovers for years with Randolph's indifferent blessing. Pleasure was too great a game not to play. As long as the rules were observed, it was completely safe. Only once had she made a mistake—years ago, in Ireland—and her younger son, Jack, was the result. Randolph claimed both boys without hesitation. He preferred Jack to Winston, his own child.

It was vital to teach Kinsky her one rule: Pleasure was delightful, but love was never allowed. Love was misery. Love destroyed lives. The value of an *affaire* was that both parties were free—neither could trap or ruin the other. They could part ways at any moment without hard words or hurt feelings. Charles was young; he had a brilliant career ahead of him. She was the consort of a powerful man. Neither of them needed more than this.

She was thinking these things as the handle of her door turned. Every hinge at Sandringham was well oiled; Bertie made sure of it. She stared at the shadow that gradually became Charles, standing potently in her doorway.

Somewhere, a clock struck the hour.

# CHAPTER SIX

Big Ben tolled out the strokes of nine o'clock.

Randolph Churchill was bent over his desk in the library of the Connaught Place house, his pen scratching at one of his speeches. His private secretary, Alasdair Gordon, lounged with legs crossed in a club chair nearby. He was a beautiful Etonian youth of twenty-one with porcelain skin, golden hair, a poet's full lips. Alasdair couldn't write worth a damn, but he answered letters efficiently and the perfection of his Greek profile made Randolph's throat ache. His father was an impoverished clergyman in Sussex; Alasdair hoped for political advancement and a steady salary. In return, Randolph asked for nothing more than to look at Alasdair from time to time, as he might a rare object of art.

The press called Churchill Little Lord Random—he was admittedly rather short and his outbursts in Parliament were often startling—and Dandy Randy. At thirty-four he was thin to the point of gauntness; the caricatures in *Punch* showed him stoop-shouldered and bandy-legged, all head and no body. His enormous mustache emphasized the absurdity of his brown spaniel eyes. Randolph embraced and even exaggerated his physical oddities—flaunting foppish clothes and jewelry—just like his political idol, the late Prime Minister Benjamin Disraeli. Not long after they married, Jennie had given him a diamond ring in the shape of a cross. He wore it carelessly on his right hand. It flashed now in the electric lamplight as he offered Alasdair the pages of his speech.

"What do you think?"

Alasdair scanned the lines. One forefinger rested against his temple as he read. Randolph's gaze fixed on the pure lines of skull and bone until Alasdair's green eyes lifted from the page. "It seems rather intemperate to call the Government *whore-mongers,* my lord. The press is sure to seize on the vulgarity."

"For what else do we live, Gordon?" Randolph sighed. "But you're right; perhaps implication is preferable to insult."

Alasdair was gazing beyond him. A bustle from the hall informed them both that Lady Randolph had come home.

Jennie stopped short in the pool of light at the library threshold, allowing her eyes to adjust. She had insisted on electrifying the house when they bought it the previous year. Nobody in London trusted the violent new form of power. During her last visit to New York, however, she had seen how brilliantly lit the private homes and streets of lower Manhattan were. Papa had assured her electricity was perfectly safe, and paid for the generator she installed in her cellar. It made considerable noise but they had all grown used to the steady growl in the bowels of the house, as though it were the pulse of a living beast. And Randolph, whose eyes were frequently tired, had come to rely upon the light.

He and his secretary rose to their feet when she appeared.

"Hullo, Jennie. Had a good time in the country?"

"Yes, thank you. I'm a little weary from the journey." Several hours by rail, chilled with persistent rain and the tedium of having only her maid, Gentry, in the compartment to amuse her. A few periodicals. Bars of music and nagging, vivid memories of Charles skimming across her mind. "You've both dined?"

"At the Club. Would you read this for me?" Abruptly, Randolph held out several sheets of paper. "Gordon's made a hash of it as usual. You're better at fixing things than I am."

"Of course. When do you require it?" It was vital to respond when Randolph needed her; working together gave purpose to their marriage.

"I must go over the thing tomorrow night."

"My lord—"

Color flooded Alasdair Gordon's pale cheeks. He shot Jennie an agonized look.

"What is it?" Randolph asked impatiently.

"Are you *quite certain* you wish Lady Randolph to see the speech? The subject matter—that is . . . the *tone* of the debate being a trifle warm . . ."

"Venereal disease, Jennie." Randy's chin rose and he held her gaze. "Shall you recoil in horror?"

"Naturally not," she assured him, smiling.

He grinned back, her comrade of old. They had been tilting at windmills together for a decade, while Alasdair Gordon was still a schoolboy. Jennie took the speech from Randolph's hands.

She noted how pale he was. The flesh of his face had tightened over his bones. He had been ill for six months last year and they had retreated from everything to a rented house in Wimbledon until he was well. Then a restorative trip to visit Papa in New York and Newport, horse racing in Saratoga. But Randolph was still frail. He pushed himself far too hard. Her heart constricted in sympathy.

"I'll read it this evening," she promised. "Good night, gentlemen."

Gordon bowed. "Lady Randolph."

Randolph turned away without a word and poured himself a glass of brandy. His forehead was clammy and glistened in the sharp electric light. Jennie quelled the impulse to ask how he felt— and pulled the library door gently closed.

She would order some soup on a tray. She would take a hot bath while it was prepared. Then, she would stop into the nursery and kiss little Jack's cheek. She saw the three-year-old boy most often when he was asleep—his fists furled close to his chest, eyelashes fluttering in his dreams. Jack was dark, like her. Winston, her elder son, was a redhead and favored the Churchill side.

Everest, the boys' nanny, slept in a room off the night nursery, but she was used to Jennie's nocturnal visits. Sometimes they oc-curred at two o'clock in the morning. Sometimes the boys—although it was only Jack now that eight-year-old Winston was away at school—were brought to her in her dressing room while Gentry did her hair. It was one of the few times Everest knew that Jennie would be free to see her children.

She mounted the stairs wearily and made for the large room at the back of the house with the pale blue silk curtains massed around the posts of her bed. Randolph's was adjacent, with her dressing room in between. It was the usual arrangement, but for the difference Jennie had demanded when they bought the house: each of them had a private bath installed with hot and cold taps. This was commonplace in Newport and New York but extraordi-nary in England—even Blenheim Palace, the opulent marble bar-racks where Randolph grew up, made do with hip baths filled from canisters of boiling water that the servants carried up and down the service stairs.

Gentry had been before her: the bedroom fire was lit, her silver brushes arranged, and her dressing gown laid out to warm. Jennie slipped her furs from her shoulders and reached for the feathered pin that secured her upswept hat, as large as a tea tray. Her head and neck ached from supporting it all those hours from Norfolk on the train. She rolled her skull in a circular motion, easing the muscles, free of the need to perform for anyone. Relief wrapped her as close as a blanket.

Randolph's speech fluttered to the floor. Poor Alasdair Gordon might flush at the thought of a woman reading about prostitutes and syphilis, but Gordon was a delicate flower and Jennie was not. She let the pages lie. Gentry would collect them and place them neatly on the soup tray she would set across Jennie's knees as she sat in front of the fire. Gentry was as much a creature of habit as Jennie was. They had accommodated each other for years.

Her husband would not disturb her again that night.

That, too, was the habit of years.

———

"How did you come to marry Lord Randolph?" Charles Kinsky had asked her that afternoon as they assembled on Sandringham's back terrace for the final photograph. Recording his good times was Bertie's favorite ritual. Queen Victoria, his mother, had a passion for photographs, too, but the Queen's were always of family. Bertie preferred to be surrounded by friends—the Prince himself in the center of a glamorous group, staring straight at the camera while others looked away. Sometimes Princess Alix appeared in them, sometimes not. Like the Queen, she loved to record moments with her three daughters, all dressed alike, or her sister Minnie, the Czarevna, who visited only infrequently from St. Petersburg. Sometimes she and Minnie wore identical dresses in the photographs, like twins, although Alix was a few years older.

"Why do you ask?" Jennie murmured as the photographer aligned her shoulder with Charles's and spaced Hartington on the step below Louise Manchester. "Are you considering matrimony?"

"I met your husband last week at White's. I should never imagine the two of you in the same room, much less the same . . ."

*Bed,* Jennie thought.

"Family," Charles concluded.

His closeness was challenging. He maneuvered to stand beside her for the photograph, as though he wanted a souvenir of the previous night's liaison. Jennie absorbed this like an attack—a calculated provocation. A wave of heat flooded over her that had nothing to do with the sunlight on the Prince's terrace. The memory of Charles's hips between her thighs. The taut skin of his shoulder blades beneath her palms. She felt her fingers tremble, and balked at her own desire. It betrayed the firmness of her mind. She had taken Kinsky deliberately in order to dismiss him.

She said easily, "It surprises you that the Duke of Marlborough's son should choose to marry an American of no rank?"

"Not when the American is Jennie Jerome."

He had learned something about her past, then. Consuelo had

been talking. What had she told him? That Leonard Jerome loved racehorses, too, and had launched his own track? That he was called the King of Wall Street, and had helped found the Metropolitan Opera? That he was once part owner of *The New York Times*?

"All Americans are gamblers, you know," she replied dismissively. "I was simply in luck when I met Randolph."

*Luck.* Was that what she chose to call it now? The hollowness of the word smote her.

The photographer hurried back to his apparatus, set up on the lawn, and lifted a tarpaulin over his head. He raised his left hand, commanding the Prince's Set to silence. They were forced to hold this position until his hand dropped. It always seemed to Jennie to take an age. But she would not be allowed to step into her carriage and make for the station until Bertie was satisfied. He was, after all, the Heir Apparent to the British Empire.

"Did you love him?" Charles asked softly.

She could feel him staring at her. When the photograph eventually appeared, he would be captured in profile, while she gazed deceitfully at the camera.

"What makes you think I've ever stopped?"

Saturday at Sandringham was neither the time nor place to share personal histories. Kinsky was behaving like a boy. Demanding attention, when she had no more to give. Asking her to declare her loyalties, as though a few hours of shared physical passion required some sort of pledge. Jennie had a train to catch.

*Did you love Randolph?* she asked herself now, in the warm, safe haven of her Connaught Place bedroom.

*Ridiculously,* she ought to have said. But was that true? Or had she merely been a silly, infatuated nineteen-year-old girl? Randolph had known her all of three days when he proposed. And then his father the Duke refused his consent to the marriage. His Grace absolutely declined to shackle his younger son to an American nobody of dubious fortune. Good God—if anything happened to Blandford, the Nobody could be the next Duchess of Marlborough! Marrying Jennie was utterly out of the question.

Clara Jerome had whisked her daughters immediately back to Paris. Jennie, restless and furious, waited for Randolph to act during six long months. She flirted outrageously with legions of men quite ready to pursue her—across ballrooms, along bridle paths, and in the gaslit twilight of chamber concerts. Ivor Rules crossed the Channel in pursuit of her. Rode alongside Jennie's hack in the Bois de Boulogne, and fed her champagne in a box at the Paris Opera. He made the mistake of trying to undress her by force in a private dining cabinet off the Boulevard Haussmann, where she cut his cheek with a broken wineglass and called furiously for a cab. That was the end of Ivor Rules.

Jennie punished Randolph for his failed promises with detailed accounts of her insanely good times, dispatched by every post. From Blenheim, Randolph wrote back, aflame with jealousy, and argued viciously with his parents. Finally, he struck a deal with the Duke: he would campaign in the upcoming election. If he won a parliamentary seat, he won Jennie.

Marlborough agreed.

Woodstock voted for Randolph by a landslide that January of 1874.

*Ever since I met you,* he wrote Jennie exultantly the day after the final vote tally, *everything goes well with me—*

*Too well.*

*I am afraid of a Nemesis.*

Jennie feared nothing. She twirled alone before the mirror in her mother's French salon, Randy's letter clutched in her palm, giddy with happiness. She'd won the man who loved her for her mind as much as her body.

"Don't cry," she told a stunned Clarita as she kissed her wet cheek. "Everything is going to be *perfect* now. Always."

———

The Duke's solicitors discussed financial settlements with Leonard Jerome's lawyers in New York. But Leonard proved difficult—he refused to turn over Jennie's money to Randolph. *My daughter has the rank of royalty in this country,* he telegraphed the Duke from his favorite chair in the New York Yacht Club, *and as such she is entitled to the management of her funds.*

The Duke was infuriated. He declined to negotiate further with the Wall Street pirate.

"If Marlborough cannot be brought to reason," Clara Jerome declared in February, as an icy rain lashed the tall windows and distorted her cherished view of the Arc de Triomphe, "we shall simply have to end this foolish engagement." The Duke's snub rankled Mamma; she had spent too many years being cut dead by Caroline Astor in New York to tolerate English condescension. "Why can't you or Clarita find a nice French count? The French love us."

"A French count would want control of our money as much as the Duke does," Jennie retorted impatiently. "Don't you understand, Mamma, that it's money that makes us marriageable in Europe? It's only Papa who thinks a woman should be independent. I don't care a fig for his vulgar *funds!*"

"You will in time," Mamma warned darkly. "Papa knows very well that money means *freedom.* To give it up to the English would be . . . *un-American.*"

Randolph was in Paris just then on a visit to Jennie, the first he'd been able to pay since the election. But he could stay only two more days, before returning to London for the opening of Parliament.

Jennie could not bear to see him go with no date set for her wedding. She was desperate for all the *negotiation* to end. For her fairy tale to begin. She would not be thwarted by the stupidity of mere *parents.*

———

Now, nearly a decade later and alone in her bedroom on Connaught Place, Jennie tossed aside the speech she had ruthlessly rewritten for Randolph. She turned down her lamp and slipped under the coverlet. The embers of a coal fire glowed red and low on the hearth; spring rain pattered on the slates and gurgled in the lead gutters. The pale sunshine of her morning at Sandringham seemed as distant as last night's erotic battle. Jennie sighed, without regret; she had curbed her attraction for Count Kinsky by indulging it immediately. Never mind that he was the most consuming man she'd touched in months. Or that his face lurked at the edge of her mind. It was probable, Jennie decided, that she would never see him again.

# CHAPTER SEVEN

Charles Kinsky called on Fanny Ronalds as soon as he was back in London.

Fanny was notable because she dared to open her home to friends on the Sabbath, and because her friends bridged so many worlds. Actors and poets and Eugénie, the deposed Empress of France, met in her drawing rooms in Green Street. Fanny was an elitist—she absolutely refused to entertain prigs or bores—but she was no snob. Birth was far less important to her than genius. Charles suspected this was because she was American.

He found her warming a clear liquid in a brandy glass over an oil lamp's flame. Perhaps fifty people filled the double drawing rooms, like so much vivid paint thrown against the dark walls. Someone was playing the piano.

"You must give me your opinion, Count," Fanny demanded as she offered him the crystal balloon. "Is it vile or ambrosial?"

"Insipid," he returned. "What do you call it?"

"Sake. A Japanese sort of wine. Mr. Sullivan is experimenting in the Oriental vein and I'm hoping to tempt the Muse."

Fanny was in her mid-forties, a beautiful woman who had dwindled to handsome. Once, her clothes had framed a flawless face and body; now, her body framed her clothes. She was known as the finest amateur singer in London. Much of the music during her Sunday evenings was provided by herself and her lover, who paid the rent for Green Street. His name was Arthur Sullivan and he composed comic operas with his partner, W. S. Gilbert, that were immensely popular in England. Fanny was still married to a man she'd left behind in New York. She went about as Mrs. Ronalds, but she had been Sullivan's mistress for years. Before that, she'd been linked to the Prince of Wales.

And before him, to Leonard Jerome.

"I haven't seen you in an age," she scolded Charles, her fingers resting lightly on his arm. "Where have you been?"

"Sandringham."

"Good Lord. Was Alix there? Or was it a stag party?"

"The Princess was in residence. Along with a number of ladies who I presume are her friends. Some of them your compatriots."

"Let me guess." Fanny's lips pursed in amusement. "Minnie Paget. Viscountess Mandeville. Each eyeing the other like a mortal rival."

"With Lady Randolph in between."

"Jennie! Has Bertie waved a white flag, then, and declared the Churchills forgiven?" She grasped Charles's wrist and drew him aside. "Come talk to me. You've caught my interest now and God knows when I'll see you again. Everyone wants a piece of you, Count." Fanny sank down on a sofa tucked into one of her alcoves. Charles perched beside her. Amid the general clamor of conversation, it was possible to pitch a voice low and be heard. "Was Randolph there?"

"No," he replied. "He sent his beautiful wife alone. She referred to herself as a hostage. Is she a sacrificial one?"

"In Bertie's bed, you mean? Not on your life." Fanny's face filled with amusement. "Jennie does exactly as she chooses. If she travels without Randolph, it's because she prefers peace to his lordship's company. I can't blame her."

"You don't like him?"

"He doesn't like women," she said bluntly. "I merely return the favor."

"I don't know either of the Churchills." Charles eased himself into the curve of her sofa. "Tell me about them."

"Why?"

"Because they intrigue me."

"They? Or Jennie?"

"Did you know her in New York?"

"From the time she was nine years old. We were like sisters. I was a few years older, of course—"

At least fifteen years older, Charles guessed. But he did not interrupt her.

"I used to sing in charity concerts as a favor to my friends. Jennie's father—Leonard Jerome—owned what you Austrians would call a *town palace* on Madison Square, nearly an entire city block fronting the avenue." Fanny's supple fingers toyed with a knotted string of beads that fell to her narrow waist; garnets, Charles guessed. Arthur Sullivan's work must not run to rubies. "It was the most marvelous place! Had a three-story mahogany-paneled stables, a ballroom, of course, and a private opera house that seated six hundred. Leonard asked me to perform at one of his parties, years ago, in support of the Union troops. They fought for the *Northern* side in our Civil War, mind. I wouldn't expect you to know."

Charles frowned; he knew very little about the American civil war. He'd been five years old when Jennie was nine.

"Leonard was passionate about opera." Fanny's eyes glistened, her mind adrift in the past. "All the house lights were cut crystal— Waterford, imported from Ireland—and the theater seats upholstered in crimson silk velvet. That's how Leonard was. He'd leave a Tiffany bracelet at every woman's dinner place, as a memento of an evening."

"And Lady Randolph?"

"Shares her papa's love of music. The first time we met, little Jennie was playing the score of *Traviata* alone on the opera house Steinway. I was supposed to run through it that morning. She accompanied me."

Strange to think of Jennie as a child, bent intently over the keys with a tangle of jet-black curls down her back. Charles remembered her perfect seat on horseback, her ease among royals. Her careless lovemaking. Privilege as birthright.

"She was raised as a princess."

"She was raised to be Leonard Jerome's firstborn son," Fanny corrected sharply. "She's more like him than any man alive. Leonard taught her everything he knows. And he's ordered her to live life entirely as she chooses."

"Does she?"

"Of course. Lord Randolph doesn't even attempt to control her. Some people say it's because he lives on her money—Leonard gave Jennie a good deal, although he lost his fortune in a crash about the time she and Randy married. That must have been awkward for her; it was understood that Marlborough bartered his son for her bank account. Leonard righted his ship eventually; he always swings with the market. That's what American speculators do. But the Duke of Marlborough calls him a pirate."

"Preferable to a thief," Charles said dryly. "When did you leave New York, Mrs. Ronalds?"

"When Clara Jerome left Leonard." Fanny's mouth curved in a sudden smile. "You might have heard *he* left *her* for *me*. But that isn't true. Leonard has his amusements, but Clara remains his wife. When the ship sailed for France, we girls sailed together. We lived in each other's pockets in Paris, as we used to do in Newport; and after the Prussians and the Communards destroyed the city, we ended up here."

"And Lady Randolph married."

"*Eventually*. Poor Jennie was engaged to Randy for *months*. At first, the Duke refused his consent—because of Leonard's being a pirate. And then, without warning, the wedding was hurriedly staged at the British embassy chapel in Paris. I was there." She paused. "Winston was born less than eight months later."

She let the implication hang in the air between them.

A marriage at sword point, Charles thought. By whose design?

"It wasn't the worst bargain she could have struck," Fanny offered, as though she had read his thoughts. "Randy got a handsome settlement—fifty thousand pounds in trust—which as a younger son he sorely needed. I believe they live on the income to this day. Jennie got a courtesy title and a foothold in British Society. The child got a name. Thankfully, there's no mistaking his parentage—Winston's as ugly as every Churchill ever born."

"Have they been happy?"

Fanny smiled faintly before replying and lifted a finger to Charles's lips. "What a question, poppet! How many happy people have *you* met in this world? The Churchills have been a *success*. Isn't that far more important?"

"No."

Fanny sighed. "A romantic! Not everyone achieves personal perfection, Count. *Some* of us compromise. I don't love Randy, but he's certainly a political sensation. And he may well be Prime Minister one day. Jennie's smart as a whip and as seductive as her father; all of political London flocks to her parties. I applaud her for one thing—she's made herself *fashionable* again, after the horror of the Aylesford affair. In London Society, that's not easy to do."

Arthur Sullivan had taken over the piano. Strains of his latest production—*Iolanthe,* which had opened the new Savoy—filtered through the drawing room. Heads were turning in Fanny's direction.

She rose. "Arthur will want me to sing. I must fly, darling."

Charles kissed her hand.

Fanny launched into "The Lost Chord," Sullivan's tribute to his dead brother, her voice swelling as she glided across the elegant drawing room. It was her signature piece and her voice was beguiling, but Charles did not stay to listen. He slipped from the house and walked in the direction of his club. He wanted to know more about Randolph Churchill.

# CHAPTER EIGHT

On Monday, Jennie's carriage took her to Westminster. The hour was well after tea and dusk was falling. Nothing of note ever got done in the House of Commons until late afternoon, and debate was always broken by the dinner hour at the men's clubs in Pall Mall. After the wine had been drunk and the beef consumed, MPs returned to argue long into the night. Jennie rarely saw Randolph in his own home during the session, but they met as a couple at evening engagements.

She was deposited at the St. Stephen's entrance and hurried through the long passage to the Central Lobby. There she mounted the public stairs that led to the private viewing galleries suspended above the Commons floor. The Ladies' Gallery and the Speaker's Gallery—reserved for the wife of the Speaker—were usually filled with women addicted to politics. The Ladies' Gallery assigned its seats by lottery, but seats in the Speaker's Gallery were secured only at the invitation of the Speaker's wife. Jennie was on the list this afternoon.

The Speaker's Gallery was rather small and dark, set behind a carved Gothic screen fitted from top to bottom with a wire grille. As many as fifty ladies could be crammed into its chairs on important occasions, but it was far more bearable when only twenty were present. Jennie always referred to the gallery as the Speaker's Harem, because its segregated atmosphere was as profound and inarguable as an Ottoman palace. Women must not be visible to the Members below, and they must only talk in whispers, as though at church.

A clerk admitted her through a baize-lined oak door. Jennie paused as it closed behind her. The first row of chairs was separated from the second by a slim horizontal brass rod placed at neck height. The second and third ranks of chairs were elevated behind the first, stadium-fashion. The lucky few who bagged the first row of seats, their knees pressed painfully against the grille, could search out their distinguished husbands, sons, and friends below through delicate opera glasses. The rest usually gave up and listened blindly to debate, or wandered forlornly into the anteroom, where they wrote letters on House of Commons stationery and drank excellent tea sent up from the Members' Dining Room.

Today the gallery was pleasantly thin. Mrs. Gladstone, the Prime Minister's elderly wife, was in her habitual seat. She was sacred to the other political wives and always accorded the best spot, despite the fact that she was notoriously untidy and left a scattering of handkerchiefs, hairpins, and biscuit crumbs in a tidal wrack around the hem of her skirt. If she was absent from the gallery, no lady would dream of sitting in her place. Mrs. George Cavendish-Bentinck, who was several decades younger than Mrs. Gladstone and far more passionate about politics, was nestled in the far corner. There, if she leaned well forward, she could see her husband. George Bentinck, like Randolph, was a Conservative Member of Her Majesty's Loyal Opposition.

The Speaker's wife, Mrs. Henry Brand, was nowhere to be seen. Jennie felt a spurt of relief; Eliza Brand was a chilly woman in her sixties who despised what she called "foreign marriages" to American girls. She usually greeted Jennie with a brief nod and an acid glance at her carriage gown, followed by a disapproving snort. Eliza's mother had been illegitimate—the love child of the notorious Georgiana, Duchess of Devonshire, and Earl Grey—so of course, she used snobbery as a sword. Jennie had learned long ago that socially vulnerable women were the most vicious.

She tossed a smile at Prudie Bentinck in her corner, then settled into a seat in the center of the gallery's first row. Her day dress of claret-colored wool and silk brocade had thick, stiff panels embroidered with gold threads; it lapped the seats on either side of her, thankfully empty. Jennie set her leather pocketbook by her feet and folded her hands, gloved in black kid. She leaned slightly forward to glimpse the floor of the chamber. A Liberal Member she recognized as James Stansfield—a pious Yorkshireman—was protesting vehemently below.

". . . draft report was submitted without marginal reference to the evidence, and was voted *en bloc* by Members who did not take the time necessary to read and understand the paragraphs . . ."

Several men interrupted him with shouts of derision.

"That may seem ridiculous," Stansfield burst out, his face reddening, "but the Honorable Member must know that it is so."

"What exactly has Stansfield moved?" Jennie whispered.

"That the House disapproves of the compulsory examination of women under the Contagious Diseases Act," Prudie muttered back.

Catherine Gladstone sighed and bowed her head as though in prayer. The Gladstones were fervently religious and spent inordinate hours reclaiming fallen women. The Prime Minister brought girls home at night for a sermon and a cup of cocoa in his kitchen. Catherine gave them her outworn gowns. Jennie thought that was enough to drive any young girl back onto the streets.

She peered about for Randolph and found him on his usual bench at the front of the Opposition, next to Arthur Balfour. The men lounging below her would argue about the *form* of the debate for a little while—that was the cut and thrust of politics they all loved—but she doubted whether they would uphold Stansfield's resolution.

The Contagious Diseases Act had been law for nearly twenty years. It allowed policemen in British port and garrison towns to arrest any woman on the suspicion of prostitution, and subject her to a doctor's physical examination for disease. If she was found to be infected, the woman was forcibly quarantined, often in a poorhouse, for at least three months and treated until she was no longer contagious. The treatments were dubious—doses of mercury, arsenic, and sulfur that seemed to diminish symptoms for a time, but sickened the patient further. When women resisted treatment, they were simply arrested and subjected to hard prison labor. And as these women were often raising children alone, with no other means of support, families were devastated. Children were abandoned to the care of the parish and ended up in orphanages. Their mothers' names were listed for the rest of their lives on prostitution registries.

Men were not arrested or examined or confined against their will on the suspicion of venereal disease. Women alone bore the burden of what was called *public hygiene,* particularly in military centers where arrests were most common. Soldiers and sailors must have sexual relief; as heroes of the empire, they were spared the embarrassment of personal examination.

This blatant unfairness had stirred social critics to action. Some of them were women Jennie knew. The Ladies National Association for the Repeal of the Contagious Diseases Act protested that police persecution amounted to a double victimization of women who had already been degraded by men.

James Stansfield, the Liberal Member who had moved to condemn the arbitrary examinations, had a different objection to the act: by registering women and designating them as whores, he argued that the Government publicly condoned Sin. What was Stansfield saying now, from the Government benches? Jennie strained to make out his words. "The prostitution of women is the *supply* to the *demand* of the sensual appetites and vices of men . . . you offer a Government sanction to this sexual vice . . . you say by Act of Parliament . . . we will provide for you *clean* women to satisfy your lusts."

"Good Lord," Jennie murmured. "The Honorable Member is a fire-breather."

"And sadly in the wrong," Catherine Gladstone said, quite loudly. "Gladstone has *no* interest in satisfying lusts, I assure you."

There was a stirring from the benches below them; a few faces turned up toward the gallery. The Prime Minister alone was oblivious to his wife's voice; he was quite deaf.

Randolph, Jennie knew, wanted the Contagious Diseases Act repealed. He and a few others called it a damnable invasion of privacy when the law subjected anyone to an unwanted physical examination. But that was a pose for public consumption. What Randy really feared, Jennie guessed, was that Gladstone's Government might one day turn its zeal for public hygiene on *men*.

She had torn apart and reassembled his speech. It was far bolder now, if less obscene, than the one Alasdair Gordon had drafted. She had consulted the Ladies National Association's open letter to the *Daily Mail,* which almost every thinking woman of social prominence had read and many, including Florence Nightingale, had signed. Jennie ignored the Ladies' argument that men were responsible for the spread of venereal disease—Randolph would never utter such words aloud in Commons. Instead, she emphasized that the Government was brutalizing one-half of its population.

Somebody was running tediously through a column of figures. Rates of infection in the military cantonments of Devonport and Portsmouth and Chatham. These were male infections, of course—statistics on the women were not kept. It was the saving of fighting men that counted.

She waited impatiently for Randolph to rise. Instead, the Speaker recognized the Judge Advocate General, a Liberal whose job was to throttle the outraged Stansfield. Jennie caught the phrase "from the evidence of clergy, medical officers, and police ... it was clear that the condition of the unfortunate women who were subjected to these restrictive and sanitary measures had been favorably influenced, and that a comparatively large proportion of them had been *reclaimed. . . .*"

"Reclaimed," Prudie Bentinck breathed beside her. "Like parcels from the Left Luggage. Bloody ass."

Jennie peered down at her husband. He was lolling against the front bench with his legs crossed, both arms flung along the wooden back. The diamond cross on his right ring finger flashed in the gaslight. His chin rested on his chest; she could glimpse only the back of his head, the hair slickly controlled with pomade. In Commons, Randolph often looked like he was sound asleep. His neck was thin and narrow, almost too weak for the support of his skull. He had run fevers in January. But he was nonetheless an elegant figure as he rose now to address the House—lean and brilliant, like his words.

Jennie felt a surge of pride. Randolph in public, with a captive audience, was like nothing else on earth.

*He can have anything he asks for,* the late Prime Minister Benjamin Disraeli had told her years ago when she was a young bride, *and soon he'll make them take anything he's willing to give them.*

"Neither the Honorable Member from Halifax nor the Judge Advocate General have cited the most obvious objection to compulsory examination under the Contagious Diseases Act," Randolph began. "It violates all notion of *habeas corpus* and the presumption of innocence enshrined under the British Constitution. Is every woman to be presumed guilty, and shamed with a forced examination? In the name of military health and the gods of war, any outrage may be accepted! These are merely *women,* my fellow Members exclaim! And *women* ought not to be regarded as the equals of men under the law or Constitution. They have no right to vote. They are not fully Her Majesty's subjects. Have they the right to *habeas corpus,* then, as the law regards it?

"I would put it to the House that every feeling Member among us must insist that they do. There are those who believe that upon marriage, husband and wife become one, and the wife ceases to exist in any legal sense. But I would remind my fellow Members that last year this Government passed the Married Women's Property Act, which accords women the right to claim earnings, inheritance, and the ownership of property as well as the financial obligations implied in the ownership of property. Women are therefore subjects in the eye of the law. They are not dogs, to be kenneled and leashed at the whim of their masters. Nor are they cows, to be penned and dosed for the greater good of the bull."

Jennie sat upright, holding her breath as she listened to her own words. Once, when she had spoken publicly to female members of the Conservative Party's Primrose League, Arthur Balfour had remarked that her speeches were remarkably similar to Randolph's. "My husband's very sweet about my poor efforts," Jennie fibbed. "He improves my drafts when he possibly can."

The three of them—Jennie, Randolph, and Balfour—had come up with the idea of the Primrose League one night in the drawing room at Connaught Place. It was a key part of Randy's push for what he called "Tory Democracy," extending the party's appeal to common people—middle-class workers and even women—by giving them a voice in politics they'd never had. His enemies called him a rabble-rouser. His supporters called him a revolutionary. For a trifling donation, the League members got a silk primrose— the flower Disraeli had always worn in his buttonhole. They also got a personal stake in a local Conservative chapter and a voice in the formulation of its platform. Nothing like the Primrose League had ever been seen in Britain before. The Liberals were falling over themselves to discredit Tory Democracy—and Randolph Churchill.

It was Jennie, who'd been reared in the machine politics of Tammany Hall New York, who urged Balfour and Randolph to give women a role in the League, although women could not vote. "Women have opinions," she insisted. "They argue and persuade. They do it in bed and at the dinner table. Women raise future Conservatives."

"What a gross insult to privacy it is," Randolph cried now on the floor below her, "when the guardians of our streets are unleashed with whistle and truncheon upon the weaker sex—one-half of our Queen's privileged subjects—the women who ought most to be protected by the Crown—to browbeat them into submission and a brutal examination of far too intimate and violating a nature. Her Majesty, with the keenest fellow feeling for her sex, has expressed her repugnance for the Contagious Diseases Act. Even the Honorable Member from Halifax would abhor a similar practice being visited upon his wife or sister, his daughter or mother—and yet he settles his conscience now with the notion that the victims of the act are never *good women*. A whore deserves no protection, he thinks, having forfeited it with her embrace of Sin. But who is the Honorable Member, I would ask, to judge the soul of a stranger? Is he God, that he may see into a veiled heart? So long as one good woman is unjustly violated—so long as the reputation and livelihood of one good woman are sacrificed—we cannot hold up our heads. Let us resolve not only to condemn forced examinations—let us resolve to return all notions of *public hygiene* from Mr. Gladstone's kitchen, to the sanctity of the bed-chamber, where they belong!"

A chorus of *hear-hear*s from the Conservative benches.

The baize-lined door behind Jennie opened; she turned her head. The porter handed her a note. She broke the wax—the seal was one she did not recognize, a crown with a flowing mantle and three slashes like claws.

*Jennie.*
*Join me in the anteroom.*
*Kinsky*

# CHAPTER NINE

Charles Kinsky stood beyond the baize door, impeccable in a dark gray swallow-tailed frock coat and a silk top hat.

"Count! How did you guess I was here?"

He bent low over her hand. "Everyone in London knows you're obsessed with politics, Lady Randolph."

"When my husband is speaking—naturally."

Important to remind him they were in public now. That she was off-limits. The highly visible wife of a rising political star.

He drew out a chair for her at one of the little tables scattered about the gallery's anteroom and waited until Jennie settled her heavy wine-colored skirts. A waiter from the Members' Dining Room hovered, a silver tea tray in his hands. She had already had tea in Connaught Place, but after listening to Mr. Stansfield's apoplectic phrases, Jennie felt she could do with another cup.

"Lord Randolph is an impressive speaker," Charles remarked as he took the chair opposite.

"You were listening to the debate in the Diplomats' Gallery?"

"Following Parliament is one of my duties."

"Duty? A strange word in the mouth of a prince!"

His teeth flashed. "You think I only race horses?"

"Of course not. I . . ."

Her voice trailed away. She knew a bit about Charles Kinsky's body . . . but what about his heart or mind? He was attached to his embassy, a representative of the Austro-Hungarian Empire with a future in European politics. She had managed to forget all that at Sandringham. Lord help her if Charles was determined to be *intelligent* and *complicated*. She didn't need another distraction in her life.

"Although the *Times* says it's just acting," he persisted. "That Lord Randolph doesn't believe twenty words of what he says. What do you think, my lady?"

"I think the *Times* prefers its politicians dull. They're easier to ignore that way. Randolph is passionate about his beliefs."

Charles lifted his brows. "The *Spectator* calls it epilepsy, not passion. An uncontrolled spasm, from a man drunk on words."

"The *Spectator* is a Liberal Party rag."

He laughed. "I forgot. You actually read newspapers, don't you?"

"What's worse, I even understand them," she retorted. "I was raised on newsprint, Count. When I was young, my father used a Gatling gun to defend the front entrance of *The New York Times* from a riot. That's the power of the press."

"Tory Democracy, in fact!" He repeated Randolph's battle cry with mock surprise. "Lord Randolph and his friends like to talk about it—but did *you* come up with the name, my lady? It has a peculiarly American ring."

"My husband has his own brilliance, Count; he has no need of mine."

Charles eased back in his chair. It framed the beauty of his profile beneath the top hat, the clean lines of his tailored shoulders. Jennie had a swift sense of animal power, leashed and perfectly contained. Her combative impulses amused him. But his self-control stung like a challenge. *Unleash me.*

*Stop it,* she scolded herself.

"Have you any notion of the fear your husband and his rabble-rousing have sent through Europe?" Charles inquired. "England sets the tone of world politics, Lady Randolph. If the common people are allowed to think they have a voice in government, we're all doomed."

"*You* being the nobility. We Americans are absurdly proud of our common people. We even elect them."

"You're not in New York anymore." His eyes moved over her lazily. "Anyone in a position of power should be threatened by your husband's bombast. I send reams of dispatches home about Lord Randolph. He's stirring the mob to revolt. We're holding our breath in Vienna to see what he does next."

"So you're a spy, Count Kinsky," Jennie marveled. "That's why you make up to me! To learn my husband's secrets."

"I make up to you," he countered quietly, "because I'm in love with you, Jennie. You're the most consuming woman I've ever met."

Her breath caught in her throat, painfully. *"Don't."*

"I haven't slept since Friday. I'll probably never sleep again."

*Complicated,* damn him.

"That's not love, Count. That's lust. Easily satisfied."

He removed one of his gloves, finger by finger. His sensitive hand—exquisitely expressive, crying out for touch—placed the leather deliberately across her empty teacup. A twist on the traditional gentleman's challenge, to a liar or a cheat. He could hardly slap her cheek in the Speaker's anteroom.

"Go on," he muttered. "Satisfy it, then."

A tremor ran through her. She leaned toward him, furious, eyes narrowed. "Would you thrust a quarrel on me?"

"I prefer an *affair of honor*."

The air between them was singing and charged.

How much did he want of her? How much would he try to take?

"My father taught me never to refuse a challenge," Jennie said.

"I'd hoped he might." He fingered her wrist, casual, searing. "Let me drive you home."

The world swung on its axis. The two of them, in a closed carriage—darkness falling outside—her fingers in his hair—

"Jennie," he whispered, deep in his throat.

"Very well." She drew back, her skin tingling. "If you promise not to talk *nonsense*."

He eased his hand into his glove.

"Never fear, my lady. I won't say a word."

# CHAPTER TEN

The resolution condemning the physical examination of women under the Contagious Diseases Act went down to defeat in Commons. Enough Liberals and Conservatives agreed that the enforced medical treatment of prostitutes for syphilis was necessary to the defense of the realm.

Jennie was privately thrilled to see that Randolph's speech received special notice in the morning papers, particularly his exhortation that women were not cows to be penned and dosed for the bull. She had taken special pains with that line.

He was unwell for the rest of the week. He spent most days in a peacock-blue dressing gown and slippers, talking feverishly of Tory Democracy to his secretary, Alasdair. Jennie knew that the excitement of debate worked badly upon Randolph's nerves. He summoned his wit and will to consider a problem, compose an inflammatory speech, and deliver it with verve—only to be left depleted and low. For him, there was no moderation, no living in between. Randy was either up with the angels or down with the devil.

He could hurt her viciously and carelessly in this mood, irritated by the slightest lapse in his routine, or Jennie's failure to cater to his prodigious needs.

"Mary is in tears," she told him indignantly one morning as she brushed past the weeping housemaid in the upper hall and halted in Randolph's doorway. "What *can* you have done to upset her so?"

"Threw a slipper at her head," he replied furiously. He was bundled in his bed, his thin cheeks livid and his eyes red. "She dropped a coal in the grate as she laid the fire. Utterly destroyed what shreds of sleep I'd managed. Give her notice."

"Indeed, and I will not." Jennie folded her arms. "She's an excellent housemaid and they're difficult to find."

"She's a barbarian from Kerry. *Give her notice*."

"I shall apologize, as I see you're incapable of it." Jennie turned away.

"Do that, and you have my leave to pack up with her!" he shouted. "No mistress of breeding would take the part of a slattern against her husband. But I forgot—you were bred to spend *money,* not manage a *genteel* household."

As she pulled closed his door, a second slipper hurtled against the mahogany.

Jennie avoided him the rest of the day, but ventured to the library when Arthur Balfour called to escort her to an evening concert of Liszt. Her husband was smoking by the fire with a racing form on his lap and his feet propped on an ottoman. Arthur had been at Eton with Randy; he was immune to his insults.

"You'll rally, old son," he said bracingly as he clapped Randolph's shoulder. "What you need is something to take you out of yourself. An issue with teeth in it. Tell us what's next!"

"A Cabinet portfolio," Randolph drawled around his cigar. "Or the Abbey."

"I hate it when you talk like that," Jennie snorted. By Westminster Abbey, Randolph meant death. A state funeral. He was only thirty-four years old.

"Then Cabinet post it shall be," Balfour interposed comfortably, and carried her off to the Royal Albert Hall.

She listened intently to the Liszt, imagining fingering, keeping time on Balfour's sleeve. He was enough of a musician himself not to mind or notice. Jennie felt suddenly lighter, free of Connaught Place and her husband's gloom.

"You're positively radiant, my dear," Arthur told her during the interval, as they strolled arm in arm through the lobby, nodding to acquaintances and drinking champagne. He was brown-haired, tall, aloof, and indolent; a bent question mark of a figure in *Punch* caricatures. Landowning Scots forebears were the source of his fortune; his uncle, Robert Cecil, Marquess of Salisbury, the source of his political pull. Balfour would be PM one day, so the wags said—although, of course, they said the same of Randolph. "I've never seen you in greater beauty. Is that a new gown, or are you in love?"

"I never have a new gown, Arthur," Jennie mourned. "Only old ones, made over. You saw this last season, without the beads and flounce. We're too poor for extravagance, as you very well know. If only Papa would come about again! He used to be quite a wealthy man—but of late, he's rather let us down. Only two thousand a year. Think what that means! Hardly enough to order a single costume."

"If it's covered in diamonds!" Arthur scoffed. "Don't let Randy's constituents hear you pine, Jennie. Two thousand's a fortune to a blacksmith in Woodstock. I daresay the Duke hasn't much more."

"Ten times at least."

"Rubbish. His Grace has Blenheim to maintain. Whereas you merely keep the best cook in London. I hear the Prince of Wales means to lure Rosa away to Marlborough House."

"He shan't succeed," Jennie vowed. "We do not speak of *luxuries,* Arthur. Rosa is a necessity to any political hostess. I'll pay whatever she asks to refuse Bertie."

"Then if it's not the gown that's brought up your color," he said speculatively, "who's the lucky fellow?"

Jennie gave Arthur her most engaging smile. He was a dear, and had no interest in women since the cousin he'd hoped to marry had died young of typhus. Every compliment he paid her was pure. "Truly—would you guess I was a day older than twenty-four?"

"Are you?" he inquired.

"I've reached the age of danger." She dropped her voice. "My next birthday I shall be *thirty,* Arthur."

"We can't have known each other that long. You're twenty-two, at the outside."

"Don't shame me. Winston is nearly nine."

"So he is." He looked down into her laughing eyes. "Who's turned your head? Can't be Freddie Burnaby. He's well enough in an idle hour—but he's as thick as a post. And utterly unmusical."

"Perhaps he'll be *posted* abroad."

"Then it must be that Kinsky fellow—I noticed you riding with him in the park."

Jennie had come down to breakfast the day after Randolph's speech to discover a new sidesaddle waiting for her, delivered with the Count's compliments. It was a perfection of supple leather with a beautifully padded pommel; naturally, she couldn't rest until she had thrown herself up on a horse. She had ridden with Kinsky three times that week. But Rotten Row offered no scope for a good gallop—

"Dashing enough," Arthur conceded, "but I daresay he's a rake."

"I like rakes," she reminded him merrily. "But you know I never play favorites, Arthur. I can hardly remember all my admirers' names."

"You're wise not to be particular. It sets the hags' tongues wagging."

"Lord knows there are enough of them in London." She inclined her head toward Eliza Brand, the Speaker's wife, who glanced aside without a smile, as though absorbed in her partner Lord Rosebery's conversation. "I have Randolph's career to consider."

"As do we all." Arthur took her champagne from her hand. "He'll either sweep the Conservatives into power with his calculated abuse—or bring us to the gates of Hell."

"Which do you think it shall be?" Jennie asked lightly.

Arthur's gaze met hers, suddenly serious. "Even odds, my dear. But the race is bound to entertain, however it ends."

Randolph was persistently depressed through the early weeks of May. He slept badly, ran low fevers, and his delicate skin erupted in hives. The clamor of London, he complained petulantly, made thought and work impossible. He needed the complete rest only the country could provide. He packed up Alasdair and Walden, his valet, and went to his mother at Blenheim Palace, the vast treasure house of stone west of Oxford. He did not invite Jennie to join him, and she was relieved to be spared the ordeal; Blenheim was magnificent, of course—but primitive and cold. She had never been anything but miserable there. She could wave with real enthusiasm as Randolph's hansom pulled away for Paddington.

Randolph's mamma, Duchess Fanny, had borne the Duke eleven children, six of them girls. Three of her sons had died in boyhood. The two who remained were often a test to her Christian faith and principles. The Duchess abhorred the wild behavior of Blandford, heir to the dukedom, and mourned Randolph's marriage to an American of no family. She never bothered to hide her dislike of Jennie, whom she judged to be too showy, too opinionated, and far too much in the public eye. Worse, Jennie had nowhere *near* the fortune Randolph had hoped. The Duchess's greatest joy was when her son came back to Blenheim alone.

"Is it possible that your wife has *still* no notion of how to care for you?" she asked the evening he arrived, as he lounged in a chair by the Long Library fire. It was an enormous white tunnel of a room, 180 feet long and three stories high, designed by Christopher Wren. A *gallery,* really, meant to display ancestral Marlborough portraits and massive scenes of Marlborough exploits. There was not much art and few books, however; Randolph's father had been forced to sell them to make ends meet. The Sunderland Library, as the collection was called, had fetched nearly sixty thousand pounds on the auction block.

"No one cares for me as you do, Mamma," Randolph replied, amused.

"If Jeanette were not so *restless* . . . I am sure she is never at home two nights together!"

"If it comes to that, neither am I."

"Rosamund informs me that one may meet with her in four different drawing rooms of a single evening."

Randolph's sister Rosamund was a year older and utterly devoted to her little brother. She was married to William Fellowes, a Conservative MP. "Rosie is in all the same drawing rooms," Randolph said. "That's a life in politics for you."

"Impossible. Rosamund was confined barely three months since."

"And couldn't fight her way free of the nursery soon enough." He knocked his pipe tobacco onto the coals, then pressed his fingers irritably against his eyes. "I'm afraid I'm rather fagged, Mamma. Have I time to lie down before dinner?"

"Poor boy," Fanny murmured, stroking his hair. His forehead was clammy, although the library was riven with drafts. "The Commons have worn you out. I shall have Benson bring up a tray to your room."

Jennie went down to Sandringham again in Randolph's absence and galloped every day with Charles Kinsky, through woods brimming with bluebells. There was a high glow to her skin and her amber eyes sparkled brilliantly in the Princess's candlelit dining room. By day, Jennie played the piano with Alix and bowled with the Prince and his friends. She laughed often and her conversation was exuberantly witty. Harry Cust persuaded them all to write riddles and charades in the evening. This was how, on one occasion, Jennie was discovered by a scandalized footman with her right foot kicked high above her head, revealing—as he later told a shocked royal servants' hall—*a most dreadful display.* All the gentlemen were circled around her, crowing and clapping as though she were on a Parisian stage; the footman swore he had not known *where* to look. Jennie's charade was *can-can,* and she could find no other way to demonstrate it; but even Consuelo Mandeville felt she might have gone too far.

"Upon my word," Minnie murmured to Connie one evening as Kinsky played Beethoven in the Princess's music room. Jennie was turning the pages for him, absorbed in her task, her white neck arched over the Count's shoulder. "I do think Lady Randolph might practice a bit of discretion! Never mind the rest of the men she delights in leading by the nose—the way she looks at Kinsky is a scandal! Bertie will have the poor man recalled to Vienna. It never pays to hunt in a monarch's preserve."

"You think the Prince is jealous?" Consuelo Mandeville frowned.

"Don't you?"

"Not at all," Connie replied smoothly. "But I know who is."

Minnie forced a brittle smile and moved away in search of coffee. Her husband, Arthur Paget, was a soldier currently posted abroad; Minnie survived her straitened financial situation by spending months at a time in the houses of friends. She repaid them with gossip. When there was no scandal to feed on, she did her best to create one. Not everyone believed what Minnie Paget said, but her whispers could be damaging.

"Jennie," Connie murmured as she paused in the dark-paneled passage outside her friend's bedroom that night, the drafts twisting shadows from their twin candles, "you must have a care. The Paget has her knives out."

"Doesn't she always?" Jennie smiled conspiratorially. "Minnie's never learned to be happy."

"Happiness is expensive. And Minnie never spends a dime if she can borrow one." Consuelo suppressed a burble of laughter. "But seriously, my darling—you ought to consider the *costs* of this affair. The Paget says Bertie is watching. I know she's angry that Harry Cust admires you so—but she might actually be *right* this time."

"Connie! This *is* serious!" Jennie dropped a kiss on her friend's cheek, both reassurance and dismissal. "Very well. I promise. In all matters of the heart, I shall take care to balance my books. You don't imagine I *wish* to go bankrupt, do you?"

But as she blew out her candle that night, Jennie felt a finger of uneasiness along her spine. She knew the gods punished too much happiness.

# CHAPTER ELEVEN

$B$ack in London and still blessedly independent, Jennie tried to act on Countess Mandeville's warning. She tried—for at least three days, before she gave up in despair and met Charles Kinsky for a trot through Hyde Park. She told him nothing of the danger she might be running—the public scandal and utter banishment visited upon her brother-in-law's mistress. Jennie refused to believe such a shameful folly could happen to them. She was too blissful, too much under Kinsky's delicious spell.

May wore away in gusts of sudden rain. She met Charles at concerts and at dinners in the homes of friends and by arrangement in the British Museum, where they sat side by side on benches and surreptitiously held hands as they contemplated the pictures. Jennie had recently taken up painting, with Princess Alix and several of her friends—setting up easels together in the meadows of Sandringham and, on rainy days, in a studio at the Waleses' London home, Marlborough House. Jennie had a makeshift painting room of her own in the north attic of No. 2 Connaught Place, where the light was best, and implored any stray visitor to sit for her.

Charles, naturally, was one of them.

She painted him in an Austrian hussar's uniform, his expression more than usually disturbing as he stared at her while she worked. He held a plumed shako on his knee. Jennie yearned to throw away her brush and tear his military discipline to shreds. She summoned all her fortitude to concentrate.

She painted him in disarray as well, the neck of his shirt open and the strong lines of his throat springing from the canvas. It was not uncommon for the work to be interrupted when Charles rose suddenly from his seat and pulled her down on the studio's chaise longue.

After one of these interludes, as they shared a glass of wine by the makeshift fire in the attic grate, a fur throw pulled over them both, Jennie fingered the gold signet ring on his little finger.

"Your coat of arms—explain it to me."

Charles eased himself upright and settled her more comfortably on his chest. "The crown of the prince, and the flowing mantle. What is there to explain?"

"Those three slashing marks. They're painted white on your carriage crest. Are they supposed to be feathers?"

"They're teeth," he said, with an odd note in his voice. "Of a wolf. And a warning to the world that Kinsky men guard their own."

She lifted her head and looked at him. His hand came up to her tumbled black hair.

"There is a legend in my family from a very long time ago—the twelfth century, in fact."

"Tell me."

"A young man of our house—and in those times, he would have been little more than a vassal, a breeder of horses and a survivor of rampage—rode through the woods of Bohemia as dusk fell. No doubt he had been hunting—wild boar, perhaps, or a fallow deer. It was winter, because the legend tells how the snow lay white on the ground beneath the trees and cast enough glow for the man to see by, although night was falling."

"Yes?"

"His horse knew the way home and ought to have gone tamely to its feed and its stable, but for the scream that pierced the twilight and stopped both man and beast in their tracks."

Jennie said nothing. Her ear rested on Charles's chest and she could hear the measured thud of his heart, the susurration of blood surging through his body.

"The scream came again. The man knew without question that it was human.

"He wove through the leafless trees and came suddenly into a clearing filled with gray wolves, braced to spring, their lips drawn back and snarling. Their prey was a young girl with eyes of blue and a gold braid down her back."

Without meaning to, Jennie flinched. He had her firmly in the grip of the tale, his voice low and dreamlike. It was as though they were both tucked up in the nursery—or encamped in the snow on high steppes, with only the talisman of fire between them and barbarity.

"The man urged his horse forward, and because it was an *Equus Kinsky* and bred to face without fear any sort of menace in the forests of Bohemia, it carried him into the heart of the pack. The man drew a knife—he was not a knight and so had no sword, but every hunter carries a knife—and slashed at the nearest animal's throat, leaving it dead. A few of the others backed away, daunted. But the greatest of the wolves leapt onto the horse's back and lunged for the man's bare neck. They fell to the ground, rolling together, the wolf tearing at the man's arms and chest. Blood poured from the wounds and inflamed the wolf further, but the man—my ancestor—rolled uppermost and, in a scant second, plunged his knife into the beast's heart."

"And the girl?"

"The rest of the pack fled, howling, as the injured man staggered to his feet and whistled for his horse. The noble creature came at once, limping where one of the wolves had savaged its hock. The man skinned the wolf and draped its pelt over the horse's flanks, so that no *Equus Kinsky* would ever again fear a predator. Then he lifted the maiden into the saddle and led her home."

"She married him, of course."

"What else? She was a princess, the daughter of the King of Bohemia, and the House of Kinsky was ennobled from that day forward. I told you it was an old family story. But we keep three wolf's teeth mounted in gold, in a glass case, in the library of our palace in Vienna."

"I should like to see them," Jennie whispered.

"You will, my darling." Warm as velvet, his lips caressed her collarbone. "Someday."

Randolph returned to London and the House of Commons. If he noticed Jennie's preoccupation with her new riding partner, he said nothing.

On the fourth of June, Randolph's sister Lady Georgiana Churchill married Richard Curzon, George Curzon's cousin, who would one day be an earl. Georgie was twenty-three and it was high time she went off from Blenheim, but Duchess Fanny felt she had given all the honor in marriage and earned none of it. The Duke had been forced to sell the Blenheim Enamels, some eighty pieces of antique Limoges, to meet Georgie's dowry.

Now only eighteen-year-old Sarah was left at home. Sarah was restless and had notions of independence that troubled the Duchess. She had taken to wearing bloomers and riding a bicycle instead of a horse. She was to make her debut later that month with a ball at the house in Berkeley Square the Duke of Marlborough had rented for the Season. Marlborough House, built by the original Sarah Churchill as her London residence in the time of Queen Anne, had reverted to the Crown six decades earlier, a matter of intense regret and mortification to Duchess Fanny. The breathless Marlborough honors had never been equaled by their fortunes. The Prince and Princess of Wales lived in Marlborough House now.

Jennie wore a new gown of pale blue silk embroidered with silver hydrangea flowers to the wedding at St. George's, Hanover

Square. The jacket bodice had the stiflingly tight collar and sleeves to the wrist that Princess Alix had made fashionable, almost nun-like in its plainness. Her hat was a shallow straw with a masculine brim that Randolph jeered looked like a coal scuttle, but for the broad band of dark blue grosgrain dressed with massed hydrangea blooms.

Georgie floated down the aisle, a plain girl transformed by the prospect of escape into the adult world. Her color was high and contrasted unbecomingly with the ivory satin of her wedding dress. She carried a trailing spray of white lilies from the hothouses at Blenheim. Her bridegroom, a pleasant-looking fellow with a mustache to rival Randolph's, was a year younger than Georgie and had known her all his life.

On the seventh of June, Jennie wore the same blue gown to the Royal Enclosure at Ascot. There she watched the canny veteran jockey George Fordham win the Gold Cup on the powerful chestnut stallion Tristan. The horse was known to be bad-tempered and tolerated only Fordham on his back; he took the lead a full mile from the finish and won by three lengths.

"Did you bet to win?" asked a voice at Jennie's shoulder.

She turned to find Charles Kinsky, impeccable in top hat and morning dress. A walking stick was tucked under his left arm; his house's curious coat of arms was emblazoned on the knob. Jennie quelled the urge to run her fingers over the wolf's teeth. And Charles's gloved hand . . .

"Do I look like the betting kind?" she demanded, tilting the brim of her coal-scuttle hat to meet his gaze.

"All Americans are gamblers. Or so I'm told."

"Very well, then—Randolph placed a pound on Tristan for me. The lovely animal has come in handily. How shall we celebrate, Charles?"

His eyes drifted beyond her; he inclined his head and raised his topper. Jennie glanced around; a young lady, golden-haired and blue-eyed, like the girl from the Kinsky legend. She could not be more than nineteen, Jennie decided—the age she had been when she met Randolph. . . .

"My lord," Charles said, and bowed to her husband.

"Kinsky! Where did you spring from?" Randolph returned his salute and handed a slim roll of banknotes to Jennie. "Here you are, darling—your winnings. Don't be in a hurry to squander them."

"Nonsense. There's nothing else to be done with the wages of sin," she retorted cheerfully. "Are you in luck, too, Count Kinsky?"

"Always," he said equably. He did not glance at the blonde again. "As a result, I've decided to throw a party. Dinner and dancing for a few select friends—at the New Café, Covent Garden, Friday week. May I hope to have the pleasure of your company, Lord and Lady Randolph, in a toast to great horses that run their hearts out?"

Randolph pled a previous engagement—a debate in Commons he could not avoid—but Jennie accepted with a teasing curtsey, her right hand on her breast. Through the silk of her nunlike gown, she felt her heart accelerate. *A night of dancing with Charles. Could anything be more joyous?*

# CHAPTER TWELVE

"My lady," Mrs. Everest said.

Jennie caught the nanny's reflection in her dressing-table mirror. It was half obscured by the more immediate image of Gentry, who was wrestling with a wreath of silk evening flowers, cream and gold, that must be woven into Jennie's curls. They were intended to pair with the cloth-of-gold gown, slashed with cream silk, that she would wear to India House that evening, but at the moment Jennie was dressed only in a lace wrapper and silk stockings bound at her thighs with garters.

"What is it?" she asked coolly, although her heart surged a little with worry; it was unlike the nanny to seek her out at this hour.

Everest hesitated in the bedchamber doorway. She was a small, round, middle-aged woman who dressed habitually in fine black wool, with plump, comfortable hands that reminded Jennie of currant buns. Her face under her white cap was rounded, too, the cheeks usually apple red and her mouth smiling. But tonight, Everest's expression was pinched.

"Do come into the room," Jennie urged.

The nanny approached.

Gentry, who was wielding an iron curling tong that had to be heated continually in a gas flame (but not so heated that it singed and burned Jennie's hair), ignored Everest; she was disciplined in her precarious craft.

"Ma'am, it's Master Winston. He arrived home from St. George's today, as I'm sure you'll know, for his Long Vac."

"Yes," Jennie agreed. More than five hundred years old, St. George's was the school at Windsor that prepared boys for Eton. Randolph had also gone there, and his father before him. Win had been a boarder ever since they'd returned from Ireland, when he was six. "I remember something about it. But I'm afraid I was from home all the afternoon. Has Win settled?"

"He has. Proper grateful he is to be back in the nursery, with Master Jack and his soldiers."

"Very well." Jennie met the nanny's eyes in her mirror. How tiresome that the woman would not simply come out and say what she wanted! "Is something amiss?"

"I don't know as how I can say. It's properly not my place to comment. But I'm troubled in my mind, madam, and I should like you to see him. For yourself. Before the marks fade."

"Marks?" Jennie repeated, bewildered.

"Aye. Wounds, I might almost call them, but for that they're a few days old and not so raw as they might be. I discovered them when I bathed him this evening."

"Wounds? Where? Did he scrape his knees?"

"His back, madam. Though I cannot believe Master Winston came by them through any clumsiness of his own."

"Does he require a doctor?" Everest was notoriously fond of Winston—indeed, Randolph complained she coddled the boy, one reason he'd been sent away to school at the age of six. No doubt this was another instance of her excessive sensitivity.

"I've dressed the weals with salve, my lady. But I reckon it's a mother Master Win could use right now."

Jennie felt a spurt of anger. She was already late and Randolph would be furious when she failed to appear as expected at India House. She was about to rebuke the nanny when she glimpsed, in the mirror, Everest's hands. They were locked together so tightly the normally ruddy skin had blanched white about the knuckles. Jennie drew a deep breath and rose from her chair. Gentry and the curling tong jumped backward. Jennie wrapped her lace robe more closely around her. "Very well. But I have only a moment."

Everest wheeled and, without another word, led Jennie along the second-floor passage to the nursery stairs. At the top, Jennie found herself in the apartment that was her children's entire world at Connaught Place: a wide sitting room under sloping eaves, with a view of slate tiles and rain-washed square below. A table with children's chairs where the boys took their supper, and a rocker where Everest did her mending while they read or played. There were shelves of books and bins of toy soldiers; an army of these had been arrayed on the floor in mock battle—Winston had lost no time in deploying his forces. Jack's hobbyhorse sat near the fireplace, cold now in summer. A night-light burned on a dresser. Two doorways led off this cozy area, one to the bath, and the other to the bedchamber where Winston and Jack shared twin cots. Everest's room connected to it.

The nanny picked up the night-light and crossed to the bedchamber door, opening it gently.

"Woom!" Winston cried. It was the name he had given Everest as a baby. He reared up from his pillow; Jennie saw his small head silhouetted against the white linen. "Why have you come back again?"

"I've brought your dear mother," she said, "to kiss you good night before her grand party."

"Mummie!" Jack shrieked, and both boys tumbled out of their beds and hurled themselves at Jennie's legs. She was engulfed in a tangle of arms, with a pair of damp heads fresh from the bath and smelling delightfully of talcum. She grasped each boy's back and patted them fondly. "Careful. Gentry will be frightfully cross with both of you if there's a single curl displaced. I'll only remain if you get back into bed at once."

Instantly, both boys shot like cannonballs beneath the covers.

"Sit here, Mummie," Jack invited, his three-year-old face imploring under his dark hair.

"She must sit here," Win retorted decisively, "as I've only just come home, and it's on account of my triumphant return that she's consented to visit the nursery at all."

"I wish I could go away," Jack said fretfully, "so that *I* might have a triumphant return."

"You should hate school," Win informed him. "It's wretched and beastly and not worth even a chance visit from Mummie."

Jennie sank down on his thin mattress. "Everest tells me you're wounded, Win."

His freckled snub nose wrinkled in distress. "Not properly," he assured her. "Not like a Hero of the Empire. Just rather as a matter of course."

Jennie placed her cool fingers on his cheek. His blue eyes met hers. "What do you mean, darling?"

His gaze shifted to his nanny's face. "Ought I to show Mummie, Woom?"

"Yes, Master Winston."

Obediently, he turned his back on Jennie and lifted the tail of his nightshirt. An expanse of bare buttock emerged, impossibly fair-skinned, and then the frailty of an eight-year-old back. Win's ribs were visible as a kitten's and his shoulder blades were sharp angel wings. Jennie was so accustomed to seeing him dressed sturdily in his school uniform that she had forgotten how vulnerable he was.

She gasped, and raised her hand to her mouth.

From Winston's neck to his waist was a brutal scrawl of sharp red lines, cut into his flesh, layer upon layer. He had been whipped ferociously, Jennie saw—whipped not once, but scores of times. The cuts crisscrossed his shoulders and ribs and reached ugly fingers down to his buttocks. Most were old scars. Many were fresh, and red, and raw.

Trembling, she reached a tentative finger, stopping just short of touching him. Everest's salve gleamed in the light of the oil lamp. Jennie did not want to cause the boy further pain.

"Dear God. Who has done this to you?" she whispered.

"The caning?" he asked nonchalantly. "Sneyd-Kinnersley, Mummie. The headmaster. He uses a *willow* switch, *not* rattan. He assures me rattan is far more painful, and the customary tool of punishment in the British colonies. Sneyd-Kinnersley says I am to be grateful."

"Grateful." Jennie's hand hovered over the web of cuts and weals. "The man's a sadist!"

"What does that mean?" Winston demanded.

"He enjoys hurting people."

"I should jolly well think he does! He wallops all of us. Only I am beaten *every* day, I'm afraid, because I'm particularly incorrigible. Or so the headmaster says. *A boy who must be broken to bridle,* as he puts it. *Incorrigible* means incapable of correction. I never seem to do things correctly."

Winston's voice, which had been determinedly casual, wobbled on that last word. He had been trying to fend off tears, Jennie realized suddenly—for him, the blatant exposure of his back to her gaze was more shameful than the beatings. With an inner howl of anguish, she reached for his small hands and kissed the palms, one at a time.

"You're right, darling. Not even a chance visit from Mummie is worth all the cost of St. George's. Should you like to try a different school next term?"

"Could I please just come home, Mummie? With Jack and Woom here in the nursery?"

"Not at your age," Jennie told him gently. "In another year you'll be a man of ten, you know."

His eyes were bright with unshed tears. "Indeed. Ten is a *very great* age; it's double digits. But please, Mummie—if it's not too great a trouble—if you have a moment to *find* another school where the headmaster is not a sadist—I should be jolly grateful."

*"Win."* Jennie kissed his forehead and folded him tight in her arms. "You have my word."

# CHAPTER THIRTEEN

"What an innocent," Jennie whispered tartly to Charles. The blond girl she had noticed at Ascot, insipid in pale pink gauze, was making her curtsey to the Prince of Wales. Her long lashes trembled on her cheeks, and she seemed as though she might swoon at Bertie's feet. "First the Royal Enclosure, and now your party at the New Café! Who *is* she?"

"The heiress to a prodigious Midlands factory fortune," he replied. "Let's meet her, shall we?"

Charles led Jennie over to the Prince, who was standing with two of his other guests—the Duke of Braganza, and Empress Sisi's son, Prince Rudolf of Austria. Jennie dropped her deepest curtsey to the royals.

"Ah, Lady Randolph and our excellent host," Bertie rumbled. "Miss Fairfield, you will wish to thank Count Kinsky for the pleasure he gives us this evening! Such a handsome way to squander one's winnings on the turf!"

"Everything is *so l-lovely,*" the girl stammered. Her doe eyes met Charles's artlessly. "The lights! The refreshments! And such distinguished guests! It is all like a faerie dream!"

Charles kissed Miss Fairfield's fluttering hand. "May I introduce Lady Randolph Churchill?"

The girl's mouth formed a wondering O, and her slender fingers pressed her heart. "Lady Randolph! But this is *better* than a princess!"

"Do not allow your sovereign to hear you say so," Jennie advised with her warmest smile.

"But you are in *all* the Society papers! And how gorgeous you appear! I declare it is truly a *faerie dream*!"

Jennie wore sapphire-blue silk that night in tribute to Charles and his first memory of her in Ireland. The gown was hardly new, but that didn't matter. She knew she glowed like a rare gem in it, her black hair massed in ringlets at the back of her head and trailing becomingly over her bare shoulders. Her Cartier star flashed on her brow. She was simmeringly, supremely happy—and the closeness of Charles, the warm musk of his skin, sang through her veins.

*More like a panther than a woman.*

"Allow me to offer you some lemonade, Miss Fairfield." Bertie offered the girl his arm. Awed, she gazed meltingly up into his face. He patted her hand and led her away.

*So the wolf makes off with a lamb,* Jennie thought wryly. *How did the chit stumble into the heart of the Marlborough House Set?* And then, with a sense of foreboding . . . *Is it possible that Charles . . . ?*

A sigh grazed the nape of her neck; the violins were tuning.

"Dance with me," he urged.


*Tziganes* music, Charles called it. Stolen from those who wandered homeless in Transylvania, and dressed up nattily for London's West End. Jennie was to love the sound of it for the rest of her life, but she heard it for the first time that evening in June, as she whirled in his arms through the red-damask-lined rooms.

Charles had brought in a group of musicians from his own country, the Hungarian Violins: five academically trained men who caught the Gypsy strains from the eastern edge of the empire. Their music throbbed with a strange sorrow that worked its way into Jennie's blood, like the bubbles of the champagne Charles poured so freely. Tragedy and passion were the high notes; loss and regret, the harmony.

It was after midnight when Bertie claimed a dance from her, a waltz in the best Viennese tradition. She treated the Prince with the deference due to a monarch and all the sauciness permitted an American lady of rank; his eyes glowed covetously when he looked at her, his hand pressed possessively in the small of her back. Despite his girth he moved with surprising lightness, his bearded face bent unswervingly to hers. Jennie could feel the heat of his skin through his wool dress coat; too real, too human. Perspiration beaded his forehead. He had been drinking claret and smoking cigars with a clutch of cronies most of the night.

"It is not every evening I am tempted to the dance floor," he offered, in his slightly German-accented growl. "Nor every night I find such bewitching provocation."

"Your Highness is a shameless flatterer," Jennie replied with a glance from under her lashes.

"I would never deceive a lady."

"Then I am honored, sir."

They whirled past a pier glass framed heavily in gold, the reflection of the entire glittering room doubled and thrown back in Jennie's face—massed orchids and the fan of women's dresses strident against the darker figures of the men. The café was stiflingly warm. It was possible she had drunk too much champagne.

"You ought to take care, my dear," the Prince murmured. "We all permit you a remarkable degree of license, because you are such excellent company; but it won't do, you know, to run away from your husband. I won't mention his name, of course. We haven't formally reconciled as yet."

"Your Highness! What can you possibly mean?"

Bertie looked deliberately across the room at Charles Kinsky, who was bringing a smile to Miss Fairfield's guileless face with some half-considered pleasantry. "You are so very clearly smitten, my dear. Very smitten indeed, and it is never well to betray too warm a preference. Poor Edith Aylesford, you know . . . such a melancholy thing, to be forced to cut an acquaintance of such long standing . . ."

"Lady Aylesford's conduct was very sad. But it can have nothing to do with me." Jennie's tone was light but her feet were suddenly leaden; Bertie meant business. He was reining her in. She wanted to dash impetuously from the room, skirts clutched in her fingers, but she forced herself to smile at him. Her gaze serene. Her voice a lie. Dread bursting inside.

"I am sure, Lady Randy, you should never be so foolish as poor Edith." The Prince's eyes were half-lidded, the pupils enormous and black. "None of your friends could wish it. We hope for nothing but your continued success and happiness."

"Thank you, sir," she murmured, with a graceful sweep of her head, as though he had not just cut out her heart. "I hope I shall always be sensible of your goodness to me, and never do anything unworthy of it."

He squeezed her right hand, poised high in his. "I am sure you will not. These Austrians are all very well, of course, with their horses and their dash, but there's nothing like one's *real* friends. You will remember that."

"How could I forget?" Deliberately, Jennie threw him a mischievous smile. He must never know he had shattered her joy in the space of a waltz. "Now, tell me, Prince. When *does* Your Royal Highness mean to reconcile with my husband?"

She might have left the party immediately, offering a hurried farewell to Charles, but ignorant of her trouble he smiled down into her eyes and swept her back onto the floor for the final dance. She did not have the strength to deny either of them. He held her far closer than the Prince had dared and whispered in her ear.

"Come home with me tonight."

Jennie shook her head, fighting for enough calm to speak. "Impossible. I've been warned off."

Charles's hand tightened over hers. "What do you mean?"

"Bertie says I've become a worry. To him and our friends. They fear a scandal. Because I'm too obviously *enchanted* by you. Oh, Charles—we shall have to part."

"Don't talk nonsense."

"On the contrary. This is of the first importance. All our fortunes are at stake."

His head reared back; he was staring at her. "We must talk. I'll escort you home."

"No, Charles. It ends here." She gazed over his shoulder, suppressing an impulse to break from him. Unbearable to be safe in his arms and yet at war; but if she left the floor now, when every eye was on them—the moment was far too public—

"We've enjoyed a great deal of amusement together," she managed with false brightness, "but I've drawn too much notice in the wrong quarter, I'm afraid. That smacks of bad breeding—and I don't wish to pay the royal penalty for it. Or cause you to do the same."

"Are you out of your *senses*?" Charles muttered. "Jennie—!"

"Don't play the heartbroken lover!" Her voice carried over their heads to the couple turning beside them. Jennie bit her lip, tasting blood, and stared directly into Charles's eyes as they waltzed toward the far side of the room. The *tziganes* music shivered and swore. "You'll solace yourself, I'm sure, with that pretty little blonde. Wherever did you find Miss Fairfield, Charles?"

"She was invited at the request of the Prince of Wales," he said through his teeth. "He's been in pursuit of her the past month."

Jennie's eyelids were wet.

"Come with me," he repeated urgently into her ear. They moved together like two palms pressed in prayer. Like two halves of a scallop shell she'd once found on the granite shore of Newport and treasured as a child. "We'll run away from all of them. Take passage for Paris. I'll get an embassy posting there."

She thought of her boys—Winston with his lacerated back and Jack, begging her to sit on his cot.

"Do you know how they bully the small sons of notorious women, at the best public schools in England? I should be handing my boys a death sentence."

Edith Aylesford had never seen her children again, once she fled to Paris with Blandford. She had lost all maternal rights.

Jennie could feel the rest of the party watching them. The Duke of Braganza. Fidgety Archduke Rudolf. Bertie, with his lips mouthing a cigar, his hooded gaze following her like a hawk. *End it now.*

"Jennie, I love you," Charles said tensely. "Don't do this."

She laughed carelessly and sank into a curtsey before him, bringing the waltz to a close.

"Such a pleasant party, Count—as with everything you do."

She had mastered the art of protective cover years ago.

"Jennie—"

She did not look back as she left him.

# CHAPTER FOURTEEN

Hours later, she could not say what slight sound woke her. The room was filled with moonlight. Jennie sat up in bed, the lace edge of her nightdress slipping down one shoulder and the heavy weight of her black hair tangled at her waist. The windows were open to the night air. The faint breeze stirring the silk curtains was damp with old rain.

In the country near Blenheim there would be nightjars calling and the cries of fox kits, but here in London there was only the rumble of vegetable carts making for Covent Garden and iron-shod hooves ringing against the cobblestones. Her bedroom over-looked the narrow garden at the rear of the house, with its high walls and its gate giving onto the mews.

There it was again—a rustle in the ivy, which was thick and ancient and as strong as a blacksmith's forearm. Jennie tensed, her eyes probing the luminous shadows. The pale blue hangings of her bed, looped about mahogany posts, obscured her view. Fear of what she could not see suddenly knifed through her. She swung her legs noiselessly from beneath the coverlet, and reached with one hand for the drawer of the bedside table.

The rustling in the ivy grew louder; the intruder climbing it was nearing the windowsill. Jennie groped for the snub-nosed lit-tle pistol Papa had given her—a memento of a morning only a year or so ago, when the two of them had amused themselves in a shooting gallery off Bond Street. She had clipped the hearts and clubs of every playing card Papa had put up for her, then toasted him with champagne when they were done. She kept the pocket pistol loaded by her bedside. Not even Randolph knew that.

Now she rose and leveled the gun at the silhouette rising above her windowsill. There was only one cartridge. She would have only one chance. For that reason, or perhaps to test her nerve, she cocked the hammer and said quietly into the darkness, "Come an inch farther and I'll shoot."

The rising shadow hesitated, stilled.

They waited, both of them. Neither breathed.

Then he vaulted over the sill and onto the floor and Jennie squeezed the trigger, gently, as Papa had taught her long ago when she was just a child at Jerome Park. The pistol had a percussion cap and the snub nose made it anything but accurate. The cartridge fired where the intruder's head had been a fraction of a second before. Jennie's breath stopped in her throat as she waited for the thud of a body—

The intruder rolled to his feet on her bedroom floor. His hand encircled her right wrist and bent it back, painfully. She gasped and tried to smash the pocket pistol against his temple to bring him down. He laughed at her effort.

And then she knew who it was.

"Charles!"

He turned her clenched fingers so that the pistol targeted the floor, and bowed low over her hand. "Lady Randolph."

She dropped the gun with a dull thud and knotted her fingers in his dark curls, wanting to hurt him, needing to scare him as he had scared her. He lifted his head. He was breathing hard.

"You fool," she whispered, furious. "This might have been any room. Randolph's."

"It was the only one with open windows. And I just left your husband at his club." Releasing her, he stooped to pick up the gun. "Never carry a single Deringer. That's why they're sold in pairs—so you can get off a second shot if you miss the first time."

"I didn't miss!"

"No," he agreed. "I did."

He dropped the pistol on the bed behind her. Smoothed her bare shoulder and touched the pulse at her throat. She drew a calming breath, willing her pulse to steady, and said, "What are you doing here?"

"We have things to discuss."

"I said everything necessary at the café."

"Not so," Charles countered. "You never said that you love me, Jennie. Say it now." His fingertip traced her parted lips. "I want to feel you say it."

She shook her head once, a mutinous child.

*"Now."*

"I never mix emotion with pleasure, Charles."

"And I'm simply pleasure?" He drew her head close to his.

"We've both enjoyed our . . . time together. But it's done."

"That's the wisest thing to say." His lips touched hers. "But it's not enough for me, Jennie. Do you remember that night we first saw each other at Sandringham? How you looked at me, and I at you? Both of us knew then we would never be the same."

"You assume too much." She tried to laugh.

"I'm simply saying what we both know."

His mouth caressed the soft skin at the base of her ear. She tensed against him, denying his impulses and her own, and then he released her and stepped back.

One of the things she admired most about Charles was his ability to control himself. He was like her in this—completely in command of his impulses. She'd counted on that.

"You may have given your body and your bed to any number of men in the past, Jennie, but you have never done *this* before."

"Done what?"

"Lost your soul for love."

"Without a soul, who would I be?"

"Mine," he answered, very gently.

Then he moved to the window. Lifted his leg over the sill.

"When you're ready . . . when there is no other choice left for you to make . . . I'll be waiting. But I will not accept less than your entire heart, Jennie."

He grasped the ivy. She listened to his swift descent in the darkness. Then she ran to her sill and looked down into the garden.

"I won't be owned!" she called after him fiercely. "By you, or anyone!"

In the days that followed, days utterly empty of Charles Kinsky, Jennie wondered repeatedly whether she was wrong.

Had she turned him away out of good sense—or fear?

That same consuming fear she'd first sensed at Sandringham, as she listened to Charles play the Eighth Prelude?

*Loss of self. Loss of independence. Emotion so deep and wide I might drown myself.*

Unless she did as Charles demanded—gave herself over entirely to her feeling for him—he would cut her out of his life.

From the age of nine, when Jennie first saw Papa's fingers caress Fanny Ronalds's throat in the private opera house on Madison Square, she had known that love was a terrible thing. Love destroyed families and happiness.

Love was the reason Mamma had sailed away from New York with her daughters forever.

Love was violent and destructive. Good only for Austrians—and fools.

# CHAPTER FIFTEEN

On the fifth of July, without warning, John Winston Spencer-Churchill, the Seventh Duke of Marlborough, suffered an attack of angina and died. He was sixty-one years old.

He lay in state for three days in the private chapel at Blenheim, with its hideous marble walls the color of raw liver, then was interred in the crypt with his ancestors on a humid and lowering summer afternoon. The air was thick with thunder and Duchess Fanny's misery. The Spencer-Churchill family marked its grief by donning black clothes and refusing all public engagements for the remainder of the year.

Jennie and Randolph left England at the end of July with their boys and Mrs. Everest, their nanny, for cool relief in the mountains of Switzerland.

Blenheim Palace was entailed upon Randolph's brother George, but the dead Duke gave one final nod of dislike toward his ramshackle heir—he left the bulk of his remaining funds to his widow, Fanny, and his younger son, Randolph. George was now the Eighth Duke but had no means to support his rank. More of Blenheim's treasures would have to be sold.

Duchess Fanny retired to the rented house on Berkeley Square. Sarah gave up her debut for another year and spent her time bicycling in Hyde Park. At the end of the summer, Randolph and Jennie returned from walking in the Alps and sent Winston off to a new school in Brighton—Jennie's answer to the sadist at St.

George's. To her surprise, Blandford invited the Churchills to shut up their London house and spend the rest of the mourning period at Blenheim.

*Blenheim.* Jennie's heart sank as she stared at Randolph's brother, impeccably turned out and holding state over the teacups in her drawing room. His vast palace was damp and echoing and cheerless at the best of times—but particularly desolate in winter.

"I need a damned hostess," he explained irritably as he sipped his Darjeeling. "You know Goosie's obtained her divorce at long last. Just missed the chance to call herself a duchess."

"And your mother?"

"The Dowager, as she insists on being addressed, is determined to remain in London. I don't want her living in my pocket in any case; we've never seen eye to eye."

Blandford—Jennie could not yet think of him as *His Grace*—had cannily delivered his invitation while Randolph was in Commons. Desperate to avoid offending him, she settled for a faint smile. "How kind of you to think of us. But I must refuse to answer until I may consult Randolph. It is his work in Parliament that dictates our lives, George."

"You can talk him round," he urged. "Randy will give you anything you ask."

"Will he?" Jennie mocked, with raised brows.

"By God, if you were *my* wife, you could have the earth on a platter." George had always treated Jennie less like a sister-in-law than a woman to be seduced. He leaned in to kiss her cheek, but she rose hastily and left him reaching for air.

"I'm sorry to let you go, George," she attempted, "but I must change for an engagement."

He set down his cup and rose to his feet. "Does my brother make you happy?"

"Perfectly."

"After all these years?" He stepped toward her. "You don't find that familiarity . . . breeds contempt?"

*Only in your case,* she thought wearily. "I daresay Randy is more compelling than your Goosie."

George barked out a laugh. "He has only to utter a complete sentence to manage that! Do you know what she did to me? When I tangled myself with Edith Aylesford? Left a china baby doll in a chafing dish on the breakfast sideboard! Gave me the queerest start when I lifted the lid in search of kippers. She thought it was a joke."

"Goosie always had an unsettling sense of humor."

"The woman's demented. And worse luck, she's reared my heir." George studied Jennie with narrowed eyes. "Hear you've been spending a good deal of time with that Kinsky fellow. Handsome devil. Too young for you, of course. Woman like you needs a man of experience."

"Your gossips have failed you, George," Jennie said indifferently. "The Count merely escorted me once or twice in Hyde Park. As have a hundred others."

"Mind you confine him to the park, Jennie."

"As you confined Edith to Paris?" Her eyes blazed.

"City was wasted on her." He reached for his homburg and settled it on his brow. "Nothing would be wasted on you. Not even a dukedom."

"I'd say you were flattering me, George." Jennie handed him his cane. "But then, I actually know how little your dukedom is worth."

"Got the price of everything, Jennie?" he rasped, stung. "And the value of nothing? But I was forgetting. You are *American,* after all."

"Just a woman, George, like any other," Jennie replied sweetly. "Naturally we price the goods we're offered. We're forced to pay so much more heavily for our sins than men."

———

"I don't know why your brother even *wants* a hostess!" she raged at Randolph as Gentry brushed her hair that night. "He's in mourning! He may hunt and shoot this whole wretched winter, but he's not likely to throw a ball for the entire county!"

"I daresay he wants help with his grocer's accounts." Randolph was leaning in her dressing room doorway, one hand stuffed into the pocket of a quilted smoking jacket. "George is no fool. As Father left me all the blunt, he thinks I ought to pay for his butcher and wine merchant. There's a certain symmetry to the arrangement."

Jennie glared at his reflection in her mirror. "You have no intention of *accepting* his offer, I hope?"

Randolph shrugged and blew a cloud of cigar smoke, obscuring his image in the glass. "We could do with some cost-saving ourselves. Father's funds aside, I've no idea how we shall make ends meet. And with Winston's school fees . . ."

"The new place is cheaper than St. George's. If the Government were to fall . . ." Members of Parliament, such as Randolph, were paid nothing. But *Cabinet* secretaries received five thousand pounds per annum. Surely Randy would be offered a Government post if the Conservatives came in?

"If, if," Randolph sighed. "Gladstone is likely to bugger on well into the next century, out of sheer obstinance."

Jennie threw him a despairing look. "What would we possibly *do* in Oxfordshire all winter?"

Gentry reached for the hair receiver on the dressing table, her lips pursed. The maid was a native Cockney and hated Blenheim almost as much as Jennie did. She combed out the brush with stifled violence.

"You could hunt with George," Randolph suggested mildly. "You haven't had a topping season in the field since Ireland. The Blenheim pack is first-rate."

"Are you entirely comfortable, Randolph, consigning your wife to the care of a rake?"

"Old George is harmless." He frowned at his cigar. "I shan't abandon you, Jennie—I'll be poking around the dreaded barracks at your side."

"But—darling, your *work* . . ."

"That's what the British railways are for. Last I checked, there was a branch line from Woodstock. Paid for by my father." He thrust himself out of the doorway, intent on his own room and bed. "Mind you speak with an estate agent tomorrow, Jennie. There must be any number of families who'd jump at the chance to rent this house for the Season. We have so many bathrooms! And *electricity*."

Within weeks, Jennie went into a new kind of exile. The house on Connaught Place fell silent under Holland covers, and the trunks were sent down with the servants to Woodstock. On her first morning at Blenheim she galloped alone through the estate's vast park, wishing with a stab of anguish that a familiar dark figure would appear on horseback, pull up under a great cedar, and call to her.

But it would be years before she saw Charles Kinsky again.

# PART TWO

# The Dinner of Deadly Enemies

*1886–87*

# CHAPTER SIXTEEN

*Temperature 104.3, and the right lung is generally involved,* Robson Roose noted. He was sitting outside the boy's dimly lit room, writing hastily on a sheet of paper. There was no desk in the infirmary, which like everything in the Thomson Sisters' School at Brighton was not very large. Roose had propped a book on his lap to support the page and had set the inkwell on the floor. He bent down periodically to rewet his pen.

He wrote down the date—*Sunday, 14 March, 1886*—and the hour. Seven forty-three in the evening.

> *This report may appear grave, yet it merely indicates the approach of the crisis which, please God, will result in an improved condition should the left lung remain free.*

He hesitated, his brow furrowing above his neat gold spectacles. This was the third bulletin he had sent off to Connaught Place in the past twenty-four hours. He had served as the Churchills' family doctor for years and had known Winston from birth. The eleven-year-old boy's parents had descended on the school the previous day when it was clear he had contracted pneumonia. They arrived separately—Lord Randolph from Blenheim and Lady Randolph from London, with her nanny, Mrs. Everest, who would help with the nursing.

"Woom," Winston had rasped as he clung to the nanny's hand. "My Woomany. You won't leave me?"

He was flung out on his side on the narrow iron cot, a sheet kicked off and in a tangle around his feet. A spot of vivid color burned in each pallid cheek. His china-blue eyes were brilliant with fever.

"Not on your life, Master Winston," Everest replied as she smoothed the linen and drew it up under the boy's chin. "It's your mamma as must return to London tonight, on account of her party for the Prince of Wales. Think of that! His Royal Highness in *your* drawing room tomorrow evening!"

"Will Gladstone be there?" the boy demanded. "And Chamberlain? Uncle Arthur Balfour?"

"No doubt," Everest soothed. "If you're a good boy and do your best to get well, you might just catch a glimpse of all those toffs. But you must drink some broth for Woom now."

Lord Randolph had sent a note of encouragement into the sickroom, but Roose forbade him to enter—as his lordship's doctor, he could not advise Randolph to risk his delicate health. And there was the younger boy, Jack, at home to think of—his lordship could not be carrying contagion back to London. Lord Randolph waited long enough to hear Roose's assessment of Winston's lungs before driving to the Brighton station.

"You can have no such fears for me," Lady Randolph had insisted firmly, and stepped past Roose to take up a chair by her son's bedside. And indeed, he had to admit that her ladyship was in her usual roaring health—although her expression was more strained than he had ever seen it. She managed a smile as she smoothed Winston's hair, and sang him some Brahms in her throaty alto. *Lullaby and good night, with roses bedight . . .*

"Will you do something for me, Mummie?" the boy demanded as she paused for breath.

"Anything, my darling."

"Beg for the Prince's signature," he implored, "and Mr. Gladstone's, if you can. If you will only send them to me, all the other boys will be *green*."

Lady Randolph's lips quirked, but she told her son to *Hush, darling,* and *not to worry about such things now.*

She had no idea, the doctor suspected, that there was a raging market among the Brighton schoolboys for the best autographs—Winston even sold his mother's. Lady Randy was one of the PBs, or Professional Beauties: Society women whose pictures were flogged on postcards at news kiosks without their knowledge or consent. Roose rather thought Lady Randy was the one the hawkers called the Black Pearl.

But the brief plea had worn Winston out; in his pain and difficulty the boy began to cry weakly, his breathing clotted with the fluid in his lungs. Everest moved firmly between him and his mother and said, "Rest is what Master Win wants. Rest and *quiet.*"

Lady Randolph dropped a kiss in her son's palm. "Keep this for me until I return, darling."

Winston's fingers curled where her lips had been. The rasp of his labored breathing filled the room. His eyelids fluttered closed. But with a parting wistful look, Lady Randy left them in a swirl of scarlet embroidered mantle and chic doeskin gloves—her head full, Roose supposed, with plans for that party.

"Thank God for the unstinting love of nannies," he muttered as he took Winston's temperature.

By the time Saturday's dinner hour had passed, Winston had fallen into delirium. His fever mounted through the night. The words he uttered were mangled and uncertain. The delirium continued Sunday. Roose glanced toward the dimly lit alcove, screened from direct light, where Everest sat with the boy, smoothing his hot forehead with folded cloths soaked in ice water. The nanny's eyes were bright with unshed tears. Winston no longer knew that his Woomany was there.

Roose felt a stab of frustration. The Churchills thought he had all the answers. That he was someone they could trust. But there was not much he could do in cases of pneumonia—plunge the boy into an ice bath if fever threatened his brain. Give him digitalis by the mouth and rectum, to keep his heart beating. But the disease would work its course, regardless. Winston would die. Or he would live.

Roose drew his pocket watch from his waistcoat and looked wearily at the hour. He was an expert in both gout and nervous complaints; the most celebrated of Society's lions, including Lord Randolph, consulted him in his rooms in Harley Street. He would have to spend the night here in the infirmary, however, and put off his London work, until the redheaded boy muttering and choking in the bed behind him rallied—or sank.

He hoped Winston rallied. The cost to Roose's reputation, if Lord Randolph Churchill's son died, was too great to bear.

Jennie had invited twenty-four people to dine that Sunday, including—for the first time at Connaught Place—the Prince and Princess of Wales. She was imitating Fanny Ronalds by summoning the Great on the Sabbath; it was supposed to be a day of pious observance, but most people were bored silly by dinnertime and desperate for diversion. She had, of course, hurried down to Brighton with Everest the previous day, but there was no question of remaining there with Winston—a thousand details required her attention in London.

"The invitations went out weeks ago," she told Randolph. "Sick child or no, the dinner must go forward."

"Your guest list," Randolph mused, "is absurd in its optimism. Do you really expect me to trade polite nothings with Gladstone and Joseph Chamberlain—that working-class bounder from the Midlands—while Bertie tut-tuts and looks on?"

"Yes," Jennie retorted. "I'm attempting a bit of political witchcraft, Randy, and you should be down on your knees in thanks! Bertie's finally agreed to grace us with his presence. Ten years since your silly spat—and he only *now* consents to dine in Connaught Place?"

They were chatting as they often did, between the doorways of their adjoining rooms, as their personal servants dressed them for dinner. Jennie was in emerald-green velvet embroidered with ivory thread, the front of the gown draped back to reveal a tightly fitted ivory silk underskirt; it had the new round neckline and slight cap sleeves that displayed her collarbones to perfection. Gentry had wound emerald silk through her black hair, which was elaborately looped at the back of her head. Jennie thought with satisfaction that she looked like a mermaid or Siren, even if she *was* a terrifying two-and-thirty. If only she had a few emeralds to clasp at her neck! But no, simply the seven-pointed diamond star . . .

"The Irish Question is about to blow up in our faces, and you summon all my foes for soup and mutton! If there's not blood spilled by the cheese course, Jennie, I'll award you a knighthood."

"It's certainly a dinner of deadly enemies," she agreed, her eyes sparkling at him, "but where's the fun, otherwise? You know what Arthur Balfour and even Hartington think about Irish Home Rule—why not hear the Working-Class Bounder's views? Chamberlain could be Prime Minister one day!"

"Not while I have breath in my body," Randolph vowed. "The man's a flaming Radical." But he bared his teeth in what passed for a smile. Politics was the only passion he and Jennie still shared. How had he described it, so many years ago? *The greatest of all blood sports?*

"You've been called the same in your time," Jennie observed. "Perhaps Mr. Chamberlain is just another victim of the press."

"Dear God! Is it possible my *own wife* mistakes the enlightened debate of an educated man for a cur's rabid snarl? Chamberlain never darkened the door of university. He earned a fortune in trade on the backs of factory brats. And he's liable to lead them all to the barricades if we're not careful."

Jennie glared at him. "Insult the fellow as you choose in Commons, Randy, but as a *gentleman,* you will be cordial at *my* dinner table!"

"I'd sooner kiss a stoat!"

"If Bertie can meet Chamberlain, so can you."

"*Definitely* a dinner of deadly enemies." Randolph scowled as his valet eased his coat of dark gray superfine over his narrow shoulders.

"I just might prove the salvation of the kingdom," Jennie retorted.

"What news from Brighton, my dear?" Arthur Balfour asked as soon as he appeared in Jennie's drawing room, his voice pitched low amidst the throng of guests. "Is the young chap any better?"

"He's a Churchill, Arthur." Jennie summoned a smile. "Fancies himself at death's door at bedtime, then orders steak and kidney pie for breakfast."

She was surprised and touched that Balfour cared—it was rare for a bachelor to notice a woman's anxiety, much less think of her children. Jennie felt a stab of uneasiness—what if there *was* no improvement in Roose's next bulletin?—and thrust it firmly to the back of her mind.

"Lord Salisbury!" She extended her gloved hand to Arthur's uncle. If Gladstone's Government fell, Salisbury would be Prime Minister—and could put Randy in his Cabinet. "And Mr. Chamberlain! How delightful to welcome you to Connaught Place!"

"My lady." Chamberlain grasped her hand and bowed low; for an instant Jennie feared he might actually kiss the satin of her glove. He was fiftyish, she guessed—handsome enough, with penetrating dark eyes and a square jaw. Jennie ran through what she knew: Chamberlain had driven two wives to their graves, and was raising six children with the help of in-laws. There was a boy a bit older than Winston, in his final year at Rugby—Neville, was it?

A sudden stir at the door—the chatter fell away, and a footman in buff and blue livery appeared behind Jennie's butler.

"Their Royal Highnesses, the Prince and Princess of Wales!"

Everyone in the room went still as Bertie sauntered in, Alix on his arm, magnificent in pale gold brocade. The ladies' curtseys were like so many birds folding exotic wings.

"Lady Randy," the Prince rumbled as he bent over her hand. "And Churchill! It has been an age!"

"An honor to welcome you, sir." Randolph bowed.

The enemies had agreed to parley.

Deadly or not, Jennie thought, they all had to eat. There would be no turning back now.

"I understand you are an accomplished artist, my lady."

She dimpled at Joseph Chamberlain, enjoying something almost American in his brash, uncultivated voice. The self-made man was standing with a tight knot collected beneath Jennie's electric chandelier, in the broad passage outside her dining room. Six of Rosa's extraordinary courses had floated around the table, and coffee was about to be served in the drawing room. Number 2 Connaught Place was hardly a vast London townhouse, but it was modern and stylish, and Jennie's spare interior, so unlike the clutter of most Victorian rooms, was a perfect backdrop. She preferred a few good pieces of furniture and a handful of dramatic paintings, set against pale walls. Let the people in her life provide the color.

"It's a privilege to sit for Lady Randolph," Sir Charles Dilke said warmly, "but one she has never extended to me. When will you consent to take my likeness, Jennie?"

"Impossible, sir." She narrowed her eyes at him. Dilke was known to be dangerous. Any number of women were ready to die for him, but some sixth sense made Jennie's skin crawl. "I could never paint you black enough."

The gentlemen roared with laughter and raised their glasses, and at that moment Jennie spied a footman approaching with an envelope on a silver salver. *Roose.* Her fingers clenched; God give her strength if the news of Winston was bad and she was forced to take it in public.

Jennie turned swiftly, her velvet train twisting around her legs, and accepted the note. Definitely from Roose. She recognized his hand.

Sick at heart, she hid the letter against the drape of her bustle and moved hurriedly toward the drawing room. Rosa had set out fruit, pastries, and dessert wines on the sideboard at the far end, but no one had drifted toward them yet. Jennie could snatch a moment's privacy. She glanced about for Randolph, but he was nowhere to be seen. She felt a stab of exasperation; must she manage everything herself this evening? Arthur Balfour caught her gaze and came immediately to join her. Her hand dropped in frustration again to her side. The message would have to wait.

"Jennie," Balfour demanded, "what the devil has got into your husband of late?"

There had been a bad moment over the fish course, when Randy had mourned the decline of Parliament with Prime Minister Gladstone. "So many ill-educated Members," he'd sneered as his eyes drifted indolently over Chamberlain. "Riffraff from places like Birmingham, who can't understand Latin when they hear it in Commons!"

Before Jennie could turn the conversation—inquire about Neville's progress in school, and whether his father was pleased with the instruction at Rugby—the Radical did it himself. "It doesn't need Latin to explain Tory Democracy," Chamberlain declared, with a flash of teeth. "All of Birmingham knows that's nothing but a sham, put about by a duke's son to exploit the working man."

Jennie sighed at Arthur Balfour now. "Randy's not sleeping well," she attempted.

"Randy's peevish, temperamental, and rude. Even I can't manage him anymore." Balfour glanced around, afraid of being overheard. "The slightest tweak sets him off; one never knows what invective he'll spout in Parliament. It's like prodding a snake."

"He's determined to fight Home Rule," she said.

"And we're all worried about the Irish Question," Balfour

agreed, "but Randy has the power to decide the issue, if only he'll use it!"

The Irish Question—which had *not* been raised in her dining room that night, thank heaven—was whether Ireland was ready for self-government. Every single man at Jennie's table held a different opinion.

"I thought *deciding* was Mr. Parnell's job," Jennie replied mildly. Parnell was head of the Irish Nationalists, Gladstone's principal supporter. He'd forced the PM to promise a vote on Home Rule that session—or lose power completely. And as Randy wanted the Gladstone Government to fall, he made a point of thwarting Parnell at every turn.

"Parnell will shoot himself in the foot," Arthur insisted, "if Randolph will only stop baiting him—and the entire country he represents. As it is, Randy looks like he's calling for civil war every time he shouts *Ulster will fight, and Ulster will be right!*"

"Have some chocolate trifle, Arthur." Jennie drew him to the sideboard. Roose's note was burning a scar into her palm. She was desperate to read it. "Rosa made it especially for the Prince— which means it's bound to have brandy in it."

"Please talk to your husband," he urged her. "*You* could persuade him, Jennie, to soften his tongue."

"Try his secretary, if it's softening you want," she returned dryly. "Alasdair's in far greater favor than I am at present. I imagine he and Randy have run off to the library, to escape the tiresome guests."

Balfour smiled faintly. "Then I'll join them. If that's the way it is, I'm sorry, Jennie. I'm keeping you from reading your letter. I hope it's not bad news."

He had seen what she clutched in her palm, then. With a rush of gratitude, she watched Arthur leave the drawing room. Footmen were circulating among her guests with trays of coffee; no one seemed to need her. Jennie tore open the envelope and scanned Roose's few lines swiftly.

He'd written at dinnertime; it was now nearly midnight. *The approach of the crisis . . . Should the left lung remain free—*

Good God. Jennie gazed unseeing into the middle distance. Winston might actually die. Might *already* have died, while she smiled and nodded and pressed delicacies on her friends. With the sudden yawning terror came a frantic desire for comfort—a strength she could grasp. *Charles—*

"My dear," Princess Alix said behind her, in the oddly toneless voice of the deaf, "is there news? Of your dear son? Bertie mentioned his illness. I am sure you are anxious."

Alix had sought her out with the instinctive kindness of a fellow mother, aware that if Jennie stood alone on the edge of her party, something must be wrong.

"You must long to go to him. While we take up your care and time." The Princess reached out as though to clasp Jennie's arm, but dropped it again as Bertie joined them.

"You simply *must* lend me your cook, Lady Randolph," the Prince drawled. "Her worth is above rubies. And therefore, the property of the Crown."

Jennie folded Roose's note and smiled at them both. "If I parted with Rosa, Your Royal Highness would never dine here again! I must have some stratagem, Sir, to lure you to Connaught Place. I'm wagering on this excellent chocolate trifle. And now, Princess—shall I play Chopin for you?"

# CHAPTER SEVENTEEN

A telegram from Robson Roose was delivered with Jennie's breakfast tray. He had sent it at one A.M.

*The high temperature indicating exhaustion, I applied stimulants. . . . I shall stay by the boy today.*

Chilled with fear, Jennie glanced at the ormolu clock beside her bed. *Nearly a quarter past nine.* She had fallen between the sheets a few minutes after two, when the last of her dinner guests had finally departed. She sifted frantically now among the pile of letters beside her teacup—there was nothing else from Roose. Thrusting aside the counterpane, she pulled on her dressing gown and went in search of Randolph.

He was lounging over coffee in the breakfast parlor with Alasdair Gordon. The octagonal room, lined in pale green paper, was suffused with the aqueous light of a London March. Both men wore riding dress, neat dark gray coats and bowlers with breeches tucked into polished leather boots. Were they jaunting about Hyde Park together in the mornings now? Gordon's classical beauty was only ripening with age. The schoolboy frame had hardened into a man's, broad-shouldered and muscled. Randy, whose hair was thinning at thirty-seven, looked more and more like a gnome from a dark fairy tale. His gauntness worried Jennie. But she could not force him to eat; when she betrayed her anxiety, Randolph snarled.

"Up already, darling?" he asked.

Without a word, she handed him the doctor's bulletins.

Randolph scanned first one, then the other, and set both aside with a grimace of annoyance. "Very well. And?"

"I must go to Win. Even Princess Alix suggested it last night—"

"Chase back down to *Brighton* again? Don't be a fool, Jennie! Roose hadn't the slightest use for us when we were there. You'll only upset the brat. *Fussing* over him." Randy's eyes flicked to Gordon, who had pushed back his chair, ready to leave them alone. "Don't run away, Alasdair. This will only take a moment."

"Randolph, I'm afraid for him."

"Of course you are. *Mother's feelings,* and all that. But Mrs. Everest is much the properest person to care for him. I'm sure Win prefers her, in any case. And we're drowning in engagements."

*Engagements.*

"He can't breathe," Jennie said fiercely.

Randy threw up his hands. "It's not as though either of us can breathe *for* him!"

Alasdair Gordon moved gracefully to the door. "I shall be attending to correspondence in the library, sir, if you wish to ride later."

"No." Randolph reached out and grasped his wrist. "*Stay.* I shan't be another moment, dash it!"

"I'm sure your mother never hesitated in her duty when your brothers were ill." Jennie heard the venom in her voice.

Randy's cup clattered into its saucer. "I couldn't say. I was little more than a year old when Freddie died."

"You were ten when Charles and Augustus passed."

"And I was safely away at St. George's. Being, unlike our elder son, a compliant scholar who was rarely caned." Randy was furious, Jennie saw, that she'd dared to mention his dead brothers. As though his own survival were somehow shameful.

"You owe it to us all," he added with deadly precision, "to *stay away* from Brighton. Winston's *contagious*. We can't risk the threat to young Jack. Or . . . ourselves. I won't hear another word."

She whirled in the breakfast parlor doorway, hot tears stinging her eyes. What was this wave of hysteria and rage, rising from her feet to her throat, threatening to strangle her? Why the helpless wash of fear?

Jennie paused at the foot of the stairs, one hand on the newel post, the other clutching at her skirts. *Of course.* Newport. Over twenty years ago now. Randy wasn't the only one who'd lost someone dear.

Grief tightened around her heart like an iron band. *Still so fresh.* And yet she had managed to keep living. Newport was an utterly different life . . . that might have happened to somebody else. . . .

She brushed a lock of hair behind her ear and began slowly to climb the steps, her hand clutching the banister for support. Memory climbed with her.

Did anyone lay flowers at the distant grave?

### *March 1863*

She was nine years old and absorbed in a book the first time her life turned upside down.

Jennie never set foot in Papa's library when he was there, because then it was *his* place and not the secret one she kept to herself while he was at his offices on Wall Street. The mahogany paneling glowed warmly even on the dreariest days, and the draperies were crimson velvet, so heavy that not a whisper of the carriage traffic from Madison Square filtered through the glazed windows. The only sounds were the settling of logs burning behind the brass fender and the rustle of thick paper as Jennie turned the pages. A Turkey carpet splashed carmine and indigo at her feet. The library smelled of cigars and brandy and old leather bindings, the dryness of paper and the wetness of ink. It smelled, Jennie thought, of *Papa.* Bookshelves soared two stories above her head, and at the far end of the room a spiral staircase led to a gallery. The ceiling was painted midnight blue, with constellations exploding across it in streamers of gold.

Behind Jennie were enormous tables, with folios and prints set out on their shining surfaces, a magnifying lens here, a few oil lamps there. Stacks of monogrammed paper sat near crystal inkwells. Papa had discarded a pair of gold cuff links beside the silver clippers he used to cut his cigars; sometimes at night Jennie glimpsed him through a crack in the library door, shuffling the evening newspapers, his shirtsleeves rolled to the elbow. He'd filled the room with comfortable chairs like the ones in his clubs— bucket chairs covered in soft leather that adapted to the men who sat in them. Jennie was draped sideways in one of these, her stockinged legs jackknifed over the chair's arm. The library was most particularly *her* place when rain lashed the tall windows and the streets beyond, as it was doing now.

"Miss Jeanette!"

She started at her nursemaid Dobbie's voice, and the heavy old volume slid off her lap.

"*Such* a way as you're sitting in that chair! I declare I'm ashamed of you." Dobbie was a large woman with coffee-colored skin, a bright green skirt, and a red turban wrapped around her hair. Jennie had known her always. "Whatever are you reading?"

"*The Children of the New Forest.*" Jennie scrambled down to retrieve her book. "Did you know that England has civil wars, too, Dobbie? In this one, the mother and father are killed and the children run away to live in the woods. The boys take care of their sisters. It's immensely exciting!"

"Put your skirts down," her nurse scolded, "and come along right now."

"It's unfortunate that we have no brothers." Jennie set *The Children of the New Forest* broodingly on a table. "If Mamma and Papa are killed in *our* Civil War, I'll have to put on a disguise—a cap and trousers would be best—and drive us all to Newport. There must be a forest there that we can hide in."

"And where are you like to find a cap and trousers?" Dobbie demanded.

"The ragman. He comes to the kitchen door on Tuesdays. I've seen him."

"Such talk." Dobbie grasped her hand and pulled her down the passage toward the massive sweep of front stairs. "A girl in pants. What would your mamma say? Come along now."

Jennie caught a glimpse of her younger sister—not baby Leonie, who was only three and taking her nap, but seven-year-old Camille—peering down through the balusters. The bow in Camille's blond curls was askew and her face looked pinched and apprehensive. Had Dobbie found their cache of stolen sweets, wrapped in wax paper and hidden beneath the skirts of Camille's least favorite doll? Or was it the broken china teacup from the nursery service—Limoges, like everything else in the Jerome house—that Jennie had buried furtively in one of Mamma's potted ferns?

"What is it?" she mouthed, as Dobbie dragged her up the stairs.

"Bombs," Camille said clearly. "It's *bombs,* Jennie."

Dobbie made them both sort through their cherished toys while she tidied their clothes into trunks—"Only three dolls each, mind, as there's a mess of things to be packed and the Lord knows if your father's boat tries to take it all, we'll sink halfway to Newport."

"When do we sail?" Jennie wanted to know.

"Tomorrow."

Still no word about the bombs. Jennie didn't care for dolls; Camille could take extra. "Are we running from the Rebels? Are they coming to New York?"

"Not that I hear," Dobbie said. Her worn hands gathered night-dresses, shifts, and sashes into neat piles. Jennie's older sister, Clarita, had moved out of the attic nursery this year and had a bedchamber on the second floor, down the hall from Mamma and Papa, with her own dressing room and maid. At nearly twelve, she had a governess now instead of Dobbie and was learning deportment. Jennie could hear Clarita's voice lifted complainingly; she had always hated packing. "Then why leave?"

"I guess your pa's worried about those Irish, down on the docks." The whites of Dobbie's eyes rolled toward her. "They've been getting into all kinds of trouble today, on account of the draft."

"What's the draft?" Camille's fair brows were crinkled in puzzlement.

Jennie was going to explain it was a chill from an open window, when Dobbie said, "*Soldiers*. President Lincoln wants all the men in New York to sign a paper saying they'll fight for the Union, but the Irish don't want to. I guess most of 'em don't feel they've been here long enough to die for much." Dobbie reached for an armful of Jennie's winter woolen dresses. "It ain't the immigrants' job to free slaves."

"But *bombs,* Dobbie?" Jennie plunked herself down on one of the nursery tuffets, fascinated.

"Most likely bottles filled with rags and kerosene, Miss Jeanette. But they work just fine—I hear most of the lower end of the city is on fire. That's why your pa wants us all out of Manhattan."

"In case the fire spreads?" If Papa's library burned—and the stable where her pony lived . . . the theater where she played her piano . . .

"They won't hurt *you,* will they?" Camille quavered. She wrapped her arms tightly around Dobbie's waist.

"Dobbie's not a slave," Jennie declared, recovering. "She's as free as you and I are. And you know we'll be safe in Newport, Camille. There's bound to be a forest we can hide in there."

The next morning, three carriages of servants, household goods, Jeromes, and baggage rolled out of Madison Square toward Papa's berth on the East River.

Papa had owned boats before, but *Clara Clarita* was special. She was a new schooner-rigged steam yacht, graceful and swift; even the iron funnel protruding amidships failed to mar her fluid beauty. She was 130 feet long, with guns mounted on her stern and a saloon lined in pale blue satin.

"Leonard," Mamma had sighed the first time she saw the rich upholstery, "what were you thinking? This will fade in sun, and stain with salt water!"

"But the color pairs so well with your complexion, my dear," Papa replied, which was unanswerable.

Mamma shooed the girls into the saloon to escape the soft drizzle, but Jennie ignored her and remained on deck with her hand in Papa's. She could feel the steady thump of *Clarita*'s engine beneath the deck. The East River was roiling and wine-dark as they headed north toward Long Island Sound. The patches of sheen on its surface dazzled like rainbows.

"Oil," Papa said disappointingly, when Jennie pointed out the sparkling colors with her muff.

Boat traffic was heavy, the racket of commerce loud and bewildering; whistles blared. Jennie gripped Papa's hand.

"Are you cold?" he asked.

"No, Papa." Dobbie had stuck a round felt hat on her black curls with a jaunty aigrette in the shape of a feather. Her cherry-red merino coat was trimmed in sable. The fur tickled her chin and cut the wind off the river. Her muff was sable, too, and she kept her left hand firmly inside it, clutching the book she'd tucked there. It was not that she was hiding *The Children of the New Forest* from Papa, but rather the fact that she had taken a volume from his library without asking. If he discovered this, Jennie would tell the truth. *I had to know how the story ends.*

"How long until we reach Newport?" Her eyes smarted and teared with coal smoke and wind. She did not want her father to think she was crying at leaving New York. She blinked rapidly.

"It's a hundred and thirty-nine miles," he explained. "The *Clarita* averages about thirteen knots. I make this trip each year with the Yacht Club regatta, you know. It's a tradition. We'll be there in nine hours or so."

Jennie was used to traveling by train to Rhode Island each summer, and the railway took half as long. But Papa looked so pleased to be sailing luxuriously from one port to another that she merely said, "As fast as that!" He was proud of *Clara Clarita.*

"Shall you be bored?" He smiled down at her.

She shook her head. "Did you know, Papa, that there are civil wars in England?"

"Men will find a reason to kill each other anywhere, Jennie. Would you like to visit Captain Thayer on his bridge?"

It was dark and cold by the time they reached Rhode Island. Mamma and Clarita had both been sick over the side and retired to shrouded cabins. In the seventh hour at sea, little Leonie began to wail and Dobbie bore her away to sleep below deck.

"You should name your next yacht *Jeanette* or *Camille,* Papa," Jennie said helpfully, "after better sailors."

Few lights illuminated the summer cottages on the cliffs as they moored at one of the private slips in Newport, but the shops and streets around the wharves were bustling. Papa sent the servants ahead in hired carriages to the Jerome cottage, which was intended purely for summer and had no central heating, so that fires could be hurriedly lit and beds made up. Dobbie and Leonie went with them.

"We'll have a little supper, girls," Papa suggested. "Get something warm in your stomachs, or you'll never sleep."

He ushered Mamma and his three older daughters, tired and red-cheeked from the March cold, into a public restaurant on Thames Street, not far from the wharves. Jennie was conscious of eyes upon them. It was an hour when most little girls were long since tucked up in bed, and the room was cheerful with oil lamps and the warm fug of tobacco smoke. A fire roared on the hearth and the Jeromes had a table near its warmth.

It was the first time Jennie had ever been allowed in a restaurant, and she struggled to contain a bubble of excitement over everything to do with the meal—the strangeness of a waiter unfurling a napkin in her lap, the swell of male voices from the tables around them, the menu that seemed so immense in her hands. Clarita, she noticed, was doing her best to look bored, as though she were used to dining out with grown-ups. She sat very straight, practicing deportment, and kept her hands demurely in her lap. Jennie stuck her tongue out at Clarita when Mamma was not looking, and caught a twinkle in her father's eyes from across the table. His thumbs were tucked in his waistcoat pockets, and his long legs thrust out on the wood floor.

"Happy, Jennie?"

She nodded vigorously. "May I have fried oysters, Papa?" It was the most exotic item on the menu. She thought the occasion called for nothing ordinary.

"You may."

"Leonard!" Mamma protested. "She'll be sick!"

"If she didn't cast up her accounts on the *Clarita,*" he said, "she'll do fine. Oysters are one of the first refinements of Society, Clara."

It was extraordinary, Jennie decided, how black the night sky over Newport seemed after the lights of New York, and how thickly crowded with stars. She stood stock-still in the middle of the carriage drive, her head craned back, just staring.

The Jerome cottage was on Coggeshall Avenue, not far from Almy's Pond. They had passed the homes of any number of people Mamma and Papa knew, but most of the houses were empty and dark.

"The Gerrys are not yet at Seaverge," Mamma observed as they traveled down Bellevue Avenue, "nor the Wolfes at The Reefs. And you heard, Leonard, that old William Wetmore died, and left Chateau-sur-Mer to George? I'm told he plans extensive renovations, and has taken his bride to Europe. You've marooned me here, with four children, thirty trunks, and not a respectable soul to cheer me! It's very *tiresome.*"

"There are lights at Chepstow," Papa observed, as their carriage turned into Narragansett Avenue.

Jennie peeked out the side window. White stucco and black shutters, a wide lawn and circular drive. One light burned behind bow windows, another high on the upper floor.

"Chepstow!" Mamma repeated. "You must be dreaming, Leonard, if you expect me to invite the Recluse to dine!"

"You could do worse." Papa quirked his bushy eyebrows. "Schermerhorn is Lina Astor's cousin."

Even Jennie knew that Caroline Astor was the most fashionable lady in New York—and that she did not wish to know Mamma. Mrs. Astor's daughter Emily refused to say hello to Jennie in the dance classes they shared at Delmonico's. The Jeromes' money, Papa had once explained to her, was not old enough. He had made his own fortune, not inherited it.

"Her *eccentric* cousin," Mamma retorted, "who refuses to marry because of a Disappointment in Youth, travels with the side shades of his carriage drawn down, and speaks only to his servants! Edmund Schermerhorn would be poor comfort at any time, Leonard—but none at all in March!"

"Suit yourself." Papa shrugged as the carriage turned into their own sweep. "For my part, I find eccentrics interesting."

Now Jennie felt her father's hand on her shoulder as she stood alone, her face lifted to the stars. "When it's a bit warmer," he suggested, "we'll study the constellations. Would you like that?"

"Very much, Papa. But we will have to stay up *fearfully* late."

"I'll settle the matter with Dobbie," he promised. "Now come along inside, before you catch your death."

There were hot bricks wrapped in flannel in the beds that night. The next morning, Papa sailed back to New York alone.

# CHAPTER EIGHTEEN

"I love Newport, even if it *is* cold," Jennie told Camille. "Nobody cares that we're all by ourselves. We're never allowed outside alone in Madison Square."

She had banged out of the cottage's back door in her cherry-colored coat that morning, immediately after breakfast, while Dobbie was busy with Leonie and Mamma was still unpacking her trunks, to roam the tumbled granite slabs that bit into Narragansett Sound. Camille followed carefully behind, picking her way uncertainly among the rocks. At seven, she was much slighter than Jennie but she would rather die than fail to keep up. The girls had raced from Coggeshall Avenue down to Sheep Point. There was a narrow curve of sandy beach here, but Jennie was intent upon the rocks, where she could test her balance and skill.

There was only one other person on the sand when the two girls reached it: a man in a dark shooting coat and gaiters with a Scottish terrier at his feet. He wore a beaver top hat, which Jennie knew was quite wrong with a shooting jacket, and he stood with his back to civilization. His gaze was fixed on the waves curling relentlessly into the quarter-moon of cove, and he was utterly still. His terrier bitch gazed seaward like her master. Jennie disregarded both of them and mounted her first granite slab.

It was precariously pitched and led to a larger boulder where the waves lapped hungrily, but beyond this was a third and larger rock that was broad and inviting, a *king* of a rock that led farther out into the sea, where she might feel the wind and the power of the tides.

She leapt once, teetered, steadied herself with her arms out-flung like a ballerina, then leapt again.

"Jennie," Camille called.

Her sister was crouched on the beach, her long blond curls shielding her face and her delicate hands poking at something. Her flared coat and skirt and petticoats were rucked up over her black-stockinged legs.

"Come see!" she insisted.

Jennie hesitated; the wildness called to her. But Camille looked so absorbed. Jennie turned back.

"It's like a town," Camille told her. "A little town with shells for houses."

It was true, Jennie decided as she hunkered down near her sister. The tide pool was a separate world ringed with stone. There were barnacles and mussels clinging to the rocks, laced with sea-weed, but below them in the shallow stillness of sand and water, crabs scuttled sideways, absurd claws waving. She could put names to some of the things Camille's fingers hovered over—

"Those are winkles." She pointed to the whorled and striated shells of the snails. "French people eat them, Papa says."

Camille wrinkled her nose.

"And that's a sea urchin." Jennie peered under the nearest gran-ite ledge. The urchin liked to hide. It was reddish orange, all spikes that waved like a tree in a strong wind, and she had no intention of touching it. But beside it—

"That's a sea star!" Jennie pulled the horny thing toward her, curling and writhing against itself. Camille was round-eyed in fas-cination; the creature was so *alive,* yet it felt like coral when touched. "Papa says that if you tear off its leg, it will grow another. Shall we see, Camille?"

"Don't," the man said.

Jennie looked up in astonishment.

The man in the gaiters and shooting jacket was standing over them, his Scottie at his side. The little black dog looked mildly interested in Jennie and Camille but seemed to reserve judgment.

"Sea stars are so defenseless," the stranger added apologetically. "It's like maiming a lamb. Would you tear the leg off a lamb, Miss . . . ?"

Jennie hesitated. Neither Dobbie nor Mamma allowed her to talk to strangers. But this one was about Papa's age, and from his voice, was clearly Their Sort of People.

"Jerome," she supplied.

"Charmed." The man lifted his top hat from his head and bowed.

"What is your dog's name?" Jennie asked.

"Matilda."

"Matilda," Jennie repeated. She reached a tentative hand to the dog's head, but the terrier ducked and avoided her.

"Always greet a dog with a hand to its chest," the man advised. "That way you touch its heart. Pat its head, and it resents you. You might as well be driving it into the earth."

Jennie said nothing, but reached for the dog's chest. Matilda leaned into her hand and made a low moaning sound in her throat that suggested pleasure.

The man crouched down beside them. "Look at the rock crabs," he told the two children. "*Cancer irroratus.* Kingdom, Animalia. Phylum, Arthropoda. Subphylum, Crustacea. Class, Malacostraca. Order, Decapoda. Infraorder, Brachyura. Family, Cancridae. Genus, Cancer."

Matilda thrust her nose into the crease of Jennie's elbow.

"There are so many," Camille faltered. It was true: crabs large and small scuttled in swarms over the sand, in the shallows, darting under rocks where they felt safest. Jennie sensed that her sister was frightened. The crabs were like spiders. They shared the same multi-limbed, unpredictable motion, the possibility of nightmare. She took Camille's hand and squeezed it.

The man lifted a crab in his fingers, claws waving. "They have a hard exoskeleton and a fan-shaped carapace, and antennae for taste and smell. Note the eyestalks at the front of the shell: they are movable."

Jennie offered her palm and the man placed the crab in it. The eyestalks waved at her, and one claw lifted in challenge. She counted to five before she set it carefully back in the pool; there was victory enough in this.

"During the mating season," the man observed, "the male crab encircles the female with his claws, to protect her as she molts. He can only mate, you see, during molting, when the female is soft-shelled and defenseless."

Camille looked helplessly at Jennie, horror in her eyes.

"But the female wants to mate, too," Jennie said sturdily. "So that makes it all right."

"Of course. God's plan," the man agreed, as though this were obvious. "Once her shell hardens, in another two or three days, the male lets her go."

There was a deeper lesson in this, Jennie knew, but her mind sheered away from considering it.

The man rose and snapped his fingers at Matilda. The black dog and her master turned their backs on the girls and made their way up the stony beach.

"Sir!" Jennie called after him. "I should like to know your name."

The man stopped short. He seemed to consider her words, his gaze firmly fixed on the sea.

"I am Schermerhorn," he said at last, "the Recluse." And walked on.

When Dobbie found smears of seaweed and sand on the hems of their dresses, she made Jennie stand in the corner without her dinner. "Catapulting over the rocks again," Dobbie scolded. "It'll be on your head, Miss Jeanette, if your sister drowns in the waves."

Camille pushed back her chair from the nursery dining table and ran to stand at Jennie's side. Jennie ignored her so that Dobbie wouldn't be angry—Dobbie loved Camille best of all four Jerome girls. Camille took Jennie's hand anyway. They stood like that until Dobbie lost patience and sent them both to bed. They shared a room with Dutch-blue walls high up under the sloping eaves of the house, their white wooden beds shaped like sleighs.

"It was worth missing dinner," Jennie whispered after the lamps were dimmed, "just to meet the Recluse."

That night she dreamed that Papa sat cross-legged on her bedroom floor, racing crabs across the carpet.

# CHAPTER NINETEEN

In April, Papa brought his glamorous friend Fanny Ronalds and her two young sons and their nursemaid to Newport on his steam yacht, the *Clara Clarita*. Although he'd assured Jennie that the dock-yards and working-class neighborhoods were quieter now after the explosive March draft protests, Papa had urged Mrs. Ronalds to get out of New York, too. He escorted her to the Ronaldses' cottage a quarter mile from his own, and his crew saw her luggage safely trans-ferred from the yacht. This was Friday. On Sunday afternoon, the rest of her things having arrived from Manhattan (the word *things* encompassing servants and carriages and horses), Fanny appeared at the foot of the Jerome drive in a dogcart pulled by a pair of donkeys.

Jennie was already dressed and running among the bare canes of the rose garden, which were beginning to swell with pale leaves the color of fresh tea, but the instant she glimpsed the upright fig-ure in a spring bonnet, its arched brim lined with silk peonies and tied with a deep pink taffeta bow, a bubble of pleasure rose in her chest. Fanny was like a memory of *home*. The streamers of her bow were six inches wide and two feet long, and they bobbed splendidly at Fanny's breast as the donkeys jogged. She held a pearl-handled whip along with the reins; her hands were gloved in pale rose kid. Jennie noticed that Fanny's carriage dress had the new sleeves: narrow at the shoulder but as full as bells where they gathered at her wrist. *So becoming for a lady who drives,* Mamma had said as she leafed through *Godey's Lady's Book*.

Mamma did not drive.

Jennie raced across the lawn to cut Fanny off, skittering into the gravel a few yards from the team. One of the donkeys brayed and kicked out with its front leg. Fanny pulled up. Her hands sawed at the reins and her breath came in fearful gasps. She did not look at Jennie until the donkeys were under control.

Jennie waited, too, then scrambled into the dogcart beside her. "How wonderful to see you, Mrs. Ronalds," she said, offering her hand. "You look as bright as a new-minted penny."

"And so do you *not,*" Fanny exclaimed. "You should have been a boy, rolling under the wheels, all blood and dirt."

"I wish I were a boy! Papa is smoking a cigar on the porch. Are these your donkeys?"

"Do you like them?"

"I've never seen any before. They aren't exactly *handsome,* but Papa says spirit is always preferable to looks."

"They have too much of that," Fanny said feelingly.

"May I drive them?"

"With pleasure." She handed Jennie the reins. "If you can manage them, you may *have* them, Miss Jeanette." She leaned close, awash in the scent of violets. "Your father taught me to drive, did you know?"

Jennie knew. She knew a number of things, in fact, and she wasn't entirely sure how she felt about them. She knew that Fanny gave her presents, for instance, because Jennie was Papa's favorite. He had taught her to handle the reins long before he had attempted to teach Mrs. Ronalds. And he had told her once that Fanny's hands did not hold a candle to hers. Jennie had good hands and a better seat and neither could truly be taught, but she did not say any of this to Fanny.

She touched the flank of the near donkey with Mrs. Ronalds's whip, and the pair moved joltingly up the drive, where Leonard Jerome stood waiting, smoke wreathing his head.

"Their names are Willie and Wooshie," Fanny told her. "Good riddance to them."

Jennie would have liked to ask which donkey was which, but she suspected Fanny had no idea.

She spent the rest of spring rattling up and down Bellevue Avenue in the dogcart, goading the donkeys with a whip. Camille came along, of course, although she was terrified of speed and of Jennie's driving. The donkeys' raucous bray made her flinch. She clenched the sides of the dogcart, her face ashen. Nothing could compel her to stay behind, though, because Camille loved Jennie with a ferocity that was the most Jerome thing about her. In return Jennie made very sure that Camille was never hurt.

On several occasions when the two girls were down at Sheep Point that spring, Mr. Schermerhorn appeared silently beside them with his dog. They never knew when to expect him, but when he and Matilda were there, the time on the beach became a lesson hour. He found them living sand dollars, green, purple, and blue, which he called *Clypeasteroida* and explained were really flattened sea urchins that burrowed into the sand. When Jennie touched them, they felt furry.

"Spines," Mr. Schermerhorn informed her. "Or, properly speaking, *cilia*. Think of them as myriad feet that propel the urchin across the sea bottom."

He explained that the white disks that Jennie thought of as sand dollars were simply skeletons, or "tests" as he called them, stripped of living flesh and bleached by sea and sun.

"Every shore is a vast charnel house," Mr. Schermerhorn observed. "Each step we take is taken upon bones."

It was his talent for blending science with the macabre that enslaved Jennie. Entranced, heart pounding, she followed his words, holding her breath. Camille was content to gather Matilda into her lap and listen, but Jennie asked question after question. *What did the sand dollars eat while they were still sea urchins? What ate them? How long did they live before turning to white tests?* When the Recluse left them in his baffling way, breaking off sometimes in mid-sentence with a gesture to his Scottie, she did not speak to Camille immediately. She was too busy absorbing all he had taught her.

"The little girls are always so *sandy,*" their older sister, Clarita, complained when they clattered through the cottage in their stout boots. "It's so much lovelier to stroll the Cliff Walk with *you,* Miss Hallam." Clarita was wearing longer dresses this spring and never went outside without gloves or a hat, which Jennie found ludicrous. Miss Hallam was her governess—a timorous young woman, engaged to a clergyman, who relied upon Dobbie to control little Leonie and "the Middles," as she called Jennie and Camille. Jennie submitted to her lessons in French and deportment and tore out among the daffodils and blown dogwood the instant she finished her midday meal.

Papa visited from New York when he could. He visited Mrs. Ronalds rather oftener, something Jennie and Camille discovered and did not tell the others. Willie and Wooshie took them farther abroad in Newport than they admitted, and once, down near the public wharves in town, they spied the *Clara Clarita,* rocking gently at a hired slip. It was not a weekend that Papa was at home.

"One steamer looks very like another," Jennie told Camille hurriedly. "That one must belong to someone else."

"But it has the same name," Camille pointed out. "Which is very odd, Jennie. There can't be two families with a Clara and Clarita in them."

"Perhaps Papa came on business," Jennie suggested, "and must leave as soon as it is done. He would not wish to disappoint us all. So he never told us he was here."

"Shall we go see him?" Camille asked hopefully.

Jennie reached out and grasped her little sister's wrist. "Promise me you will never go near the yacht unless Papa asks."

"But why?"

"Papa will have gone to his business. But if you run down the dock calling for him, Captain Thayer will know. He'll send for Mamma. And then Papa will be in trouble for having kept his visit a secret."

The two girls looked out over the docks to the sea beyond. "Jennie, let's go home," Camille whispered. "Maybe Papa is already there."

During the stretches of rain in April and May, Mrs. Ronalds was often at the Jerome cottage, singing duets with Clara Jerome while Jennie and Clarita played the piano. The two women trimmed hats and sewed embroidery. They read to each other from *Godey's Lady's Book*. They ridiculed outlandish fashions and practiced new dance steps together and taught them to the girls. Fanny's sons, who were two and four years old, remained firmly at home in their nursery. Jennie was not entirely sure that she had ever seen them. Although Fanny's gowns were as elaborately hooped as Clara Jerome's, the gauzy fabrics and colors she wore gave an impression of lightness, Jennie decided, of petals fluttering in a breeze. When she left them, ducking hurriedly into her carriage under cover of an umbrella after dinner on a wet evening, Clara invariably murmured that *dear Fanny is like another sister,* and *What a comfort that she left New York.*

Sometimes when Jennie was alone, she paraded in front of her mirror with carefully gliding steps, practicing Fanny's charm.

In June, the first trickle of summer families returned to Newport. Minnie Stevens (who would one day be Minnie Paget and entertain the Prince of Wales with her scurrilous stories) arrived with her parents and her little brother, Harry, and a passel of servants to stay in a hired house on Bellevue Avenue. Mrs. Paran Stevens was building a new place on the heavily treed lot behind Mr. Bennett's Stone Villa, in a style known as Steamboat Gothic, and she spent most of her time bullying her architect. Minnie spent most of her time careening up and down Bellevue Avenue with Jennie and

Camille in the dogcart. There was always room for another passenger; the girls were adept at squeezing together and the donkeys were game to pull anything.

When Alva Smith (who would one day be Alva Vanderbilt) arrived with her family, and Consuelo Yznaga and her three sisters moved into a third rented house next door to the Smiths, Jennie briefly considered charging a penny per dogcart ride, but Camille was so shocked by this mercenary impulse that Jennie never acted upon it. Alva was a pugnacious and wiry redhead. She rode her horse recklessly about the town and engaged in fistfights on street corners with boys, who lived in terror of her. The girls went bathing together at Bailey's Beach, wearing navy-blue wool flannel dresses with long sleeves over full-length flannel bloomers. Jennie's was trimmed in red nautical braid, Camille's in white. They had bathing shoes to match. None of the girls could swim but they loved to jump up and down in the rollers where the sand met the granite rocks. In the dusky June evenings, cleaned and fed, they met in one another's backyards and chased fireflies. Alva was the only one who insisted on keeping them, stifled in a jar until one by one the lights flickered out. Her lack of mercy both appalled and fascinated Jennie. Alva, she realized, enjoyed her power over weaker creatures. Jennie decided never to be one of them.

Papa arrived on the first true summer weekend prepared to squire both his wife and Fanny to a dance at Bateman's Hotel, which was the center of Newport's social world. He brought with him his great friend August Belmont, a fabulously wealthy Rothschild partner who was rumored to be Jewish. Belmont and Papa both loved racehorses and were members of the same clubs. Jennie watched Mr. Belmont arrive that night from her perch on the upstairs landing. He had dark hair and eyes and a trimmed set of black whiskers curving along his jaw. Mr. Belmont liked to wear elaborate silk waistcoats, and his topper was always cocked at a jaunty angle. He smelled deliciously of something she identified years later as ambergris. Mr. Belmont liked to hoist Camille in his arms and spin her around in the air; Jennie, at nine, was too tall to twirl.

Papa had explained to Clara Jerome that Belmont was a bachelor here in Newport until his wife, Caroline Perry, moved north with her summer household. The Belmonts had built a brand-new cottage called By-the-Sea, which sat on an immense lot at Bellevue and Marine Avenues. Mrs. Belmont was a descendant of Commodore Perry, and, being from a naval family, had always summered in Newport as a child; but now she brought liveried footmen in powdered wigs from New York to serve her in July and August.

From their bedroom window later that evening, Jennie and Camille avidly studied the four grown-ups as they entered Papa's carriage. Mrs. Ronalds had flowers in her burnished hair. Mr. Belmont hovered at her elbow, his hands on the verge of caressing her shoulders where they sprang whitely from her evening gown. His voice had a brutal quality that fascinated Jennie; she decided it might be like a leopard's.

Mamma was handsome rather than pretty, she thought; *a fine-looking woman,* Papa always said, which signified something deeper and far better than beauty, Jennie knew. As the consort of the King of Wall Street, it was Mamma's duty to inspire envy in men and women alike. She wore a fortune in Tiffany diamonds that night.

"Once the grown-ups are gone," Jennie whispered to Camille, "let's play dress-up." She loved to steal into Mamma's room and plunder the wardrobe. Camille would wrap herself in elaborate shawls, while Jennie hobbled in high-heeled slippers with her mother's hoops swaying around her waist. The glimpse of a different self in Mamma's mirror—tall and strangely curvaceous—excited her. And it scared her, too.

Now that it was June, Newport had a thrillingly festive air. Lights blazed in every cottage window. Bellevue Avenue was choked with carriages in the afternoons as ladies paid calls and took their airings. Jennie and Camille did not see Mr. Schermerhorn at the beach anymore. The crowds of outsiders, bathing and picnicking and promenading across the sand, had driven him back behind his drawn shades at Chepstow House. Jennie imagined him there, turning shells in his fingers. She ran down to Sheep Point very early every morning in case he was walking Matilda now at dawn, but she never caught him.

It was also in June that the Rebel general Lee moved his troops into the Shenandoah and J. E. B. Stuart won a dreadful cavalry engagement against General Pleasonton. The Union garrison was attacked at a place called Milliken's Bend, Papa read aloud, as he sat over his coffee and newspaper in the breakfast parlor. *Hush, Leonard,* Mamma scolded—she did not like him mentioning the war in front of the girls, but Jennie listened to every detail. The idea that men were fighting each other while she jumped from boulder to boulder below the Cliff Walk in the mornings was difficult to believe. She had finished *The Children of the New Forest* and kept its survival lessons in mind. Unlike Alva Erskine Smith, she did not punch Newport boys, and had actually allowed a few of them, like Minnie Stevens's brother, Harry, into her donkey cart—although she never let him drive. This was a calculated gamble on Jennie's part: if the Rebels reached Rhode Island and she was forced to hide as an orphan in the woods, Harry might sell her a pair of trousers.

In Winchester, Virginia, Confederates surrounded and slaughtered six thousand Union men. By the end of June, as Rebel forces crossed into Maryland at Harper's Ferry, the Union general, Hooker, was relieved of his command, Papa told Jennie, and someone named Meade took over the Army of the Potomac.

Papa showed Jennie the columns of dead men's names printed in *The New York Times*. In the days after July 3, when the battle in a place called Gettysburg seemed to be finished and Lee had retreated south with his survivors, the lists of War Dead were endless. The battle began on a Wednesday, the first of July. When Papa received the Saturday edition of the *Times,* shipped by Sunday's train to Newport, the whole space above the fold was one enormous headline:

THE GREAT BATTLES.; Our Special Telegrams from the Battle Field to 10 A.M. Yesterday. Full Details of the Battle of Wednesday. No Fighting on Thursday Until Four and a Half, P.M. A Terrible Battle Then Commenced, Lasting Until Dark. The Enemy Repulsed at All Points. The Third Battle Commenced. Yesterday Morning at Daylight. THE REBELS THE ATTACKING PARTY. No Impression Made on Our Lines. The Death of Longstreet, and Barksdale of Mississippi. Other Prominent Rebel Officers Killed or Wounded. A LARGE NUMBER OF PRISONERS. Gen. Sickles' Right Leg Shot Off. OTHER GENERAL OFFICERS WOUNDED. OFFICIAL DISPATCHES FROM GEN. MEADE. THE BATTLE OF WEDNESDAY. REPORTS FROM PHILADELPHIA. THE BATTLE OF THURSDAY. YESTERDAY'S BATTLE. Our Special Telegrams from the Battle Field. NEWS RECEIVED IN WASHINGTON. NEWS RECEIVED IN PHILADELPHIA. THE ASSOCIATED PRESS DISPATCHES. REPORTS FROM HARRISBURGH. REPORTS FROM COLUMBIA, PENN. REPORTS FROM BALTIMORE. THE GREAT BATTLE. COL. CROSS, OF NEW-HAMPSHIRE, KILLED.

Jennie ran her index finger under the lines of type. They did not tell her the one thing she wanted to know.

"Did we win, Papa?"

"I suppose," he replied, scowling. "But at terrible cost, Jennie."

That morning there was a solemn celebration of Independence Day. Gentlemen clapped each other on the back as they met in front of the tables where ladies poured out lemonade and tea. A band played and children raced down to the sea's edge, trailing kites. There was an archery competition for the ladies, and Fanny Ronalds competed. She wore a white canvas archery coat with pagoda sleeves over her hooped skirt and looked breathtakingly fetching with her quiver of arrows at her back. Jennie longed to look as dashing and begged Papa for archery lessons.

"You must ask Mrs. Ronalds to teach you," Papa told her.

The idea made Jennie feel, for once, shy. She had enjoyed being superior to Fanny with her driving hands and her riding seat. But when she asked if she could try to nock an arrow in her bow, Fanny was instantly serious. She held Jennie's hands in her own to guide them.

"Relax your shoulders," she said, "and turn your face slightly to the side, just so. You must let the bow do the work for you, Jeanette. Start by standing only a few feet away from the target."

When Jennie managed to hit the cotton-battened sphere on her fourth attempt, Fanny removed her pin from her carnation corsage and handed it to her with a smile. Jennie gasped. It was the prize August Belmont had presented to Fanny that very afternoon—a gold arrow with diamond head and tail.

"You must drive over every morning in the dogcart after breakfast and practice with me," Fanny told her.

By the seventh of July, the Union's relief at having turned the tide of war was so great that celebrations broke out all over Washington. But Papa said immediately that he must head back to New York on the *Clara Clarita*.

Jennie overheard her parents late that night on the staircase landing.

"Stay, Leonard. A gentleman has no real business in New York in summer. Particularly *this* summer. You could have such a lovely time sailing here. We've received so many invitations—"

"Somebody has to fiddle while Rome burns," he interrupted tiredly. "I'm as good a Nero as any."

Jennie had never heard that depth of weariness in Papa's voice before, and she felt a creeping chill in the pit of her stomach—a whisper of desolation—that he would have to travel all by himself while the rest of them stayed in the Newport sun. She got up early the next morning to kiss him goodbye, running downstairs in her bare feet and nightdress.

Papa held her close, his whiskers like a boar-bristle brush against her cheek.

"Why must you go, if we won the war?" she implored.

"We won a battle," he corrected. "Remember the list of War Dead I showed you?"

She nodded.

"Mr. Lincoln will need more Union soldiers now. That means he'll call the draft."

Jennie frowned. "Dobbie says the Irish don't want to fight. That it's not their job to free the slaves."

"More than just the Irish feel that way."

"And they'll throw bombs?"

"I hope not." Gently, Papa released her. "Don't you worry about me, Jennie. I can take care of myself. You hold the fort here, understand?"

She felt his kiss on the top of her head. She stepped back as he climbed into the carriage. Papa rolled an unsmoked cigar between his long fingers, shredding the tobacco, as the horses pulled away. Jennie realized with a small jolt of pride that he meant to save New York. And if Papa couldn't, no one could.

Days passed without a word from him, however, or none that Mamma shared. Jennie fretted at the silence. She longed to know what was happening in the world. *The New York Times* never came to the house unless Papa was there.

"Do you know where I can buy a newspaper?" she asked Dobbie one morning, when she could no longer abide her ignorance.

"Now, Miss Jeanette, what would you be wanting with one of those?"

Dobbie was ironing a pile of white muslin shifts. She was responsible for the care of the younger girls' clothes, and the scents of iron and linen and lavender water, which she used to dampen the shifts before she pressed them, filled the upstairs room. Jennie was sprawled on a window seat overlooking the trees that surrounded the house. The rustle of leaves made her feel like a bird in a secret nest. She imagined climbing out onto the nearest limb and swinging from one branch to another.

"When he left here, Papa said he was fiddling while Rome burned. I should like to know what he meant."

Dobbie snorted. "I suspect your Papa fiddles most days. Can't be the King of Wall Street without leading a whole band."

"Is New York burning?" Jennie demanded fiercely. "I *must* know."

Dobbie folded a square of linen deliberately and set it on a pile. Her dark eyes flicked across Jennie's face; she was deciding, Jennie knew, how much to say. "There's mobs in the city, from what I hear tell."

"Are they near Papa, Dobbie?"

A pause, while the hot iron passed to and fro. Jennie stared implacably at the nursemaid; at last Dobbie relented. "Two nights ago, they attacked his newspaper office."

Jennie's stomach somersaulted, and suddenly she couldn't breathe. "Why?"

"The *Times* backs Mr. Lincoln. Some folks don't like that."

"Is Papa all right?"

"I guess we'd have heard if he wasn't."

She thought of her piano. Her library. "What about our house?"

"The trouble's all below Union Square," Dobbie said.

Jennie's sense of the city was limited, but she thought Dobbie meant to reassure her.

She ran to find Camille. They must write to Papa. They must tell him to come back to Newport as soon as he could.

Her little sister was curled up on her white sleigh bed in the Dutch-blue bedroom, fully dressed. Her eyes were half-closed and her whole body shuddered. At first Jennie thought Camille was crying, but then she saw that the wetness on her face was sweat. She touched Camille's forehead. Her little sister was burning with fever.

# CHAPTER TWENTY

*London, March 1886*

Jennie sat at her writing desk, attempting to answer the flood of congratulatory notes that had arrived in response to her dinner. It was gratifying, of course, that the Deadly Enemies had thoroughly enjoyed themselves—or their proximity to the Prince and Princess of Wales—but her replies were perfunctory. As her hand moved across the thick linen notepaper, Jennie's stuttering mind was on Winston. She was aware of her breast rising and falling with each breath. Any second, this simple power might be denied her son. Any second, the footman might appear with another note from Robson Roose, announcing that Winston had ceased to breathe. Fear made Jennie frantic. Her hand trembled and she blotted her words.

Of course, Roose was the properest person to care for Win. Randolph was right—the doctor did not need an anxious mother hovering at his elbow. But as Jennie addressed her polite nothings to a score of friends and left them in an unruly pile for Randolph to frank—postage was free to Members of Parliament—panic rose like floodwater in her throat. Her husband was useless to her now. He had no comfort to give. He made the slightest request for support or concern seem like an outrageous imposition on his attention. Jennie was desperate for someone who *cared*. About her anxiety, her guilt, her animal need for reassurance.

She set down her pen and sank back against her chair. *Damnit*. She wanted Charles Kinsky.

How to think about the Count?

Jennie had tried to avoid him since their private rupture. Over the past three years, she'd thrown herself into Randolph's work. Her husband's political career was important to her sons; it was all the foothold in British Society they had. But it was impossible to cut Charles Kinsky entirely—he was a fixture in London's best drawing rooms. There were moments when Jennie glimpsed him across a crowded salon, felt his cool eyes upon her like a finger drawn suddenly down her back. Then she curtseyed in his direction, talked lightly of him to strangers, pretended there was nothing more between them than a love of horses and mutual friends. He was always surrounded by his entourage. He escorted a series of beautiful women, some married, some not. He never met her alone after that reckless climb to her bedroom window. She had burned her bridges when she told Charles it was impossible for her to love *only* him.

Jennie had tried to take other men into her bed, out of a need for affection and human warmth. Edgar Vincent, Viscount D'Abernon, a Cambridge-educated soldier who adored art; Henri, Marquis de Breteuil, with his dreamlike chateau southwest of Paris. She had even briefly enjoyed a flirtation with young Harry Cust, whose way with words had charmed her as much as his roguish smile. All useless. Jennie had driven away the one man she loved. And, Lord help her, how she wanted him now—

She drew forward a sheet of blank notepaper embossed with her monogram, and hesitated over it, her pen suspended.

*Dearest Charles, Winston is gravely ill at school—indeed, as I write this, he may already be . . .*

Jennie crumpled the sheet and tossed it to the floor.

*My Dear Count Kinsky—Although it has been some years since communication of a personal nature has passed between us, I feel compelled to let you know that I am in great trouble at present. My son, Winston, is gravely ill at school in Brighton, and . . .*

She tore the sheet in two.

Absurd, to ask anything of a man she'd sent away with such ruthless precision. He would toss her letter on the fire without even breaking the seal.

Jennie rose from her desk and stared at the spring rain coursing down the windowpanes. Her pulse throbbed relentlessly in her temples. Nobody would be riding in Hyde Park today. A full-blown gallop would calm her nerves, and to hell with the wet. At least she'd be far from the threat of Roose's next bulletin. She hurried upstairs to change into her oldest boots and riding habit.

From Connaught Place, the park was due south. As always, Jennie was obliged to guide her gelding, a showy chestnut she'd named Uncle Sam, through the traffic of Edgeware Road to the Cumberland Gate. From there, she had a choice of paths down to Rotten Row, which ran along the park's southern edge from Hyde Park Corner to the Serpentine Road. She met few riders as she trotted briskly beneath the dripping trees, which were flushed with the first acid green, but as she turned Sam's head into the sanded expanse of Rotten Row and collected herself to gallop, she glimpsed a scattering of horses ahead. No matter. She was adept enough in the saddle to weave her racing mount through a handful of plodders. She had done it often enough in the hunting field. She urged Sam forward.

A half mile in, her breath tearing in her chest and the gelding at full stretch, she blew past a pair of beautifully mounted riders. Jennie barely spared them a glance—they were moving at a walk, well to her right, the gentleman shielding the lady, whose horse was close to the inner rail. But the man's dark head turned swiftly as she bowled by him, and Jennie caught the straight blade of the nose, the unmistakable blue eyes, the strong line of his chin. *Charles.*

And beside him, her mouth a perfect O, the blond Miss Fairfield, heiress to a prodigious factory fortune.

Did Charles urge his horse forward, before his mind checked the impulse and reined in pursuit? Jennie felt it was just possible. She felt his surge in the saddle, his eyes boring into her back. But she did not glance behind in her flight. She would not stop, to be patronized by a *Miss Fairfield*. She kicked Uncle Sam harder, tears whipping down her cheeks.

# CHAPTER TWENTY-ONE

*Newport, July 1863*

When Camille had been sick for three days, Clara Jerome at last sent Jennie in her dogcart into town with a letter for Papa. Clara thought he ought to know that a fever of this kind, in summer, was out of the ordinary. Dr. Winslow, she wrote, was not entirely encouraging. She did not tell him that Camille tossed in sweat-soaked sheets or that her breathing was labored. One of the women from the kitchen sat by her bed and fed chips of ice between her cracked lips.

Jennie was no longer allowed to sleep in the same room. She hovered on the threshold constantly, checking to see if Camille was better. Her little sister's cheeks were mottled and her pale peach eyelids were translucent as shells. She whiffled when she breathed, like a dreaming dog.

Jennie brought her bouquets of Queen Anne's lace and black-eyed Susan she gathered along the roadsides and tied with her hair ribbons. She played the piano for hours each day, in the hope that Mozart and Bach would sooth Camille. She wrote stories in her scrawling hand about the donkeys and Alva Smith and Consuelo Yznaga, who had fallen over when a big wave hit them at Bailey's Beach and gotten drenched to her ears. She pressed these jokes on Dobbie, who read them to Camille and swore her sister always smiled when she heard them.

After Jennie turned in Mamma's letter at the post office that third day, she lashed Willie and Wooshie until they galloped along Bellevue Avenue. There was too much traffic now at the height of the Season for such behavior to be safe. She careened past carriages frothy with women's parasols. It would take at least a day for Mamma's letter to reach Madison Square, and another for Papa to answer it. Jennie wished Mamma had sent a telegram instead. She was sure Camille would get better once Papa was there to smooth her hair.

She pulled up the donkeys on a small bluff above the streets of town, under the shade of a tree. From here she could see the sweep of ocean, the wharves stretching out into Narragansett Bay. The sun flashed brilliantly on the deep blue-green of the sea, riffled with whitecaps. Schooners dipped and turned under their widest sail. Jennie felt her heart surge and something of her joy must have communicated itself through the reins to the donkeys; Wooshie flicked an ear back at her and tossed his head. In a world so fresh and beautiful, surely nothing could be wrong for long. Not even Camille.

Jennie's eyes roamed appreciatively over the wharves, then stopped dead. For an instant, she thought she had imagined *Clara Clarita,* lying sleek as a cat at her usual mooring. She craned forward to study the slip. But it was no mirage. There was the steamer, dark-hulled and merry with its striped awnings. Papa was already in Newport. It would be days, now, before he received Mamma's letter.

"I was ready for them," Leonard Jerome said.

He wore a smoking jacket and his collar was undone. Fanny was in one of the loose day gowns that Jennie would later order herself from Charles Worth in Paris, called a déshabillé, and her chestnut hair was unpinned down her back. Leonard was stretched out on a chaise longue in her boudoir, and Fanny was curled on the rug at his feet. Somewhere in the house a child wailed. All the windows were open to admit the sea air, because the late July weather was close this year. An insect bumped repeatedly against the picture moldings. Leonard's hand stroked her head as though she were a prized retriever. Fanny felt a trickle of sweat between her breasts. She leaned into his hand.

"The first thing I did when I got back to New York was hunt down two of the new Gatling machine guns that the War Department has been fashioning. They're not for civilian use but I'll say I made my case. The *Times* has backed Lincoln. It's fitting that he should back the *Times*."

"Leonard," Fanny murmured.

"I had them mounted right at the newspaper's main doors. Drawing a bead on the whole of Times Square. When that vicious crowd came for us, meaning to lynch the editors from the trees, I manned one of the guns myself. Raymond"—Henry Jarvis Raymond was the *Times* founder—"manned the other. They left us alone after a while."

He stroked her head methodically. Cigar smoke curled to the ceiling and stunned the insect meandering there.

"Six days," he went on. "Six days of looting and fighting, Fan. Negro neighborhoods burned. Some dozen Negro men dragged from their homes and murdered. Bodies dragged behind carriages. Cobbles torn from the streets and hurled through windows. They haven't begun to count the dead or the cost of the destruction."

"Leonard," Fanny said again. Her voice was soothing, soporific.

"They torched the Negro orphanage, did you know that? And the little children running in their nightdresses through the dark, screaming. I hope never to see another week like it. I am so grateful to God my own girls are safe."

"Stay here now," she urged. "You've done your part."

"I can't. The city's a smoking ruin."

Fanny stiffened under his hand, suddenly alert. Her ears had detected an uproar at her door, a persistent demand for admission. Perhaps August Belmont . . . She half rose, Leonard's fingers slipping to her shoulder.

"Papa," Jennie burst out as she thrust open the door of Fanny's boudoir, "I am sorry to disturb you and Mrs. Ronalds, as I know it is not the done thing. But poor Camille is terribly sick and she needs you! Will you come now in the dogcart, please?"

She never knew what her father told Mamma. Some variation on the theme of a desire to join his family, without ever having received Clara's letter. This argument would place him in the most charitable light, and leave Fanny entirely out of it.

Jennie never knew what he said because she fell ill herself that evening.

The talk of the grown-ups became echoes and murmurs, distorted by fever. Dobbie going on about orphan children lynching policemen in their nightshirts. Dobbie talking about ice, and crooning that she should mouth it. A cool cloth grazed her forehead and swiftly turned warm and sodden. Miss Hallam and Clarita stood on the fringe of sight, faces distressed and swimming through waves of heat. Miss Hallam refused to enter the sickroom. It was not her place, she informed Clara Jerome; besides, her fiancé forbade her to endanger herself.

Clara set Miss Hallam to amusing Clarita and little Leonie with elocution and exercise along the Cliff Walk. Neither sister was allowed to enter the Middles' room. They were told only good news. Clarita tried to mother four-year-old Leonie but she was frightened and made a poor job of it. Jennie's throat was swollen and most terribly painful; a rash spread across her stomach. She woke desperate for water and groaning from the pain in her joints.

*Rheumatic fever,* the kitchen maid Hannah mumbled as she bathed Jennie's forehead. *Got it hanging around the stables, and passed it to that angel there.* No one would ever call Jennie an angel. Mamma called her "young lady" and Papa called her "a sad romp," but it was Camille who was angelic, Camille for whom they had no words.

Jennie lay spellbound and dreamed of burning. Of Papa with a fiddle in his hands. Camille cried tunelessly in her torment, and the sound wove through Jennie's mind like a dirge. *Some dozen hanged from trees. As good a Nero as any.*

Her fever broke the fifth night. The next day she was moved to a separate room, a disinterested bed with cooler sheets.

Camille's fever did not break. Her heart and lungs grew weaker. The doctor told Mamma that the fever was afflicting her brain. Clara Jerome took Dobbie's chair and fed her baby ice, refusing to leave the room. Papa, as Jennie expected, smoothed Camille's hair, but she had traveled far out on the Narragansett waters and the tide did not appear to be bringing her back.

Jennie disobeyed orders that night. She climbed into her sister's bed and curled protectively around her. Camille's frail body was a furnace. She did not open her eyes but her stiff frame relaxed at Jennie's touch. Jennie laid her cheek against her sister's neck, listening fiercely to her heart.

She was still holding Camille when it stopped.

Camille's coffin seemed so terribly small. They placed it in the morning room and set flowers all around it. Mrs. August Belmont sent white lilies from her gardens. Camille looked like a doll nobody played with anymore, and her skin when Jennie touched it had the senseless quality of bisque. For three days, the ladies of Newport came to pay their respects while Clara Jerome received in the drawing room. Mamma wore a black so dense it seemed to absorb light and sound.

Fanny Ronalds held Clara's hand in silence. Papa kept his distance from them both.

Nobody visited Camille except Jennie. She stole down the back staircase while the grown-ups were all busy trading sacred nothings in the front parlor, and crept into the morning room at the rear of the house. Camille lay silent and still, her head toward the fireplace and her feet toward the bow windows that overlooked the garden. They had been draped in black crepe, like the mirror over the mantel, so that Camille's soul would not be trapped in the shiny glass. Dobbie had explained this carefully to Jennie when she draped the mirror in the girls' bedroom. All over the house, every inch of glass was covered.

Jennie edged between the masses of Mrs. Belmont's lilies and looked into the coffin; Camille was wearing her favorite white voile dress with the broad blue satin sash. Jennie was in black cotton that itched at her neck and felt far too hot for the July day. She reached a finger and smoothed Camille's sleeve. Then, carefully, she slipped a rounded beach stone into her sister's new bed. A favorite shell. The silver dollar Papa had left in the toe of Camille's stocking last Christmas that she had never spent. Jennie's was long since gone.

"It should have been me," she whispered. "*Hanging around the stables*. Not you, Camille. I'm so awfully sorry."

She was the only person who knew that Mr. Schermerhorn came.

She found him kneeling on the prie-dieu before her little sister's casket on the second day of mourning. He had changed from his usual shooting clothes to a dark suit, and his black top hat did not look at all out of place. Matilda waited patiently by his knee.

Jennie hesitated in the doorway, thinking he might wish to be private with Camille, but like all recluses, he was sensitive to the sound of others breathing. He turned his head. After an instant she ran toward him. He did not get up or pray for Camille. Jennie waited for him to say something about carapaces or tests bleached of flesh, but instead he reached into his breast pocket and withdrew a shell. Jennie had never seen one like it before. It was the size of her hand, curled like a horn, cream striated with caramel. "Where did you find it?" she asked, entranced.

"It was sent to me from the Andaman Sea. *Nautilus pompilius*. It swims only in tropic waters. I like to think your sister is there."

"So do I," Jennie decided. "She is certainly not *here* anymore. I wish I knew exactly where she has gone. It would help when I talk to her."

He placed the shell inside the casket, being careful like Jennie to put it where only Camille would find it. Then he rose in his abrupt way and walked to the door.

"I'm sorry," he said without turning to look at her. "You will be lonely now."

Jennie was not allowed to go to Trinity Church with Camille; only Papa did that. Funerals were considered too distressing for women and children. Miss Hallam read the funeral service to Clarita and Jennie as they sat stiffly on their schoolroom chairs. Clarita had a black silk handkerchief to dab at her wet eyes. Little Leonie was napping and Mamma refused to leave her room.

Papa did not come home from the funeral, or indeed all that night.

Jennie watched for him through the stairs. She could not sleep in any case because she kept opening wardrobes and staring under the beds, looking for a shadow that might be Camille. Her sister's bedding had been burned in a bonfire at the bottom of the garden, to banish the sickness, Dobbie explained, and one side of their room was stripped. Jennie stretched herself out on the bare mattress and reached her arms wide, like an angel.

It rained that night. She thought of water trickling through the earth of Trinity churchyard.

Early in the morning, before anyone was up, she harnessed Willie and Wooshie and drove to Fanny Ronalds's house.

She found Papa in the barn, sitting in the hay in one of Fanny's stalls. He still wore the black clothes he had put on for Camille. He stared as Jennie pulled up.

"You should be at home with your mother," he said.

"So should you. Fiddling while Rome burns."

She got down from the cart, holding the reins. Tears of anger spattered her face, the first she had cried for Camille. She was furious with Papa for deserting them all, and with Camille for leaving her behind.

"Come here," Leonard said gently.

"What is it?" she asked.

"Puppies. Fanny's cairn had a litter last night."

She swiped at her eyes with a black cotton sleeve, then walked toward them and went down on her knees. Not touching. Just looking.

So many blind things, fighting for life.

"It's my fault she's dead," Jennie whispered. "I made her sick. Hanging around the stables."

"No."

"It should have been me. Not Camille."

"I guess God plays favorites." Papa reached down and lifted one of the sightless pups into Jennie's outstretched hands. Its small body was smooth as a pigskin glove and the weight of its head like a stone in her palm.

She remembered to touch its chest first.

"If He had taken you, too, my Jennie, I could not have gone on," Papa said.

Her hands clenched and the pup gave a faint cry. She held it against her and it relaxed.

"But if I'd been taken, Papa, I could have helped Camille. How will *she* go on, with no big sister? She couldn't even drive yet."

"I know." Papa touched Jennie's head gently. "But she could ride her pony like the wind. Remember? How Camille threw her heart over, and took all her fences, though she was just seven years old? She needed nobody then."

"Yes," Jennie said, relieved. "I will think of her on horseback. Perhaps she does not have to drive, in the Andaman Sea."

If her father found this reference puzzling, he asked no questions.

"Listen." He crouched down beside her and looked into her

eyes. "The only way to fight death, Jennie, is to *live*. You've got to do it for two people now—yourself and Camille. Take every chance you get. Do everything she didn't get to do. Live two lives in the space of one. I'll back you to the hilt."

"I know you will, Papa. You always have."

The tiny fawn-colored thing peed wetly in her hands and she did not mind. This was what she'd been searching for under the beds last night. Some sign from Camille.

"Isn't he a dear?" she crooned. "Isn't he cunning?" The puppy nuzzled her neck blindly.

Papa smiled. For the first time in days, Jennie smiled back.

# CHAPTER TWENTY-TWO

*London, March 1886*

Jennie received a third bulletin from Robson Roose within a quarter hour of her return from galloping through Hyde Park.

> *We are still fighting the battle for your boy. . . . As long as I can keep the temp. under 105 I shall not feel anxious.*

Randolph had already left for Commons. Unable to eat, with dread gripping her throat, Jennie changed out of her riding dress hurriedly and summoned a hansom cab. Randy might scoff at her anxiety, but she was determined he must know that Winston was fighting for his life. She drummed her heel impatiently on the floor of the hansom as it made its way through the heavy afternoon traffic to Westminster, jumping down to press Roose's message on a porter at the St. Stephen's entrance. *Deliver this immediately to Lord Randolph Churchill.*

Now what? Wait for an answer?

There would be none soon. Randolph was on the floor of Commons. Shivering, Jennie glanced at the rooks wheeling in the leaden sky above the spires of Parliament. Their plaintive cries chilled her to the bone. She would *not* think of Charles, although the glimpse of his profile was seared on her brain. But she wanted comfort. And a friend.

"Take me to Charles Street," she ordered the cabman. Connie Mandeville would give her tea.

---

The Viscountess welcomed Jennie in an ivory satin gown picked out with black ruffles, loose and becoming, with ivory lace at the plunging neck. Jennie had thrown on a carriage dress of purple velvet and brocade at random, too distracted to think of what she wore, but she wished now that she could kick off her half boots and curl up on the sofa with Connie as they had when they were girls in New York. She was aware of an immense weariness and the desire to be held on someone's lap, like a dog. She was afraid if Connie was too kind to her she might burst into tears.

"What news of your boy?" Connie asked once the maid had poured them each a cup of tea and left the tray on the ottoman before the fire. She had a son herself, three years younger than Win.

"He's worse," Jennie said bluntly. Her throat tightened and she swallowed hard. "Both lungs are inflamed."

Connie offered her a macaroon. "Forgive me if I don't embrace you, then, dearest. I have the girls to consider." Connie's twins were the same age as Jennie's son Jack—just six—and still in the nursery.

Jennie set down her untouched tea. "Randolph insists there's nothing I can do for Win if I race down to Brighton. But I can't stop thinking about that summer in Newport. . . ."

"When you lost your sister?" Connie murmured sympathetically. She had known Camille, of course. "Such a sprite. All gold and ivory. It was only a few weeks after Gettysburg, wasn't it?"

"Yes," Jennie said. "And the draft riots in New York."

"I don't recall those." Connie reached for a pot of Devonshire cream and spooned a little next to her biscuit. "All I remember is bathing with the other girls. And your donkeys pulling us up and down Bellevue Avenue."

"I thought I was to blame. For Camille's death. That I'd picked up germs in the stables," Jennie remembered. "But Mamma was sure my father brought infection with him from the city. All those conscripts, and the wounded evacuated to New York—I'm not sure she ever forgave him."

Connie lifted one dark brow. "Shall you forgive Randolph?"

Jennie looked at her swiftly. "Or myself, you mean? If Win dies while I'm sitting here? What a comfort you are, Connie! You know it's not the English way to hover over children."

"We're not English," Consuelo reminded her.

Papa might have brought rheumatic fever to Newport, Jennie thought as she tossed endlessly in her bed that night, *but he was with Camille to the end.* She remembered how desperately she had wanted to send Papa a telegram when her sister was ill, but had not known how. Remembered her crashing joy at the sight of *Clara Clarita,* and the way she had whipped her donkeys straight down the hill to Fanny Ronalds's house. She had known instinctively at the age of nine what Camille needed most: Papa's hand on her cheek. How had she forgotten something so vital in the years since?

Gentry's tea tray appeared at eight A.M. *We have had a very anxious night,* Roose's bulletin informed Jennie, *but have managed to hold our own. . . . On the other hand we have to realise that we may have another 24 hours of this critical condition, to be combatted with all our vigilant energy.*

Twenty-four hours. She could not endure it.

She went in search of Randolph, but he was in neither the breakfast parlor nor the library. She discovered only Alasdair Gordon instead, writing letters of business at her husband's desk. Jennie felt a wash of relief; Papa always insisted it was preferable to ask forgiveness than demand permission.

"Alasdair, would you inform Lord Randolph that I have been called to Brighton? And cancel all my engagements for the next few days?"

"*All* of them, my lady?"

"Every one," she said briskly. "I shall send word when I mean to return. Oh, and Alasdair—could you be a *dear* and summon a cab?"

She saw Win immediately, immobile in his bed with the sheet drawn up to his chin. His eyes were closed and his thin face impossibly pallid. Jennie's heart stopped as she halted in the doorway— was he even breathing?

"My lady," Everest whispered.

The nanny rose from a chair behind a screen near Winston's bed and moved soundlessly to join her. She had lost her starched white cap in the interval since Saturday, and her black dress, high in the neck and long in the sleeves, was unusually creased. "You're just in time."

Jennie's lips parted. *For what? Good God—for what?*

"His fever's broken at last," Everest told her. "He's sleeping for the first time in days."

Jennie pressed her hands to her mouth to stifle a choking sob. Everest reached out as though she were a little girl and gathered Jennie to her ample bosom. "Master Winnie took some broth before he went off, like the dear lamb he is. I daresay you're chilled through, my lady. I'll fetch a cup of tea, shall I? If you'll watch with him?"

Jennie nodded, unable to speak.

She crossed swiftly to the foot of the sickbed and looked down at Winston.

His lashes were ginger-colored. They fluttered in his dreams. The skin beneath his eyes was sunken and blotted with purplish shadows. His lips had cracked with fever. She had seen that look before. Was it possible he would survive? What had she done to deserve such a miracle?

Tremulously, Jennie set down her pocketbook and unpinned her hat. She placed it on Everest's chair with her gloves. Then, careful not to wake the sleeping boy, she lay down on the narrow cot beside him and wrapped him in her arms. He felt impossibly light, a gathering of twigs instead of limbs, but he was not burning with fever like Camille. He was not a blistered husk. With tears of relief rolling unheeded down her cheeks, she listened for the rhythm of his heart.

# CHAPTER TWENTY-THREE

His army numbered nearly fifteen hundred lead soldiers now, all the same size and British-made. Winston had arranged them on a vast table made of planks, laid across trestles, that nearly filled the entire room: an infantry division with a brigade of cavalry. They were assaulted by such projectiles as came to hand—marbles, pebbles, even dried peas—which he shot out of a catapult that Old Farnham, the chief carpenter at Blenheim, had whittled for him last Christmas. He had eighteen field guns and a handful of fortress pieces placed in mock castles. Flags flew from their turrets and from the hands of gallant standard-bearers. There were rough roads and even bridges, which were useful to blow up and bring down upon the heads of the Enemy.

Jack, who was six, sometimes commanded the hostile army, but his troops were Colonials and weren't allowed to use artillery. Jack never won these battles, of course, because of his inferior numbers (he had been collecting soldiers half as many years as Winston) and the fact that the British Army was invincible. Any Colonials who chose to challenge Victoria's rule were damned rebels, and bound to die inglorious deaths. Jack understood in principle that he was a traitor to the British Empire, but was frequently known to bury his head in Woom's lap when his losses were too great to bear.

Jack was starting at the Thomson Sisters' School in the autumn, but first Woomany was taking them both away for a fortnight to her sister's house in Ventnor, on the south coast of the Isle of Wight. Woom's brother-in-law was a prison warder who led them on bracing walks along the cliffs and told exciting stories about inmates who rose up and broke for freedom. He also read aloud to them at bedtime from Macaulay's *History of England,* and it was the most thrilling thing Winston had ever heard, although lately he'd discovered Rider Haggard. Haggard's books were brimming with adventures and near-death escapes and odious brigands who deserved to be Put Down. *King Solomon's Mines* was Winston's favorite. He read it in bed at night until Woom put out the light.

He studied the trestle-table landscape now, assessing whether it might be possible to introduce the element of water, in a self-contained bed that might serve for perilous river crossings when the bridges were blown. It probably would not be possible to do such a thing without soaking the carpet beneath the table and being scolded for it. Old Farnham at Blenheim would know how it should work, but nobody at Connaught Place knew anything except how to cook and arrange flowers—except for Papa, who spoke in Parliament and held the key to everything worth having. Winston tried to cadge letters from him so he could sell Papa's signature to other boys at his school and even to the porters, who would pay a shilling for Lord Randolph Churchill's fist.

As though he had conjured him, Winston's father thrust open the nursery door and stuck his head around it. This was such an extraordinary occurrence that Winston cried out, "Sir!"

"Steady on," Randolph said easily. "What are you playing at, Win?"

"Soldiers." He grasped a cavalry captain, fully horsed, in his right hand. His fair, freckled skin flushed painfully. He'd had only two glimpses of Papa since reaching London—or rather, of the crown of his top hat, from the nursery window. Winston was not allowed to enter the library or even knock on the door while Papa was working. The boys ate with Woom in the nursery. Sometimes they were allowed to watch Mamma dress. They were permitted to fetch her evening slippers—she kept countless pairs of them, brilliantly colored satin and velvet, scattered with flashing glass jewels or silk ribbons—on her boudoir shelves. The boys pretended the slippers were ships, careening in mock naval battles across the sea of her carpet. But even those visits had grown infrequent; Mamma said they were growing too big to be indulged.

"How old are you now?" Papa demanded.

"Eleven and a half, sir."

"I thought you had a tutor during this vac. You're supposed to be swotting Latin. For the exams."

"He comes in the afternoons," Winston explained, "as I'm still Delicate from my illness." Mamma had engaged a topping crammer, just sent down from Cambridge, who was meant to get him ready for school, whichever school he was meant to try for next. The Thomson sisters would wash their hands of him once he turned twelve, in November. If he crammed well and passed his examinations, he might start spring term at the next school. That could be Winchester, where his cousin Sunny boarded—Sunny was Uncle George's son and would be the Ninth Duke one day—or it might be another place. No one had told Winston yet and he did not like to ask. All schools were terrible. He wanted to be left alone in peace in his nursery with Woom until the Long Vac ended, and not think about it.

His father took a step through the doorway and halted; there was truthfully not much room with the unwieldy trestle table. He walked the length of it, his hands shoved into the pockets of his narrow trousers, his enormous mustache moving up and down as he frowned. He bent to peer closely at a detachment of troops crawling through the mud toward the piers of the castle bridge—crack sappers, all of them. It was a frightfully delicate maneuver and Winston hoped Papa did not disturb any of them.

"Do you like soldiers?"

"Very much indeed."

"Your army appears to lack for nothing."

"Except what every military lacks, Papa."

His father quirked an eyebrow.

"Sufficient *transport,*" Winston explained. "We're frightfully embarrassed for troop carriers. Your friend Sir Henry started a Transport Fund when he visited."

"Drummond Wolff?" Papa frowned. "When was *he* last in the nursery?"

"Three days ago," Winston said promptly. "He is a great friend of Mamma's. She is painting him at present. He gave Jack and me three half crowns. We gave them to Woom to save. She's the Transport Fund *bank,* actually."

"Ah," his father said. He jingled the change in his pocket. "The First Duke was a military man, you know."

"Yes, sir. Grandpapa told me once, before he died. He said our House's Fortunes were Founded on the Battlefield."

"Did he?" Papa snorted. "If only they had been salvaged there, too. But we dropped our swords and took up pens, worse luck. *Fiel pero desdichado,* as the ducal motto goes."

Winston stared at him.

"Spanish," his father snapped. "It means 'Faithful but unhappy.' Or 'miserable.' Or 'wretched.'"

"That's our family motto?"

"Well—it's the House of Marlborough's."

"Why is it in Spanish?"

"I have no idea, old chap. Most ducal mottoes are Latin." His father sighted along a turret gun. "Not much good at Latin, are you, Winnie?"

"I'm all right except for the Ablative Absolute. I detest the Ablative Absolute, Papa. I far prefer its alternative—*Quum,* with the Pluperfect Subjunctive."

"Not as elegant a form of expression, though, is it?"

"I have frequently been assured as much."

His father nodded and, for the first time Winston could remember, looked directly into his eyes instead of past him.

"Should you like to go into the Army?"

Startled—he had never been asked about his own wishes before—he said, "Yes."

Papa drew some loose coppers from his pocket and dropped them carelessly on the trestle table. "For your Transport Fund."

# CHAPTER TWENTY-FOUR

In the early hours of the morning of the eighth of June, after a full month of polarizing debate, William Ewart Gladstone called for a vote on Irish Home Rule.

"Go into the length and breadth of the world, ransack the literature of all countries, find, if you can, a single voice, a single book . . . in which the conduct of England towards Ireland is anywhere treated except with profound and bitter condemnation," the Prime Minister declared.

Jennie had arrived at Parliament after a dinner engagement, still wearing a rose silk evening dress, to watch the debate from the Speaker's Gallery, which was packed full of both gentlemen and ladies. She remained until well after Big Ben had struck midnight. Louise, Duchess of Manchester, sat by her side, magnificent in eau-de-Nil brocade. The Duchess was agonized for her lover, Lord Hartington.

"He might have been Prime Minister three times already," she whispered fretfully to Jennie. "And again he is throwing his chance away!"

"What has he done?"

"He has utterly broken with Gladstone," Lottie explained. "Over poor Freddie, of course."

*Of course,* Jennie echoed. Hart's younger brother, Lord Freddie Cavendish, had been brutally murdered a few years before in Dublin, within hours of his arrival to take up the post of Chief

Secretary—an appointment he owed to Gladstone. He was walking across Phoenix Park, where Jennie and Randolph and Winston had lived years before, toward the Viceregal Lodge. The Permanent Undersecretary, Thomas Burke, was the real target of the assassins—two men who belonged to a rebel Fenian group called the Irish National Invincibles—but Freddie was walking with Burke and so he had to die, too. He was stabbed through the ribs with a twelve-inch surgical knife.

"Hart's never got over it," Lottie whispered, reaching for Jennie's hand, which she grasped with painful force. "He refuses to set foot in Ireland again—not even for Lismore."

Lismore was one of the Cavendish family's eight enormous estates, this one in Waterford: a twelfth-century castle built by Prince John on the ruins of a seventh-century abbey. Jennie had visited it during her years in Dublin, at Hart's invitation. She had liked Freddie and his wife, Lucy—who was more earnest than fashionable, and a bit of a bluestocking, if Jennie was honest. Lucy was Catherine Gladstone's niece, and although she did not go out into the streets in search of prostitutes, as the Prime Minister did, or give them her cast-off gowns, like her aunt, she was dedicated to the cause of women's education. Jennie suspected that Lucy had loved her husband and been devastated by Freddie's death. But the night before his murderers were hanged, she had sent a gold cross she wore round her neck to one of them, as a sign of her forgiveness. She still supported Home Rule, as her uncle Gladstone did.

Jennie could not fathom Lucy's sort of compassion. Indeed, she felt scathing contempt for it. If any one of her family was hurt or killed, she'd shoot the villain responsible herself.

She watched now as Hart rose and was recognized by the Speaker.

"I must oppose the bill put forward by my own party," he said bitterly. "I would remind the House that I will never make common cause with those who stand by and watch the Fenians grow in violence; moreover, I regard the Irish as having no practical sense, unbalanced temperaments, and a complete inability to manage the economy. They are dedicated to perpetual war with England, to be fought in the shadows with broken bottles and knives. To imagine that they might ever be capable of governing themselves is a folly of criminal proportions. It calls into question all rational basis for this Government."

He walked over to the bench occupied by the Radical Joseph Chamberlain and sat down beside him.

"Good Lord," Jennie breathed. "He's made a clean break with Gladstone."

"He feels betrayed," Lottie sighed. "All the years he's worked with the PM have gone up like paper."

"But he can't divide the Liberal party *and* form a Government," Jennie protested. "Even with Chamberlain beside him. Their numbers are too few. What do they mean to do?"

"Why—support your husband, of course."

Jennie sank back in her seat, so that her face was in shadow. If one man intended to bring down the Grand Old Man, it was clearly Randolph. The Irish faction accused him of starting a civil war. *Ulster will fight, and Ulster will be right.*

As she watched, Randy rose from the front Opposition bench. He was impossibly thin, but beautifully tailored in his dark gray frock coat, which flowed like a second skin over his narrow back and shoulders, so that his gauntness seemed like a deliberate choice, a conscious honing of a body given over entirely to the force of its formidable mind. Randolph did not glance at the Speaker or seem aware of the thronged galleries behind his back—his spaniel eyes were fixed instead, with a terrifying purpose, on Gladstone himself.

"I would point out that the Honorable Member from Midlothian"—this meant the Prime Minister—"has spent all of three weeks in Ireland," he began. "While I myself have spent nearly *three years* there. I think I may claim to know a good deal about the country."

"Fox-hunting country, perhaps!" one of the Irish benchers sang out.

Randolph ignored him. "I would say to the Honorable Member from Midlothian—as Sir Robert Peel once said—that to maintain the Union, we ought not only to use the scaffold, but if necessary, deluge the plains of Ireland with blood."

*Good God,* Jennie thought. *He's going for the PM's jugular.* She drew a quick breath and glanced at Catherine Gladstone, who for once was eating nothing in her accustomed chair at the center of the gallery. The PM's wife sat with her head bowed and her gloved fingers tightly clasped. Jennie's pulse quickened. Randolph had no intention of making peace with the Grand Old Man. Blood and war served his purpose—which was nothing less than to take Gladstone's place.

"The allegiance of Ulster is given to this Parliament on the condition that it *protects* the inhabitants of Ulster," Randolph declared.

Hart shouted, "Hear, hear!"

Louise Manchester gripped Jennie's arm.

"No, no!" others cried.

"Certainly," Randolph persisted, his head up and his eyes flashing. He was transported by his own prominence, by the voice he could unleash to sway the entire kingdom's opinion. Jennie was struck, once more, by how Parliament transformed him—he stood easily at the front of the Conservative benches, his hands on his hips, more relaxed than when he was alone in front of his own fire. "If this Parliament transfers the lives and liberties of the inhabitants of Ulster to a body over which this Parliament will have no control—*absolutely none*—and if that should lead to civil war, we *cannot* charge those who take part in it with treason. They are loyal subjects to a man, dedicated to Queen and Empire. That is my view, and I shall *never* be ashamed of expressing it."

A roar went up from the Conservative ranks.

*Civil war.* Jennie had lived through one she had not fully understood at the time. Lincoln, too, had soaked the plains in blood to preserve his Union—but he had done so in the name of freedom. Wasn't Randolph on the side of oppression, in the Irish case? Jennie shook her head slightly to clear her mind. He had not asked for her help with this speech. She had no business questioning his line, when good men like Hart and Balfour supported it. But she felt uneasy all the same.

"Motion to divide," the Speaker said.

Louise Manchester had closed her eyes; her hand still clutched Jennie's arm. Jennie patted it consolingly. Lottie was anxious that Hart had backed the wrong horse, of course. So was Jennie. Excitement and adrenaline coursed through her body as though she had just run pell-mell downhill. Randolph had wagered all his political capital to beat Gladstone. It remained to be seen if he won or lost.

"What's happening?" Lottie muttered.

"They're going out."

The Duchess's eyes flashed open and she leaned forward. MPs filed like ants through the twin doors of Commons into the division lobbies below. Jennie watched as Randolph, Hart, and Chamberlain disappeared together into the *No* Lobby; Gladstone and the Irish leader, Parnell, into the *Aye*. As each man passed through, his vote was counted.

"We must have tea," Lottie said briskly. She had found strength now that the die was cast.

"What time is it?"

"Nearly one o'clock in the morning. They will require a quarter hour for the division, at least."

Jennie joined the Duchess in the anteroom, which was so crowded with onlookers that there were no free chairs. With a sudden pang she thought of Charles Kinsky. What had he said that day they'd had tea here? That he reported constantly on Randolph to his ministry in Vienna? What would he have said about tonight? That it was just another fit of epilepsy and rabble-rousing?

"They're coming back in," Lottie said, snatching Jennie's cup from her hands.

The two women took their seats hurriedly in the Speaker's Gallery, craning toward the wire grille.

"Ayes, 313," the Speaker called. "Nos, 343."

Ninety-three members of Gladstone's party had voted with Randolph—and against Home Rule. Jennie felt a sick excitement rise through her rib cage. It was only a matter of hours, now, before Gladstone's Government fell. Randolph had won.

When the PM called a general election for the month of July, Jennie left the boys in Everest's care and campaigned on Randolph's behalf. He was standing for South Paddington. She drove herself through the streets in a sporting gig, her harness decorated with pink-and-chocolate ribbons, Randolph's racing colors. She wore a deep pink muslin carriage dress run up deliberately for campaigning, trimmed with chocolate bows, and a portrait straw hat tied with chocolate ribbon. The crowds, mostly men who could vote and hordes of gawkers avid to glimpse Lady Randy, roared with approval when she pulled up the gig before the campaign platform and handed the reins to Alasdair Gordon. Jennie ran up the hustings' steps, waving her gloved hand to the crowd. *Lady Randy!* they cried. *Give us a kiss and we'll give you our votes!* Jennie laughed and tossed primroses—the symbol of Tory Democracy—into their outstretched hands, and signed picture postcards of herself for eager young clerks and solicitors and children and their mothers. And Jennie shouted—rousingly and at length—about the need for all good Britons to support the Conservative Party and her husband.

It was the most exhilarating and exhausting campaign she'd ever experienced. The hems of her skirts were filthy by the end of each day, and the speeches she'd long since had by heart ran round and round in her brain as she lay in bed at night. Newspapers printed accounts of her appearances and sent photographers to capture her piquant face, framed by the portrait bonnet. Her sporting gig was mobbed ten deep.

"You're jolly good at this, Jennie," Arthur Balfour praised her when they met one evening for a cello concert. "Would you consider coming north to speak for me?" Arthur was running for Manchester East on an anti–Home Rule platform.

"I'd have to give up my chocolate ribbons," she told him. "And you haven't any racing colors, Arthur."

Randolph himself spoke in South Paddington only twice. Then he left hurriedly for a fishing trip to Norway with his old friend Tommie Trafford. *The weather has been rainy and raw, but on the other hand we have no flies,* he wrote Jennie. *I've had no election news since Tuesday, when things seemed to be going very well. . . . I expect the Tories will now come in. . . . It seems to me we want the five thousand pounds a year very badly.*

Randolph was counting on a Cabinet post.

On the eve of the campaign's final day, which was July 27, six-year-old Jack was sailing Jennie's slippers across the carpet of her boudoir while Gentry dressed her hair for dinner. Winston was sprawled at Jennie's feet with newspaper clippings and a pot of paste.

"What is all that mess, Win?" she asked.

"My scrapbook." Her son glanced up at her, his round face flushed with July heat. "I must have a record of Papa's triumph, once he is PM."

"Let's hope he's returned first." She rose from her dressing table and crouched down, sifting through the treasures Winston had collected. Cartoons from *Punch.* A rather good illustration from *Hansard's Parliamentary Debates,* of Randolph speaking in Commons. Various articles from the *Daily News* and the *Evening Standard* and the *Times.* Something stirred in her heart. "You're a staunch admirer of Papa's, aren't you?"

"Of course! Papa's a Great Man. I've learnt some of his speeches by heart."

She smoothed his unruly red hair. "How is your chest?"

"Topping. Woom says it wants only a visit to Ventnor to make me entirely well again. Darling Mummie, may I campaign with you tomorrow?"

"Certainly not. The hustings are no place for a boy." Neither were they the place for a lady, of course, with the amount of drink that flowed during campaigns. Only yesterday a gang of Liberal supporters—engine stokers and rail workers, by the look of their clothes and hands—had jeered her speech, catcalling insults and obscenities. *Lady Randolph? Dandy Randy's Fancy Piece, more like! Aye, she's free with her favors! Ten votes'll get you a tumble! Her man would as soon put his hand in yer pockets, boys, as she'd put hers on your cock!* Cheeks burning and eyes flashing with anger, Jennie had forced her voice to rise over the drunken heckling. But when a group of Conservative hearties turned and pummeled the inter-lopers, launching a bloody brawl that threatened to tear down the hustings themselves, she gave up and allowed Alasdair to race her to her campaign gig. The men's foul words had echoed in her head for the rest of the day.

Jennie could stare down the ugliness. She knew that Win could not. He was still too young. His brush with death was too recent.

"*Please,* Mummie." He caught at her wrist. "I promise I won't take ill."

He was always begging for some indulgence, pleading for her time and attention. It was the same when he wrote home from school—demanding she attend his plays and Class Days, or send for him on holidays. Jennie wondered if she had spoiled her boys by giving way to them too often; she was conscious of how rarely Randolph did. He had forgotten Win's pneumonia as readily as he forgot the boy's existence. And yet Win desperately wanted to campaign for his father. The *Great Man.*

She held the boy's head against her breast for an instant. "Have I mentioned how glad I am that you're here, my darling—instead of sailing far out on the Andaman Sea?"

He wrinkled his nose. "Where's that? I don't know the Andaman."

"Look it up."

"I shall. Aunt Leonie gave me a topping atlas." He reached for his paste.

"There will be other campaigns, Winston." She released him. "Recruit your strength for the next battle."

Randolph was returned for South Paddington with 77 percent of the vote. The Conservative Party won in a landslide.

Queen Victoria summoned Robert Cecil, the Marquess of Salisbury, to Buckingham Palace and asked him to form a Government.

When the royal audience was over, Salisbury invited his nephew Arthur Balfour to join him for a cigar at the Carlton Club.

"I now have four crosses to bear," he said through a cloud of tobacco smoke. "The Prime Minister's portfolio, the Foreign Office, the Queen—and Randolph Churchill. The burden increases in that order, Arthur."

Balfour examined the spirits in his glass. "Randy's brought us in with a sweep, sir."

"And he wants my job," Salisbury pointed out.

"Only the Queen could give him that—and she declined. What are you going to do?"

"Name Churchill Leader in Commons. And Chancellor of the Exchequer."

"Sir!" Arthur was startled. "I'm not sure that's wise."

His uncle stared at him coldly. "The two posts generally go together."

"Because they're portals to the prime ministership," Balfour agreed. "But the Treasury portfolio is the most powerful position in Government, behind yours."

"And?"

Balfour hesitated. He'd been a few forms ahead of Randolph at Eton. "Randy was never very good at sums."

Salisbury discarded his ash. "So much the better," he said.

# CHAPTER TWENTY-FIVE

Jennie went looking for a dress on the last day of July, in a sudden shower of rain. She and Randolph were expected at Cowes for Regatta Week in August, and she absolutely *had* to be new-gowned for whatever entertainments the Waleses were sure to offer. With Randolph back in Cabinet it was essential that she represent him in as glittering a fashion as possible. Princess Alix spent Race Week in a variety of sailor dresses, navy blue and white, with closely fitted high necklines to disguise her scar, and neatly tailored bodices, masculine in style. Jennie was thinking of something lighter and altogether more suggestive of France. Bertie loved Paris and French women; a looser style would surely please him.

She patronized a modiste with a salon in Piccadilly, a Mademoiselle Antoine who had probably never seen Paris but could buy the latest French fashion plates and had the cleverness to copy them. Even with the prospect of Randy's Cabinet salary, Worth was much too expensive to consider this summer.

But when she entered the salon, Jennie's heart sank. Most of the mannequins circling the room seemed to be in thrall to Princess Alix, wearing necklines that hugged the throat—whether for sailing, casino, or walking. Worse, the half bustle at the rear of the gown had become a veritable shelf, while the fronts were elaborately draped over underskirts that clung to the legs. A warmer, more uncomfortable, and more constraining costume for August Jennie could not imagine.

Two girls—in their early twenties, from the simple lines of

their white dresses—sipped tea indolently on a settee. Jennie recognized the Miss Tennants, Margot and her elder sister, Laura, who were suddenly at the glamorous center of Society. The pair had formed a sort of club they called the Souls, a group of men and women who sometimes gathered (scandalously) in the girls' night nursery on Grosvenor Square to discuss Art and Life's Meaning. Laura was lately married to Arthur Lyttleton but Margot was still a debutante—George Curzon, Jennie understood, was deeply smitten with her. All the daring and expensive young people in London had collected around the sisters, but she had not been introduced to the Tennants herself. Perhaps at thirty-two she was too old for the Souls. . . .

"Lady Randolph! Where *have* you been hiding?"

And there was Fanny Ronalds, elegantly composed in an upright chair, with a straw hat like a Turkish fez perched on the top of her head. The chestnut curls betrayed a few streaks of gray. Her liquid dark eyes were as vibrant as ever, and her figure never strayed from its rigid discipline—she must be a few years short of fifty, Jennie calculated, but she wore it well. Always exquisitely gowned, of course. Her men saw to that. Today she wore a white linen carriage dress with a broad windowpane check in peacock blue, trimmed with peacock-blue silk in a Greek key design eight inches deep along the hem. Perfect for high summer.

Jennie kissed Fanny's cheek, and felt a sudden rush of warmth that had everything to do with childhood and memory.

"My dearest Fanny, how is it that in a circle as small as London, we never come to meet?"

"You're political and I'm bohemian," Fanny replied. "The two rarely mix, I find. Particularly when that husband of yours is rocketing to his predestined heights. It wouldn't do to be seen with music-hall riffraff; Dandy Randy might end up parodied in one of Arthur's shows!"

"He'd make a beautiful Pooh-Bah. 'Lord High Everything Else,' am I right?"

W. S. Gilbert and Arthur Sullivan's *Mikado* was all the rage that year; Jennie had seen the comic opera three times. As Arthur Sullivan's acknowledged companion, naturally Fanny gloried in his success.

"You look well, Jennie," she said. "How are your dear father and mother?"

"Mamma remains in Paris, and Papa in New York—where he is consumed with horse racing," Jennie told her. "He and August Belmont have launched yet another track. In Sheepshead Bay, of all places."

"August Belmont," Fanny repeated reminiscently. "It has been an *age* since I heard that name. Do you know that on one occasion, Belmont bankrolled the most *elaborate* party for me? And that your poor papa paid for it, too? He and dear August were bound to discover my sad confusion over expenses, but neither was so ungentlemanly as to tax me with it."

"A kinder age," Jennie suggested, smiling. "No one may claim the title of gentleman anymore, Fanny—least of all those born to it. Self-made men are best."

"Now, now." Fanny pressed her hand. "You must except your marvelous Charles Kinsky! The manners of an Austrian prince in the body of a dashing Englishman; I cannot think of a more elegant flirt. I was desolate to learn he's been posted to Paris. How will you do without him?"

"I've managed quite nicely to date." Jennie's heart began to thud painfully. *Charles.* Leaving England?

Fanny's brows rose. "I *have* put my foot in it! I thought you were the best of friends."

"We met once or twice, a few years since. But nothing more than that."

"Well, well. I ought to leave my bohemian set rather oftener. I am clearly behindhand with all the choicest bits of news. Tell me, my dear—what do you think of these *hideous* necklines for summer?"

"I hate them," Jennie said cordially.

She chatted of fashion for as long as she could bear it, then fled Mademoiselle Antoine's.

How to think about Charles Kinsky?

She had seen nothing of him since that bruising gallop through Rotten Row, but her mind had been filled incessantly with his voice. His hands. The elusive scent of him. She had expected Kinsky's fascination to wane with time. She had expected to recover her self-possession, her sturdy bulwark against love and its tragedies, the longer they were apart. But love had crept up on Jennie unawares. Her yearning for Charles was as deep as her perpetual loneliness for Camille—as though Death had parted her from both of them.

Why, she asked herself, had she fought him so much? Why was the deepest emotion she had ever felt in her life a force to be thwarted and feared?

*Fanny,* she thought. *Fanny and Papa.* They had shown her long ago what the end of love looked like. And she had vowed never to be trapped in that kind of rubble.

## *New York, January 1867*

"You must push off with enough speed to complete the figure," Fanny Ronalds told Jennie as she skated beside her, "and raise your left ankle above your right." Fanny was teaching her figure skating on the frozen pond at the Jerome country home in Bathgate, near Old Fordham.

At twenty-eight, Fanny remained one of Mamma's dearest friends, and was spending the week with them. There were three children in the Ronaldses' nursery now, but except for a few lines at the corners of her eyes, Fanny looked as girlish as ever.

Jennie was now thirteen. She studied the older woman's example as she spun like a ballerina on the ice. "You're dancing!" she exclaimed. "Even though it's so slippery, and you should have tumbled long ago. How do you keep your balance, Mrs. Ronalds?"

"I fight for it." Fanny twirled slowly to a halt, her arms flung wide. "The key is to ignore your fear. Fear nips at the edge of the mind, Jeanette. You must knock it off its pins."

"I didn't know you were afraid of falling." Jennie was sharply afraid herself when her feet slid too fast to prevent disaster—and in the middle of the night, when she awoke from a dream of Camille, and remembered all over again that her sister was dead.

"That's because I refuse to show it." Fanny skated over to Jennie. In her short-hooped skating costume, she might have been an enchantress from an Andersen fairy tale, Jennie thought—the Snow Queen perhaps. Her skirt of gray cashmere fell just below the knee, so that her shapely legs, clad in wool stockings and delicate boots with silver runners strapped to them, were partially, tantalizingly visible. The skirt had an over-draping of blue moiré silk that fluttered when Fanny sailed across the pond's shimmering surface. A gray cashmere jacket trimmed in ermine and an ermine hat with a veil finished the costume. Her muff swung carelessly from one hand.

"It's never the ice that brings us down," Fanny confided. "If you *must* tread a slippery path in life, Jeanette, self-confidence is vital. It can look like balance, even when you have none."

"And suggests you'd never dream of putting a foot wrong in the first place," Jennie added, giggling.

The Bathgate cottage they were sharing this January was barely a year old, and, unlike the Newport house, was designed for winter comfort. Papa had built it along with the rest of Jerome Park, his latest venture with August Belmont. The crown jewel of the sporting ground was Jerome Park Racetrack, where the two men's passion for horse racing could be enjoyed in style. Papa's racecourse had a grandstand that seated eight thousand, a clubhouse with a ballroom and bedchambers for overnight guests, and a dining room with its own chef.

Jennie and Clarita had been allowed to attend the opening-day ceremonies the previous fall. Adelina Patti—the Italian soprano who was Papa's latest flirt—had sung for the crowd. Jennie was allowed to watch the first horse race, which was called the Belmont Stakes because August Belmont had put up the prize money. When Papa's thoroughbred, Kentucky, won, Papa ran with Jennie to the winner's circle and hoisted her onto the horse's back. She felt as giddy as though she'd won the race herself.

"Have you heard anything from your father?" Fanny asked, a little abruptly.

Which meant, Jennie knew, that Papa was no longer writing to her. The thought caused a dull ache, the way the frigid air coming off the ice pained Jennie's bare hands.

"He expects to dock in New York at the end of January," she said in a rush. "Mamma received a letter last evening. I am sure she means to show it to you."

This was the first Christmas Jennie could remember without Papa—and the first time he had missed her birthday. He had left New York for Cowes in late November, following a transatlantic schooner race with his friends from the New York Yacht Club. The American boat had won, and Papa and his friends had remained in England to celebrate. Jennie wished with all her heart that he had come home.

"You are more beautiful than Adelina Patti," she said impulsively as Fannie spun in a final graceful figure. "I cannot think why Papa is smitten with her. Perhaps it is her voice, which we must acknowledge is very fine."

The look of careless freedom faded from Fanny's eyes. "No one can equal her *bel canto* technique," she replied. "Compared with Patti, I am an aging matron with no claim to talent or beauty."

She left the ice slowly, tearing off her gloves. After a moment, with a pang of regret for her thoughtless words, Jennie followed her. Fanny found a free spot on a bench and began to work at the laces of her runners. Jennie put her arms around her neck and rested her cheek against Fanny's cool one.

"I am sure Papa admires you," she said. "So does Mr. Belmont."

"Never mind me." Fanny's eyes were fixed on her boots. "I do not want your pity, Jeanette, of all people's. I know how much I have figured in your mind as a rival. Leonard loves you best of anyone in the world, because you are so much like him."

"You are not my rival!" Jennie protested, wounded. "Mamma's, perhaps—"

"Your mother should thank me." Fanny met her gaze directly. "I have kept your papa amused and content and in no mood to find another family. We both know divorce is shameful—it bars one forever from Society. That's why I've never sought one from Mr. Ronalds. But *après moi, le déluge,* Jeanette."

Coldness settled in the pit of Jennie's stomach. "After me, the flood," she said. "I understand what you said, but not what you mean."

"I mean that I have contained your father's impulses for years. I shudder for all of you, now that he has done with me. God knows where he will look next."

She rose from the bench and smiled mirthlessly at Jennie. "I have been practicing my French, as you see. I am moving to Paris in September—did you know?"

Mamma was mad for the Paris scheme once she learned of Fanny's plans.

"Clarita will be sixteen in April, and would benefit immensely from a little cultivation before she is brought out," she mused over her magazine in the Bathgate parlor that evening. The fashion plates were French; Mamma studied them with new interest. "You know, Fanny, not even Mrs. Belmont invites us to her *best* parties. Certainly, the Schermerhorns and the Astors do not."

"The girls will find their prospects of marriage very limited in a few years' time," Fanny agreed, "if they are consigned to the second tier."

"No daughter of Papa's is second-rate," Jennie objected. She was reading *The Mysterious Key and What It Opened,* a dime novel by Miss Louisa Alcott, in a chair by the parlor fire. From Mamma's sudden look of exasperation, she had forgotten Jennie was there.

"Go up to bed, now, Jeanette," she ordered.

"But, Mamma—"

"That is enough."

Jennie thrust herself out of her seat, but took her book with her. In the hallway, she lingered, her ears pricked.

"Think of the advantages," Fanny murmured. "The best music masters, the best art instructors, a thorough immersion in the French language . . ."

"A tour of European capitals, to aid the girls' general knowledge and sophistication," Mamma breathed. "The most cultivated circles at the Emperor's court . . ."

"It will be the making of Clarita."

"*And* Jennie. I fear, Fanny, that she is becoming a hoyden."

"A lady can have no finer education than a period in Europe."

"And consider the gentlemen they will meet! From the nobility, perhaps! Fanny . . . a Vanderbilt or even an *Astor* will be as nothing to a French count!"

Jennie shut her eyes tightly. *Papa, Papa, Papa,* she prayed. *Hurry and come back.* She did not want to leave him, or New York.

She moved noiselessly to the stairs. Clarita was crouching in the shadows above. Listening to every word. Her older sister's hands were clasped and her blue eyes were shining.

"Jennie," Clarita whispered when she reached the top step. "A Season in Europe! Isn't it a *dream?*"

By the time Papa disembarked in New York at the end of January, the flood Fanny predicted had drowned them all. Mamma was tired of being second best, in every aspect of Leonard Jerome's life. He had settled a fortune on her that even the Depression of 1867 could not touch. Mamma decided to leave Leonard. None of his promises could sway her.

From the wreckage tossed up by the flood's retreating waters, Jennie gleaned shards of her childhood. A simpler happiness, of fierce loyalties and convictions. A lost copy of *The Children of the New Forest*. A beloved pony she would never be small enough to ride. Soiled beauties and broken faiths.

She would never sleep again in any of the houses she had loved, where Papa had sheltered her.

Leonard Jerome made the crossing with his girls that September on the *City of Paris,* the first of the great screw-driven steamships. Jennie was allowed to take Nero, her cairn terrier. He had a basket in the stateroom she shared with Clarita and loved to brace himself against the wind when they strode the promenade deck. He was Jennie's greatest friend.

Fanny Ronalds crossed on the same ship. She had left her children behind. Her husband, though happy to fund her sojourn, clearly expected her back. Fanny never admitted she had no intention of returning to New York, but Jennie saw it in the carriage of her head and the way she smiled so broadly at the world. She was still teaching Jennie things. That it was possible to reinvent yourself—several times, if necessary. That you could find joy despite the death of your heart's desire.

Papa remained with them in Paris for a month, long enough to see his girls established in a *hôtel particulier* on the Rue Malesherbes. He engaged French tutors and music masters. He opened Clara's bank accounts. He left letters of credit to be drawn on his funds in New York. He paid Dobbie's salary in advance for a year; she had agreed to remain with Leonie, who was now eight, for at least that long.

On his final afternoon in Paris, Papa took Jennie riding in Napoleon III's new pleasure ground, the Bois de Boulogne. It was filled with fashionable carriages and gentlemen on horseback. Jennie was riding a four-year-old gelding Papa had just given her— sixteen hands, a black horse suited to her coloring. Her hair still hung down her back like a child's but she rode better than any woman who passed them. The eyes of Frenchmen followed her as she and Papa cantered through the Bois.

"You will write to me," he said as they drew up near the Grand Cascade.

"Every day, Papa. I shall have so much to tell you."

He touched her cheek. "You'll be too busy being a madcap. I'll never hear from you."

"You will be busy, too. You always are." She met his gaze squarely, determined to be cheerful. But her voice quavered.

"Shall you miss me?" he asked.

"Of course." Pain shafted through her, and a yawning desolation. Much later, she would have words for such a sensation. *Grief. Loss. Betrayal.* Right now, however, she knew only that she was both sad and furious at being forced to part from Papa. "Nothing exciting ever happens in a household full of women!"

He threw back his head and laughed. "I shall miss *you* dreadfully, dear heart."

She fought the urge to clutch his arm. To keep him from leaving. To keep herself from falling. Was it Papa's fault that Mamma had carried them all off to France? Was Fanny Ronalds to blame? Or . . . if Jennie had been less of a *hoyden,* would Mamma have let her stay in New York?

Was she the cause of her own misery?

If so, she must take responsibility for it.

Jennie laid her hand gently on Papa's sleeve. He placed his own palm over hers, strong and warm.

*When fear nips at the edge of your mind, knock it off its pins,* Fanny's voice echoed. *Self-confidence is vital. It can look like balance, even when you have none.*

"You must visit us at Christmas, Papa," Jennie said evenly. "Clarita and I will be home from school then."

"You can count on it. I've learned my lesson about missing holidays."

She dimpled. "I hope you will bring vast quantities of presents."

"For a change?" he joked, then grew suddenly serious. "Is there anything I can give you now, before I sail?"

She hesitated, her cheeks flushing. "I should like to have a cigar, Papa."

"A *cigar*?"

"To roll between my fingers. The scent will remind me of you. And our library on Madison Square."

He reached into his breast pocket and offered her a Havana.

Jennie took it from him, her eyes suddenly dancing. "Now teach me to smoke, Papa," she commanded.

She hesitated now, two decades later, under the canvas awning in front of Mademoiselle Antoine's. Rain still fell on Piccadilly and the paving stones streamed with water. A dark head swam in her mind, his hair falling vagrantly over the brow. The blue eyes that held her own—the strong hands that could sketch an image of herself simply by touching her. Jennie's flesh thrilled with longing suddenly, as though he had traced his finger from the corner of her mouth to her clavicle. *Charles.*

Posted to Paris?

And what then?

To Berlin, next?

Ensnared in the politics of *Mitteleuropa,* the push and pull for primacy between Prussia and Austria, Bismarck and the Emperor?

She unfurled her umbrella. She was done with running from love. Done with the fear of what she could not control.

The patter of rain increased.

"Shall I summon a cab, ma'am?" the porter asked.

"No, thank you," she said.

Charles's rooms were off Piccadilly.

"I prefer to walk in such lovely weather."

# CHAPTER TWENTY-SIX

The most exclusive group of bachelor digs in England began life in the eighteenth century as a private home for the Melbourne family. The Albany, as it was now known, was a three-story mansion, seven bays wide, converted by Henry Holland into sixty-nine sets of rooms for gentlemen of taste and means. Lord Byron had lived there, and Prime Minister Gladstone in his youth.

Jennie entered by the main door off the central courtyard. A liveried steward inquired her name. Ladies had only been allowed onto the Albany premises in recent years, and the privacy of the male residents was still jealously guarded. The steward took her dripping umbrella, offered her a chair at a writing desk, and suggested she pen a note to be sent up to Charles's digs. Jennie sank down on the seat and drew off her gloves. They were pale yellow doeskin and quite ruined by the rain. The toes of her boots were capped with wet.

Charles's set lay beyond this central part of the building. She had visited his rooms more than once in the past—by daylight, to take tea, and at night, heavily veiled, although the gentlemen lodgers of the Albany were not the sort to spy on their neighbors. They all had secrets to respect and keep.

In converting Melbourne House, Holland had designed two perpendicular wings that ran the length of the back garden along Sackville Street. A covered and paved path the residents called the Rope Walk led down the center of the courtyard. The sets gave off a group entry, rather like rooms at Oxford or Cambridge; Charles lived off the "C" stair. The sets were notoriously small, but their ceilings were high, their windows bowed and filled with sunlight. One could be sure of being left in peace.

Jennie wrote two lines.

*Dear Charles—I must see you. I'm waiting below.*

The steward took her note and went.

Odds on he was out. He would be at the Austrian embassy. He would be at his club. It was a Thursday afternoon and he might even be riding through the woods at Sandringham, for all Jennie knew. But she had to find out for herself. It was possible Fanny Ronalds was wrong about everything, in her bohemian eyrie, and that Charles was fixed forever in London. Jennie had to tell him that she regretted nothing so much as sending him away.

The courtyard door was thrust open; the steward returning, and behind him Charles's valet, a ruddy-faced fellow in his fifties with close-clipped gray hair. He appeared to have thrust himself hurriedly into his black coat.

"Lady Randolph." He bowed.

"Foster." She had remembered the man's name. English; it was a precept of Charles's that one always hired servants native to one's diplomatic post. They were, he claimed, vital to mastering the language and customs of a strange country.

"I regret to inform you, ma'am, that my master is from home."

"Ah," she sighed. "Then pray give him my missive when he returns."

Foster's pale eyes skittered away from hers with what Jennie realized, to her horror, was *sympathy.* "I'm afraid that will be impossible, ma'am. I will no longer be in His Excellency's employ in another hour, once the last of the packing cases are shifted." The valet glanced down at the floor. "I did not fancy a removal to Paris at this time of life. I will be taking up a position with young Lord Clavering, the Earl of Markham's heir."

"I see," she said unsteadily. Clavering was one of Charles's racing friends. They shared a club.

She rose. "Thank you, Foster."

"My lady." He bowed again.

She nearly asked him for Charles's address in Paris, but the steward would overhear her, and the thought was somehow shaming. The small flame that had carried her down Piccadilly flared and died.

*Charles had left London without saying goodbye.*

That was the way with people she cared about. Like Papa. They picked up their lives in other countries, leaving her to go on alone.

What would she have said to him, in any case?

*Don't leave me.*

*Take me with you.*

Either was absurd. She and Charles had nothing to do with each other, now.

"I wish you the very best with Lord Clavering, Foster," Jennie said.

"Thank you, ma'am. Please accept my best wishes for your ladyship's health and happiness."

This time, she let the steward fetch her a cab.

# CHAPTER TWENTY-SEVEN

In September, Winston took the train back to Brighton. Little Jack went with him for his first term at the Thomson Sisters' School. Jennie and Everest rode in the hansom with them to the station. The two boys held hands as they walked down the platform behind the porter. Winston's trunk was shabby; Jack's was brand-new.

Everest buttoned the collars of their coats, although it was still quite hot and Jack insisted he was *boiling*. "If you or your brother has the least need, Master Winston, tell those school-ma'ams to wire for me," she said.

"I shall, Woom."

"And don't be waiting until you've a temperature of a hundred and four."

"I shan't." He flung his arms around her comfortable bulk and hugged her tightly.

Jack's face was very white. He clutched his bear. Winston fingered a soldier in his pocket. Over Woom's head he saw his mother's face, carefully shielded with a veil against the steam and soot bursting in gasps from the train. She was gazing at something far down the platform. Her navy-blue twill dress had military-style epaulettes and beautiful brass buttons. He thought she looked splendid as a hussar.

"Goodbye, Mummie."

Her brilliant eyes came back to his, and softened. "Goodbye, darling. Do write."

"I shall. And I'll make Jack. But you must remember to answer!"

"Of course," she replied.

Which meant, he knew, that they would each of them receive one letter for every six they wrote.

"I shall be very busy, you know, with Papa back in Government," she added.

"Please say goodbye to Papa for me. And assure him of my very best wishes for his success at the Exchequer."

"Better him than you, eh, Win? Work on your maths this term." She leaned down to kiss his cheek, fluid and fleeting. He caught her familiar scent: a mix of tuberose and saddle leather. "Look after your brother."

He nodded, his throat too tight to speak.

"Now hurry along!" Everest scolded. "You'll want good seats by the window, if Master Jack is not to be sick."

As they mounted the carriage steps, Jack uttered a faint and despairing sound. Rather, Winston thought, like a rabbit taken in a snare.

"It's out of the question that I should propose him for Eton," Randolph said brutally. He had stopped into Jennie's boudoir that afternoon as she changed out of her riding habit. She had invited Consuelo Mandeville and Fannie Ronalds to Connaught Place for tea. The two women rarely met but enjoyed each other.

"I thought you put him down for a place when he was born," she objected, as Gentry repinned her hair. Six generations of the House of Marlborough had attended Eton College.

"That was before I knew Win was a dolt."

"Randolph!" Was this his idea of a joke? "His latest reports from Miss Charlotte are quite good. He's taken a prize in recitation and one in French—"

"The Thomson Sisters' School hasn't a patch on Eton." Randolph smoothed his hair in the large gilt mirror that hung over her dressing table. In the weak autumn sunlight, his cheeks appeared sunken; his eyes protruded from their sockets, the whites glassy and reddened. His hand trembled in a way she doubted he could control. Being Leader and holding the Treasury portfolio were very bad for Randolph's nerves. He'd stayed in bed the whole of Sunday, from his morning tea to his evening brandy, newspapers drifting among the rumpled sheets.

*You really must take more care of yourself,* Arthur Balfour had told him worriedly. *You're looking devilish knocked-up.*

"The poor chap can't manage Latin," Randolph persisted. "He'd be at the bottom of his form at Eton, bullied and fagged to death, and sent down within weeks."

"Not if you put in a word with the headmaster. Asked for a kinder Head of House. Explained how sensitive Winston is."

Randolph threw her an incredulous look. "And embarrass the little sod beyond belief? Do you want Win *hanged* by his own form with a bedsheet? Good God, Jennie—if you think the boy's as soft as all that, send him to Anglican seminary and be done!"

"Too much Latin," Jennie retorted in clipped tones. Then she sighed in frustration. "You're not being fair, Randy. The boy isn't soft—he's a stoic. You didn't see the weals on his back."

"A stoic would never have mentioned them."

The injustice of this lashed Jennie. "He didn't! We'd never have known of his scourging if Everest hadn't spilled the beans."

"Then he'll think twice next time before he winges to his nanny," Randolph said callously. "It's not done for boys to blubber, Jennie. *Especially* at Eton. In any case, I thought we'd agreed on an Army career."

"And? Are all soldiers assumed to be uneducated?"

"Well," he temporized, "they go to Sandhurst instead of 'varsity, where they spend all their time drilling and taking apart guns."

Jennie threw up her hands in defeat. "*So much the better.* He'll adore it. But Winston can't stay with the Misses Thomson forever.

Where do you intend him to go next? Winchester, with George's boy?"

"I wouldn't give George the satisfaction."

Randolph was not speaking to his brother at the moment. George had sold off *three hundred* of Blenheim's Old Masters.

"Let's have a crack at Harrow," he suggested. "It's only a dozen miles or so from London, it's respectable, and the entrance exams can't be *nearly* as hard as the ones I endured. They'll take him in any case because he's *my* son."

She frowned at him. But at least he was offering a solution. "Very well. Harrow it is."

Who did she know, Jennie asked herself, who had gone to the school? Of course—all Randolph's cousins, the Spencers, and through them, the Hamiltons, the Duke of Abercorn's family. Liberal Party members, and all Harrovians. She must talk to Charlotte Spencer. Charlotte was one of Princess Alix's ladies-in-waiting.

"Tell Win it's for his chest," Randolph suggested. "The air at Harrow is better than Eton."

"How can that possibly be true?" Both schools were within shouting distance of London.

"Harrow's on a hill," Randolph said vaguely.

*A hill.* She would have to find out when the entrance exam could be offered. What the fees and uniforms ran to. How many boys were under the care of each master, and which were the best houses. Jennie's head was full of plans as Randolph turned for the door.

"Mind you get Win a crammer over the hols," he said.

She saw little of her husband during the next few weeks. He cared passionately about his leadership in Commons, and sent detailed reports on the debates to Her Majesty the Queen, who answered with a personal letter of commendation from Balmoral. He loathed his Treasury portfolio, however. The ministry was populated with civil servants dedicated to producing the annual budget. Many of them viewed Randolph with suspicion. He was unknown to them and had never worked with budgets before. He was supposed to provide *vision* and *policy,* not actual sums, but he had begun to scribble endless rough figures in columns on sheets of paper. The process was perplexing to him—"I never could make out what those damned dots meant," he said bitterly of decimals to his secretary—but Randolph was certain his ministry would not accept mere vision without hard math behind it. The British Crown and Government allowed no shortfalls or debt. Expenditure must strictly adhere to revenues.

Randolph, who had lived on credit and in continuous debt for most of his life, was ambitious with the Government's funds: He craved a budget *surplus*. As for his vision? "Cut taxes for the poor, simplify the death duties on the rich, and find savings in the Army and Navy budgets."

"But those are Gladstone's ideas," Arthur Balfour objected in horror.

Randolph shrugged. "He wasn't wrong about everything."

His fellow Cabinet members, including the PM, were not amused that Churchill was borrowing from the Opposition.

"It is frankly impossible," Salisbury told him, "with the world in the state it is, to trim the Admiralty and War Office."

In direct conflict with the Prime Minister and Cabinet, Randolph gave a speech in Kent to twenty thousand people, supporting closer ties with Germany and Austria. He delighted the Queen—Victoria had relatives scattered all over the German parts of the world—but infuriated Salisbury.

"He's deliberately challenging me, Arthur," the PM complained at their usual drinking hour. "He thinks his Tory Democrats will come out in the streets and lift him as high as Prime Minister."

Reporters tailed Randolph from his home to his club and everywhere in between, speculating on his loyalty to Government.

Jennie's initials appeared in the *Spectator*—the chief Liberal gossip sheet—with sly aspersions on her voracious pursuit of other people's husbands. She shrugged it off and tried not to mind; it was common in politics to savage families.

And then, one morning, Randolph simply disappeared.

It was Alasdair Gordon who told Jennie he was gone.

He appeared in the breakfast room with the sick look of a cat that has been left out all night in the rain.

"What is it?" she asked, her brow furled.

"I beg your pardon, my lady, but did Lord Randolph mention when he expected to return?"

"From his club, you mean?" She rose to refill her coffee cup. "Have you breakfasted, by the way?"

"No, ma'am," he said. "That is—I *have* eaten, but I was *not* referring to the Carlton Club. Lord Randolph appears to have left town. Walden tells me he took only a single valise, and refused to accept his services for the journey."

Walden was Randolph's valet.

Jennie bit her lip. She was too used to her husband's unpredictable hours and hectic schedule to track his comings and goings every hour of the day. But it was unlike him to leave his valet behind, and it was clear that Alasdair was worried. "Send Walden to me, if you would be so good."

The secretary inclined his golden head and left her to her coffee. She sipped it tentatively—it was still quite hot—and wondered if Randy had simply gone home to Blenheim. Surely there was a reasonable explanation—

"My lady." Walden bowed.

"Ah, there you are," she said briskly. "Did Lord Randolph tell you where he has gone?"

It was a bald question. Spouses rarely interrogated each other's personal servants; that was poor taste and worse breeding. A lady's maid or a gentleman's valet often overheard conversations or witnessed scenes that were meant to be forgotten and were certainly not meant to be shared. Walden had known Randolph longer than Jennie had, in fact. She had been married to him nearly thirteen years; Walden had been in Randy's employ for fifteen.

"No, ma'am," he replied.

Jennie set down her cup. "But his lordship was *quite definite* that he did not require your services?"

"He was emphatic, my lady."

"I see. That will be all, Walden."

It was probable, she reasoned, that Randolph was at Blenheim—he was too fastidious about his clothes to do for long without a valet. George employed fewer servants in his bachelor household than Duchess Fanny's fifty, but no doubt there was at least one who could safeguard Randy's wardrobe while he was there. But it was odd that he had mended fences with George— and odder still that he hadn't left word.

Jennie went about her day.

No message came in the evening mail, and none in the next morning's post. Jennie dispatched delicate inquiries to Blenheim and to Duchess Fanny, who now leased a home on Grosvenor Square. She hated betraying her ignorance to the Duchess, who reveled in every hint of marital discord between them, but Jennie was uneasy. By that evening she learned that none of the Churchills had heard from Randolph in days.

"Arthur," she said, when she met Balfour at the Albert Hall for a spectacular Beethoven concert that night, "where is Randy?"

"I haven't the faintest," he replied. "I'd hoped you'd tell me."

Jennie turned the comment aside with a smile and was more than usually glittering that evening, but once alone again in her bedroom at midnight, she stared unseeing at the coal fire, wondering with an edge of panic if Randolph was lying dead somewhere. If he had thrown himself into the Thames, or under a train. Or if he had fallen into one of his fevers, and no one knew who he was—

*Nonsense.* His face was the most recognizable in Britain.

The next morning, she found the answer in the copy of the

*Times* her butler had placed, carefully ironed, at the breakfast table.

> "Mr. Spencer" and Mr. Trafford, two travelers whose every step is watched by the European press, have been residing at the Imperial Hotel in Vienna since yesterday. One of those who glimpsed the gentlemen disembarking from a train insisted that "Mr. Spencer" is none other than the British Chancellor of the Exchequer, Lord Randolph Spencer-Churchill.

Jennie closed her eyes an instant before reading further. Randolph and Tommie Trafford. Tommie and Randolph. Running away together under an assumed name so ridiculously childish even a random Austrian on a railway platform could see through it.

A random Austrian.

She pushed away the sharp stab of Charles Kinsky and read the rest of the article. Randolph had passed through Paris and Berlin. The newspaper speculated he had been on a back-channel mission to Bismarck, but Buckingham Palace revealed nothing. He had looked at picture galleries and attended theaters in Dresden. He appeared exhausted and ill and told his landlord in Vienna that he would receive no one. He had worn a dark green coat and a trilby hat and browsed through the exquisite leather-goods shop of Herr Weidmann. He was dogged everywhere by journalists.

*I am hopelessly discovered,* Randolph wrote in the letter she received from Vienna the next day. *This pottering about Europe would suit me down to the ground if it were not for the beastly journalists.*

He said nothing about Tommie. To Jennie's fury, he offered her no apology or explanation. She tore the letter to bits and went out to gallop recklessly through Hyde Park.

# CHAPTER TWENTY-EIGHT

"My dear," Louise Manchester said as she settled herself in the drawing room at Connaught Place one November morning and removed her delicate fawn gloves. "I'm so glad I found you at home. And alone."

It was true that Jennie was rarely indoors at eleven o'clock, but the autumn sky had threatened rain, and she had put off riding. She sank onto the opposite end of the sofa and smiled with real affection at Louise, whose bone-deep beauty never wore thin. The German-born Duchess was nearly fifty-five, but her elegance—and, Jennie suspected, her fundamentally optimistic nature—gave her a perpetual appearance of serenity.

"A true morning visit!" Jennie said cordially. "This is treating me like family, Lottie."

"I would know better how to proceed if you *were* my relation," the Duchess replied abruptly. "But lacking a blood tie, Jennie dearest, I must simply blunder forward. No matter how much I bruise you."

Jennie felt her happiness ebb. "What is it?"

"I've just returned from Sandringham, where I'm afraid you were the subject of gossip. . . ."

"Is that all!" She tried to look indifferent, but repressed an uneasy shiver. Louise would only mention such talk if it had truly turned ugly. Jennie's mind raced. What damage had she done? Had she earned a new enemy?

"I could have put this in an envelope and mailed it to you." Louise reached into her reticule and withdrew a folded square of paper. "I brought it myself because I am angry on your behalf."

Jennie smoothed the creases. It was a column of print—from a journal, she guessed, rather than a news sheet.

"That was cut from *Town Topics,*" Louise told her. "A New York publication, I believe."

"Call it a scandal sheet and be done. When I was a child, it was a literary review with an emphasis on music and culture. But the current editor has considerably altered the tone. He has black-mailed some American friends, Lottie, who pay ridiculous sums to stay out of his paper."

"Did he attempt to extort money from you?"

Jennie shook her head. Pulse leaping, she scanned the brief paragraph.

> Society has invented a new name for Lady R. Her fondness for the exciting sport of husband-hunting and fiancé-fishing, when the husbands and fiancés belong to other women, has earned her the title of "Lady Jane Snatcher."

It reminded her of something vague and far less damning she had glimpsed in a recent issue of the *Spectator.* She had dismissed that as a Liberal jab at Randolph. But if the same rumor had surfaced in New York—

Jennie glanced up. "Who gave you this?"

"I wish I knew," Louise said crisply. "The column was left on the Prince of Wales's sideboard, beside the covered dish of quails' eggs. Each of the guests—there were sixteen this past week—was privileged to read it as they progressed through the buffet. Naturally, it was the first topic of conversation."

"Random spite," Jennie said bitterly.

"Of course. But some people took it quite seriously. It was said that if your behavior was outrageous enough to cross the Atlantic, someone ought to warn your husband. As a Cabinet member, Lord Randolph cannot afford a scandalous wife."

"Damn their impertinence!" Jennie's lips were white with anger.

"Indeed." Louise studied her bleakly. "Those were Hartington's exact words, when it was suggested that *he* should speak to Randy."

"Please offer Hart my deepest thanks."

"We are both your friends. As I hope you know." Louise reached for her hand. "But I would dearly love the answers to two questions: Whom have you offended, Jennie, with connections to the American press? And who hopes to turn the Prince of Wales against you by leaving this rubbish in his breakfast parlor?"

"No man would waste his time this way." Jennie met the Duchess's eyes. "Both the tone and the tactic are female. Which ladies were at Sandringham last week, Lottie?"

"Lady Brooke. Gladys de Grey. Mary, Lady Jeune. My daughter-in-law Consuelo. The Wyndhams. Minnie Paget. And a lady you have *not* met, I think . . . a wealthy widow. From New York."

"Ah." Jennie drew a deep breath. "And the widow's name?"

"Lily Carré Hamersley. Quite a shy and well-bred young woman. Consuelo tells me her late husband left her a considerable fortune—which his family has fought in the courts. Mrs. Hamersley has quitted New York in an effort to put the distress behind her."

"And may have brought a copy of *Town Topics* in her baggage," Jennie mused. "As the lady is a complete stranger to me, however, she can have no reason to savage my reputation. Particularly among a social set entirely new to her."

Louise hesitated. "I can think of one possible cause. . . ."

"Can you?"

"Mrs. Hamersley—or her fortune—is an object of great interest to several impecunious noblemen. Among them is your brother-in-law the Duke of Marlborough. Does Randolph *still* refuse to speak to him?"

"Who is that child?" Minnie Paget demanded of Daisy, Lady Brooke. "She's come out in her nightgown!"

"I daresay no one told the poor thing the Prince of Wales was expected," Daisy suggested. "What a shame."

Both women were sipping sherry in Jennie's drawing room a few weeks after Louise Manchester's sudden morning call. The Marquess of Hartington and Louise were standing by the fire. Near them, Randolph was arguing with George Curzon. The gentlemen were in unimpeachable evening dress: cutaways and starched white cravats. Lottie wore a gown of maroon velvet and one of the Manchester tiaras, set with rubies. Daisy Brooke was sporting the Warwick emeralds with her silver evening gown— she would be Countess of Warwick one day, and the jewels complemented her golden curls and misleading expression of sweetness. At present, Daisy was Bertie's reigning mistress, a fresh and witty young woman of twenty-five, only a few years older than the "child" in the nightdress.

Jennie had decided that the best way to combat *Town Topics* was to flaunt her friendship with the Waleses, so she'd invited Bertie and Alix to dine. Having Randolph there, along with most of the Marlborough House Set, would put a stop to malicious gossip. But as she hurried past Minnie and Daisy to welcome her guests, she caught the snide remarks about children and nightgowns. She hoped Margot Tennant had not overheard them.

Sir Charles Tennant had sent round a note only an hour before, to explain that his wife was indisposed but he would like to bring his younger daughter to supper. Jennie had immediately replied that he *must*. She had been wanting to meet Margot, the mysterious founder of the Souls, for some time.

"My dear Sir Charles," she exclaimed as she greeted them, "welcome to Connaught Place!"

He was, Jennie thought, a man after her father's heart—a self-made industrialist from Glasgow whose fortune was larger than anyone else's in the room. The breathless aristocracy Jennie had gathered was inclined to patronize him. Tennant was a Liberal Party MP.

Sir Charles bowed and touched his daughter's elbow. "May I present Miss Margot Tennant, Lady Randolph."

Boldly sculpted cheekbones, a sharp blade of a nose, a heavy square chin, and penetrating eyes. Margot's dark hair was parted in wings on her forehead. She had a reputation for cleverness. Other people sometimes called her *intellectual,* which was not a compliment. The look Margot gave Jennie was full of intelligence—but something else as well. Reserve? Resentment? The girl probably *had* overheard Minnie's insult.

"You were lovely to join us on such short notice," Jennie told Margot warmly.

"My father assured me this was to be an informal supper." Her voice was a deep contralto, almost grating, her diction precise—to avoid any suggestion of a Scottish lilt?

"And so it is," Jennie declared. "I'm an American, you know, and can't know what ceremony is." The "nightgown" was a white muslin dress with transparent chemise sleeves and a blue taffeta sash. Margot had tucked a bunch of rose carnations into her fichu with three diamond duck pins. *Unusual.* It was the sort of word frequently attached to her.

George Curzon was staring, transfixed, from his position at Randolph's side. Jennie had heard that he was one of the Souls who gathered in the Tennants' night nursery. She dimpled at George and said, "You know Mr. Curzon, I think? But Sir Charles, you must introduce Miss Tennant to Lord Randolph—your sparring partner of old!"

The Tennants moved toward the knot of gentlemen near the

mantel. Curzon flushed and bowed low over Margot's hand. He must be in love with her, Jennie decided. But even Randolph looked alert and intrigued.

"Cultivating tradesmen, Jennie?" a voice murmured in her ear.

Minnie Paget had drifted over in her noiseless, catlike way. She was magnificent this evening in black lace over a champagne silk underskirt, elaborately draped with knots of passementerie and black jet. A parure of topazes glittered in her hair and at her throat. It was unusual for Minnie to look so fine—or so expensive.

"Sir Charles is a political ally of Randolph's on Home Rule," Jennie explained. "His manners are refreshingly like an American's, don't you think?"

"I confess I cannot see the likeness," Minnie retorted with a bleak smile. "But it has been so long since *you* were in the States. You would find it remarkably changed. The rougher class of persons aspiring to Society—the *speculators* and *pirates*—have been entirely cast down by the Wall Street slump."

Jennie bit back a sarcastic response. Minnie's father had owned hotels, for heaven's sake—a grade less distinguished a profession, one might argue, than Leonard Jerome's. But anything she might have said was forestalled by the fresh acid dripping from Minnie's lips.

"One meets only people of quality in New York now. I was fortunate enough to spend a few weeks there this autumn—some part of my father's estate has, at long last, settled. Did no one mention that to you?"

*Six million dollars.*

"I think everyone has mentioned it," Jennie said wryly. "But unlike the rest of London, I know the tragedy behind the truth. No amount of money, Minnie, could possibly be worth the loss of your only brother." The sole male heir to the vast Stevens' fortune had died the previous year of tuberculosis, barely twenty-five. His inheritance had gone to his two sisters. With typical Stevens' rapacity, Minnie's mother was suing her daughters for the balance of the estate.

"He was a dear boy. I shall always regret that I returned to New York too late to see him." Minnie's gaze hardened. "I wonder you have time for sympathy, Jennie. You've been so taken up with Harry Cust. I assumed you had quite forgotten your *old* friends."

Startled, Jennie frowned. *Harry Cust.* Whom Minnie still pursued. He'd idled away a few weeks in Jennie's company, it was true, but neither of them had taken the affair seriously. He was the Duchess of Rutland's lover now. But perhaps Minnie really cared about him—and resented everyone he'd touched? It would be like Minnie to lash out from the pain.

Had she spent her time in New York stabbing Jennie in the back? Feeding scandal to the press?

*Lady Jane Snatcher . . .*

"I always knew you had a vicious streak," Jennie breathed wonderingly, "but I never thought you could occasionally be *clever*! You left that piece of newsprint on Bertie's sideboard, Minnie— and were smart enough to do it when there were other American guests I could suspect."

"I don't know what you mean." Minnie's green eyes were alight with triumph. "And I resent your tone, Lady Randolph."

"How you have the *gall* to show your face in my drawing room! But your tricks never work, Minnie! You really think your millions will secure your place in Society? I am happy to say that I have more *friends* than you do!"

Minnie's face drained of color. "You overestimate your power, Jennie. There are some things Society does not forgive. A woman who can't keep her legs closed is one of them."

The chatter around them fell silent. Heads turned. Jennie caught a glimpse of Margot Tennant's shocked face and Louise Manchester's stricken one.

"Get out of my house," she ordered, her voice guttural with fury.

But before Minnie could move, a royal equerry strolled into the drawing room.

"Their Royal Highnesses, the Prince and Princess of Wales!"

Jennie stepped back. So did everyone else. With a faint rustle, the men bowed and the ladies curtseyed deeply as the royals entered. When Jennie rose again, Bertie stood before her.

"Lady Randy! How sorry we were not to have you at Sandringham last month! But how delighted to join your party this evening!"

"Your Royal Highness is far too good." Jennie dazzled him with a smile and accepted Alix's hand. "Lord Randolph and I are sensible of the very great honor you do us."

"And Mrs. Paget," Bertie rumbled to Minnie. "You are looking well, my dear."

"Unfortunately," Jennie interjected as Minnie bowed her head in acknowledgment of the Prince, "Mrs. Paget is obliged to leave us. A summons from home that may not be ignored. Your Highness will forgive her, I know, though I cannot!"

She made this last sally sound like a joke, but from the taut expression on Minnie's face, Jennie knew her cut had gone home.

"There is my young friend Miss Tennant," Princess Alix announced in her toneless voice. "Such a sweet creature."

Bertie beamed at Margot. "Ah, Miss Tennant—the Princess has spoken much of you! You must sit right by me at supper, eh? And tell me all about yourself?"

"Oh, no, Sir," Margot replied clearly. "I am not dressed for the part. I expect some of the ladies think I have insulted them by coming in my *nightgown*."

So the girl *had* heard, Jennie thought. Seething, she stopped a passing footman. "Mrs. Paget requires her cloak, James. You will escort her to the door."

"But I have not the slightest desire to leave!" Minnie protested shrilly.

"Alas, where duty lies, desire must give way." Smiling, Jennie met her gaze implacably. "Mrs. Paget has no alternative but to go. James? If you will?"

Several hours later, while the Hungarian Violins crooned their melancholy song and her guests waltzed beneath the electric lights, Jennie slipped from her saloon. She had tamped down on her ill-timed anger and smoothed over the ugliness of the public spat. Her friends were too well-bred and too conscious of the royals to mention it. But Jennie would breathe a profound sigh of relief only when the evening was over.

She discovered the Tennants in her foyer, putting on their wraps.

"You cannot be leaving!" she said in dismay. "And I haven't had a moment to speak with you!"

Sir Charles twinkled at her. "You know I don't dance and I detest sitting up, Lady Randy. I ought to have been in my bed long ago. Margot's presented me to her Prince, which is enough for one night."

"You must return, Miss Tennant, when you've more time at your disposal," Jennie urged. "I long to paint those cheekbones."

"Only if you promise to visit Grosvenor Square and attend a meeting of the Souls," Margot replied.

"The very invitation I've longed for! But it's too bad you won't waltz with us this evening."

"Another time—when I'm wearing a ball dress." Margot cast down her eyes at her fichu of carnations. "The Prince referred to me as an *original,* and I should hate for the name to stick. Lord knows what damage it might do beyond these walls."

"I have never been anything *but* original." Jennie glanced over her shoulder, toward the distant hum of her party. "I cannot be one of *them,* after all. Much better to be the best possible version of myself."

Margot studied her appraisingly. "I should say you've taken Lady Randolph to a high level of art."

Impulsively, Jennie hugged her. "I look forward to watching Miss Tennant do the same."

# CHAPTER TWENTY-NINE

"I call it infernal cheek for Salisbury to turn up his nose at my budget, when he's never been out of his tailor's debt in his life. . . ." Randolph broke off his querulous tirade to glare at Jennie across the breakfast table. "You're *not listening*. Confound it! If a man's *wife* can't be bothered to show him respect—"

"Randolph, look at this."

Abruptly, Jennie passed him a letter from her stack of morning mail.

He scanned the few lines rapidly, his mustache working. "Who and what is Arthur Brisbane when he's at home?"

"He claims to be the London correspondent of the New York *Sun*."

"Is that a reputable paper?"

"Extremely." Unlike the *Times* and the *Herald,* which only wrote about finance and politics, the *Sun* published articles about real people's lives as well—their tragedies, romances, triumphs, suicides. It was the most widely read newsprint in New York. Jennie pressed her fingers against her eyes. Brisbane's words scintillated behind the closed lids.

> *. . . must call to your attention, rumors of a separation pending between yourself and Lord Randolph . . . allegations of infidelity on both sides. . . . The writer is assured that divorce proceedings are presently to be entered into . . . have attempted to obtain*

*information from Mr. Leonard Jerome of Manhattan, in New
York, who has refused to comment. . . .*

"No reputable paper would send this." Randolph tossed the letter aside. "I'll threaten the rotter with libel."

"That's not enough!" Jennie thrust her chair away from the
breakfast table. "Don't you *see* that it's the *rumors* we've got to
stop? This . . . *Arthur Brisbane* . . . is merely a symptom, not the
disease! More queries will follow. We must draw out the poison
*behind* the words, Randy, or watch your reputation and career be
savaged on both sides of the Atlantic!"

Randolph shrugged. "I shouldn't worry overmuch, darling. No
British journalist would dare to print such trash."

"If this kind of talk has reached New York, matters have gone
far enough." It was the *Town Topics* threat enormously amplified.
Jennie paced angrily back and forth before the sideboard, her
hands fisted at her sides. "*Divorce,* Randy! I cannot *believe* that
Papa has been embarrassed by inquiries of this sort. It is *beyond
intolerable* that the *Sun* is badgering him."

"I'll have Alasdair draft a reply," Randolph sighed. "Assuring
Mr. Brisbane of our complete *marital cordiality.* And threatening
him with the full force of British law if he suggests otherwise."

"Is that *all*?" Jennie was astounded at Randolph's indifference.
The press was hounding them in their own home. Didn't he understand it was too late for denials?

"Failing that, I can always have the man horsewhipped," her
husband drawled. "But forgive me, Jennie, if I have more important things to think of—such as the passage of the *annual budget* of
Great Britain!"

Watery sunlight gilded the London streets that December afternoon as Jennie slipped from her hansom onto the rancid paving.
She had driven to an address in Fleet Street, heavily veiled and
warmly cloaked against inquisitive eyes and the yellow coal-laden

fog that curled around her ankles. The offices of the New York *Sun* were on the building's first floor. Stifling a fit of nerves that nearly made her turn back, Jennie hastened up the narrow flight of battered wooden stairs, her black leather pocketbook tucked under her arm.

A door with opaque glass panels confronted her. She hesitated, then rapped on the wooden crosspiece.

"Come," ordered a voice heavy with drink and cigar smoke.

Her gloved hand turned the knob. She stepped into a room that was larger than she had expected. Broad windows at the far end shed a liminal glow. Four men were scattered about the office—one with spectacles and wildly untamed blond hair, bent over a monstrous ledger propped on a desk, his pencil furiously adding sums; another smoking a pipe, with his hands thrust into torn trouser pockets; a third, bearded and gray-haired, lying on a settee with his booted feet crossed and his eyes firmly closed. An empty bottle of spirits sat on the floor at his elbow beside the stub of a cigar.

The fourth man was leaning out of an inner room. He wore a green eyeshade on his balding pate and in his right hand he held a sheaf of scrawled paper. As Jennie watched, he scattered the pages unceremoniously on the slumbering man on the settee.

"It's too long by eighty-six words." Then his eyes fell on Jennie's veiled figure. "*Hello*—who's this?"

"I am looking for Mr. Arthur Brisbane," she said clearly.

"I'm the chap," he retorted. "What have you got for me?"

She assessed his face. Lined with hard living, grim about the mouth. The eyes were small and gave away nothing. He didn't look like the sort of man who'd strike a bargain. For an instant she regretted her impulse to come. But what choice did she have?

"I wish to speak with you," Jennie commanded, "in *private*."

There was a pregnant silence. With a tubercular cough, the scribbler set down his pencil. The man with the pipe pulled it from his mouth, smoke spiraling to the ceiling.

"Lift your veil," Brisbane challenged.

Jennie complied.

The newspaperman whistled. "Lady *Randy,* calling *special* on Our Arthur! Come along into my private office, *my lady*."

"I received your distressing communication this morning," Jennie quavered from behind the handkerchief she had pressed to her eyes. She had worn black for the occasion, as though she were in mourning.

"I expect you did," he agreed. "I had it delivered by special messenger. I make a rule never to spare expense in matters of national sensation. And divorce in a Cabinet household certainly qualifies! Lord Randy might've been PM one day, if it weren't for your careless ways, my lady."

"It takes two to ruin a marriage. But I cannot tell you how your message *worked* upon me, Mr. Brisbane. I am *prostrate* in all my trouble! I do not know whom to trust—to whom I may turn. . . ."

"Matters have reached a crisis, then?"

Jennie heaved a convulsive sigh and bowed her head.

"You may repose complete confidence in me, your ladyship."

"If only I could believe that! You have no notion, Mr. Brisbane, how difficult my life is! With my husband in the public glare— and the *vultures* of opinion, so entirely unsympathetic . . ."

"I'm sure it isn't easy for a lady in your position," he soothed. "And handsome as you are, it's no wonder you've a surfeit of beaux. If I may ask, does Lord Randolph know that you are here?"

He was greedy, Jennie saw, for exclusive information. Brisbane wanted to be first to publish the Churchill bombshell.

"I daren't tell him!" she gasped. "He abhors newspapermen. And we meet so rarely . . . my husband practically *lives* at the Carlton Club. I can only imagine:"

*'Friends of the illustrious couple reveal that Lord Randolph no longer resides at home.'*

"But as you are a representative of the *American* press—and have consulted my beloved father—"

"An openhanded gentleman if ever I knew one," Brisbane agreed.

"—I felt I could trust you. I need not say that the courage required to come to this office has *quite* drained my slender reserves."

Jennie raised her crumpled scrap of linen to her eyes. From his derisive look, Brisbane obviously had the poorest possible opinion of her morals and intelligence. He would not hesitate to take advantage of her vulnerability.

"I have here in my pocketbook a signed statement"—her voice was low and ashamed—"which I am prepared to turn over to you, Mr. Brisbane, detailing the state of my marriage and the proceedings Lord Randolph and I contemplate, in the very near few days."

"Indeed?" Brisbane reached across his scarred desk. "If I might just glance at it?"

"Of course!" Jennie kept her grip on the pocketbook and managed a pathetic smile. "You will understand that in my position, the wife of the Chancellor of the Exchequer—*the target of unbridled speculation*—I have taken particular pains with my statement. It is *extremely important* to me that it be published by a *friendly* organ, such as the *Sun,* with all the sympathy due to American brides exiled on these cold English shores. My husband will no doubt find other allies."

"You have my word, Lady Randy," Brisbane assured her. "You shall be accorded the delicacy and honor due to a daughter of New York."

Jennie pressed her hand fervently against her breast. "You are very good, Mr. Brisbane. Before I may entrust you entirely with my statement, however, I must inquire . . . which friends of mine were so kind as to confide my trouble to you?"

Brisbane's mouth curled sardonically. "A good pressman never gives up his sources."

"But I wish to thank them!" Jennie's voice throbbed. She

reached out a gloved hand and pressed the journalist's wrist. "The knowledge of their support has given me strength to come to you today! To know that there are those willing to take my part . . . to offer a sense of solidarity, and *fellow feeling* . . . Please, Mr. Brisbane—do not deny a broken woman her last possibility of returning a kindness?"

Brisbane hesitated.

"If you will not speak," Jennie urged, "surely you might *write down* the name of the friend to whom I owe so much? It would relieve my mind immeasurably. And, I need hardly add, my father's. Leonard Jerome might do much to advance your career in New York, Mr. Brisbane, if he knew his cause for gratitude. I am sure his interest in your work would be as warm and eager as mine."

Jennie watched Brisbane waver, her breath suspended. Would he take the bait?

"If I might just see your written statement—"

She took up her handkerchief again and gave a stifled sob.

Roughly, Brisbane tore off a sheet of foolscap and scrawled a name. He thrust it toward Jennie.

*Mrs. Arthur Paget.*

She met Brisbane's gaze, her eyes limpid with gratitude. "You swear to this? On your oath as a gentleman?"

"Of course."

"I cannot be surprised," she said with a catch in her voice. "Dear Mrs. Paget is my *oldest* friend! We met as girls, you know, Mr. Brisbane—mere children—in the Family Dancing Class at Delmonico's. She has always thought first of *others* before herself."

"Indeed."

Delicately, Jennie pressed his ink-stained fingers with her gloved ones. "Pray do me one last favor, Mr. Brisbane. *Attest to the truth of what you have told me*. I wish to make the communication to others more powerful, in a position to help your career."

The King of Wall Street hovered in the air between them.

"With pleasure, my lady." Brisbane signed his name beneath Minnie's.

"Thank you," Jennie breathed. Her gloved hand trembling, she folded the foolscap carefully and secured it in her pocketbook. Exchanging, as she did so, a sealed envelope with Brisbane's name on it.

The journalist's hand closed over it avidly.

"I authorize your exclusive right to publicize this statement, Mr. Brisbane, on both sides of the Atlantic," Jennie said earnestly. "I hope we may always regard each other with the same *depth of respect* that has characterized our meeting today."

"Your servant, Lady Randolph."

Brisbane rose from behind his desk and bowed. Jennie dropped her veil over her face and swept from the inner office.

Heart racing, she ran down the flight of stairs. It was vital to reach the safety of her waiting hansom before Brisbane tore open the envelope flap and unfolded the stiff sheet of letter paper embossed with the Connaught Place address.

*In light of recent rumors impossible to meet with a dignified silence, Lord and Lady Randolph Churchill are pleased to assure a wondering Public that they are happier than ever in their Union, and, if spared by a benevolent Providence, look forward to many more years of marital accord.*

Jennie drove straight from Fleet Street to 35 Belgrave Square. When the Paget butler blandly informed her that Minnie was not at home to callers, Jennie pushed past him and stormed furiously up two flights of stairs to her old friend's boudoir.

"My father was a great student of Niccolò Machiavelli," she announced as she thrust open the door, her veil thrown back and her eyes flaming. "He assures me, Minnie, that the Master's teachings may be distilled to a single sentence: *Keep your friends close, and your enemies closer.*"

Minnie turned from her mirror, aghast. "Have you gone mad, Jennie Jerome? Get out of my house at once!"

Jennie crossed the pale rose-and-white room in three strides, heedless of the lady's maid clutching vainly at her arm. "I have Arthur Brisbane's written and signed testimony of your attempt to destroy my life. I shall not hesitate to use it."

Minnie's mouth opened slackly, then snapped closed. She uttered a dry cackle. "There is nothing you can do. A mere *journalist's* word, indeed!"

"That is where you're wrong." Jennie held up her bit of paper triumphantly. "I intend to show this to the Princess of Wales. Alix abhors blackmail, Minnie. She will know immediately how to deal with you. The Polite World will cut you dead from this day forward. You will never enter Sandringham or attend the Queen's Drawing Room again."

A strangled sound formed deep in Minnie's throat. Her fingers tensed upon her hairbrush, as though she longed to hurl it at Jennie. "Give me that paper!"

"Never." Jennie whirled for the door.

"Wait. . . . *Wait*." Minnie held out both hands in supplication. "Tell me—what must I do? What *can* I do?"

Jennie made her burn with suspense. She paused a moment to tuck her precious paper inside her pocketbook. Then she looked shrewdly at Minnie.

"You will apologize for your willful and vicious attack. Immediately."

"I am heartily sorry, Jennie. I don't know how—"

"And you will scotch *every poisonous rumor* of divorce you have circulated through the drawing rooms of Mayfair."

"As God is my witness," Minnie muttered fervently.

"And, finally . . . regardless of whether you are otherwise engaged . . . you will attend the opening of *Ruddigore* this Sunday evening."

"I shall?" A line appeared between Minnie's plucked brows.

"As *my guest*. Expect my carriage to call for you at seven."

That Sunday night when Jennie, magnificent in a gown of peacock-blue brocade, entered a box at the Savoy, Randolph was by her side. The crowd of Fashionables surrounding them rose to their feet and spontaneously applauded the Churchills. Jennie managed to look astounded and thrilled as she acknowledged the tribute, and Randolph gallantly kissed her hand. As she had suspected, gossip about their marriage had flown all over London. But Minnie Paget, who could be counted upon for the truth, smiled brittlely at Jennie's side.

There was nothing so valuable, she reflected as she slipped her arm through Minnie's, as the support of old friends.

# CHAPTER THIRTY

Charles Kinsky settled his black derby on his head and swung through the broad front doors of the Austrian embassy. A pair of uniformed officers stood at attention as he passed; Hungarian boys, they stared unwaveringly from beneath their visors at the cobbled courtyard, framed by two broad wings of the building that reached toward the narrow Rue Las Cases.

The *hôtel particulier* had been built for a relative of the Sun King around 1700; his heirs had met their deaths on the guillotine, and after the Revolution the serene and classical city palace with its columns and Palladian windows had passed into strangers' hands. A century later, most of the great homes in the seventh arrondissement—one of the oldest and most exclusive quarters of the Left Bank—had been converted to embassies or French government ministries. The Bourbon Palace, where the National Assembly met, was within walking distance. The great dome of Les Invalides hovered at the edge of sight. Charles associated the *faubourg,* as it was commonly called, with work and governance and entrenched medieval sensibilities. He preferred to spend his free hours across the Seine, on the Avenue de l'Opera, in the midst of all the light and whirl of the Right Bank.

He passed through the massive courtyard gate. The porter saluted him. Outside, on the Rue Las Cases, the buildings encroached on one another. The stone street was empty. It was two days before New Year's, dusk was falling and with it a flurry of snow. Charles paused, rubbing his gloved hands. The cold air was scented with roasting chestnuts and burning wood. It irresistibly recalled other towns and other times: winter in Vienna and Prague, candles in leaded windows and fires burning in the midst of the market. A soprano's voice filling Wenceslaus Cathedral, his father carving a suckling pig while a private orchestra played Mozart. His younger sisters in gowns of crimson and emerald velvet. Waltzes and czardas in the baroque confection of a ballroom, angels peering down from their plaster lozenges in the vaulted ceiling. The scent of bruised hothouse flowers, and mulled wine with cloves. His mother's jewels glittering in her hair.

He ought to have requested leave. He ought to have gone home for Christmas. He was struggling with an emotion he had never suffered so much in all his life: *loneliness*.

The snow kissed his cheek, settled on his eyelashes and mustache. He could walk, of course. Take the streets running toward the Seine until he ended at the Pont de Solférino, and cross the river to the huge blasted ground that had once been the Tuileries. He might stop for a *fine*—a cognac—at one of the cafés on the Rue St. Honoré. But the snow was increasing. He would be chilled to the bone as dusk turned to night.

He glanced toward the Rue de Bellechasse. A fiacre—one of the Parisian cabs drawn by a single horse—was pulled up at the corner. The horse was a worn-out gray and its nose was shrouded in its feedbag. There was no established cab stand in the Rue Las Cases—it was far too narrow—but the fiacre driver was pacing the paving at the horse's head with his hands thrust into his greatcoat pockets as though he owned the ground, shoulders hunched against the cold.

Charles walked toward him.

As he came abreast of the man, the cab's door opened from within.

Charles stopped short. He stared into the fiacre's depths.

Her hand, white against the surrounding darkness, reached toward him.

"Charles," she said.

---

Jennie had gone to the wrong address that late December day in her hunt for Count Kinsky. The Austrian embassy she remembered from her girlhood in France fifteen years before had been on the Rue de Grenelle, a few blocks away.

"It had a wonderful garden—acres and acres of trees and formal beds," she explained as Charles stared at her, unspeaking, inside the fiacre. The cab had not moved; the driver awaited instructions. "Pauline de Metternich used to hold receptions there when I was a girl."

"Prince Metternich left Paris when the Prussians invaded," he told her. "So did you, as I remember. But you didn't come here to talk history or houses. What are you doing here, Lady Randolph? Ordering a few more gowns from Worth?"

*Lady Randolph.* He did not intend to make it easy for her.

"I . . . needed to get away. From London."

"At Christmas? Why aren't you at Blenheim with your boys? Or doesn't the Duke of Marlborough gather his family for the high holidays anymore?"

"George is from home these several weeks. So, as it happens, is my husband."

"So, as it happens, are *you*. And from the fact that you were searching for me at a defunct address—then lurking here by the curb in the hope of catching me unawares—"

"Why did you leave London without calling in Connaught Place?" she demanded abruptly.

"I thought I had. That night in your bedroom, after the *tziganes* party at the New Café."

"You left the country without a word of farewell."

Charles leaned toward her. "Because I couldn't bear to live there any longer. In constant sight of you. Unable to touch your skin or speak to you. Don't you know what hell it was?"

"Naturally I know," she whispered. "Do you think I'm made of stone?"

"I had waited. Hoping for some change on your part—some sign—and when it never came I was afraid of what I might do." He glanced away from her, through the tiny fiacre window at the curtain of snow. "I had to get out of Britain. Having made that decision—knowing that you had made yours—I thought a clean break best."

"It felt like a slap to the face. When I understood you were gone . . ."

"You had it in your power to call me back in an instant." His unyielding gaze swept her face, the kiss of her chinchilla collar where it met her chin, the piquant hat perched over her temple. He touched her cheek lightly. His fingers were cold with the winter and Paris. "You knew the terms. So I ask you again, Lady Randolph: *Why have you come to France?*"

She drew an uneven breath, fighting her panic and the desire to feel his arms around her. "Charles—I need your help."

His expression changed; instantly he dropped his hand. "In what way?"

"There's no one else I can ask. . . . No one I really trust."

He laughed sharply.

"Don't," she said in a stifled voice. "I have allowed no one alive so deep into my heart as you."

He was silent, assessing. Then he nodded. "Where are you staying?"

"The Hôtel des Deux Mondes, on the Avenue de l'Opera."

"That's on my way home." He frowned. "I thought titled Englishwomen always stayed at the Grand—or the Meurice?"

"I'm not really titled. Not really English. I can't bear to overlook the Tuileries . . . that vast empty scar where Eugénie's palace used to be. . . . *Besides,* one meets too many people one knows, in such places."

"And you want to be . . . unmet?"

"So far as is possible. Yes."

He smiled at her faintly, his eyes still watchful. "And yet your face, once seen, can never be forgotten. If we are to talk, we need someplace private. Will you dine with me before I return you to your hotel?"

She glanced down at her carriage gown and fur cloak. "I'm not dressed to dine."

"Neither am I. But this is Paris. No one will ask impertinent questions." He thrust open the fiacre door and said to the driver, *"Allons. Quai des Grands Augustins, s'il vous plaît."*

Charles took her to Lapérouse, on the very edge of the Seine's Left Bank, where generations of lovers had found refuge in discreet *salons privés,* small private dining cabinets lined with etched mirrors and red damask and mural-painted panels. He was not so unwise as to ask for one of these—it would ruin Jennie if she were seen entering one of them. Instead he secured a table upstairs with a view of the Seine. The Île de la Cité filled the river beyond the windows: the buildings of the Conciergerie where Marie Antoinette had waited for death, and farther downstream, the cathedral of Notre-Dame, gently lit in the greenish glow of gaslight.

"None of your friends will find you here," Charles promised her. "The English only dine in their hotels. French restaurants are too risky for them."

Jennie knew he was right. She was free tonight of English fears. Exhilaration filled her the way a fresh gust of wind unexpectedly fills a sail. She looked around at tables given over to chic Frenchmen and their women, exquisitely dressed and coiffed. This was the Paris she remembered from childhood. It had been ruthlessly overlaid in her mind with images of destruction and violence. But that darkness was gone. She smiled without being entirely aware of it.

Charles said, "Praise God."

"What?"

"I thought you'd never smile again. Tell me what's happened."

She reached impulsively for his hand. "Not yet. Pour me champagne, Charles."

They shared perfect foie gras and langoustines; sole meunière and roasted lamb; salad with shaved black truffles. With the sole they had a respectable Sancerre and with the lamb a *premier cru* Bordeaux. They talked of Paris, as only two people who love that immortal city can talk: about riding through the Bois in the cold hour just after dawn. Walking the narrower streets of the Latin Quarter while a cello's strains drifted through an open window. They talked about nights at the Opéra and stag hunting at Fontainebleau, which had become a French artillery school now that it was no longer a royal château. Jennie told Charles how as a girl of sixteen she had ridden through the Compiègne woods in the company of Napoleon III, dressed in the Emperor's required green-and-gold livery. In ten days, she would be thirty-three.

They talked of chestnut trees, which were slowly returning to the siege-ravaged boulevards, and of the art within the Louvre's walls. Jennie mentioned her progress in painting and how Winston had asked for his own paint box. She did not tell Charles that she had turned his portrait to the attic wall at Connaught Place— the portrait she loved, with his collar undone and his eyes caressing her.

He told stories about his horses, and the hopes he had of a certain three-year-old filly he thought might go the distance at Longchamp that spring.

He did not mention the past, or the current state of his heart.

Neither of them discussed politics.

Finally, as the demitasse was served and she declined a sweet, Charles asked her again.

"What has happened, Jennie?"

Her pulse quickened at the use of her first name.

"A good deal. You told me once that you followed my husband's career—and reported to your superiors."

"Yes."

"Is that still true?"

He cracked open the walnut he'd been turning between his fingers. "What do you think?"

She drew a sharp breath. "Then you know. That Randolph resigned last week from Government. He gave up both his posts—the leadership of the House and the Treasury portfolio. Without warning. Without explanation."

Charles studied the walnut's shell, its brainlike folds. "Three days before Christmas. Yes. It was in all the newspapers."

His voice was casual, as though he weren't talking about the end of Jennie's world. The crushing loss of all she'd worked for, at Sandringham and in the glittering salons of London, on the hustings during campaigns and through countless hours in the Speaker's Gallery. When she continued to stare at him, stricken to silence by all that was still unsaid, his eyes flicked over her curiously.

"You had no warning?"

"None." Her voice wobbled, nearly broke. "I learned about Randolph's resignation from the *Times*. Do you know how infuriating that was?"

He set down the walnut and dusted off his fingers. "It was certainly unthinking of him."

"He'd been to visit the Queen at Windsor, that last Friday. He dined with her, talked with her, bade Her Majesty good night—and never even *hinted* he meant to resign. But he wrote his letter to Salisbury before bed, on Windsor Castle paper. Infernal cheek, the newspapers called it."

"Well, your husband has always been reckless. And he just returned to London the next morning? As though he hadn't tossed a match in a hayloft?"

She bit her lip. "He made himself scarce that Saturday—traveled directly from Windsor to the Carlton Club. We met at a production of *School for Scandal* that night, but Randy said very little about his Windsor visit—only natural, I thought, in a public place. He left after the first act. I know now that he went to the offices of the *Times* and handed the editor a copy of his resignation." She drew a shaky breath. "It was printed in the morning edition."

"And be damned to Lord Salisbury," Charles observed.

"The PM never had time to answer Randolph's letter." Jennie took a sip of coffee; it was hot and rich, utterly unlike the swill she got in London. "Charles, he dashed himself down from a great height! It was an act of sheer madness. He says the Government forced his hand, by rejecting his budget. But *damn* his *insane* impulsiveness! Surely he might have found a compromise?"

"Compromise? That is not a word I associate with Lord Randolph," Charles said dismissively. "In point of fact, he committed political suicide. But that was always going to happen. Wasn't it?"

"You think so?" Jennie asked, startled.

"I'm certain of it. Randolph has always had a death wish. Why else would he have married *you*?"

The depth of his bitterness was like a slap in the face. But Jennie knew she deserved it. She had forced open a wound he'd struggled for years to heal. Her sudden appearance in Paris was brutally selfish. Unforgivable.

But as she stared at Charles, desire in every cell of her body, she regretted absolutely nothing.

# CHAPTER THIRTY-ONE

She was acutely conscious of his body next to hers in the closeness of the cab as they rolled toward the Hôtel des Deux Mondes. Aware of the silent rise and fall of his chest, of the tautness of his thigh as it deliberately did not touch hers. The tenseness of his gloved hands, which rested on his knees. The interior of the fiacre was turbulent with thwarted emotion.

But when Charles spoke, his dispassionate tone chilled her.

"Your husband burned his bridges. After barely five months in Government. He must have been very sure he was finished with politics. Must have hated them, in fact."

"Quite the reverse," Jennie retorted, her gaze fixed on the lights of the quay beyond the carriage window. "All Randy's ever dreamed of is being Prime Minister of Great Britain. He expected Commons to rise up when he resigned, and demand that he replace Salisbury."

She felt Charles smile in the darkness. "But instead?"

"The PM merely named another man to replace Randolph," Jennie faltered.

A snort of derision. Charles had grown cynical in the years since they had last met, she realized. No matter. They lived in cynical times.

"You asked for my help, Lady Randolph?"

Distant, again. He must be put off by her obvious distress at her husband's difficulties. Charles could have no idea how desperately she longed for him—the unswerving presence in her life that had once made her feel joyous . . . and loved . . .

"He's gone missing."

"What do you mean?"

"Randolph has simply vanished. *Again.*" She tore her eyes from the passing streets and looked at his profile, just visible in the darkness. The straight line of his nose. The jut of his brow, and the fall of curls over it. Impossible not to yearn to touch them. "He hared off to Vienna a few months ago, with Tommie Trafford. But this time, it was Tommie who told me Randy was gone. I thought he was still lying on his library couch, receiving condolences from his mourners. . . ."

"I'm afraid I don't see—"

"Why I want your help?" she interrupted. "Of course you don't! You don't know my husband. Randy only comes to Paris when he wants to die. It's his version of Hell, Charles. He throws himself into the lowest circles and tries to immolate himself. And I don't know where to begin to look for him—"

"Why bother?" Charles demanded. The killing coldness still in his voice. But he was looking at her now. "He's treated you shamefully."

"Yes," she admitted. "But that's been true for years. I've been fighting for my family's survival any way I can—and Randy's just smashed years of work to pieces. I could strangle him, I'm so angry."

"And hurt, I daresay." Charles edged closer, his shoulder brushing hers. A pulse of current, instantly, where they touched. "*Jennie.* When will you stop trying to save the bastard?"

"I have two sons. Two lovely boys who've done nothing to deserve this abandonment. I refuse to let their lives be ruined by a suicidal father."

The gleam of his eyes in the darkness. "You're that worried?"

"I am." Panic rose in her chest. She forced it down.

Charles sank back against the hard leather seat. "Very well. You must tell me the truth. If I'm to help you."

"Do you honestly think I've ever told you anything else?"

"There's all you haven't said," he pointed out. "These circles of Hell—what do you imagine they hold?"

"Whores," she answered succinctly. "It's impossible for me to enter such a place. I would never get past the door."

"Even if you knew where the best houses were. In Paris."

"Or the worst. I think those are the kind Randolph likes."

Charles laughed sourly. "You're certain you want to find him?"

It would be so much easier to do nothing. To wait at home for the prodigal to return. Or be found dead in a Paris gutter, God help him. But Jennie had weighed and rejected those options days ago.

"I have to, Charles. His life is at stake." She grasped her gloved hands together to keep from reaching for him. "Even if he's in no physical danger, Randolph's not thinking clearly. He risks utter social ruin if the wrong person discovers him in such despicable circumstances. You know how recognizable he is. And how the press follows him . . ."

"You want me to run him down in a whorehouse and say that his *wife* sent me?"

The fiacre drew up to the curb. She did not reply.

"You don't ask much, do you?" Charles said.

Gentry had turned down her bed and built up the fire. The maid had been given a cot in the dressing room that formed a part of Jennie's suite, and when her mistress entered the room she instantly appeared, a piece of mending in her hands and a pair of spectacles perched on her nose.

"I'm very tired," Jennie said tersely. "Once you've helped me out of this gown, you may leave me. I shan't want anything further tonight."

Gentry set down the mending, removed her thimble, and

swiftly unbuttoned the back of Jennie's dress. "When you didn't return to dress for dinner, I was that worried you were set upon by thieves. Tossed in the river with your throat cut, my lady, and how I was to manage the bill here at the hotel, nor break it to the young masters back home, I didn't dare think."

Jennie made no answer. She knew Gentry considered it indecent to travel alone in foreign parts, but she had not explained her errand to her maid. Gentry would approve even less of a woman who chased after her straying husband.

"And not a word left with the hotel porter, which you might have done if you'd spared a thought."

The gown slid to the floor; Jennie stepped out of it. Gentry gathered up the mass of silk and wool and draped it over a chair. Jennie felt her fingers an instant later, undoing the tapes that held her half bustle at her hips. This folded together like an accordion and was propped at the chair's foot. Then Gentry's fingers again, loosening her corset laces. Jennie's waist still measured eighteen inches, despite two pregnancies. She drew air deep into her lungs as the confining whalebone eased. Gentry placed a silk dressing gown over her shoulders and waited until she was seated before a mirror.

"I made do with some soup and cold fowl," the maid said grudgingly as she loosened the pins in Jennie's hair. "They've a good enough servants' dining parlor near the kitchens, and the folk come from all over. Not as many from home as I'd like, but respectable. Few of our sort are wishful to leave home in this season."

Jennie closed her eyes as Gentry began to brush her hair. The maid's strokes were swift and thorough. It was the one habit that recalled childhood, Dobbie moving from each of the four girls in the Newport nursery, *shooshing away the cobwebs,* as she liked to say, their scalps tingling and their minds drowsy. Camille's curls looped around Dobbie's fingers. The translucent gold of the nautilus shell the Recluse had tucked in her coffin—

Jennie did not tell Gentry that she had come to the Deux
Mondes because it was Randolph's favorite hotel in Paris and she
had hoped to find his scrawling signature in the guest register. She
had looked; it wasn't there. Neither was the careless *Mr. Spencer.*
The clerk at Reception had shown no interest in her name.

The maid left her.

Jennie settled herself in bed and took up a book—Rimbaud's
*Illuminations,* published a few months before. She had been longing to read it, and had purchased a copy almost as soon as she
reached France. But now the lines of poetry swam before her eyes.
Shadows of memory loomed in the corners of her room.

She had entered this hotel only once before—as a girl of twenty,
in the spring of 1874, impatient for the man she was determined to
marry.

## *February 1874*

It was unusual for an engagement to run six months without a
wedding date. Jennie was allowed to write to Randolph. And he
found a way to visit Paris in February, after he won his seat in Parliament.

Clara Jerome invited him to dine at her comfortable home in
the Rue de Presbourg. But the visit was short—Randolph was expected in London for the opening of Parliament. And the Jeromes
were being mulish about the marriage settlements.

Jennie did not argue with her mother anymore or write another
letter to Papa. It was time to take matters fearlessly into her own
hands. Heart hammering, she slipped out of the garden entrance
of her mother's house after breakfast, while Clara was still dressing. In a matter of minutes, she was at the Hôtel des Deux Mondes.

Randolph's valet, Walden, opened the door of his suite and stared
at Jennie in surprise.

"Darling?" Randolph said.

He was in a silk dressing gown, paisley figures in scarlet and blue, seated at a small breakfast table. He had been bathed and shaved and already wore a white shirt and collar beneath the gown.

"Walden, fetch my laundry from the nether regions, there's a good chap."

"Very good, my lord." The valet's eyes shifted uneasily to Jennie's, but he was not in the employ of a duke's son for nothing. He moved noiselessly through the door and Randolph made sure it was locked behind him.

"What are you doing here, Jeanette? Trying to provoke a scandal?"

"Yes." Jennie stood defiantly in the center of the room and looked around her, intensely conscious of how masculine Randolph's things were. Leather-bound books. Tobacco. A traveling case with whisky in it. Like Papa's library on Madison Square, another sanctum she had violated.

"What is it?" He reached for her hand. "Has something happened?"

"No. It's just . . ." Color bloomed in her cheeks. She could not say to him: *Mamma is hateful. Mamma is against us.* "You're leaving tonight. And it could be months before I see you again. If ever! They may succeed, Randolph."

"Who?"

"Everyone. All the people ranged against us. What if we are parted forever?"

"Would that make you unhappy?"

"I shall die if I can't be with you!"

He reached for her narrow waist. She clutched at his lapel, turning her face up to his. And then he kissed her.

It was the first time she felt hunger in Randolph. The first hint of what she would later identify, as a more experienced woman, as passion. Perhaps he responded because she was so eager, so untutored—so clearly a creature to be molded to his need. He prolonged the kiss and allowed his hands to roam across her pelvis, her narrow shoulders, the small of her back. She was encased in so many clothes. Contained in a structure of whalebone and cloth and steel. Her absurd hat came between his forehead and her own. She reached up and tore it off, though her careful chignon was destroyed in the process.

She slid her hands beneath the edge of his silk dressing gown and wrestled it off his shoulders. It pooled brightly at his feet.

He was breathing quickly but his expression was strange—almost disgust. Surely she was wrong? Surely he did not *despise* her? She thought suddenly how *male* that seemed—that he should be capable of detachment when she herself felt swept helplessly into a raging current.

"How long will your valet be gone?" she whispered.

"I've locked him out." He met her eyes then, his own dilating slightly. "What do you want, Jennie?"

"You."

"You're sure?"

"Help me, Randolph."

He undid her myriad small buttons. She loosened his collar with inexpert fingers. So many clothes. She found his skin before he found hers—shifts beneath petticoats beneath corsets that must be removed. They made a bed of them. Their hands slid over each other. Jennie was surprised at how fragile Randolph's bones felt beneath her fingers—as delicate and pliable as the baleen in her stays.

"I have never wanted anything so much as you," he muttered.

And in her determination and need, she believed him.

At the end of that March, Clara Jerome suddenly dropped every objection she held to the match between Lord Randolph Churchill and her daughter Jennie. The wedding was hurriedly set for

April 15, Clarita's birthday. It was also the birthday of Duchess Fanny, but Her Grace had no intention of wasting it in Paris. Randolph might run his ruinous course without his parents. She and the Duke would remain at Blenheim, and content themselves with a telegram.

Clara Jerome had set her heart on a large Society wedding. Seven hundred of England's notables, at St. George's, Hanover Square. She settled instead for a ceremony at the British embassy chapel in Paris. The guests were an intimate group, composed of the Jeromes and three of Randolph's sisters—the older, married ones—who crossed the Channel for the occasion. Randolph's brother Blandford came, without his wife. Sir Francis Knollys, secretary to the Prince of Wales, stood up as best man.

Jennie's trousseau had been ordered with a different wedding in mind. Piles of embroidered lingerie, seven outrageously fetching hats, twenty-three dresses, and countless shoes, shawls, capes, and gloves. All heroically finished in record time by the seamstresses who slaved for Charles Frederick Worth.

Which was the main reason Jennie was hustled off to the British embassy chapel: Madame Worth, the couturier's French wife, had discovered her secret.

She was being fitted for her wedding gown, white satin with a long train and rivers of expensive Alençon lace. Satin was very new in 1874, as far as milliners' stuffs were concerned—an invention of Worth's and the silk weavers of Lyon.

This was Jennie's second fitting, the third week in March. She had chosen the gown soon after Randolph left Paris for Parliament, on the superstitious hope that if her dress was ordered, nothing would stop the marriage. But something was wrong. The *vendeuse* in attendance eyed the girl fitting the pins in the seams of Jennie's bodice. She was letting out the delicate fabric across the breasts and pelvis.

"My word, Jeanette," Clara said crossly as she watched in the long mirror. "Have you been indulging yourself on cakes and bonbons? Or did this stupid girl take your measurements wrong?"

The *vendeuse* made her way to Madame Worth.

Madame came on noiseless feet, magnificent in pale lilac. She stood silently at Clara's shoulder, studying the girl's body, the flush of her cheeks.

"When is the wedding to be, Miss Jerome?" she asked softly.

Jennie shrugged. "We have not yet decided. Before June, I hope—or this satin will suffocate me."

"Decidedly before June," Madame murmured. The girl was either abysmally ignorant or shameless. "Mrs. Jerome, would you take coffee with me in the salon? We must discuss the lamentable error in your daughter's fitting."

# CHAPTER THIRTY-TWO

When Charles left her in the Avenue de l'Opera, he gave his fiacre driver a simple order.

"Number twelve Rue Chabanais."

The most famous brothel in Paris was only a few short blocks from Jennie's hotel. Run by an Irishwoman known as Madame Kelly, it was a luxurious and sprawling townhouse fully licensed for business. Prostitution was legal and closely monitored in France. Sex was one of Paris's greatest confections, and the entire world knew it. Tourist guides like *The Pretty Women of Paris,* by an anonymous Englishman, and *Le Guide Rose,* by a Frenchman, were sold out in European bookstores. Precious copies passed from hand to hand among upper-class men and the servants who procured for them. The pocket-sized books provided addresses and descriptions of the principal whorehouses, according to personal inclination or fetish, and physical descriptions of individual courtesans—the *grandes horizontales,* as they were called—who might be kept for a month or a year if one had the money to spend.

Madame Kelly was backed by a tightly knit group of investors, most of them members of the exclusive Jockey-Club de Paris. Le Chabanais, as Kelly's *maison close* was called, had cost millions of francs, but there were rich profits to be made from this world. It housed thirty young women of every physical description and taste, who entertained their wealthy clientele in exotically decorated rooms—Moorish, Japanese, Hindu. They charged breathless fees, and Madame Kelly's investors pocketed most of them.

Bertie, the Prince of Wales, had his own room at Le Chabanais with his coat of arms mounted over the bed. Charles had glimpsed him there only the month before, mingling with friends and elegant, if loosely gowned, young women in the house's main salon. The Prince had a copper bathtub, too, that was filled with champagne at his request; he liked to bathe two girls at once in the sparkling wine. Near the tub was a special upholstered chair that suggested something out of an operating theater—the back reclined, and there were stirrups for a lady's feet. Bertie had designed it himself. He preferred to stand between the stirrups when he ministered to one of Madame Kelly's girls; his bulk was best accommodated upright.

Charles paid off the driver and approached the door, drawing a token from his pocket—a gold coin engraved with the image of a grotto on one side and *No. 12* on the other. He handed this to the porter, and Le Chabanais, like Ali Baba's treasure cave, was opened to him.

The entrance hall was carved out of stone to resemble the yawning mouth of a cavern. It was lit by torches set into niches on either side. There were fur skins underfoot, tossed opulently over marble. Charles removed his hat and coat and handed them to a bare-breasted Nubian slave; her tawny skin gleamed with oil and her eyes were rimmed with kohl.

"Where is Madame Kelly?" Charles asked.

"She is not to be disturbed."

Charles drew a card from his case and offered it. "Please. Beg her to join me for coffee and cognac."

"Monsieur le Comte is quite early." The girl eyed him dubiously. "Madame never takes cognac at this hour."

Charles handed her a franc. "Oblige me."

She swiftly tucked the note behind the leather cord that bound her waist and left him.

Charles wandered into the main salon. This was a high-ceilinged space with low couches and cushions scattered about the floor between the double fireplaces, which were burning brightly. The gas jets in cut crystal were kept low, bathing the women lounging throughout the room in something like moonlight. Most looked at him languidly as he passed; they could sense he was uninterested in sport this evening. Some were smoking from long cigarette holders; others were glancing through magazines. All were jeweled, exquisitely or nakedly dressed, their hair elaborately coiffed or flowing freely. Some were in costume. Some wore only corsets and stockings.

A girl with brilliant gold hair and sumptuous breasts wore nothing at all except a pair of high-heeled pink slippers. She crouched on her hands and knees in the center of the room, a massive gold chain looped around her neck. Her buttocks were perfect: smooth and muscled as a stallion's. Another girl, equally naked except for a pair of high black boots, held the long end of the chain like a leash. She was spanking the blonde's sleek bottom with a rolled copy of *Le Figaro* while two men in white tie and tailcoats watched.

"Monsieur le Comte."

The scent of lilies of the valley; a voice as cool as springwater. Charles turned. "Madame."

She offered her hand. He bowed low and kissed it.

Alexandrine Jouannet had been born in Dublin and she had taken the surname of the Irishman who deflowered her at fifteen, but no one would mistake her for anything but a Frenchwoman. She was tall and lean in a daring black gown that was emphatically *not* from Worth. She had expressive features and artistic, long-fingered hands carelessly dotted with emeralds. Her eyes were wide and violet and thickly lashed. Her nose and chin were harsh. She was a *jolie laide,* a beautiful ugly woman, with vivid hair the color of mahogany. She appealed to young men searching for an older woman to adore and to those who found most women distasteful. Her discernment in matters of business was unquestioned.

"Welcome to Le Chabanais. You wished to see me? You have an acute and *particular* desire, perhaps?"

*I do,* Charles thought, with a fleeting sense of Jennie's skin as it had looked in the candlelight of Lapérouse. *And nothing you can offer will satisfy it.*

"Will you do me the honor of sitting down for a moment?" he said. "A little conversation. On the most discreet terms."

"But of course."

She led him through a cut velvet portiere in the far corner of the room. He recognized the fabric as from the Venetian silk house of Bevilacqua, a weaver his mother patronized. There was a table and two chairs in the mirrored alcove. The small space was lit by branches of candles on the wall and on the floor. A carafe of wine and two glasses rested on the table.

"Your every need is anticipated," she said simply, and offered him a seat. "Château Haut-Brion?"

"No, thank you. May I smoke?"

"Naturally."

Charles drew a gold case from his pocket; cigarettes were very chic now in France, only recently mass-produced and sold to the masses. But like his father, he still preferred Cuban cigars. He clipped the end of his Havana with a pocketknife and bent over the flame of the candle to light the tight wand of tobacco, mouthing the smoke as it rose.

"I shan't waste your time," he said to Alexandrine. "You've given me too much already."

*"Pas de tout,"* she said, and snapped her fingers.

The Nubian peered around the edge of the silk velvet portiere. *"Oui, madame?"*

"Bring me cognac. Monsieur is smoking tonight."

No Frenchwoman would desecrate Haut-Brion with tobacco,

Charles reflected; it had been his subtle test. A measure of whether Alexandrine Jouannet could be trusted.

"How may I serve you?" she asked him, as the girl with the oiled skin and the kohled eyes poured her three fingers of brandy.

"I'm in search of a dear friend," Charles replied. "Urgently. I simply wish to know whether you've seen him."

Alexandrine took a sip of amber liquid. Charles watched as she rolled it about her tongue. She was inviting him to kiss her, he knew; but he restrained himself. Seduction was second nature to her, every encounter a subtle contest for power.

She set down her glass and reached for Charles's cigar. This, too, a form of seduction; the Havana as phallic substitute. Her lips caressed it. She drew deeply and swallowed the smoke.

When he did not respond, she said abruptly, "You understand that the sort of discretion I give to you, I give to all my clients?"

"Yes. That is why Le Chabanais is unrivaled."

"How, then, can you ask me to betray your friend?"

"With an appeal to your compassion. I believe him to be in personal danger. It is vital that I find him."

Alexandrine waited. She continued to smoke Charles's cigar.

"I shall, of course, make it worth your while."

"Monsieur understands the conventions."

"What price do you put on your discretion?"

Her eyes narrowed. She studied him. "I could ask for money."

"Of course. And up to a certain limit, I would agree."

"Or . . ."

There was a pause. Alexandrine sipped her cognac.

"Or?" Charles said.

"An introduction to certain figures in Vienna. Who might be interested in investing in a lucrative business, managed with the utmost professionalism."

"You're seeking to expand?"

"Diversify, let us say." She set down her glass. "To expand, I need merely buy the neighboring property. Whereas to attract an entirely new clientele—one drawn from St. Petersburg rather than London—I must have an entirely new foundation."

"I see."

Charles had no interest in serving as Madame Kelly's noble pimp in the land of his forefathers. But time was passing and he had not even asked his questions yet. Somewhere, Jennie was sliding between lavender-scented sheets and turning out her light. . . .

He drained his brandy. "I am happy to consider it—and explore the notion further—in deference to my friend's considerable danger. Now, Madame Kelly, will you tell me if you have lately seen Lord Randolph Churchill?"

# CHAPTER THIRTY-THREE

The vast structure of glass and iron that housed the central Paris market of Les Halles came to life in darkness, three hours before dawn. Fires flared in coal braziers and stall keepers brewed coffee. Burly carters and stout ponies drew heavy drays from the countryside into Paris, where butchers' apprentices and market porters unloaded crates from the backs of wagons. They kicked their way through straw and horse dung to the brightly lit pavilions, where they set up pyramids of root vegetables and hung trussed rabbits from their paws. Poulterers unloaded wire mesh crates of squawking fowl that would be plucked and boiled within hours. Set out on trestle tables were sacks of lentils and dried peas and rice and tea; roasted coffee beans; saffron and cardamom seeds and milled corn and olives. A thousand scents mingled and perfumed the frigid night air—animal, vegetable, mineral. The din was ferocious.

A Renaissance church, Église Saint-Eustache, rose at the market's edge, and in the streets surrounding it young wrestlers grappled in the light of open fires for anyone willing to place bets on their bodies. Cafés served stews and fried potatoes and bottles of wine all night long, and at the *buvettes*—makeshift market bars set up inside Les Halles—the porters and sellers snatched quick glasses of cognac. Prostitutes, both male and female, worked the shadows. So did pickpockets and hungry children.

To Randolph Churchill, the quarter's noise was almost unbearable. He baffled his ears with a goose-down pillow and slept poorly, regardless; during his few days in Paris he had been crippled by constant pain in his joints and muscles. His legs refused to obey him. His hands shook with palsy. His sheets were damp with sweat, although the bed itself was luxurious enough—a four-posted affair at the rear of a house on the Rue Rambuteau, at the northern end of Les Halles. He had come to it immediately upon his arrival in France two days before Christmas, but he had lost track of how long he had been lying here in the semidarkness. He refused to allow the shades to be raised. Night followed night as he burned with fever.

Occasionally a boy of about thirteen peered around the door and stared at him, or an older one in his twenties, hair carefully pomaded and skin freshly scented with musk, sidled into the room with a tray. Randolph declined everything except *premier cru* Bordeaux. He thought the alcohol might kill whatever was killing him.

Charles Kinsky halted outside the house on the Rue Rambuteau a little after three o'clock that morning. The numbers of the address set in faience over the doorway were different from the blue and white ones that graced most houses in the French capital. They were exaggeratedly large, colored green and red, and bordered with yellow rosettes. Places of prostitution in Paris were discreet out of respect for their neighbors, but all of them signaled their existence with gaudy address tiles.

It was the third house Charles had visited that night. Alexandrine had sent him about his business as soon as he uttered Churchill's name.

"Lord Randolph?" She'd smiled at him with her ugly mouth and startling eyes. She shook her head. "That one finds nothing to amuse at Le Chabanais."

Alexandrine suggested he drop into Miss Betty's first if he wanted word of the Duke's son. Miss Betty was English herself and her *maison close* sat directly across from the side entrance to the Église Saint-Sulpice, on the Left Bank. It counted numerous priests among its clientele, their clerical garments flapping like crows' wings as they hurried across the street. Betty understood their tortured relationship with pleasure and sin, guilt and temptation. She offered rooms especially designed for Catholic tastes. She specialized in mock crucifixion.

Charles gained admittance and made his way swiftly through the parlors, with their mournful subjects, and lingered in the doorway of a firelit chamber. A nude young woman lashed a whip over the back of a prelate violently enough to draw blood. He thought that might appeal to a man like Randolph, schooled at Eton.

But when Charles conferred with Betty, who comported herself as a nun and ceaselessly fingered the beads of a rosary, she, too, shook her head. "I 'aven't seen Churchill." The accent was pure East End. "You might try the Satyr for *that* one. Near the market, it is."

He had not expected children in this place, although later—when he was alone and able to consider all he had done, not just now on Jennie's behalf but in the course of his male life—he admitted this was foolish. Girls were everywhere in whorehouses. They were apprenticed. They served as acolytes at a young age, and sometimes—for a special price—they were sacrificed to the whims or needs of men before they were fully grown. Why should it be any different with boys?

But he had not expected it. Choirboys with angelic faces, slim arms, wide eyes. Boys of eight and ten. Some were dusky-skinned in a way that might tempt colonial overlords. Two led him from the Satyr's entrance down a brief hall to a firelit salon at the far end, where the *maison close*'s proprietor received: a former British officer of the Rifle Brigade named Hobhouse-Jones.

He was tall, correct, mustachioed in a way that might inspire confidence at the card tables of a dozen St. James clubs. He was also equipped with a sword at his belt and a pistol in a holster. Charles wondered how often the Satyr had been attacked. He offered the man his card. Not the diplomatic one but the card with only his title and crest.

"Count Kinsky," Hobhouse-Jones mused as he fingered it. "It has never been my pleasure to serve anyone of your house. What may I do for you?"

"The matter is delicate."

"I see. Please, will you take a chair?"

Charles remained standing. "I am in search of a dear friend on a family matter of some personal urgency. It is vital that I find him and communicate news of extreme import. I have reason to believe he may enjoy your hospitality at present. A Mr. Spencer? From London?"

"Mr. Spencer," Hobhouse-Jones repeated slowly. "That is not a name *commonly* used."

"By a duke's son, no. Only when his lordship is anxious to deflect notice."

"Indeed." The man's eyes shifted from Charles's card to his face. "And why do you search for Mr. Spencer? In place of, let us say, a member of his noble family?"

"Let us say that I have been seconded to the duty by one who commands my soul and allegiance, at the highest possible level."

Charles was royalty himself, after all. Let Hobhouse-Jones think it was Queen Victoria, not Jennie, who had sent him searching for Randolph.

The words transfixed the brothel keeper. He did not speak for a moment, but twisted Charles's card in his long, nervous fingers. "Of course. I beg your pardon—Mr. Spencer's intimacy with Government..."

"Take me to him now," Charles said.

———

He had glimpsed Randolph Churchill in the early hours of the morning on other occasions, of course: at the Carlton Club or White's, as he gambled at cards. But nothing could have prepared either of them for this particular encounter.

It was the pomaded twenty-year-old who led Charles along a crimson-carpeted corridor with flaring gas jets to the rear bedroom on the second floor. He scratched delicately at the door. There was no answer and the youth had no intention of waiting for one; he turned the knob and ushered Charles inside.

He waited for his eyes to adjust to the dim interior. Two windows were cracked open and a draft of icy air wafted in a current through the room. The remains of a coal fire burned low. A figure in the bed pushed itself upright and growled a few words.

They were unintelligible.

"He cannot speak clearly," the youth informed Charles *sotto voce* in French. "A convulsion of some kind. We have done our best, monsieur."

"Leave us," Charles ordered, and handed his guide a few centimes.

The door closed behind him.

The man on the bed struggled to free himself from the sheets, still growling in hoarse syllables. Charles could see, now, that he was bare above the waist. A slight figure, with a hollow chest and rickety shoulders.

Charles reached for a lamp on a nearby table and turned up the flame. And found himself facing the muzzle of a gun.

The sick man had found a pistol somewhere in the sheets and was leveling it at him, still barking nonsense. The gun shook uncontrollably in his hand. Charles felt a sudden spasm of fear: at least when he'd faced down Jennie in similar circumstances, he'd suspected she was an accurate shot.

He lunged at Randolph and wrenched the pistol from his hand.

"Kinsky!"

The first articulate word the man had managed. But distinguishable only to Charles, who had heard his surname uttered in a dozen different dialects.

He tucked the pistol safely into his coat. "Kinsky indeed. I've come to fetch you a doctor, Randolph."

# CHAPTER THIRTY-FOUR

When he called at the Hôtel des Deux Mondes the following morning, Charles found that Jennie had already gone out. He asked to speak to her maid, and was met in the lobby by a tearful Gentry. They were old acquaintances.

"Oh, my lord," she said as she curtseyed, "can't you persuade my lady to stop gallivanting alone around this wretched city? A quiet spot of dressmaking was what I thought we'd come for, although why such business had to be done at Christmastide I *couldn't* say, when most decent folk are happy enough to be close to their own hearths and in the hands of their dearest kin—but if she meant to have her measurements taken, then she did ought to have carried me along with her to Mr. Worth, for I'm sure I'm a better judge of fit and quality than he is."

"Do you know where her ladyship has gone?"

"To them painters," Gentry said darkly. "Wild she was to see them, and nothing would do but she must set out immediately after breakfast, on account of the light. Or so she said. Insisted it would be better in the morning, and quite gone if she waited until a decent hour. Although the way such people carry on, I don't suppose they know what *decent* is."

"Which painters?"

Gentry shrugged. "I can't make out foreign names. But I wrote down the direction, in case Lady Randolph was kidnapped, and the gendarmes did have to be sent for."

The scrap of paper she handed Charles was printed in block

capitals, *128 b, Bull Clishy,* which he rightly interpreted as standing for 128 *bis,* Boulevard de Clichy. An address in Montmartre. He pressed a few coins into Gentry's hand, but she shook her head.

"Thank you, sir, but I've no use for foreign money. It's good enough for me that you mean to go after her."

"Buy yourself some chocolate," he ordered, and left.

There were any number of artists' studios in the quarter known as Pigalle, but women of Jennie's social class were rare. This was a district that slept by day and came alive at night, full of *caf'concs,* as they were called: song-and-dance cabarets that served a raw clientele. Charles's fiacre driver carried him north from the Place Pigalle to the very end of the Boulevard de Clichy, hard by the quiet Montmartre Cemetery. On the hillside above, the vanes of numerous windmills turned in the stiff breeze, grinding grain and pressing grapes. The quarter remained working class.

Number 128 *bis*—the word indicated a secondary entrance to a street address—led to a narrow stair rising straight up, six stories. The hall smelled of fish. Somewhere, a baby wailed. No carriage stood at the curb for Jennie and there was no sign of her on the paving. There was a street brazier of burning coals, however, and a man turning sausages over the fire.

"Do you know whether any painters live there?" Charles asked him.

The sausage turner grunted. "Are there rats in a sewer, monsieur? This is Montmartre."

"Did a lady enter in the past hour?"

The black eyes flicked up to meet his. Took in his impeccable top hat, the well-cut coat he wore to the embassy, his dove-gray gloves and ebony stick. Took in, as well, his flawless French and something not quite French about him. "I couldn't say. Would you like a sausage?"

"No." Charles handed the man a few centimes. "Where did the lady go?"

He pocketed the money. "Fifth floor."

Charles told the fiacre to wait. He entered the smelly hall and began to climb, conscious of the street cook's stare as he mounted the steps. He was tired of chasing after Jennie and the men she could not control. And impatient, after only a few hours, to be with her again.

When he glimpsed her through the studio's open door, her face seemed lit from within. She was gazing at something beyond Charles's range of vision, her lips parted and a slight furrow between her darting brows. Her cheeks were faintly flushed. A ravishing face, framed in black-dyed ostrich feathers. In her eyes was an expression that recalled his time before her own easel: she was weighing shadow and light.

He stepped into the room.

It was high-ceilinged and stood far enough above its neighbors to capture the sun. On a winter day like this, the atmosphere was gray, aqueous, sterile but for the vivid color dotting the large canvases set against the walls. Jennie stood well back from them, as though she needed distance. She was marooned in an island of bare floorboards.

Her head turned at the sound of his step. Her expression changed. The rapidity of it jolted him. She had been trancelike; now she was alive.

"Charles!"

She held out her hands, gloved in black suede. He bowed low, aware that they were not alone.

"Do you know Monsieur Seurat?"

"I have not had the pleasure," he said.

"Monsieur—allow me to introduce you to *le comte* Kinsky, of the Austrian embassy," she said, in her rapid French. She led Charles to the bearded man leaning against the far wall, a narrow-shouldered, composed figure roughly his own age. "He's a neo-Impressionist," she murmured, in English this time. "A founder of the Society of Independents, along with Redon and Signac. I've been dying to see their work—Monsieur Seurat calls it *pointil-lisme*."

The names meant little to Charles. Had she asked about music, he could have given her a tour of Paris few Englishwomen were allowed, but art was another country. He watched Jennie enthuse over the large canvases. She placed smaller studies in his hands, all of them compositions of jabs and dots in myriad colors that blurred too close to the eye and resolved themselves only when viewed at a distance. A line of cliffs by the sea; a figure upright in a boat. The compositions were painstakingly detailed, complex, rigorous. Under examination, the mass of dots bewildered; everything solidified when he stepped back.

"Like dreams," Jennie mused. "Real as houses while you move through them—lost once you wake. Did you know, Charles? Monsieur Seurat tells me there are any number of *women's* studios here in Paris—where women take instruction, and paint together, as professionals. I should dearly love to visit such a place."

"Professionals?" Something in Charles baulked. "But women aren't admitted to the École des Beaux-Arts. I may have seen a few female pictures in the annual Salon . . . but do admit, Jennie—true genius is male."

Jennie threw him a smoldering look. "Not another word, you philistine."

She bought three of Seurat's studies and arranged to have them sent to her hotel. "I don't intend to show them to Randolph," she confided to Charles. "I mean to keep these in my studio, and learn from them."

Something in his face must have reached her. The glow in her eyes flickered and went out. "What is it, Charles? You don't mean . . . Have you found him?"

He inclined his head.

"Of course," she breathed. "That's why you're here. How stupid of me."

She waved in parting to Monsieur Seurat, who was busy with brown butcher's paper and twine, and swept out of the studio. Charles followed her to the street. She allowed him to help her into the fiacre and waited until he was seated beside her before she spoke. "Well?"

The horse pulled into the traffic of the Boulevard de Clichy. The noise of carriage wheels on stone was considerable; it was now nearly noon, Charles judged, and even Pigalle was awake. He leaned close to the black ostrich plumes to speak into her ear.

"I found him in a house near the market."

"A brothel, you mean?"

"Of sorts. Are you aware that your husband prefers men to women?"

*That first encounter at the Hôtel des Deux Mondes, nearly thirteen years ago. Her silk dress bunched beneath her. His hands lifting and turning her roughly onto her stomach, her breasts pinned to the floor. Her thighs, lean and muscled and boyish from hours of riding, gripped painfully in his hands. And then the thrusts, too soon, agonizing and endless, her teeth biting the crumpled silk, as he entered her from behind.*

Jennie's nostrils flared; she glanced away. "Yes."

Charles waited for her to fill the silence.

"I don't expect you to understand."

"On the contrary, I understand quite well," he said. "I have lived in the world. It's rarer for a lady to . . . recognize and accept."

She shrugged slightly, still avoiding his gaze. He realized suddenly that she was embarrassed not for Randolph but *herself*, as though it were her fault that her husband could not physically love her. As though she were not attractive enough. As though she had failed him as a woman.

"My darling," he said urgently. "I have known a number of similar stories. Both in Vienna and London. Here in Paris, even. Don't blame yourself."

"How can I not?" she burst out. "He loved me enough to *marry,* once. We came together long enough to have a child. . . . But after I discovered I was pregnant . . ."

"I am sure that for Lord Randolph, men have always mattered most." Charles did not want to prolong this conversation, have her voice all the doubts that had poisoned over a decade of marriage. "He's very ill at the moment. I called in my own doctor to examine him. How long have you known?"

"That Randolph prefers men?" She was frowning. "I just *said*—"

"That Randolph has syphilis."

He watched the color drain from her cheeks.

"That's why he opposed the Contagious Diseases Act years ago, isn't it?" he pressed. "Because one day, the Government might come to quarantine *him?*"

She glanced at Charles, could not speak. Her eyes drowning.

"Jennie—*how long have you known?*"

It was as though he had thrust a knife into her. He set his heart in stone and refused to feel.

"Since Winston's birth," she whispered. "Randolph believed himself cured when we married. He thought coupling with a virgin—it's an old wives' tale. . . ."

He grasped her shoulders, appalled. "He took your maidenhead *knowing* he had the disease?"

"He hoped my virgin blood would cure his illness! But I failed him. His symptoms recurred while I was pregnant with Winston."

*Almost thirteen years,* Charles thought savagely. Well before she had invited him into a bedroom at Sandringham or their trysts in the attics of Connaught Place. Before he had fallen so hopelessly in love with a woman who refused to love him back. She had known her husband was infected with a fatal disease. That she might be as well. She had told him nothing.

"Did he give you syphilis, Jennie?"

She shook her head. "He never touched me after that first time.

From the day we married, I seemed to physically repel him. I thought it was because pregnancy made me hideous, or that he feared damaging the child. But even after Winston's birth he remained distant. I tried to act as though I didn't care; as though he hadn't hurt me to the core. Four years ago, Randy had . . . a relapse."

"Just before I met you at Sandringham."

"The year before," she agreed. "Randolph broke out in hives—ran perilously high fevers—developed open sores on his body, and aches in all his joints. Robson Roose—Randolph's doctor—sat me down and explained exactly how it was. The name of his disease."

"You should have left him then!"

"How, in God's name? With a public statement that the rising Conservative star was, in fact, a leper? No! I wanted him *cured*. Roose had a plan—the only possible one. Randolph would take the Mercury Cure: mercury rubbed in his sores, inhaled in steam baths, taken by mouth in pastilles. We rented a house in Wimbledon for six months. I had no choice but to retire with him while he underwent treatment. Our future depended on it."

"But he wasn't cured."

She met his gaze bleakly. "The medicine was worse than the disease."

"It always is." Mercury, Charles knew, poisoned the nervous system and brain. He laughed bitterly. "Would you honestly tell me, Jennie, if you carried syphilis? Or is your whole life a series of lies? Am I already doomed?"

She stiffened and her eyes blazed. "I have been neither admirable nor respectable in our dealings together, God knows, but I would never expose you to mortal danger. I am not viciously careless with the people I love, Charles."

"You've been nothing else since the day we met!"

She gasped and her pupils dilated. In them he finally read all her pain and regret, her yearning and her pride. "Since the day we met, you've ruined me for anyone else. I go through the motions of living, Charles, and can't say why. I'm *lost*. Utterly lost. When will you find me again?"

And now it was he who was drowning.

He took her back to her hotel and made love to her in the great bed set out before the fire. A declaration of faith on a cold late-December afternoon, when all faith ought to be dead.

"I've fought you for years." He swept her into the curl of his body, beneath the eiderdown. "Tried to forget you, Jennie, with a hundred other lovely bodies. But it's your soul I'm after. Your soul I can't forget."

"No other bodies, Charles. No other soul. I tell you now what I never allowed myself to say out loud—*I love you*. Only you. Forever you."

At midnight, they heard bells all over Paris ring in the New Year. He had forgotten that it was *le Réveillon*—New Year's Eve.

"We should have champagne," he said.

"Drink to me only with thine eyes," she whispered.

"And I will pledge with mine." Ben Jonson's old song, still true. Charles's words blurred as he kissed her mouth. Still drowning.

"This French doctor of yours," Jennie asked much later. "Can he be trusted?"

"To keep your secret? Of course. He does not know Randolph's name. Only that he is a friend of mine."

"Randolph is recognizable the world over," she said despairingly. "You understand that the word *syphilis* can never be spoken?"

"Yes," Charles said. "It would end his career."

"It would destroy our whole family. His mother—she believes him to suffer only from nerves."

"And there's your place in Society," Charles suggested.

She turned her head on the pillow. "My boys. Ridiculed and

whispered about. A child can be born with the infection and develop the disease later in life—the idea haunts me. People—cruel people, vicious people, like Minnie Paget—already talk about how Win is *different*. Because he had to leave St. George's. That's why Randy sets Win at such a distance. It's nothing more nor less than *guilt*."

"The sins of the fathers." Charles twined his fingers through hers and kissed her palm. "I know. I'll pay the doctor whatever he asks to hold his tongue."

"What did he say? After he'd seen Randy?"

He cupped her cheek in his hands and met her gaze squarely. "That your husband has reached an advanced stage. The disease has begun to infect his spine. His brain. He is having difficulty walking, darling. It is hard for him to speak. Hold a spoon. The present fit will pass with more mercury—but he will not improve."

"It will only get worse." She said it flatly. "Until he dies."

"You must leave Randolph, my love. Before the disease is so obvious that all of London knows."

"I can't."

His grip on her tightened. "You must. You'll be cast out, otherwise. Suspect. *Shunned*."

She shook her head. "I've told you. Divorce is England's only sin. Having married Randolph, I have a duty toward him. And in the morning, I intend to go to him."

## PART THREE

# Happy Families

*1890—91*

# CHAPTER THIRTY-FIVE

After decades of solitary buccaneering, Leonard Jerome came back to England in the autumn of 1890 to die.

When Papa landed at Southampton just before Christmas, Jennie was shocked to see how much he had changed. He was seventy-three years old now, and his hair was white. Gout had crippled one leg, and cigars had corroded his lungs. *Galloping consumption,* Robson Roose told her once he had examined Leonard at Connaught Place. There was another name for it: *tuberculosis.*

Leonard joined his wife in her rented London home off Park Lane and spent his last days in the small spare bedroom, coughing blood into a handkerchief and dining on oysters and champagne. Leonie and Clarita, who had married Englishmen and lived in London, too, sat by his bedside and reminisced about their mad escape from Paris years ago. Jennie read aloud to Papa from *Ruff's Guide,* the British racing form, and placed bets on horses he pegged as winners.

And before he grew too weak to talk, she brought Fanny Ronalds to say goodbye.

Jennie did not invade the meeting between the two old friends, Fanny seated by Leonard's Bath chair, his gouty leg raised on a cushion. He was smoking a cigar and smiling, as though Fanny had come to him in a dream. She would always be matchless in his eyes, Jennie knew, no matter how many years fell between them.

The soprano raised her wrist and turned it before Leonard's gaze. A spattering of gemstones glinted in the sunlight, incongruous with her neat carriage dress of plum-colored wool. "The bracelet from Tiffany's you gave me, on the night of the Union League charity concert," she told him fondly. "Twenty-eight years ago, Leonard. *Before Gettysburg.* Can you believe?"

"I'd have thought you sold it long ago, to keep yourself in furs," Papa growled.

"Sell a gift from you, darling? *Never*."

As Jennie closed the door gently on the pair of them, Fanny began to sing. "Sempre libera," from *La Traviata*.

In her last hours with Papa, Jennie tried and failed to ask him about love: why some men made a symphony of women, and others had no use for them. She had never found the words to explain her marriage to her father. But as always, he sensed when she was troubled.

"What's preying on your mind, dear heart?" he asked. "Is it young Winston?"

She seized on the excuse. "He's so aimless, Papa," she managed. "Full of bravado and promises. His reports from Harrow are dreadful. Thank heaven he's in the Army section—no more Latin."

Winston had been at Harrow nearly three years now. He had entered as the last-ranked boy in the lowest form. It hurt Jennie to see the Harrovians forced to march in and out of school according to their rank—and Win at the very end of the line. Complete strangers whispered about his stupidity within her hearing when she visited her son, unaware that Jennie was his mother. *Look*, they chattered. *Dandy Randy's boy comes last of all! He must be half-mad, like his father!* Jennie longed to strike their blank and avid faces, their vicious mouths, glistening with the hunger to bully.

It was obvious, Winston's headmaster said, that he possessed high intelligence—even some brilliance. But to Jennie's immense frustration, Win could not be *made* to do what he did not *want* to do. He failed at everything except writing, but was capable of stupendous feats of memorization. He had won a prize for reciting twelve hundred lines of Macaulay's *Lays of Ancient Rome* flawlessly. Before his transfer to the Army form, Win had also been caught bartering his perfectly crafted English essays for another boy's crack Latin exercises. He had nearly been sent down for that offense. It didn't matter whether he was flogged, threatened with expulsion, or derided as an idiot by his form-mates. Winston blindly plowed his own obstinate furrow, in defiance of nearly a thousand years of English public school tradition.

"He'll turn all our hair white." Jennie managed a smile for her father; she did not want him worried, in his last weeks.

"He reminds me of myself at that age," Leonard answered. "If you leave boys alone, Jennie, they find out what they're good at."

"He seems to be good at nothing," she retorted in exasperation. "Except boasts and exaggeration. He's convinced he was born for greatness, on the basis of no excellence at all. And *desperate* for his father's attention, of course. But he goes about winning it in *precisely* the wrong way. Randolph has long since decided Win's hopeless. He's washed his hands of him."

"Randolph has washed his hands of most things," Leonard observed.

It was true; despite still being a Member of Parliament for South Paddington, her husband had spent the winter far from England, in a houseboat on the Nile, with his friend Harry Tyrwhitt-Wilson. When he returned, he planned a year of gold-prospecting in South Africa. "Randolph is too impatient, too easily angered—"

"And never at home," Papa snorted. "So the hell with him, I say. Mind Winston spends more time with Count Kinsky. He's worth ten of that husband of yours."

Perhaps, Jennie thought as she left him to sleep, Papa had answered the question she did not know how to ask. Perhaps love could not be explained. Only recognized. And cherished.

She was thinking of her father now, as she rode out over the North Downs on a fresh June morning, in her light summer habit of pale blue twill, the sun coming up. Leonard Jerome, more than anyone alive, had shaped her passion for riding, her familiarity with race-courses, her exuberant wagers—her fearless attack of every sort of ground. Papa had been dead and buried three months already, but Jennie refused to wear black for him. Mourning was contrary to the pirate's creed.

Banstead Manor, the Churchills' rented home near Newmar-ket, was a sprawling old redbrick manse on the Cheveley Park estate, inhabited since the fourteenth century. It was only a few miles as the horse ran from the heath where Randolph's trainer exercised his string. It was Jennie's secret gift to herself, hours be-fore her sisters or the boys awakened, to rein in her mount on a hillside and watch the stable lads put the beautiful creatures through their paces. The air smelled of dew-wet grass, bruised by churning hooves; of trampled mud; of hay-making, somewhere in the distance; and of the deep tobacco musk of sweating horse-flesh.

A lark sang to the sunrise. A fragrant breeze kissed Jennie's cheek. She shaded her eyes and gazed toward the gallops. Over a thousand horses were exercised on the Downs daily. But she could pick out the Abbess even from a distance: a compact and elegant black mare they had bought at Doncaster four years ago, for three hundred pounds.

Jennie had named her for the main character in a French novel. As a three-year-old she had won the Oaks at Epsom; as a four-year-old, the Manchester Cup, beating out seventeen other con-tenders; and at Sandown last year, the Abbess had triumphed at the Princess of Wales's Stakes. Jennie herself had accepted the cup from Princess Alix, curtseying prettily to her friend in a morning dress of jonquil silk and a chip-straw hat. This race season, however, was to be the Abbess's last. She was five years old. At the end of the current season, she would turn brood mare—kicking up her heels in the fields that lapped Banstead Manor.

"And you'd love to kick up your heels with her, wouldn't you?" Jennie crooned as she patted the muscled neck of her mount—a roan gelding, six years old and fifteen hands high. Cyclops nickered yearningly. She'd named him for the noticeable cast in one eye. His ears were pointed toward the pack of racing horses and lads, and Jennie could feel his rib cage shudder with longing to take the bit between his teeth. But he stood obediently, lifting one foot and then the other, with Jennie curled around the pommel of her sidesaddle.

Stocking a race stable had been the best choice Randolph had made after their return together from Paris that grim winter four years before. By the end of that January, he had recovered his speech enough to formally resign as Chancellor of the Exchequer and Leader of the Conservative Party.

"I've thrown away my career in politics, of course," he admitted to Jennie, "but the stress of office, on top of this bloody illness, would kill me."

Jennie had watched from the gallery as her husband rose from the front bench and sneered at his friends and enemies. For all the long years of effort, the end came blessedly fast. As she swept through the Central Lobby of Parliament afterward with her chin held high, her smile wide and fearless, she could not help but overhear the insults. *Having got rid of a boil on your neck, would you ask for it back again?* And—more damningly, from Salisbury himself to his nephew Arthur Balfour—*Randolph Churchill is a woman. And I can never deal with women.*

She had no outlet for her rage and frustration that day, nor for months afterward—and no use for the skills she'd learned as a crack campaigner and speechwriter. She could only smile and lie, with false serenity, when friends inquired about Randolph's plans. "He found Cabinet a dead bore, I'm afraid. But Randy always has adventures in view."

"Pity they're not with his wife, in England," Minnie Paget observed loudly in Jennie's hearing. "But perhaps in this case, absence makes the heart grow fonder?"

"For someone else," Daisy Brooke tittered.

Only one other MP resigned from Salisbury's Government in support of Lord Randolph: Windham Thomas Wyndham-Quin, Fourth Earl of Dunraven and Mount-Earl. It was Dunraven who invited Randy to set up a racing stable with him. The Abbess was the first yearling they bought together. No one was more startled than Jennie when the filly ran her heart out.

The sound of racing hooves came to her suddenly now across the Downs—not from the mass of training horses, but nearer at hand. Cyclops turned his head and skittered sideways, despite the pressure of Jennie's calves. Her grip on the reins tightened. She peered in the direction of the horse's ears and saw a beautiful chestnut galloping toward them, a lean figure crouched low over its neck, urging it on through the rising morning and the living heath. Jennie's heart lurched, as it did every time she saw him. *Charles.*

He had leased a house nearby. In the fall, he was quitting Paris to take up a senior post back in London. But for now—and all of July and August—Jennie had him entirely to herself. Randolph was two months gone already to South Africa.

Charles galloped past Jennie and then wheeled, his horse rearing, his arm raised in salute. Every eye would be upon them; the Downs were filling with other racing spectators. But Jennie no longer cared.

He leaned in and kissed her hard on the mouth. "You're the most beautiful sight in all of England."

"Come back to the house for breakfast," she said breathlessly.

"Is anyone up yet?"

Jennie glanced at the sun. "I doubt it."

"Good." His eyes glinted. "We can go back to bed. Race you to Banstead—"

And he reached out and slapped the rump of Jennie's horse.

# CHAPTER THIRTY-SIX

With the help of the gardener, Winston had built a two-room hut of logs and mud close up to the edge of Banstead's ancient moat, which was disused and foul smelling. He had set the younger boys—his brother, Jack, and his cousins Jacky and Hugh—to digging out the moat right near the hut, which they had agreed to name the Den, while he himself hammered at a drawbridge. It must have real pulleys and gears, so that it could be raised and lowered, and it was essential that the catapult he had just finished be set near enough to the Den's defenses so that the catapult operator was not annihilated in battle. The catapult fired green apples stripped from the adjacent orchard.

The plan, once the drawbridge could be sealed against the Enemies of England, was to defend the Den against all comers. These would probably be a gaggle of farm laborers' sons, or the canny boys who haunted the Cheveley racing stables, carrying water and hay for the grooms and exercise lads; in moments of extreme need, the Enemy might even include a girl, like cousin Hugh's little sister, Clare. But Winston must always be General of the forces commanded to defend the Den. At sixteen, he was the eldest and the only one in possession of sound military strategy. Jack was eleven, Hugh was nearly eight, and young cousin Jacky only six, but they would make do. The catapult, and Audacity, were everything.

———

Jennie was painting *en plein air* near a paddock stream beloved of the horses when she heard Jack's high-pitched cry. She cocked her head and listened for a moment; the cairn at her feet—a dog named Bonaparte, generations descended from the pup she had taken from Fanny Ronalds's Newport stables—jumped up and raced in full-throated bark across the meadow. Jennie dropped her brush and followed him.

Charles Kinsky was holding her younger son high in the air, shielding his own body as he faced down the remaining forces ranged inside the Den: Winston, little Jacky, and Hugh. The three faces could be glimpsed through the slits cut in the Den's turf walls, paralyzed and uncertain. The drawbridge was up, the moat churning with fresh water, the catapult already discharged. Presumably what Jennie had heard was an apple, intended for Count Kinsky, striking her younger son. Charles had his Austrian hussar's saber raised high in one hand. The other firmly grasped Jack Churchill's waist.

"Parlay!" Charles yelled. "Or my hostage dies before your eyes!"

Poor Jack's face was very white under his summer tan, and his eyes were squeezed shut so that he would not have to witness the ultimate sacrifice visited upon his own neck. Jennie nearly went to him—nearly pulled him from Kinsky's arm and roundly scolded them all—but something of Leonard Jerome whispered in her ear. She dived instead for Bonaparte's outraged body and smothered his barks in her chest.

She had asked for a man in her sons' lives. Papa had told her she already had one.

Suddenly, Winston's red hair knifed through the Den's doorway. He was waving a strip of white linen, probably torn from one of his cousins' shirts. Everest would be furious.

"Parlay, agreed!" he yelled.

"Terms?"

"Hand-to-hand combat. Have you another sword?"

Charles laughed, and set Jack down on his feet. "No, as it happens. This is a family heirloom. Would you like to see it?"

"Very much, sir," Winston said. "Let us exchange prisoners. My person shall be forfeit for my brother's."

"Very well." Charles glanced at Jack. "Off you go, back into the Den."

The drawbridge began to lower, Winston working the pulley rope hand over hand. Little Jacky and Hugh had peashooters trained on Charles. Jack stood anxiously on one leg as Winston emerged, then scuttled across the drawbridge. His cousins cheered.

"Golly," Winston said as Charles handed him the saber. "It's ever so heavy. Is that a ruby in the hilt? What are the three slashes for? Are they ivory?"

"Yes, it's a ruby—an ancestor brought it back from the Crusades. The slashes are meant to be wolves' teeth." He glanced sidelong at Jennie. "They're fashioned from an elephant tusk. My father, the Prince, presented me with this when I came of age."

"Has your family got a motto?"

"Yes," Kinsky said, "but you wouldn't understand it."

"Ours is 'Faithful but Unhappy.' I should rather have wolves' teeth." Winston glanced up. "Did you know that I'm a jolly good fencer? I've been learning at Harrow. I was School Champion last term."

"Were you?" Charles's eyebrows rose. "And I am a knight of the Holy Roman Empire. Have you got a foil here at Banstead?"

"In my room. But it has a cap on the tip. It's not a real sword like this."

"All the better. I shouldn't like to be scarred. Fetch your weapon, Winston—and we'll have a go, shall we?"

Jennie's sisters Leonie and Clarita came out of the house to watch the combat from lawn chairs drawn up to the strip of grass. The children settled themselves cross-legged on the ground, boisterous with excitement, until Winston told them firmly that they must keep quiet so that he and Count Kinsky could concentrate. Kinsky stuck a wine cork on the tip of his saber so that it would not cut Winston, and laid down the rules: the target area was solely the chest. He had removed his coat and was in vest and shirtsleeves. He towered over Jennie's son, and for a moment she was sure that the episode would end in humiliation and disaster. But she had not counted on Harrow.

When the two fencers faced each other and Kinsky cried, *"En garde,"* she was astonished to see Winston move as lithely as a cat, springing forward and back with his arm extended—lunging into Kinsky's reach to touch his chest, only to retreat just as Kinsky parried. He really *had* learned how to fence, a claim she'd discounted when he boasted of it in his letters from school. Her heart accelerated, and suddenly, as Winston lunged again and Kinsky said *"Riposte"* and flicked Winston's breast, she could no longer sit still. She got to her feet and began to pace, her eyes trained on the combatants.

Back and forth the two figures went, first one scoring and then the other. Winston fell behind—Kinsky had found his chest three times—until suddenly he danced furiously toward the Count, forcing him to retreat, and then raced past him with his foil extended. *"Flèche!"* Winston cried.

*"C'est une touché,"* Kinsky agreed. He narrowed his eyes against the sun, his jaw set. Jennie realized he regarded Winston with utter seriousness. She glanced at her younger boy: Jack's fists were clenched and his whole face alive with hope.

On the next action, Charles scored again. Then Winston beat aside Charles's blade and grazed his sternum. The score was tied. Kinsky halted and raised his saber in salute; Winston did the same. *"La belle,"* he said. That was what they called the next touch, the tiebreaker that would decide the victor.

Winston retreated, his foil held high. Retreated again, and again. And then as Charles lunged in attack, Winston parried and thrust forward. His foil bent in a shining arc against Charles's waistcoat; his tip had struck one of the horn buttons. Charles fell back and dropped his guard. *"Et là,"* he said, and held out his hand. A concession of defeat.

For an instant, Winston stared at him. Then he swished his foil up through the air and touched the guard to his forehead in salute.

The rest of the afternoon, the boys were absorbed in fencing lessons, the younger ones clamoring to be taught everything Winston knew, using sticks cut from the orchard. The ladies sat about in the lawn chairs drinking tea. Charles Kinsky lay on the grass at Jennie's feet, tossing a leather ball for Bonaparte. When the shadows began to lengthen, and Leonie and Clarita went inside to dress, calling to their children, Charles said, "Stay a moment."

Jennie glanced down at him. "What is it?"

He threw himself into a chair beside her, turning the cairn's ball moodily between his fingers. Bonaparte had already moseyed toward the kitchens, his nose to the turf. "That lad of yours," Charles said.

"Winston? What about him?"

"He's too old to play with little boys."

Jennie shrugged. "That's all he has, I'm afraid. Sunny—George's son—is nearly twenty, and already up at Cambridge. The future Duke of Marlborough can't be expected to show a schoolboy of sixteen any interest."

"Hasn't Win any friends? Boys his own age, from Harrow?"

"None that he mentions."

The ball spurted angrily into the air, was caught in Charles's fist. "And I'm correct that he has no mount? Here in Newmarket?"

"Randolph doesn't think it worth the cost of board for a horse, when both boys are away at school most of the year."

"Win's never taken out a gun?"

"He says he's had Riflery at Harrow. But real shooting? On an estate? Good Lord, no."

"And yet the preserves at Blenheim must be among the best in the kingdom."

"Win doesn't live at Blenheim." George had married the widowed American, Lily Carré Hamersley—who was indeed a shy and lovely woman, entirely friendly to Jennie—and was busy refurbishing his estate with his second wife's fortune. He and Randolph were back on speaking terms, but in her husband's absence, Jennie avoided Blenheim.

"He visits the place enough. It's his ancestral home." Charles thrust himself out of the chair and began to pace before her, raging. "For God's sake, Jennie, what is Randolph about, to neglect his son's education so completely? It should have been his first duty to teach Win how to go on—as a gentleman and a member of his class. The boy ought to have been given a pony at the age of three and schooled to take any fence. He should have been hunting with the Blenheim pack from the age of ten or twelve, as I dare swear Randolph was. And as for guns—what does Randy expect him to do on the Glorious Twelfth? Play with his toy soldiers?"

He meant August 12, the opening of grouse season.

"I doubt Randolph expects him to do anything," Jennie replied mildly. "George and Sunny will be in Scotland, of course—"

"Winston is sixteen! Has he ever touched a fowling piece? Or even walked out with a party of beaters?"

"No."

"It's a bloody disgrace," Charles snarled. He stopped short and glared at her. "Tomorrow I'll bring over a target and a few shotguns. Jack's old enough to learn, and so is Hugh. We'll set up a range. And you may tell Winston he's welcome to ride any horse in my stables while he's here in Banstead. I'll teach him to jump. He can teach me to fence like a champion. I can't do more than that until hunting season, but—"

Jennie held out her hand.

He took it and raised it to his lips.

"Thank you, my darling," she said.

"It's what any man would do." He strode off toward the Den. "Winston! Jack! Come dress for dinner!"

# CHAPTER THIRTY-SEVEN

In September, both boys returned to school and Jennie moved regretfully into Duchess Fanny's house in Grosvenor Square. She had found a lessee willing to take No. 2 Connaught Place furnished, and with Randolph still away in Africa, the savings in household expenses were too great to ignore. Living alone with a quantity of servants was crushingly expensive, and Duchess Fanny's establishment was decidedly good. Jennie's new position as a dependent chafed at her, however—the Duchess could not help mentioning every time she received a newsy letter from Randolph. He wrote only rarely to Jennie, but complained to his mother of Africa's flies, which plagued him in unceasing swarms; of the poor coffee and the dirty water and what he regarded as the unimaginable crudity of Boer life. He was constantly on the move, camping throughout the veldt, prospecting for gold and writing articles for the *Daily Graphic*. The paper had paid him two thousand guineas for twenty articles of four thousand words each—enough to keep him in funds for the year. He hadn't shared his largess with Jennie. Nor, she reflected, had he asked for her help with writing.

Duchess Fanny still knew nothing of Randolph's disease. His mother ascribed his poor health, his ravaged features and fits of temper, to the burden of an unfaithful wife. An ungrateful nation. A Conservative Party that had betrayed its greatest voice. Randolph was a victim of a general conspiracy, Fanny believed. Taking Jennie under her own roof only deepened the Duchess's contempt.

"You might make yourself useful while you're here," she suggested over the breakfast table one morning. "I am sure you have nothing better to do, Jeanette, with your children from home and your poor husband martyring himself in Mashonaland to keep you all."

Jennie sipped her tea, counting silently to ten. Was there no end to the humiliations she was forced to endure to protect Randolph's secrets? "Did I mention I met Lord Winchester in Bond Street yesterday?" she asked brightly. "He is just back from Africa, where he had a glimpse of Randolph—being carried across a river, in a litter filled with champagne bottles."

Duchess Fanny stared at her. "I am sure it is the best thing he could choose to ward off dysentery. Were he to drink from those filthy rivers, he might contract any sort of disease!"

"True." In her stifled fury, Jennie almost burst out that it was *far too late*—Randy was already doomed from a sickness he had probably contracted at Oxford—but she bit her tongue and set down her cup. "I interrupted you, Mother Duchess. You wish me to make myself useful?"

Fanny sniffed. "Whatever your more *variable* qualities, Jeanette, you do have a talent for *exhibition*. You might lend your flair to my concert scheme, in support of the Paddington Recreation Ground."

This was the Duchess's pet charity in Maida Vale, an open-air park designed to improve the lot of Randolph's borough constituents through healthful exercise. The Ground offered cricket pitches, a bowling green, tennis courts, and a cinder track for foot-races and cycling. It had begun life purely as a cricket club, but in 1887, the year of the Queen's Jubilee—a year of economic slump in Britain when so many of the local people suffered from want—the plan had been enlarged by a benefactor. Some five hundred out-of-work men were employed for months, clearing the ground for the courts and tracks and building an actual gymnasium. Now there was a Churchill Gate at the entrance.

Randolph might not have appeared in Parliament as the Member for South Paddington for most of the past year, but Duchess Fanny was eternally watchful. The charity must not be allowed to lapse, or the Churchill Gate might be pulled down.

"Very well," Jennie said. "When is it to be?"

"At the end of October. I thought perhaps the twenty-ninth, as it is a Thursday."

"And what are your plans?"

Duchess Fanny's pug eyes started and her lips set in a thin line. "*Plans?* I have none. I leave all that to you, Jeanette. You are the one who professes, after all, to have *connections* in the artistic world."

Somewhere, the Duchess had apparently heard of Arthur Sullivan. Perhaps she had even heard of Fanny Ronalds.

"I do think it is the least you could do in support of poor Randolph, after all he has sacrificed for you," Fanny added.

Although she would never admit as much to her mother-in-law, Jennie *did* know how to organize a charity concert. She had learned at the feet of the best—Leonard Jerome. She allowed it to let slip during a visit to her milliner that she required a dress for a highly select charity event she was planning—and within hours, the fact had appeared in a gossip column. Sir Henry Irving, who managed the Lyceum Theatre and was himself a notable actor, offered Jennie his stage for the event. The Prince of Wales called in Grosvenor Square, astounding the Duchess, to announce he would sponsor the performance, and he carried a note from Princess Alix with an offer of help. Julian Story—an American portrait painter a few years younger than Jennie—volunteered to design the sets. And a flood of fashionable but tiresome friends clamored to be included in the performances: reciting, pantomiming, or playing instruments with dubious skill.

Jennie tactfully turned down most of them in favor of Margot Tennant, who was as accomplished a ballet dancer as she was a

rider to hounds; the Australian soprano an aging Papa had admired, and considered his discovery—Nellie Melba; and the
thirty-year-old Polish pianist Ignace Paderewski, who was a personal friend of Charles Kinsky and only recently introduced to
London. Paderewski sported a wild head of orange hair and a
badly mended broken nose. He loved to play duets with Jennie,
without having the slightest romantic interest in her. Jennie found
him refreshing.

On the night of the charity concert, two of the scheduled performers inexplicably failed to appear, and Jennie was forced to seat
herself on the Lyceum's stage amidst the potted palms, in a dress of
bright green that showed up well from a distance. She played a
Chopin polonaise for the nine hundred guests. She got through it;
the wayward performers arrived, replete with apologies; and the
benefit went on to rousing success.

It was Duchess Fanny, however, who rose to accept a massive
bouquet of roses from the Princess of Wales, as the lady sponsor of
the Paddington Recreation Ground. She was at her most austere as
she sank into her deepest curtsey, and murmured her thanks to
"the dear friends who have shown their support for my beloved
son Randolph and his constituency."

She did not acknowledge Randolph's wife.

"So *like* Lady Randolph to seize the stage," Minnie Paget sniped
as Jennie made her way through a crowd of well-wishers, "when
there were so many others of real talent available! I myself had offered to declaim a portion of *Antony and Cleopatra*. But apparently
my poor efforts were not wanted."

"Never mind," the Prince of Wales told Jennie when he took
his leave of her. "You shall have a greater reward than one of my
wife's posies. Shall I tell you, hmm? The treat we have in store?"

He was patting her hand, his twinkling eyes roving from Jennie's face to Charles Kinsky's. If the Prince still regarded the Count
as a threat to Jennie's reputation, he no longer told her so. The
years between his warning at the New Café and the present eve-

ning of Paderewski had convinced Bertie that Jennie was not the sort to elope to Paris with her lover.

"I am charged with an invitation," the Prince added, "on behalf of Baron de Hirsch. He has invited us all for a month of shooting at St. Johann, his estate in Hungary. Even Kinsky is included."

Baron Moritz von Hirsch was a German financier who kept a residence in Paris (where he was known as Maurice de Hirsch), a château in Saint-Cloud, a twelfth-century castle in Moravia, and Bath House in Piccadilly. He also rented Grafton House near Newmarket, where he bred his fabulous racehorses. Jennie had often met him on horseback just after dawn, in halcyon summers, watching the gallops across the North Downs. At the end of last season, he had confided to her that he intended to sell his entire string and shut down his stables. It was Lucien, his son, who had loved racing—and Lucien had died suddenly.

"My heart has gone right out of it, my dear," de Hirsch told her pathetically.

He was nearly sixty years old, but he counted among his friends the much younger Charles Kinsky and Randolph's childhood friend Natty Rothschild. Like Rothschild, Hirsch was Jewish. His grandfather had been the first Jew allowed to own land in Bavaria, and as banker to the King, the first to be ennobled. The Baron was one of the five wealthiest men in Europe. Having no child any longer—no son and heir—he had begun to give away vast sums to persecuted Jewish communities throughout Europe. No one in London knew what that meant, and most were too well-bred to ask. They accepted the Baron and people like Rothschild because the Prince of Wales did.

Bertie needed Hirsch's money. The Baron held enormous mortgages on Sandringham.

"I suppose, if you have been invited in the company of the Prince of Wales, you must certainly go," Duchess Fanny said doubtfully, when informed of Jennie's plans for November. "It would never do to slight the Prince. The Queen cannot live *forever*. And Randolph's political future hangs in the balance."

Jennie did not believe her husband had any sort of future. But she had no desire to argue with the Duchess. She set Gentry to packing.

# CHAPTER THIRTY-EIGHT

The journey to St. Johann began in Paris with a special train. The Baron owned the Imperial Turkish Oriental Railway, an Ottoman line that connected Vienna to Istanbul through the Balkans. They would not be taking that line—or the brand-new train that traveled it, the Orient Express—because the Baron's hunting lodge was located in Upper Hungary, an area Charles called the *Felvidék*.

"That means 'upland' in Hungarian," he explained to Jennie. "You'll have a glimpse of the Carpathian Mountains while you're the Baron's guest. We'll change lines in Vienna for Pressburg, and after that, it's all overland by carriage, I'm afraid. It may be tedious for you."

"In such magnificent terrain?" she retorted. "Nonsense."

Three cars were reserved for the Prince of Wales—a royal sleeping coach, a dining coach, and a saloon where Bertie and his equerries smoked their cigars, read the newspapers obtained at every station stop, and occasionally commented on the scenery. Jennie and the rest of the guests had less private but equally sumptuous spaces assigned to them. They shared a dining car—although they were often summoned to Bertie's—and a variety of saloons. One was designated as a "smoking" and another as a "ladies'" car, rather as they might have been aboard ship.

They stopped in Reims, Strasbourg, Stuttgart, and Munich. Jennie donned her furs at each halt and walked briskly along the platform to stretch her legs, mourning that there was not time enough to venture into the towns.

The third morning out of Paris, Jennie pulled aside the curtains of her sleeping compartment to find they had crossed into Austria during the night and had arrived in Salzburg. The air on the platform was sharply colder.

"From now on, we skirt the Alps on our right hand until we reach Wien," Charles told her over breakfast, using the German name for Vienna. He became more Austrian, Jennie thought, repressing a smile, with every mile that passed.

"I wish we could stop there," she said impulsively.

He glanced at her. "Let's."

"We can't leave the Baron's party!"

"Not on our way to St. Johann, perhaps. But we might manage it on the way back."

She studied him. "Charles, you can't be serious!"

"Always, where you're concerned." The words were light but his expression was not. He reached for her hand and brought it to his lips. "I want to show you my home, darling. And introduce you to my parents. Normally they'd be in Bohemia at this time of year, but the Archduke is being tiresome and the Emperor has asked my mother to intervene."

*The Archduke* meant Franz Ferdinand of Austria-Este, Royal Prince of Hungary and nephew to Charles's Emperor. He was in his late twenties and as yet unmarried.

"Your mother has an archduchess up her sleeve?" Jennie asked, amused.

"It's not that simple. Franz is a member of the Imperial Hapsburg dynasty. He must marry a princess of rank."

"The poor man's had his life turned on end," Jennie protested. "Surely he might be allowed to *marry* as he likes?"

Franz Ferdinand had been plucked without warning from his comfortable world of stag hunting and mock soldiering two years before, when Crown Prince Rudolf—who had danced with Jennie to the strains of *tziganes* music at the New Café—had shot himself in the head, along with his seventeen-year-old mistress, at his hunting lodge in Mayerling. The girl's body had been buried within hours at a nearby monastery, and the murder-suicide was hushed up. Charles knew the truth, however, and he had told Jennie. She had thought immediately of Sisi, Rudolf's mother. The beautiful Empress would wander forever unconsoled now.

"Jennie," Charles had said when he explained Rudolf's suicide. "You know that it's possible . . . that his condition . . . It ends in madness."

"Yes." Rudolf's *condition,* like Randolph's, was syphilis.

"You must break with your husband," Charles had urged. "If this curse leads to violence . . ."

"That's hardly warranted." She had smiled into his eyes faintly. "Randolph's so rarely in England!"

Charles had grasped her shoulders. "Don't you understand, I'm *afraid for you*. God knows what the man might do when his reason is deranged—"

"Hush." She placed her fingers on his lips in a wordless caress. "I keep a Deringer beside my bed, remember?"

They arrived at St. Johann as night was falling. The mile-long drive was lit every ten yards by torches. A liveried servant stood guard with a rifle by each flame.

The main house on Baron von Hirsch's vast estate was a square and generous old building dating to the twelfth century, with peaked roofs of dark-stained wood and deeply overhanging eaves that shouldered snow in winter. The walls were clad inside and out with the white stucco pervasive in the region, incised with curlicues and whorls of *sgraffiti* to reveal a red undercoat beneath. Jennie was charmed by the patterns, and when she was not walking for miles during the day with the men and their dogs and guns, she was absorbed in studying an artisan who maintained the decorative technique. She had decided to attempt *sgraffiti* in her dining room at Connaught Place.

The Baron, like Jennie, believed in luxury and convenience. Although there was no electricity at St. Johann, there was infinite hot water and a bath attached to every bedchamber. The beds were blanketed with eiderdowns. An army of servants tended fires and answered every bell, and the refrigerated game locker in the kitchen wing was the largest in Europe—capable of storing seven thousand fowl.

There was a reason for this.

Each morning during the shooting party, the Baron and his guests were loaded into victorias accompanied by postilions clothed in blue hussar jackets, and driven out into the field. They were met there by six hundred beaters. Hirsch's chief gamekeeper would sound a bugle, and the party would advance in a line across the Hungarian plain. Most of the ladies remained at the house, bent over needlework or riding the Baron's beautiful horses, but Jennie walked out with the men, wrapped in furs, her gloved hands swinging and her cheeks brilliant with exercise. The beaters flushed blackcock and partridges, pheasants and blue hares. Roe deer bounded away in startled panic. At times the huge coveys overhead darkened the light.

"Have you ever fired at a bird on the wing?" Kinsky asked as he handed his gun to his loader and accepted a fresh one. Every man walked with a bearer and two guns. Speed of reloading was essential.

"Besides you, you mean?" she flashed, remembering his silhouette in her bedroom window so many years before. "A long time ago. My father had a trap-shooting range at Jerome Park."

Charles raised his fowling piece at a forty-five-degree angle, his left arm quite straight as he tracked a partridge, and fired. The bird tumbled out of the air and one of the Baron's pack of Vizslas sprang to retrieve it.

"Guns have changed since then," he said, "but as a former target, I suspect you still have the touch."

He took his reloaded gun from the bearer and offered it to her. "Go on. No one will mind."

It was an elegant fowling piece, a "London best," as they were known in sporting circles, made by Holland and Holland. A twelve-bore, double-barreled, breech-loaded, sidelock shotgun with a chased action and walnut stock. Not above seven pounds in weight. Elegant and exorbitant. The sort of gun she could never afford to buy for Winston and that Randolph ought to have given him on his sixteenth birthday. Fathers were meant to pass guns on to their sons, along with the skills to fire them. Randolph had been a great sportsman in his day, before nerve tremors destroyed his reflexes.

"Do you know," she said slowly as she took the gun, "I was out at a driven shoot the day my pains came on with Winston—the day before he was actually born. The Duchess blamed the dogcart jerking over Blenheim's ruts, which was her way of blaming me for joining the shoot. But she was wrong."

"Isn't she always?" Charles flashed.

"I went into labor because I danced all night at the Blenheim Hunt Ball."

He threw back his head and laughed.

Jennie set the fowling piece's butt against her right shoulder and sighted a gray partridge. She tried to track the bird's flight, tried to anticipate where it would be by the time the burst of shot reached its body, but when she had fired she glanced up and saw the partridge still in the sky.

"Bird away," Charles said. "Have another go."

After that, they shared his guns as they walked, and by the end of the day Jennie had brought down three birds.

The rest of the party bagged nearly three thousand.

That night, Charles slid her velvet dressing gown from her clavicle and kissed the purple stain where the gun's recoil had bruised her.

# CHAPTER THIRTY-NINE

They passed back through Vienna the third week in November. At Charles's urging, Jennie had consented to leave the Baron's party and break her trip in Austria for a few days. But when they stepped down from the special train at Vienna's main station, and Jennie had collected both Gentry and her numerous trunks, she turned to the Count and held out her hand.

"This, my dear, is where we part for a time."

"What the devil do you mean?"

He was frowning, eyes furious under his dark gray homburg.

"I am greatly fatigued, and although I am wild to be introduced to your dear mamma, I must recruit my strength a little. I will take a cab—there *are* such things in this city, I assume?—to my hotel and rest."

"Your *hotel*?"

"It's called the Sacher. Have I pronounced that correctly?"

"Directly opposite the opera house," he said impatiently. "But you can't stay there."

"Bertie assures me it is quite respectable."

"Bertie?"

"Are you going to repeat every other word I utter, Charles? It grows quite tedious." She smiled at him with false mischief. "Naturally I accepted the Prince's advice on accommodation when I informed him I was leaving the train at Vienna. He swears the Sacher is in an unobjectionable part of town. Which reminds me:

What is the German word for *cab*? Gentry will need to know."
Jennie glanced over her shoulder at her maid, who stood by the
porter and a cart full of cases in her black coat and hat, her nose
reddening in the cold.

"Indeed, and she will not," Charles retorted. "No one speaks
German here; the dialect is Austro-Bavarian and Gentry will
never master it. You are both coming with me to Palais Kinsky. It
is absurd to think of you staying anywhere else."

"Darling Charles." Jennie placed her gloved hand on his sleeve.
"If you think I am going to descend upon your ancestral home,
entirely unaccompanied by my husband, in the figure of a schem-
ing mistress—expecting to be established opposite the heir's bedchamber and eyeing the family jewels across the dining table—you
are utterly mistaken. I shall go discreetly to the Sacher, with the
Prince of Wales's approval, and call upon you tomorrow."

"I wired ahead to my father to expect us. Preparations will have
been made." The wolf look was in Charles's eyes.

"And the relief will be infinite when I demonstrate that I am,
after all, a lady of breeding." Jennie drew a deep breath, summoning all her resolution. She refused to enter Charles's palace as his
*indiscretion*. "If you persist in arguing the point, I shall catch the
next train west."

He held her gaze a moment, saw no hint of weakness in her
face, and threw up his hands. "Very well! My mamma receives
between one and three o'clock in the afternoon. She does not speak
English, but her French is excellent. Never mind the word for
*cab*—I shall order yours, and accompany you to the Sacher, while
sending my baggage to the *palais* with my man. Gentry can go in a
third carriage with your things."

Jennie tilted her head and smiled. "Thank you, Charles. You're
very good."

"And you make me feel like a thief in the night."

She affected surprise. "But that's exactly what I want to *avoid*!"

He leaned close and growled into her ear. "When will you learn, my beloved Jennie, that scandal touches only those who fear it? Stare down the gossips and they have no power."

"If you're a man," she retorted, feeling a pinch of anger as she turned away from him. "Women are the gatekeepers of Society, Charles. Your mamma knows this better than anyone. Only *you* seem not to understand the laws that make or destroy women's lives!"

The *stadtpalais,* or city palace, of the Kinsky family sat on a triangular park known as the Freyung. The word, Charles had told Jennie, meant "free area," because next door to the palace was an ancient monastery of Benedictine monks. By law, neither the Emperor nor Vienna's burghers could impose tax on the clergy—so the name stuck, even after the quarter became the very heart of the city.

Jennie was startled to see that the Freyung was filled with peddlers' stalls and people browsing among the wares. Carriage traffic around the park was thick and slow. When her cab finally arrived at No. 4 and she made to pay off the driver, he offered her a single word of apology.

*Christkindlmarkt.*

German was her least accomplished language, but even Jennie could parse the idea; it was a Christmas fair of some kind. She wished, suddenly, that she could wander among the people selling baskets and blown glass and finely turned wood carvings and find treasures for the boys' Christmas stockings—but she had a duty call to pay. Resolutely, she turned her back and studied the Palais Kinsky.

It was a baroque confection of a building, soaring some seventy or eighty feet above the street, the stucco painted pale yellow and overlaid with decorative white plasterwork. Marble statues gazed down at Jennie from their position on the edge of the roof, as though contemplating suicide. She made out the Kinsky crest above the portal, with its three slashing teeth. She smiled.

A porter stood at attention behind the massive iron grille that filled the palace entryway. She handed in her card. *Lady Randolph Churchill.* The porter glanced at it, then swept her with an assessing gaze. She had taken care with her dress that afternoon; she was beautifully turned out in a midnight-blue velvet coat with deep collar and cuffs of Persian lamb. Her toque was the same blue velvet, pitched forward on her forehead, with a plume of black ostrich dangling fetchingly over her ear. A luxurious Persian lamb muff concealed her gloved hands. The porter bowed, stepped back, and opened the portal. Jennie entered.

She was standing beneath an enormous entrance portico with a second door directly opposite. It was thrown open, and she glimpsed a long courtyard enclosed on all four sides by the soaring walls of the palace. Jennie glanced to her right; a footman in a powdered wig and Kinsky livery was waiting. From his earnest and attentive expression, he had been instructed to convey her immediately to the Princess. There was no loitering here while her card was scrutinized and debated. He bowed, and turned up a massive baroque staircase as wide as a ballroom. Jennie followed him up the marble steps to a principal floor above. Two stories higher still floated a painted ceiling that must have been executed by an Italian master. The space reminded her of Chatsworth—Hartington's Derbyshire seat.

The Palais Kinsky was magnificent. One day, it would be Charles's.

It was almost as extraordinary as Blenheim.

Jennie had long been accustomed to England's most glorious palaces. She had moved through their rooms and dined at their tables in the company of British royals. Before that, she had known the Tuileries and Compiègne. So why did her stomach lurch and her fingers clench with anxiety? Papa used to say that in America, she was a princess's equal! She had learned enough over the past two decades to know that he was utterly wrong, but his puckish words gave her courage. Americans made their own rules. As the footman threw open the last set of doors, Jennie lifted her head.

The first thing she saw in the opulently draped salon was Charles, staring broodingly into the fire, his booted foot resting on a massive bronze firedog. He was dressed in some sort of Austrian uniform—he had once been a cavalry officer, Jennie knew, before his diplomatic career—and looked as though he were expected at court. His head swung around at the sound of the opening doors and his eyes met hers, searching and intent.

"Lady Randolph Churchill," the footman announced.

"My lady," Charles said, and crossed rapidly to her. "Mamma, Papa—may I present to you my friend Lady Randolph? Lady Randolph—Prince Ferdinand Bonaventura Fürst Kinsky and the Princess Marie of Liechtenstein und Kinsky."

Of course his mother was royal. It must be an actual law in this empire, not just for the Hapsburgs but for all nobility. Royalty married royalty. Precedence and power and position were lost otherwise, not just for oneself but for generations.

Jennie curtseyed low and bowed her head, as though she were in the presence of Victoria.

Prince Ferdinand stepped forward, clicked his heels, and kissed her hand. *"Enchanté."*

In his black frock coat and gray trousers, Jennie decided, he might have been any gentleman of means sauntering through Piccadilly. He had neatly clipped hair that had once been as dark as Charles's, and a trimmed beard that had begun to gray. He was tall, broad-shouldered, fit from years of riding punishing horses—Charles at sixty, in fact. She felt her heart lurch as she met the Prince's blue eyes.

*Charles at sixty.*

Princess Marie was a small woman with a prominent nose and snapping dark eyes. Her lips were thin and colorless, her cheeks gaunt, and her hair a dark brown shot with silver. She was gowned in a rich saffron-colored velvet trimmed with mink, a woven silk shawl draped about her elbows. She inclined her head to Jennie but did not offer her hand; her fingers were clasped. One flashed a ruby that glowed dully, like clotted blood. It matched the decoration of the room, which was oval and enormous: crimson draperies trimmed in metallic gold, paneled walls painted with trompe l'oeil marble. The ceiling, forty feet above, was covered with draped classical figures disporting themselves in a vivid sky.

A brief visit. Chillier than the heat thrown out by the massive tiled stove in one corner. They sat, the Princess rather farther from Jennie than was conducive to conversation, Prince Ferdinand in an Empire-style armchair at her right hand, his thumb and forefinger stroking his beard. Charles took a seat on Jennie's other side.

"I hope you find the Sacher comfortable," the Prince said in French.

"Entirely so," Jennie assured him, smiling. "It offers every convenience, as one must expect of a hotel that ranks so high in the Prince of Wales's estimation."

"A hotel, nonetheless," he remarked disparagingly. "I should not like to see any of my daughters or my wife alone in one. But my son assures me that American ladies"—he glanced at Charles—"are far more daring."

He might have chosen *confident* or *independent;* but this was a deliberately charged word. Prince Ferdinand was insulting her.

Jennie quelled a spurt of anger. "I have been fortunate enough to live and travel for much of my life in Europe, Your Excellency. The Princess Metternich, a very old acquaintance of mine, was once forced to escape from a violent mob at her dressmaker's in Paris by lying on the floor of her carriage, with a horse blanket over her head. That may be *daring,* to be sure, but I confess I admire her. *Daring* is so often synonymous with *courage* and *common sense,* isn't it?"

"Pauline von Metternich once fought a duel with another

woman over the matter of flower arrangements," the Prince snorted, "*naked from the waist up*. Do you also fence, Lady Randolph?"

"Only with words." She would *not* betray that she felt his contempt. "But my son is quite an adept swordsman, as Count Kinsky may attest."

"He nearly spitted me last summer," Charles volunteered.

"Indeed? Your husband is a son of the Duke of Marlborough, is he not?" Prince Ferdinand inquired. "Absent this year from his home, I understand, hunting gold and sensation in Africa? I have seen the news reports."

"Yes," Jennie agreed amiably. "Although Lord Randolph is his own best advocate—he has written most of the reports himself. And it appears he has actually *found* gold, and claimed it for the Rand Company. We expect him to reach London early in the new year."

"How providential," the Prince murmured, looking profoundly bored. "Domestic matters will claim your attention, when one might most wish it."

"Mamma," said Charles, turning to the Princess, "shall we show Lady Randolph the music room?"

"If you wish." Princess Marie rose immediately and glided to the door, where she turned and waited.

Prince Ferdinand stood and bowed. "It was a pleasure, my lady. I wish you a safe journey home to England. You leave tomorrow, I assume?"

"The following day, Your Excellency."

"Tomorrow, Lady Randolph has kindly agreed to accompany me to the Royal Opera," Charles broke in.

His father smiled faintly. "Mascagni's new work. *L'Amico Fritz*. Have you seen his *Cavalleria Rusticana,* Lady Randolph?"

"Yes—in Paris, with the soprano Emma Calvé."

"Not even the divine Calvé can rescue *Fritz*. It's a slight story, about a misalliance—between a wealthy landowner and a nobody." His blue eyes met hers squarely. "But perhaps *you'll* enjoy it."

Jennie fought down her hurt and fury—her desire to strike the smug complaisance from Prince Ferdinand's face—as she followed the Princess through the corridors. She had not taken Charles's arm. He seemed to sense her mortification, and kept his distance.

The music room's windows overlooked the interior courtyard. It had the same breathtakingly high ceilings, which Jennie thought must affect the acoustics. The walls were painted in cream, with white and gold boiseries depicting musical instruments. A harp was placed to one side of the tiled stove; a piano filled the other end. In between was a music stand with a violin resting on it.

"Is this where you learned?" Jennie managed to ask Charles in English, when his mother had led them into the room's center. The Princess's cheeks were faintly pink as she studied Jennie's profile.

Charles shook his head. "Most of my instruction took place in Prague, where I spent much of my childhood. All of us prefer Bohemia to Vienna; the land is in our blood."

"Not *all*, Charles darling," the Princess said suddenly in French. "I am no Bohemian. Now, Lady Randolph, my dear friend Princess von Metternich informs me that she was recently privileged to advise you on the arrangement of a charity concert—which I believe you lately held on behalf of the Duchess of Marlborough. Pauline told me so much about the arrangements—the tableaux, the sets, and the remarkable appearance of Paderewski. Did everything come off to your satisfaction?"

Jennie stared at her in surprise. The snapping black eyes were bright with interest. The thin lips were smiling.

"Indeed," she stammered. "The Princess von Metternich offered a great deal of excellent advice—by letter, of course, once Count Kinsky informed her of my event. Her management of such things is effortless, as no doubt you know. When I was a girl in Paris, her soirees and picnics at the Austrian embassy were a particular treat."

"So, too, with her parties here in Vienna. You *must* play for us," the Princess insisted. "The instrument is old, but well tuned."

Jennie glanced at Charles; he leaned in and kissed his mamma on the cheek. "Ask for Mozart. Then you might accompany her."

Princess Marie hesitated an instant. "The Piano Sonata in E-flat Major? Or perhaps C Major?" she asked Jennie.

"I could attempt one or both," Jennie said, "but I warn you, I have not looked at the music in ages."

"Neither have I." The Princess raised her violin. "We shall stumble through together. How very *daring* of us, my dear!"

Long after Jennie had rolled away from the Freyung and the Kinsky family had dined—Charles's youngest sister, also named Marie, being allowed to join them for a glimpse of her dashing eldest brother—Prince Ferdinand summoned him to his library and offered him a glass of apricot brandy.

Charles held the glass aloft and said, *"Na zdraví."* He downed the digestif in a single draft, as was the custom.

His father repeated the words. Then he set down his glass. "Come home to Vienna this Christmas," he urged, his voice unwontedly gentle. "Indeed, as soon as possible, Karl. Your mother has agreed to assist the Emperor with his young heir—and you might be infinitely useful, as Franz's companion. You know the world, you know men—it would be a natural role. I'm told the Archduke loves horseflesh and hunting. You excel at both."

"Franz Ferdinand slaughters more animals than any decent man should countenance—it's madness," Charles retorted. *"And* he's tubercular. I'm told he isn't expected to live long enough to take the throne."

"Your mother says he is quite passionate about roses."

"Wonderful! He can present them to every girl he hopes to

marry." Charles waved his hand dismissively in a gesture that echoed, had he known it, his father. "I have only just returned to London from my Paris posting."

"And that was a mistake," the Prince said. "You are my eldest son. You'll be thirty-three next week. You ought to give up this diplomatic nonsense and tend to our estates. Spend some time in Vienna. Go to balls with the Archduke and meet all the pretty young women. Marry one of them, even, and take her with you to your embassies in Berlin and Paris. But settle down, my son. I won't live forever."

"Nonsense. You look fitter with each passing year."

"*Karl.*" The Prince slammed his desk with his fist.

Charles stiffened.

The Prince took a deep breath, poured himself another brandy, and offered the bottle.

Charles shook his head.

"Your brother has been married already for ten years," his father pointed out. "*He has only daughters,* Karl. I need an heir. *You* need an heir."

"Do I?" Charles asked levelly.

The Prince tossed back his drink. "If you want to inherit my title—my power in the Emperor's court. My *palaces.* My stud farms and hunting lodges. My dignities as a member of the Order of the Golden Fleece, and my knighthood in the Holy Roman Empire—*yes,* Karl. If you wish to be the Eighth Prince Fürst Kinsky von Wchinitz und Tettau, *you must come home,* and take up your duties as my son."

There was a silence. The two men, so terribly alike, studied each other.

"I pay an unending stream of bills." Prince Ferdinand lifted a few papers from his desk. "Your hunters. Your *racers.* Your lodgings in London. Your flat in Paris. Your carriages. The cost of your guns—do you *really* have to buy them in Bruton Street, Karl? Not to mention your bootmaker and your tailor. I wonder how you would contrive to live if I suddenly *stopped* meeting your obligations?"

"Are you threatening to disinherit me?"

The Prince smiled sadly. "Well. I do have other sons. Far less expensive, I might add."

Charles rose and bowed.

"Lord Randolph Churchill's wife is an extremely beautiful and accomplished woman." Prince Ferdinand's eyelids flickered. "Your mother tells me that you are in love with her."

"More than I have ever loved anyone."

His father shrugged. "Keep her on the side if you must. But by God, Karl—you must find an acceptable wife. One of impeccable birth and breeding. *Of your own*."

# PART FOUR

# Ship of Ghosts

*1894—95*

# CHAPTER FORTY

Winston sat on Chobham Common, the empty heath not far from the Royal Military Academy at Sandhurst, with a piece of charcoal in his hand and a large pad of drawing paper on his knees. He was wearing the scarlet coat and pillbox-shaped forager's cap that made up a subaltern's uniform, and he was utterly absorbed in his task: the composition of a topographical map. He had always possessed a facility for drawing—a skill not much valued among dukes' grandsons, although his mother encouraged it. Frowning furiously, he alternately scanned the horizon and peered back at his paper. It was a bright June day—Tuesday, the twenty-sixth—and the short-brimmed forager's cap did nothing to shield his eyes from sun. His Topography instructor expected the map tomorrow, and though Win longed to chuck it and return to his quarters for tea, he compressed his lips and narrowed his eyes. Most of his fellows couldn't draw half so well. He'd get full marks for the map if it killed him.

He had been at Sandhurst nearly a year. It had taken him three tries to pass the final entrance examinations, but once admitted, he had found the academy to be glorious. It was as unlike Harrow or any other boys' public school as could possibly be imagined. Although the schedule was grueling, Winston thought Sandhurst was as good as a holiday. He was allowed—*commanded,* even—to dig trenches and construct breastworks. He revetted parapets with heather and sandbags. He cut railway lines with something called guncotton, which was explosive, and he was taught to set charges

that blew up masonry bridges. He learned how to replace the rubble with pontoons, so that horses and men could cross, and he
learned to construct *fougasses*—primitive land mines. It was the
world of his nursery soldiers magically brought to life, and he was
ecstatic at his luck.

His entrance score was low, of course—too much maths and
French—which placed him in the cavalry instead of infantry. A
cavalry commission meant Winston would have to set up a stable—
not just several chargers, but also hacks for every day. Lord Randolph had written him an unhappy letter upon learning the news.
Horses cost too much.

The charcoal faltered for an instant in Winston's fingers and he
felt almost physically sick. The handwriting had been shaky—
Father was always unwell lately—but he could read the fury in the
half-legible words.

*In that failure is demonstrated beyond refutation your slovenly
happy-go-lucky harum-scarum style of work for which you have
always been distinguished. . . . Never have I received a really
good report of your conduct. . . . With all the advantages you had,
with all the abilities which you foolishly think yourself to possess,
with all the efforts that have been made . . . this is the grand
result. . . . I no longer attach the slightest weight to anything you
may say about your own acquirements and exploits. If you cannot
prevent yourself from leading the idle useless unprofitable life
you had during your schooldays and later months, you will
become a mere social wastrel, one of the hundreds of public
school failures, and you will degenerate into a shabby, unhappy
and futile existence. If so, you will have to bear all the blame for
such misfortunes yourself.*

"Churchill! Mr. Churchill!"
He threw aside the drawing pad and scrambled up, brushing

the seat of his trousers with his hands. "Oy!" he called. "Over here!"

A messenger boy he recognized was running across the Common, his bicycle tossed behind in the heath. Winston felt a flicker of apprehension. Why were they looking for him? Had he done something wrong? He bent to gather his things into his rucksack and felt again the glancing blow of sunlight on his cheek. *Damn.* He had been so close to finishing—

"Mr. *Church*ill." The boy came up panting, then bent in half with his hands on his knees, wheezing.

"What is it, Sid?"

Sid reached into his shirt, open at the neck, and withdrew a sealed envelope—slightly dampened from his exertions. He flourished it at Winston.

"From the adjutant."

Winston tore open the letter.

*By order of the Secretary of State for War, Sir Henry Campbell-Bannerman, you are to proceed to London immediately upon receipt, there to bid your father, Lord Randolph Churchill, farewell on his last day in England. Special leave is hereby granted at the request of the Secretary of State for War, not to exceed thirty-six hours from the issuance of these orders.*

"My father is leaving England," he told the messenger boy blankly.

"Is he indeed, sir? And where is he bound, then?"

"I have no idea," Winston said.

Randolph had decided on a world tour three months before, in March, when his old friend Archie Primrose, the Fifth Earl of Rosebery, replaced Gladstone as Liberal Prime Minister. Arthur Balfour was Conservative Leader now, and Randolph was still going into Parliament and attempting to make speeches, but his words were unintelligible. When he rose to speak, his voice snarled forth in bursts of grunts and wheezes, choked and spitting. He no longer had control of his motor functions. His arms and legs shook; he stumbled when he walked. Arthur Balfour sat with his head in his hands on the front bench while the rest of Parliament fled for the exits, the Speaker begging for "Order!" It was a waking nightmare for anyone who had ever loved Randolph Churchill.

"There's no curtain," Rosebery muttered to Balfour. "No retirement. He's dying by inches in public."

It was Rosebery, not Arthur, who paid a difficult call on Jennie that spring. Finances were tight enough that she and Randolph had sold No. 2 Connaught Place entirely and moved in with the Dowager Duchess in Grosvenor Square. After Jennie rang for tea and she and Archie had exchanged news of their racing strings—Rosebery was a formidable owner and his horses were always Derby contenders—he came to the point.

"Have the doctors told you what to expect?" he asked.

Archie had been at Eton and Oxford with Randolph; he knew the nature of his friend's disease, although nothing would ever compel him to name it.

"They call it General Paralysis of the Insane," Jennie answered evenly. "A nerve sickness. It cannot be cured. And it will end in death. What am I to do about it, Archie?"

"Get him away—to Blenheim or somewhere else in the country."

"Blenheim is difficult now," Jennie explained, "with George gone." She was quite pale, but her voice was firm.

Randolph's elder brother Blandford had died suddenly in 1892, at the age of forty-eight. Despite his second wife Lily's fortune, George had left his affairs in deep disorder. To everyone's horror and no one's surprise, he had bequeathed twenty thousand pounds to his last mistress. Winston's cousin Sunny was now the Ninth Duke. He had entered the House of Lords at the age of twenty-one, but was persistently anxious about money. Sunny was casting about for a rich wife; he wrote to Winston in despair that if he failed to find one, he would be forced to sell Blenheim, bringing dishonor on the family.

"Could you take Randy abroad? To Biarritz, perhaps?" Rosebery suggested. "Somewhere out of the way, in the sun? His health might improve if he lived more *quietly*."

"But he doesn't live quietly," Jennie retorted, her inner flame of anger flaring. "Randy cannot sleep, he cannot sit still. At times he cannot read or write. He cannot ride a *horse,* Archie, or shoot a gun. He can barely eat without spilling food down his shirt. He is still invited to political dinners, of course, and it's sheer torture to accompany him—he terrifies the entire table by the time the first course is served. How am I to lock Randy away, I ask you, when what he craves is constant movement?"

"I see." Rosebery stared at his clasped hands. "Have you consulted with the Dowager Duchess? Has she any thoughts on the matter? What do Randy's doctors advise? Might there be some sort of medicine that would render him more . . . *malleable*?"

"You think I should drug him with morphine? Stun him to immobility, so the rest of us can get on with our lives?"

She rose abruptly from her seat and walked rapidly to the drawing room windows, staring blindly out at Grosvenor Square. She knew Rosebery was no idle gossip; he loved Randolph, and was sincerely concerned about all her family. Which meant Randy had done something unforgiveable in public.

"Why this sudden concern, Archie?" She wheeled to face him. "Has my husband embarrassed you?"

"Not me," he said quickly. "Never me. But there are those in Commons, Jennie—younger men, who do not know what he was—who have no reason to value or understand him . . ."

"Ten years ago, he commanded the world." Her voice trembled with anguish and despair. "Has Randy become an object of fun?"

Rosebery shook his head, still refusing to meet her eyes. "Of pity, rather. And horror."

Jennie's heart lurched. She reached behind her, grasped the back of a chair. "I see," she said faintly.

Rosebery stood and reached for his hat. "Somehow, my dear, you must try to save Randolph from himself. You are the only one of us with the strength and courage to do it."

Jennie consulted with the Duchess.

Fanny would always despise and resent her, but Randolph was a problem both women wanted to solve. That made them temporary allies.

"Cannot one of his doctors remove with him to the South of France?" the Duchess suggested.

"Roose would never do it," Jennie told her. "The demands of his practice are too great. And Dr. Buzzard is equally besieged."

Thomas Buzzard specialized in diseases of the nervous system; he was a consulting physician at London's National Hospital for the Paralyzed and Epileptic. Jennie had called him in to advise on Randolph's case immediately after her husband's return from South Africa, two years before. Randolph had descended to the dock at Liverpool, haggard and bearded, a refugee from his private war. He had refused to shave the beard; it hid the syphilitic chancres that had broken out on his face.

Buzzard suggested that Randolph go to Norway for a fishing trip, perhaps with a friend. . . . But Harry Tyrwhitt-Wilson had died, and Jennie doubted that Tommie Trafford would be willing to leave Paris, where he seemed to live permanently these days. They had not met in months. Norway was likely to end only in frustration, in any case: Randolph screaming incoherently by the side of a lake, unable to bait or cast his line.

"What about Dr. Keith?" Duchess Fanny attempted.

"*My* Dr. Keith?" He was a medical man who dealt in women's

matters. "He's far too busy," Jennie told her. "Every lady in London consults him."

"He has a *son,* doesn't he? A rising fellow in medicine?"

Jennie glanced derisively at the Duchess. "*George* Keith? Not very young; he's older than Randy! And last I heard, he was working in New York."

"He has returned to London," the Duchess said with evident satisfaction. "Buzzard told me so—you know what a gossip the man is."

Jennie considered the idea. George Keith was, like his father, a specialist in female complaints. The Duchess still had no idea that her son had syphilis. In her mind, any doctor would do for a man with a nervous disorder. But it was possible, Jennie realized shrewdly, that Keith could be lured by the prospect of research: Women died of syphilis as well as men. He could learn something from her husband.

"Young Keith might be the very person to undertake a protracted journey with poor Randolph," Fanny persisted.

*Young Keith. Fifty years old if he's a day.*

"Very well," Jennie said. "I'll write to him."

"I want to see Burma before I die." Randolph kept his eyes fixed on her face, ignoring the medical specialist.

"He wants to see Burma," Jennie explained.

She was serving as interpreter of her husband's garbled words. Much as she had once translated his political speeches to a common, and accessible, brilliance. They were sitting in George Keith's consulting rooms. Keith was a man of middle height and thinning hair, already gray. His heavy spectacles glinted in the light.

"Burma," he repeated. "That is a considerable distance from England. Perhaps a trip of less ambitious extent . . . ?"

"I annexed the bloody kingdom to the empire," Randolph spluttered. "I refuse to die without seeing it."

"My husband brought Burma into the empire," Jennie explained, "while serving as Her Majesty's Secretary for India in 1885. It is his heart's desire to see the kingdom. Is it not possible that with such a goal, his health might rally?"

"Possible, indeed," Keith said uncomfortably. He was studying Randolph as he spoke, not Jennie; Randolph absorbed all his interest. Bitterly, she knew Keith was already seduced—the chance to intimately chronicle the last stages of General Paralysis of the Insane, with a captive subject, was too great to turn down. Keith was imagining academic papers, submitted to scientific journals, with the subject's name elided, of course. "Would the object of the trip be to sail directly to the Subcontinent? And then sail east to Rangoon? Or break the journey en route?"

"We thought to begin our journey in New York," Jennie said.

"New York?" The doctor was plainly startled; it was, after all, the opposite direction from the British Raj.

"Yes," Jennie said decisively. "I must visit my father's grave in Brooklyn. We'll spend a week or two in Manhattan, then travel by train to Bar Harbor, Maine. After that we intend to cross Canada, with stops at the principal towns—Ottawa, of course, and Banff Springs. Then we'll descend from Vancouver to San Francisco, where we will embark for the Orient, with scheduled halts in Yokohama, Hong Kong, China, Singapore, and eventually Madras."

"Good Lord!" Keith exclaimed. "And how much time do you expect to devote to such a scheme?"

"Nine months," Jennie answered. "Perhaps a year."

The doctor fingered his pocket watch fretfully. "A year! I am not sure I may give you an immediate answer, Lady Randolph, as to the feasibility of such a project—or my own willingness to undertake it."

"Damned fool," Randolph growled. "You should be on your knees begging for the chance to see such remote parts of the empire! And without the slightest expense to yourself!"

For once, inexplicably, the words were clear as a bell.

Keith stared at his lordship, his lips parted.

Definitely seduced.

"We'll leave you to consider our proposition." Jennie rose gracefully and, with one of her roguish smiles, extended her hand to Keith. "If you could let us know by tomorrow evening? We would not wish to delay our search for the perfect companion. Come along, darling."

# CHAPTER FORTY-ONE

Winston reached London by seven o'clock in the evening that Tuesday. He was able to dine at Duchess Fanny's in Grosvenor Square, with his mother and Jack, who had been summoned from Harrow to say farewell. Bonaparte lay in ecstasy on Jennie's lap, unaware that she was deserting him the next day. Duchess Fanny was too much overcome by the imminent departure of her son to join them; she took her dinner on a tray with Randolph in his room.

"How jolly that you shall see India at last," Winston crowed. "I remember how you *longed* to go, Mummie, when Father was Secretary. You must bring back some rubies!"

"Sapphires, I think."

"And by the time you reach the Raj," he added, "Father will have entirely recovered his strength, and be able to visit the temples with you."

"Yes, indeed." His mother grinned at him with abandon, looking like a carefree girl. "We'll see all the sights, and I'll send you sketches. Now tell me more about your riding, Win—are you truly learning to play *polo*? And what in God's name will your father say when you demand the price of a few polo ponies?"

The next morning, they all traveled together by hansom to Euston Station, where his parents would catch the Southampton train. Winston sat next to his father, who did not speak, but at one point, as the carriage slowed before the station, his trembling fingers hovered and descended on Winston's knee. They had shaken hands on rare occasions in their lives, but Randolph had never touched him with affection. Never hugged or kissed him. Winston blinked rapidly and stared straight ahead as his father's fingers closed on his thigh. Cadets of nearly twenty did not cry.

Some of their old friends were waiting on the platform to wave goodbye: Archie Rosebery, who was now Prime Minister, and Lord Goschen—who had taken Randolph's place as Chancellor of the Exchequer years ago when he'd resigned—and Mary, Lady Jeune. She had promised to invite Winston to her London home as often as possible in Jennie's absence; she was a notable political hostess, and Win would love dining with her powerful friends. Poor Jack would be rather at loose ends on his holidays, Jennie realized—Everest had been sacked a few years ago when she was no longer needed—but Duchess Fanny would take care of him. The Duchess never minded having Jack to stay; he was a quiet boy who caused no trouble.

Lord Frederic Wolverton was standing on the platform, too, next to Margot Tennant, who had recently become Margot Asquith. Her husband, Henry, was one of the principal members of the Souls—but also a member of Cabinet, and a widower with five children. Margot had astonished the world by marrying him. Which meant, Jennie thought, that it must be a love match.

"You will be too busy to write," she said as she embraced Margot, "but I shall send you reams anyway."

"Send watercolors instead," Margot advised. "Then I shall be able to picture exactly how you are."

Freddie Wolverton was a dashing fellow of thirty, Margot's age and the sort she'd been expected to marry. His hair was blond, his eyes were warm, and his teeth were very white. He was a member of the Marlborough House Set and had been paying Jennie a great deal of attention in recent weeks. When she held out her hand in parting, he drew her close and kissed her cheek. "I depend upon a steady correspondence to cheer my broken heart."

"Of course, Freddie, if you promise to reply," she retorted.

"I shall have nothing better to do," he mourned. "I'm desolate that you are abandoning me."

Jennie laughed. "You'll have your hands full, keeping Bertie in order!"

As the train pulled away from the station, she stood in the first-class compartment window, blowing kisses to Winston, who had his arm around his brother, and to the rest of the known world dwindling too swiftly behind her. Soon enough she would smile on Dr. Keith and Randolph and attempt to make some conversation, but for now, she needed all her rigid self-control.

She was keening silently for far more than her friends and family. She feared she had lost what mattered most on earth.

Charles Kinsky had not come to say goodbye.


"He will kill you," he had muttered into her ear when she'd told him of her plans in April.

They were waltzing at Consuelo Yznaga's ball the week after Easter—Consuelo, who was no longer Countess Mandeville, but the Dowager Duchess of Manchester. The old Duke had died in 1890 and thankfully released his wife, Louise, who had finally married her lover, Hart. Lottie was now Hart's Duchess of Devonshire; the press liked to call her the Double Duchess. But her son, Consuelo's husband, George, had survived his father by merely two years, dying of drink at the age of thirty-nine. Connie's only son, William, whom everyone called Kim, was the Duke of Manchester now. Connie lived anything but quietly with her fifteen-year-old daughters at 17 Charles Street, and surveyed her intimate parties from a chaise longue. She was, as always, too lazy to waltz.

"Or you will kill *him*," Charles added. He was staring at Jennie while she gazed determinedly over his shoulder, a fixed smile on her face for the benefit of anyone watching. "It's sheer folly! A *year* of wandering, Jennie, with a man who's losing his mind? I won't let you go."

"You must."

"Nonsense! No one would blame you for staying behind. We've all seen how Randolph treats you—the *rages,* the threats. . . . He's come near to striking you any number of times in public. Let this medical man you've hired be responsible for him! Why else pay the fellow's passage?"

"Randolph is *dying,* Charles." She said it bluntly. "He may not survive the voyage. What kind of wife would I be if I abandoned him now?"

She felt his hand tense on the small of her back.

The waltz ended. They clapped and moved to the edge of the room. Charles placed her arm through his and led her toward the supper table. "The sort of wife who has done everything she possibly can, Jennie. No one would reproach you."

"Except myself."

He handed her a coupe of champagne. "Has Duchess Fanny bullied you into this?"

"Duchess Fanny is utterly opposed to my going! She says I'm the cause of Randolph's *nervous complaint.* The Duchess believes that if her son were only free of me, he'd recover. She wants Keith to manage Randolph alone."

Charles stared at her. "The woman has given you *permission* to stay behind? And you haven't swooned in gratitude? If Randolph dies, Jennie, she'll tell all of London that you drove him to his grave."

"I know." She set down her glass and drew a deep breath. Surely, if Charles could be made to understand anything, it was the notion of *honor*. "But you see, my darling, I made a vow twenty years ago. *In sickness or in health*. Would you have me show no faith or loyalty, in the worst of all possible times?"

"Yes," he snarled. "I damn well would."

"Someone has to fiddle," she told him, "while Rome burns."

He came to her three days later, on an afternoon of chill spring rain when the fires were lit throughout Duchess Fanny's Grosvenor Square house. Jennie was writing letters alone in the library. She received him there, and when she had told the footman to bring brandy, and the door had closed on the two of them, she took Charles's hand and drew him down to a sofa.

"What is it, my dear?" she asked.

He had a look on his face she'd only seen a few times before, as he schooled his horse over the jumps at Aintree—a reckless mix of joy, resolve, and dread. Her heart sank.

"I've secured a transfer to Brussels," he said.

She felt the light die out of her. "When?"

"The usual time. The end of June."

"After I've gone, then." She managed a smile. "How long is the posting? Will you give up your London flat?"

"Jennie." He grasped her hands tightly. All the world in his grip. "*Listen to me.* I secured the post for both of us."

"*Both* of us?"

"Come with me. Leave London when Randolph does—and take a place in Brussels. You'll love the city, darling. The musical world is exactly what you'd wish, and there are *painters*. Even women painters. Professionals, of genius. It's an easy distance to Paris if you wished to study—"

She rose and walked to the fire, holding out her hands, which were suddenly cold. "What are you saying, Charles?"

"Marry me, my love."

"I'm *already* married."

He shook his head. "Not in your heart."

"You've always commanded that," she told him softly.

"I won't, when you're on the other side of the world."

A shaft of fear went through her. Had he listened to gossip?

Minnie Paget's poison? That she took her pleasure at the slightest opportunity, regardless of vows?

"Nonsense." She glanced at him. "Is this some sort of test, Charles? Must I choose Brussels over duty, to prove my love for you?"

"Duty!" He downed his brandy in a single draft and crossed deliberately toward her. "Do you know what Randolph's friends say, Jennie, over cards in their private clubs? That he's not just sick, but insane. *Insane.* You have no duty to live with a madman!"

"So I should live as your mistress instead?" She faced him. "Until Randolph *dies*? A fine spectacle that would make!"

"No." He grasped her shoulders. "Sue for divorce. As soon as possible."

"On what grounds?" The usual cause was desertion—and she could hardly claim that. Since his year in South Africa, Randy had practically lived in her pocket.

"Anything you like!" Charles cried. "Rape—sodomy! Lord Randolph cannot possibly refuse to release you. Think of the secrets you could tell."

"Never!" She stared at him in shock. "How can you even *suggest* it? The damage to my boys . . ."

"Jennie, demand your freedom," Charles pleaded. "The world will hold you blameless."

"And shun me regardless! Worse yet, the world would shun *you,* Charles. I will *not* be the reason your career ends in scandal."

"Let me worry about that," he said impatiently. "I've thought it all through—I've thought of nothing else since you told me your plans." He roughly pulled her close and spoke into the black mass of her hair. "Come away with me to Brussels, my darling. We'll secure your freedom and be married quietly. After that, we can live anywhere in the world that Austria has an embassy. The United States, even."

For an instant, Jennie's knees nearly gave way. His vision was bewitching. Life as Charles's *wife*—not the indiscretion she'd been for the past ten years. No hurried meetings, broken off too soon. No pretense, or *lies,* or subterfuge. No persistent loneliness at the core of her being. Just love. With her soul mate and equal.

*She would become the Princess Karl.*

Impossible. She stiffened, and stepped back.

"No."

His brows furled. His dark head dipped over her. "Jennie—you understand? I'm offering you *all that I am.* All that I have."

"Which is immense. And it's too much," she said.

He was scowling now, anger gathering on his brow. "What do you mean?"

"The cost."

"Your place in Society? You'd gain a higher one in mine. The cost to your sons? I'd be a far better father than they've ever had!"

"Yes," she admitted with difficulty. "Winston and Jack love you. But they would not be *your sons.* They would not be your father's *heirs.* Marry me, Charles, and your parents will cut you off with tuppence."

"Bollocks," he said brutally. "My mother admires you."

"Your mother barely speaks in your father's presence."

"I will persuade him."

"You can't," she laughed. "He's a creature of his class and his world! And he despises me. Under your Austrian laws, I am *not* your equal, Charles, in blood or birth or status! I am not of the *High Nobility.* You cannot marry me without dishonoring your house. Isn't that true?"

He drew a sudden breath, but said nothing.

"Pauline de Metternich explained it all in a letter a few weeks ago. Ours would be—what do you call it? A *left-handed* marriage?"

"A morganatic one," he muttered.

"Which means you could not pass on your title, your wealth, or your estates to any child we might have?"

"Those laws are outmoded. They'll change in our lifetime."

"You may be right," Jennie conceded. "But you can't give up your birthright on the chance."

"That's my decision, not yours," he flashed.

"One you'd regret, and come to hate."

*"Never."* Charles reached for her with a kind of desperation.

"Eventually you'd hate *me* for what I've cost you," Jennie persisted. "I couldn't bear your hatred, Charles."

"Never," he said again, and pulled her mouth to his.

She felt the fury in his body, barely leashed; fury at the truth of all she'd said, at the perversity of it, the despair they both felt. Another instant and he would lay her down on the rug right in front of Duchess Fanny's fire and plunge into her body, as though that could change things.

She pushed away from him.

"Go, Charles," she breathed. "Just go."

And to her dismay—with a goaded look—he *went.*

Throughout May and much of June, Jennie planned the trip with Randolph and his doctor. They sold their share of the Abbess to their racing partner, Lord Dunraven, as well as some of Randolph's African gold stocks, to pay for the year abroad. When she was not poring over maps or Baedekers, Jennie made sure to go out as often as possible—to the theater, or concerts, or the myriad parties that filled the London spring. She needed brief bouts of freedom. In a few months, there would be no escape.

And she spent a good deal of her time, in public and on purpose, with Lord Frederic Wolverton.

Whenever Charles Kinsky called in Grosvenor Square, Jennie was "not at home." Whenever she encountered him in public, she was on Freddie Wolverton's arm, and determined to look as though she hadn't a care in the world. The gossip sheets began to hint slyly at her latest flirtation. She hoped that would incense Charles—humiliate him, even. Maybe then he'd give up *her,* instead of his future.

The night before she left for Euston Station, Jennie received a letter by the last post.

*Come to me tonight,* he'd written, *or never come to me again.*

The exact words she had uttered on their first night together, long ago, at Sandringham.

Charles knew, none better, how to twist a knife in her heart.

She did not send a reply.

# CHAPTER FORTY-TWO

In Bar Harbor, Maine, she danced the Boston—a slow, American version of the waltz—at the Kebo Valley Club, a broad-eaved, comfortable restaurant and theater built in the Shingle style. The summer people of Mount Desert Island played croquet there as well as tennis, the women in tidy white shirtwaists and cinched linen skirts they were forced to clutch in one hand while they held a racquet in the other. Jennie preferred to walk the island's rough trails after breakfast, her memory stirred by the massive granite shelves jutting into the deep, deep waters of the bay. On more than one occasion, in secluded places, she allowed herself to spring from rock to rock as she had done so long ago in Newport—and hoped some shadow of Camille followed her.

The fashionable world in Maine was both freer than, and yet as consciously formal as, the Newport one Jennie had once known—indeed, many of the principal New York families had homes in both places. There was the same round of pointless dressing for the business of paying calls and leaving cards, which Jennie engaged in like the others simply to avoid being isolated. If she skulked alone in her rooms with Randolph, people would talk.

George Vanderbilt invited the Churchills to dine one evening in the house he called Pointe d'Acadie, set in the pines above the rocky shore. He was younger than Jennie—perhaps Charles Kinsky's age—dark-haired and slender, with sensitive eyes and the ivory skin of a man who studied too much indoors. He was rumored to be cold and aloof; Jennie found him merely shy.

"I understand you paint," he remarked as he handed her a coupe of champagne. "What do you think of my pictures?"

Instead of the usual seascapes and family portraits, Jennie saw, to her surprise, that the walls of the airy saloon were hung thickly with paintings in the Impressionist style. She stopped still, her glass forgotten in her hands. "Is that a Seurat?" she asked. It was all gold and lapis paint, the figure of a juggler or clown at the center. Nothing like the studies she had bought years ago, but recognizable as the painter's all the same.

"Got it in one," George said softly. "Nobody gives it a second glance, usually. Too difficult for most people to comment upon."

Jennie smiled. "I once visited his studio in Pigalle. How often do you get to Paris?"

"Once or twice a year. We've houses there, you know."

*We* being the Vanderbilts. George was the youngest child of the current generation; it was his much older brother William, whom Alva Erskine Smith had married. William and the eldest brother, Cornelius, had inherited the inconceivable sum of two hundred million dollars *each*. They had both built palaces in Newport on the strength of it. George had inherited far less, but Jennie thought he made the most of what he had.

"Let me show you the gardens," he suggested. "We've just time before dinner."

Thankfully, Randolph was having one of his better nights. Jennie glanced over her shoulder at Dr. Keith, who gave her a slight nod, his protective gaze on his patient. Randy was actually talking *politics* with another of George's guests.

She walked out onto the house's terrace, where the hillside fell away to the rocky shore and the last light of summer shone brilliantly on the distant sea. Her silk chiffon gown—in a shade that echoed the Atlantic—swirled about her ankles. Once the sun went down, the nights were sharply cooler in Maine, and Jennie had tossed a fine wool wrap about her bare shoulders. "What a glorious prospect," she said, breathing greedily. The clear air filled her lungs with the scent of roses, and salt, and the fresh smack of pine.

George led her through a landscape deliberately shaped to look wild—"I *adore* Frederick Law Olmsted, don't you?"—to a clearing where he stopped short, his hands in his pockets. "We all swim here on hot days," he said.

"Do you?" Jennie gazed at the rectangular pool, its waters as dark as the sea. There was a fountain at the far end, gushing whitely against the backdrop of Olmsted's shrubs.

"It's the first of its kind in Bar Harbor," George told her. "Seawater, piped up from below the cliff. Quite refreshing. Go on—try it."

He might have expected her to dip her hand in the fountain. But impulsively, Jennie slipped out of one silver sandal and, holding her skirt clear of the water, drew her toes across the pool's surface. A trail of bubbles followed, like a ship's wake. She saw George's eyes widen as he stared at her foot and the line of her leg, draped in chiffon. Then his shy gaze flicked up to her face. He swallowed convulsively. Jennie remembered he was unmarried. She had unnerved him.

She slipped her sandal back on. "And you *all* swim here? Men and women together? In bathing dress?"

"Yes."

"How very daring." She took a ruminative sip of champagne. "I had no idea that Americans were so . . . promiscuous."

Randolph was not always well enough to leave. There were hours at a time that Jennie sat with him in a shrouded room, the shades pulled down against the light that hurt his eyes. Dr. Keith made a point of relieving her after such periods, when his patient had taken a dose of laudanum and was profoundly asleep. Jennie usually sought out the company of other people then, from a desperate need for simple conversation. Sometimes she played duets with chance acquaintances, or wrote deliberately light letters to Freddie

Wolverton, whose replies occasionally reached her as she sat in a straight-backed rocking chair on the hotel's covered porch.

She never heard from Charles.

Jennie was reading a novel on the Kebo Valley Club's shady lawn one afternoon when she met up with a lost Siren from her past: George Vanderbilt's sister-in-law Alva.

It was her voice Jennie noticed first—unmistakably imperious, yet softened by a Southern drawl.

"Naturally," Alva said to an invisible minion, "I shouldn't wish to sit in such bright sunlight. I'm sure my delicate skin would suffer immeasurably from the insult. There *must* be some chairs in the shade, and if not, you may carry these two over and just shove 'em right in among the others. No one will mind. *Much*."

Alva had always known how to command her subjects. Jennie closed her book, leaving her finger between the pages as a marker, and fixed her eyes expectantly on the corner of the clubhouse. And in an instant, there was the procession: a quartet of male servants, shuffling under the weight of two lawn chairs; an expensively dressed woman with a face as broad and red as the side of a barn; and behind her, under a frothy sunshade held aloft by a frail gloved hand, the most famous eighteen-year-old Beauty in all of America.

"Alva Erskine Smith," Jennie called, rising from her chair and smiling with true affection. "What in the name of heaven are you doing in Bar Harbor?"

And that quickly, she was a girl of nine again, back in New York.

*Manhattan, February 1863*

There were several new girls in the Family Dancing Classes at Delmonico's that winter, standing in corners and against the walls, stiff with apprehension and uncertain where to leave their wraps.

Some had bored maids or nurses sitting behind them. One girl with a pugnacious expression and a head of red hair was chaperoned by an enormous black man in a powdered wig and eighteenth-century livery, who refused to take a seat. Jennie found his whole appearance astounding and smiled at him shyly in greeting. The man returned her gaze impassively, not a muscle of his face moving.

"Who are they?" she'd whispered to Minnie Stevens (later Paget). Minnie's father had built the most modern hotel in New York, the Fifth Avenue, which sat on the southwest corner of Madison Square, not far from Papa's house. It had cost two million dollars, an unfathomable sum to spend on a single building, Mamma said. Every room had a private bathroom with indoor water closets, which some doctors said were dangerously unhygienic. Papa took Jennie and Clarita to the Fifth Avenue when it opened so that they could ride the "vertical screw railway," the first elevator in New York. Within months, Mr. Stevens's hotel was the political and social center of the city. The Stevenses had entered Society on the strength of it.

"Southerners," Minnie said succinctly. "I pinched them both. My father says Southerners are damned Rebels."

"Minnie!" Jennie was shocked and secretly envious. Papa never swore in her presence. She remembered suddenly that Mamma had said the Stevenses were not really "our sort."

"The red-haired girl said she'd heard my mother was a chambermaid before Papa married her," Minnie added. "I'd have slapped her, but the Negro scared me."

"Was she?" Jennie asked, fascinated. Mamma had once repeated this rumor, too. Jennie assumed there was something Not Quite Right about Mrs. Stevens.

Mr. Percival, the piano master, sat down on his bench. Mrs. Andrews, who conducted the Family Dancing Classes, motioned for the girls to find partners. Jennie put her arm around Minnie's waist and held up her hand, ready to lead her in the waltz.

"Of course not!" Minnie retorted. She had dark hair like Jennie and green eyes that were very sharp. Although she was slightly older, she was shorter and thus at a disadvantage; she had to cling to Jennie's hand and shoulder. Jennie thought this was only reasonable. Most men Minnie Stevens would eventually dance with would be taller than she was. "Mamma married Papa in Lowell, long before the hotel was even thought of. She could not possibly have worked for Papa as a chambermaid."

"Where is Lowell?"

"New England." Minnie shrugged petulantly. "And everyone knows New England is better than the South. I should like to *hurt* that girl."

"What's her name?"

"Smith." Minnie's green glare bored into Jennie. "No one of distinction is *ever* named Smith, Mamma says."

Jennie glanced over her shoulder. The Smith monster was paired with another stranger, a girl with sparkling black eyes and elaborate ringlets of dark gold piled high on her head. She had a laughing mouth and an aquiline nose. Something about her puckish face made Jennie want to laugh out loud. "*That* one looks like a princess," she told Minnie. "Wouldn't she be perfect in fancy dress!"

Minnie followed her gaze. "She's another Rebel. I couldn't possibly remember her name—it's fearfully foreign. Her father's from some island. And her mother grew up on a plantation. Cotton people."

Jennie was leading vigorously, too absorbed in Minnie's gossip to pay strict attention to the other pairs of girls as she swept buoyantly around the room. She loved the waltz; it was as good as skating or driving, so long as you didn't step on your partner's feet. "Do you think they're all moving north because of the war, Minnie?" she asked. "Maybe they're ashamed of being Southerners. Maybe they never wanted to leave the Union. We should—"

"No," Minnie said. She stopped abruptly in the middle of the dance floor and dropped Jennie's hand. "Don't you know that black man is a *slave?*"

Her young voice was piercing. Every head in the room turned swiftly toward Jennie and Minnie, and with a jangle, Mr. Percival crashed his hands down on the keys.

A body collided sharply with Jennie's. She turned, and looked straight into the Delft-blue eyes of Miss Emily Astor. Emily was as fair as Jennie's sister Camille. Her mother, Caroline, ruled New York Society. The Astors had never recognized any of the Jeromes.

"You have trod on my toes," Emily said. "But of course, how could you possibly know how to behave? *Your* mother is an Indian. And *yours*"—her gaze drifted three inches over Minnie Stevens's head—"is a shopgirl from Lowell."

"Girls, girls!" Mrs. Andrews cried in exasperation. "Have I not told you repeatedly, *there is to be no conversation during the figures?* Miss Astor, are you injured?"

"Not at all, Mrs. Andrews," Emily replied with an angelic look, "but I fear Miss Jerome has said the most *shocking* things. I dare not repeat them."

"Snake," Jennie breathed.

"Miss Jerome, Miss Stevens, pray sit out the next dance." Mrs. Andrews hurried over to the side of the room and seized the girl named Smith by the hand. As Jennie passed them, she heard the dancing mistress say strenuously, ". . . *cannot* allow it. Must insist . . . against my Republican principles and those of this establishment . . . a note to your mother . . ."

Jennie sank into a chair. She longed with all her heart to box Emily Astor's ears, not so much on her own account as on Minnie Stevens's. At Emily's words, Minnie had flushed red and then dead white, as though she might faint. It must be true, Jennie decided, that Mrs. Stevens had worked in a shop before Mr. Stevens married her.

The two Southern girls also sat out the dance. Miss Smith looked, indeed, as if the Civil War had come to Delmonico's. Her hazel eyes were flashing dangerously and her arms were crossed over her thin chest. She had a blunt, square face and a very strong chin. Behind her, the black man held out her coat, waiting for Miss Smith to allow him to place it over her shoulders. The plantation princess stood hesitantly beside her. Jennie studied them and comprehended the situation in an instant: the princess had been delivered to the dancing class in Miss Smith's carriage. She had no other chaperone. If Miss Smith left, so, too, would her friend.

Jennie took Minnie's hand, rose from her seat, and walked resolutely over to the two new girls. As they were Southerners, she curtseyed carefully, as though she were on the stage of Papa's theater.

"I'm Jennie Jerome," she told them. "I should very much like to meet your . . . footman."

"Why?" the red-haired girl demanded.

"I have never known a black man before."

Dobbie was colored, it was true, but she was a woman—and had always been free.

Miss Smith smiled faintly, as if in pity at the stupidity of Northerners. "This is Monroe," she said. "He's been with me since I was born. I guess he'd die for me. Wouldn't you, Monroe?"

"I'm not so sure about that, Miss Alva," Monroe said. "Don't you go putting on airs before the other girls. Pleased to meet you, Miss Jerome."

"I'm Alva," Miss Smith admitted. She offered Jennie her hand. "Alva Erskine Smith, of Mobile and Fifth Avenue."

The way she said it, her name came out *Owl-lvuh Urhs-kee-yin Smee-yuth*. Jennie was enthralled.

"That's Con*swell*-a," Alva added offhandedly with a wave at her friend. "It means 'comfort' in Cuban. She told me."

The princess dimpled at Jennie and dropped into her own delicious curtsey. "Consuelo Yznaga del Valle y Clemens at your service."

"This is Minnie." Jennie pulled her friend forward. Minnie's body was rigid with stubbornness but she relaxed under the strength of Consuelo's smile. "Minnie lives at the Fifth Avenue Hotel, which is a little like an enchanted castle and Heaven all at once. She invites her friends for hot chocolate and sweet buns on Saturday afternoons. Don't you, Minnie?"

"I do," Minnie said defiantly. "Miss Astor is *not* one of my friends."

"She's not one of ours, either," Alva said.

Jennie danced with Alva next and Minnie partnered Consuelo. It was the first time that Minnie had danced the lead, and she was pink with pleasure at the end. Consuelo was perfectly happy to be led and spent the remainder of the class displaying her small white kitten's teeth in a broad smile.

Alva insisted on playing the role of boy. She and Jennie almost came to blows about it—Miss Smith revealed an alarming tendency to use her fists until Monroe called her to heel—but Jennie wisely gave way. She sensed that in a world ruled by Astors, Alva might come in handy someday.

Now, thirty years later, Alva Vanderbilt stopped short on the Kebo Valley Club's porch, stared hard at Jennie, and let out a crow. "It's true! I saw the news in the gossip sheets—*Lord and Lady Randolph Churchill Make World Tour*—and when I noticed you'd no intention of stopping in Newport, I said, 'Well, Con*swell*-a, we'll have to go rusticate at George's in Maine!'"

She was referring, of course, to the Beauty, who had been locked away in the schoolroom when Jennie last glimpsed America. Consuelo Vanderbilt was now Officially Out. Jennie dropped her book and stepped forward into Alva's bosomy embrace. The two excessive deck chairs were ranged beside Lady Randolph's and fresh lemonade and macaroons were brought for all three of them. Alva introduced her daughter. She had named her after Consuelo Yznaga, to give her a bit of continental flair.

The Beauty had not much to say for herself. But then, she could never have gotten a word in edgewise; Alva talked for ten.

"Sad about poor Connie," she mused. "A widow so young. And I hear her scoundrel of a husband left nothing but debts."

"I'm sure Consuelo will rally," Jennie replied. "She has her children to live for. There is young Kim, of course—the present Duke—who is barely twenty, and May and Nell are but fifteen years old. They are beauties, the pair of them, with the same gold hair Connie had as a girl."

"I wish her well rid of both," Alva declared, "though with no fortune to speak of, she'll have a time sending them off. It's a deal of trouble, Jennie, raising daughters—but you wouldn't know that. Finding a suitable husband! Which reminds me." Alva leaned closer. "What do you think of Minnie Paget these days?"

"I rarely see her," Jennie managed, after an instant's surprise. "She has inherited her fortune at last, and cultivates *other* friends."

Alva smirked knowingly. "She offered to introduce me and Con*swell*-a around the English aristocracy next fall, when we tour the Continent. *If I pay her expenses,* Jennie. What do I need with Minnie Paget, when I've got you and Dowager Duchess Connie?"

"I cannot presume to advise you." Jennie gathered her thoughts. She must be careful; Minnie had visited New York recently, and might be closer to Alva than either admitted. Marietta Stevens, Minnie's mother, was one of Alva's social acquaintances. "She certainly is received everywhere, and knows everyone."

"But?" Alva demanded.

Jennie faced her old friend squarely. "Her tongue is a double-edged sword, my dear. One is never quite certain whether she is a friend or an enemy. I imagine that her English acquaintance might wonder the same about *you*."

"If that isn't the old Minnie! Tell me something I don't know!"

Jennie smiled faintly. "Minnie may certainly admit you to the highest circles, Alva. She trades on her intimacy with the Prince of Wales."

"I doubt His Highness is much of a stranger to *you*, Lady Randolph. Nor Connie, neither. I read the papers. What I want to know is—is Minnie Paget worth her price?"

"It is possible," Jennie replied delicately, "that her price is the best guarantee of avoiding her *poison*. If you reject Minnie, Alva, she has the power to ruin your daughter's chances."

She watched Alva absorb her warning.

"Thank you, Jennie. Nothing more need be said."

"What's your real object, darling?" Jennie asked. Her eyes drifted to the Beauty. Consuelo Vanderbilt was an exquisite piece of girlhood, as utterly unlike her mother as two creatures could be. Where Alva was virulently red-haired and freckled, with forthright hazel eyes and a pugnacious chin, her daughter was sublimely dark, with almond-shaped eyes that suggested the Orient, or perhaps Slavic blood. Her full lips were red and pouted. Her cheekbones, delicately tinted with a virginal flush, were divinely high. Her neck was a phenomenon of swanlike slenderness, adorned with a diamond collar to rival any of Princess Alix's. Consuelo was a freak, Jennie decided—a complete accident of Nature—aligned with a fortune that exceeded any debutante's on the planet.

The girl's thick eyelashes fluttered like butterfly wings beneath Jennie's scrutiny. Upright as though a sword were plunged down her spine, Consuelo gazed wanly at the horizon. Not even her sunshade trembled as she held it aloft. But she had neither animation nor conversation. Insipid, Jennie decided—and probably a peagoose. No brains.

"Con*swell*-a," Alva said, "you go on into the Ladies' Saloon and write that thank-you note to Mrs. Astor. Tell her we'll call when we're back in Newport, mind."

"Yes, Mamma."

The Beauty smiled at Jennie—who felt as though a curtain had parted, so brilliant were the girl's perfect teeth—and drifted elegantly away.

"Mrs. Astor?" Jennie inquired sardonically.

Alva fluttered a hand. "Oh, me and Caroline have been on sparring terms ever since I threw a Society ball ten years ago. She was pushing off her youngest, who was dying to come to our party. Needed an invitation. Lina had to recognize us. Changed all the Vanderbilts' lives, I don't mind saying, and they owe it to a *Smith*. But you asked what I want for my girl."

Jennie nodded.

"I want a noble title," Alva declared. "Con*swell*-a's worth a hundred million dollars. As God is my witness. She thinks she's in love with some polo player here in Bar Harbor, but it won't last. Love's Young Dream always turns out to be a nightmare, and when you wake up screaming, you need something to live on. Aren't I right, Jennie? Wasn't she born to be a duchess?"

"Weren't we all?" Jennie observed mildly. "But, Alva—money and titles aren't everything. They don't secure happiness."

"As if we both don't know." Alva eyed her speculatively. "You've got the title, and I've got the money. I saw *Town Topics* suggest you're a two-bit floozy. That's just so much horseshit, Jennie. But I guess neither of us is the picture of wedded bliss. If I catch Mr. Vanderbilt sailing off to Europe in the *Alva* with one more dancer on board, I'm suing for divorce."

"Really?" Jennie was startled. "But the scandal . . ."

"I'll risk it. I'd like a little happiness before I die. Money certainly doesn't buy that, but I'm willing to bet it buys freedom."

Jennie studied her, tempted. England was definitely more cautious than America. "Wouldn't a divorce hurt your daughter's chances?"

"Oh, I'll wait until Con*swell*-a's gone off," Alva replied comfortably. "With her looks and her fortune, it won't be long. Do you know any available dukes? And can Minnie Paget bring 'em up to scratch?"

"My nephew Sunny is hanging out for a rich wife." Jennie smiled broadly. "He's the present Duke of Marlborough and decidedly presentable. But you can't mean to sell your daughter to the highest bidder, Alva!"

"Don't I just?" Alva's eyes flashed. "How old is this Sunny, anyway?"

# CHAPTER FORTY-THREE

In early August, the Churchills left Bar Harbor and traveled by private train car across Canada. They were welcomed in Ottawa at Government House, a vast stone monstrosity of nearly two hundred rooms. It was built in a bewildering mix of Regency, Norman, and Florentine styles, placed high on a bluff overlooking two rivers. The current Governor-General of Canada was John Hamilton-Gordon, the Earl of Aberdeen. His wife's brother was married to Randolph's sister Fanny.

Which meant that a number of the Aberdeens' English friends in Ottawa knew the Spencer-Churchills.

Jennie could feel them talking behind her back whenever she entered a room. There was the sudden cessation of noise—the lifting of heads—and the equally studied aversion. A few of the men tried to include Randolph in cards and cigars and drinking in the billiards room. They ignored his inarticulate grunts and shaking limbs, the way he set each foot down carefully as he moved glacially across the floor. He could not hold a hand of cards without dropping them on the table, could not lift a glass without it chattering against his teeth. Everyone spoke cheerfully over his head as though he were a half-witted child.

And then there were the women.

"Duchess Fanny's uncle was Lord Castlereagh, you know, who slit his own throat with a penknife," Jennie heard one of them murmur—a Mrs. Fitzherbert, whose husband was something at the embassy. "The Duchess's brother went mad, too, and had to be *restrained* before he died."

"It runs in the family," her friend agreed, "but the American strain can hardly help. I hear the elder Churchill boy is tragically slow! He was asked to leave St. George's—and never tried for Eton."

Jennie rose, intending to move away from them, her eyes brilliant with anger. Mrs. Fitzherbert called out to her, as though only just aware of her presence.

"Lady Randolph! Are you missing all your dear friends during this protracted tour?"

Jennie halted, and turned back toward the two women. "Friends are everywhere, when one travels through the empire. But I confess that it is my sons I long to see. The younger is still at Harrow, and the elder has earned a distinguished record at Sandhurst. Lord Randolph and I expect great things of both. Have you any children, Mrs. Fitzherbert?"

The lady's expression closed. "Sadly, I was never blessed."

"You have my *deepest* sympathy." Jennie allowed a certain self-satisfaction to creep into her voice. "Nothing in my life has equaled the gift of my two remarkable boys! The young demand a great deal of trouble—spirit is, after all, the mark of *genius*—but as my sons mature, they prove such a support and comfort. Far deeper than that of mere *friends*."

"How remarkable, then, that you have chosen to abandon them so long." Mrs. Fitzherbert's gaze hardened. "You are acquainted with my cousin Freddie Wolverton, I believe?"

"A little," Jennie replied. "How is Lord Wolverton? Have you any news of him?"

"Only the most delightful!" Mrs. Fitzherbert exclaimed. "He is engaged to be married—to dear Lady Edith Ward. He has been besotted with her these several months, you know. Quite the pursuit—it has set all of London talking. I am so happy to be able to wish him joy!"

Jennie had met Lady Edith, a plain girl of twenty-three who had languished on the marriage mart for the past five Seasons.

Jennie gave Mrs. Fitzherbert her most artless smile. "Joy indeed. Lady Edith will never figure as a beauty, but she *is* a considerable heiress. And as the son of a banking family, Lord Wolverton will know just how to *value* her charms! When next you write to your cousin, pray offer him my sincerest congratulations."

She would not be writing to Freddie again herself.

They left Ottawa abruptly two days later, after Randolph tried to strangle their manservant, Job, when he offered his lordship the newspaper after breakfast. It was a Canadian journal, not a British one, and Randolph was outrageously offended. He put his hands around Job's neck and throttled him, squealing all the while.

The fit occurred in the library at Government House, and at least seven gentlemen witnessed it. Two of them intervened and pulled Randolph off his servant's neck.

"His lordship appears seriously unwell," Lord Aberdeen warned Jennie that afternoon when they met privately in his study. "Have you considered that travel only worsens his condition? Cannot you return home?"

"I appreciate your concern," she told him, meeting his troubled gaze squarely. "But our plans are quite fixed. Job, naturally, will be sent back to the Dowager Duchess of Marlborough's home in London—at Lord Randolph's expense."

"You will wish, I am sure, to take dinner in your rooms," Aberdeen said.

It was a command, Jennie knew—not a request.

September wore away while they visited Banff Springs, where the railway line was lit at night by the crimson glow of vast forest fires no one bothered to battle. They reached Vancouver, Victoria, then San Francisco—where they stayed some days, and Randolph was well enough to leave in Dr. Keith's care for a few hours. Jennie might have done some shopping or found the salons of a few artists, but as she prepared to leave the hotel lobby one afternoon, drawing on her gloves, a slim, dark Eurasian boy darted forward and bowed.

"If Madame would like to see Chinatown, I can promise to lead her through it in safety. You might buy jade. I assure the best prices."

Jennie stopped short, assessing him. He was neatly dressed and his speech little different from hers; they were countrymen, however divergent their circumstances. Chinatown was regarded as an infamous and vice-ridden place, dangerous for any white person to enter, much less a lady alone. The boy might hand her over to confederates, who would steal her purse. Or worse. Jennie glanced through the hotel's double doors at the sharp sunlight on the paving; an innocuous day. And she was restless, fretful . . . to be brutally honest, *lonely*. If Charles were with her, they would plunge into the mysteries of this raw and exotic city without a backward glance. She had no Charles, but she had all the courage Papa had taught her. Her spirits surged. "What is your name?"

"Edgar."

"And your price?"

"One dollar."

It was steep enough, but Jennie was oddly reassured; Edgar valued himself highly. "Very well," she decided, "but I can spare only two hours."

He grinned at her. His right front tooth was made of gold. "It will be enough," he promised.

She had expected the Chinese quarter to lie somewhere near the great shipping piers, and was surprised to discover it was in the beating heart of the city. Her immediate impression was of a throng of humanity, all utterly unlike herself, all dressed as they might have been in Shanghai or Peking. The narrow streets were crowded with men whose foreheads were shaved to their crowns, the rest of their hair gathered into trailing braids that reached the waist. The women wore heavy silk embroidered gowns that brushed the paving, and gripped children by the hand—tiny girls with elaborate gold headdresses shaped like pagodas, and boys with bald skulls and peaked caps of silk. Many of the men smoked long clay pipes. One, in pantaloons and a black vest, danced with a pair of swords, skittering backward along the street in front of Jennie and her guide.

Vendors were everywhere. Jennie had never entered an Eastern bazaar, but she imagined this must be what one was like: odorous from meat turning on open braziers, and dark from awnings overhead; bins and sacks of rice; smoked fish hanging by their tails; chests of tea and dried roots and vegetables she could not name. Edgar led her to three jade shops and she bought a pair of bangles for her wrist and carved seals for Winston and Jack.

He showed her glimpses of gambling houses where crosslegged men, young and old, clicked colorful ivory mahjong tiles, and opium dens where the dreaming and desiccated bodies of addicts lay fetuslike on bare wooden platforms. Part of her envied their escape—longed, even, for a similar peace and oblivion. She was spooked by the eyes of the den lords, which lingered on her insanely and covetously. When she backed away, Edgar's hand was at her elbow and a few coins passed between proprietor and guide.

Jennie drew in great gulps of fresh air once out on the street again and felt her dizziness pass, and then Edgar stopped short before an elaborate gate painted in red and black lacquer. "Joss house, madame."

This was a Chinese temple, she knew, named for the sticks of incense that the faithful burned in order to gain luck, or *joss*. The clouds of smoke when she passed through the gate were dense and overpowering; she pressed a handkerchief to her eyes.

"Here, lady." Edgar handed her a length of bamboo. "You are

in need of joss, yes? I see it in your face. You must light the stick and ask for your heart's desire."

"Do we go inside?" Jennie glanced about, blinking her streaming eyes; all around her, people were swaying and chanting, their faces turned to the temple's walls.

"No. The temple is for monks. You must light the stick and leave it here, lady. They will intercede for you."

Jennie did as she was told. The end of the bamboo flared like a firecracker, a pungent scent of sandalwood rising into her hair. What should she pray? *Let him die soon.* Surely to wish for another's death must violate the ritual?

She prayed for freedom instead.

The next morning was the first of October. They set sail for Yokohama on the *Empress of Japan.*

# CHAPTER FORTY-FOUR

Winston raised his pen from the fine sheet of linen notepaper, pilfered from the Dowager Duchess's writing desk and emblazoned with her address. He had brought a stack of it back to Sandhurst, meaning to write to his parents, but now the bouyant phrases and his breathless excitement had begun to falter. That was due, he suspected, to the fact that he was writing to Papa, who had ordered him not to address him as *Papa* any longer, because Winston was too old for childish affection and must only call him *Father*. In his haste to convey his extraordinary success to the man on the other side of the world he had probably bungled and addressed Lord Randolph as *Papa* again. Winston glanced back at his salutation, swore under his breath, and tore the Duchess's engraved sheet in two.

He had been explaining about the riding competition. The entire class of cadets had been put through their paces on a set course, urging their mounts over jumps without using stirrups or reins, their hands clasped behind their backs. It was a test of balance and strength and communion with a powerful and sometimes wayward animal that Winston found both nerve-wracking and exhilarating. Only ten cadets from the class of one hundred and twenty-seven had advanced to the field chase. Only four of those survived for the final test.

When it was done, Winston had earned one hundred and ninety-nine marks out of a possible two hundred, placing second. It was the greatest performance of his young life.

But as he stared at the blank page of his letter, Winston knew that Papa would not care. Lord Randolph would never know what it meant to leave one hundred and twenty-five men to eat one's dust. Lord Randolph despised the cavalry.

Winston's grades were good enough now at Sandhurst to be eligible for infantry, but he wanted desperately to join the Fourth Hussars, a light cavalry regiment commanded by an old friend of Lord Randolph's, Colonel Brabazon. Brab had seen action in the Afghan Wars and around the Red Sea ten years before, and he'd invited Winston to dine with the regiment several times at their billet in Aldershot. The officers wore blue and gold. The Fourth had campaigned for nearly two centuries. An air of discipline and affluence and superb power pervaded the mess. Winston lost his heart to the hussars. And his second-place performance in the exhibition—out of 127 cadets in his Sandhurst class—meant he could have his pick of regiments.

His father insisted on the Duke of Cambridge's Sixtieth Rifles.

He took up his pen again. Better not to reopen the debate about his future when all possibility of answer was on the other side of the world.

*Was it too much to hope that Papa would be pleased?*

The only acceptable place to buy horses was Tattersall's in Knightsbridge. On his bimonthly half day of leave, Winston took the train into town and made his way to the vast new auction ring presided over by the family's fifth generation. The first Tattersall had founded the business long ago on Hyde Park Corner, when that was the rural edge of London. All manner of horses came under the gavel at Tatt's: carriage horses, riding hacks, hunters, Thoroughbred racehorses, the entire contents of deceased noblemen's stables. And on days like this one, polo ponies.

Winston was passionate about polo. Sandhurst prohibited the sport on the grounds that it required cadets to buy a string of mounts in order to participate, and thus relegated the poorer subalterns to the sidelines, but Winston and his friends circumvented the rules by hiring hacks from a local livery stable and playing polo on Cobham Green, not far from the military academy. It was a sport he'd mastered with relatively little effort—he who had never been any good at cricket or the field races so vital to public-school boyhood. The bruising, high-speed game had something of the dash and thrust of fencing, the polo mallet taking the place of his foil and the pressure of his calves on the flanks of a horse controlling the speed of his advance and retreat.

It did not occur to him that his mother was an effortless rider, and Leonard Jerome a polo player long before him. Winston discovered everything in life as though he were the first man to exit Eden.

He would graduate from Sandhurst in less than two months, at the end of December. The Fourth Hussars were famous for their polo squad. He meant to join the regiment—and play for Colonel Brab.

London was bustling this last week in October. The Tower Bridge was newly completed, and just along the Embankment from Westminster Bridge, New Scotland Yard was rising like a refugee from the Loire Valley, a Château-on-the-Thames. He eyed a few of the young women seated nearby on his omnibus— the bustle had quite gone out, he noticed, and most wore neat skirts and blouses rather than carriage gowns. That would be the influence of the bicycle craze; he'd heard girls wore bloomers now beneath their skirts instead of petticoats, but he had no way of knowing whether this was true. Their hair was piled effusively on the top of the head, rather than coiled neatly at the neck, and their hats perched precariously on the downslope toward their foreheads. He would have liked to have had a jolly girl on his arm, and taken her to see Mrs. Patrick Campbell at St. James's Theatre, or perhaps Oscar Wilde's *Woman of No Importance* at the Haymarket—but he could not risk missing the last train and being absent from morning reveille. Besides, he knew no jolly girls. He had come to town for one purpose: to buy, on his father's credit, a pair of polo ponies. He meant to stable them at the livery near Sandhurst and school them throughout the winter once he had graduated.

Tattersall's sat on the southwest part of Knightsbridge Green, on the site of what had once been an old townhouse. There was a stone archway with iron gates, and side entrances for people on foot. These were flanked by a pair of functional, if unlovely, buildings in sulfurous brick that hid the rear of the premises from unprivileged eyes. The building on the left housed the off-site betting rooms run by the Jockey Club, with a gloriously tiled floor and a telegraph office to alert the cognoscenti of the results of races throughout the kingdom. The building on the right was reserved for Tattersall's managers and partners. In between the two was a granite walkway that led to the auction yard—an enormous court housed within a plain two-story building, roofed with iron girders and soaring patent glass. Superb modern stabling, with gas and water laid on, surrounded this enclosed ring—enough loose boxes to house over a hundred horses.

Winston accepted an auction billet and found a seat. One of Colonel Brabazon's junior officers had told him about this sale. A member of the Fourth Hussars had broken his neck on the field, and his widow was selling his string.

The ideal polo pony was of no particular breed, although many had Thoroughbred blood in them. Winston required an agile sprinter who could stop and turn quickly—but the sport demanded intelligence and heart as well. A young or untrained horse was difficult to assess from a walk round an auction ring. Bloodlines were helpful—a few breeders were beginning to produce horses specifically for polo—but Winston had no time to train a raw horse. He needed a mount previously owned and schooled by a crack polo player.

The first few lots were for riding hacks. Then carriage horses—a beautiful set of match grays. Winston allowed himself to dream of what sort of neat little conveyance he might purchase one day, when he was able to set up his own stables—although God alone knew when that would be. And then his attention was drawn by a figure raising his arm to bid on the pair.

There was something familiar about the set of the narrow shoulders and the elegant folds of the fellow's cravat. One of his father's friends—Mr. Trafford. Winston had dined with him a few years ago in Paris. It had been the week after Christmas, and Mummie had exiled him from home to bone up on French before his Sandhurst exams. Trafford had been very sporting and had taken Win to a cabaret.

When the gavel came down on the grays, Winston moved through the stands to join the older man. Papa would wish him to be civil.

"Sir—Mr. Trafford?" He extended his hand.

Tommie glanced toward him and Winston felt his stomach suddenly drop. The man was dreadfully changed—looked quite ill, in fact. His face was gaunt, the skin marked by obvious sores. His pupils were dilated. Beneath his carefully trimmed mustache, his lips trembled and his tongue moved restlessly. He stared at Winston without recognition.

"Who is it? What does he want?" he asked his companion querulously.

The man—an upper servant of some kind, Winston guessed, in a plain dark suit and bowler—glanced at him. "Your name, sir?"

"W-Winston Churchill," he stammered.

"Good Lord! Young Churchill! How are you, my boy?" The words emerged slightly slurred. *Not as bad as Papa's,* Winston thought, *but still . . .*

Tommie grasped his hand. "You're a young man now."

"Yes, sir. I am about to leave Sandhurst."

"Years since we met in Paris."

"Indeed. Have you returned to London permanently?"

"For as long as I have left," Tommie muttered. His gaze slid away from Winston's face. "Takes us all in the end. Your father, me, poor Harry . . . still, must have horses. Go about in style. What's the next lot, Simms?"

"Lord Fenton's chestnuts, sir."

"We missed the grays?"

"We did, sir."

"Don't like chestnuts as well."

"No, sir."

The manservant's eyes met Winston's. He shook his head almost imperceptibly—in apology or warning, Winston could not say.

"I shall tell my father we met," he said to Trafford.

"Yes, yes. Old man still kicking, what? Must call round and have a chat."

"My father is from home, sir. En route to Burma. My mother is with him."

"Took him out of the public eye, did she?" Trafford's expression changed. "Poor bugger. Poor old Randy. Those whom the gods love, and all that. It'll have us both in the end."

Winston sat through the bidding for the first polo pony as though carved from stone, his arm and his paddle fixed at his side. He could not concentrate on the auctioneer or his calls. When the horse had been sold, he rose from his place and left Tattersall's.

He hailed a jarvey and took a hansom to Harley Street. Robson Roose had his London consulting rooms there. He was without an appointment, but that could not be allowed to matter. Roose had saved his life when Winston was a boy. He had known all the Churchills for years. He would not refuse to see him now.

"I must speak to the doctor," he told Roose's nurse, "on a matter of the gravest importance."

Charles Kinsky slipped into his father's library and quietly closed the massive door. The strains of orchestral music filling the Viennese palace faded behind him. He had seen Archduke Franz Ferdinand safely bestowed on a respectable young countess—a girl named Sophie Chotek, who could do him no harm—for the latest waltz, and felt he was entitled to take a few moments to himself. If he was lucky, no one—not even Lise—would miss him.

The gas in the library's chandelier was turned low, but a fire burned in the grate. Charles ignored it and all the books set out on the large leather-topped tables and crossed slowly to the glass cabinet positioned to the left of the hearth. A sconce set into the wall shed enough glow to illumine the objects laid out on ink-blue velvet.

There was the gold chain and emblem of a sheep's skin that signified the Order of the Golden Fleece. A sword that had belonged to the Kinsky who had served King Wenceslaus centuries ago. A tiara from a long-dead princess. And a gold-trimmed enamel box with three white fangs, displayed on a bed of silk.

Charles opened the glass case and removed the wolf's teeth.

Impossible to know if they were truly twelfth-century, truly a relic of the house. But he carried them over to the firelight and crouched down. The flames flickered over his face and the elaborate dress uniform he wore; threw the shadow of his profile against the wall. He touched one of the fangs with his fingertip. What had he told Jennie all those years ago? *Kinsky men defend their own.* He would still tear the throat out of anyone who tried to hurt her, regardless of time or distance.

Behind him, the door opened with a slight sigh on its hinges. He glanced round and saw his mother. She was regal this evening in a ball gown of bronze silk with the new leg-of-mutton sleeves.

"Karl. I saw you leave the ballroom. Are you unwell?"

"Not at all." He replaced the teeth and set the enamel box back in its spot in the case. "I must congratulate you on an exceptional entertainment, Mamma—you have outdone yourself. So many beautiful young ladies! The Emperor can hardly reproach you if his heir fails to marry *this* Season, at least."

"Franz is in love with that little Countess," the princess said impatiently, "and she is entirely unacceptable."

"Countess Sophie?" Charles asked, surprised. "They make a charming couple."

His mother crossed the carpet to his side and cupped his cheek in her hand. "Poor darling. Charm is not the point. The Chotek is not a princess! Worse for Franz if he contracts a *mésalliance* than if he never marries at all."

"I see." Charles grasped her small hand in his and kissed the palm. "Let me escort you back to the ballroom, Mamma."

"You were looking at the wolf's teeth," she said, frowning.

"Yes."

"Does it hurt you so much?"

"Duty often does."

"Duty has its compensations," she suggested.

"So I'm told."

"Karl," she said impulsively, "please try to be happy. I cannot bear you to live in regret."

He smiled down at her. "But isn't that the human condition? Why should I be any different from the rest of the world? Come along, Mamma. We must dance together before I return to Brussels."

# CHAPTER FORTY-FIVE

She stood on the steamship's promenade deck not far from the stern, where she could watch the bearers. There were six of them, native Gurkhas. They seemed too slight for the thing they carried. The quay's surface was uneven and slick and the bearers wore no shoes. She waited for one of them to stumble, for the oblong casket to cartwheel obscenely to the ground. But the men came safely to a halt near the cargo hold.

Which meant that their burden was hers now.

Jennie turned and stared out over the ocean. Burma was at her back, the setting sun invisible behind a bank of cloud. She was moored in the midst of the Andaman Sea.

*The Andaman Sea.*

*Oh, where,* she thought, *are you floating, Camille?*

No answer came back from the waves.

Did Mr. Schermerhorn still live behind his drawn shades at Chepstow House, turning over the shells of creatures he would never see? Had he ever thought of her or Camille again, as he walked in the winter months along the granite-strewn shore? Matilda must have died long ago.

*I have tried to live for us both,* she told her little sister. *I tried to carry you forward, Camille.*

It was early November. Spring or fall? Naming the season this close to the equator was pointless, like so many of the habits she'd abandoned over the past four months. Simpler to say that the air was both hot and moist, the harbor a basin of steam. That it might be any day of the week. That she hated the way her silk dress, soiled from too much wear and impossible to really clean, stuck to her back like flypaper. She had been sitting below in the cabin with Randolph for hours, and when he fell asleep, she had ducked up the gangway for air. Only there was no air. Just mist as warm as a kiss on the nape of her neck.

*Keep him below if you possibly can,* Keith had warned. *The bearers might unsettle him.*

She should have followed her instincts and ignored the doctor's advice. Nothing infuriated Randolph more than being idle. She should have hired a native guide and a pair of mules and set out with him up into the tea plantations, where they could have clawed their way above the clouds and felt the cool sunlight. There might have been a breeze. He would have boarded the boat this evening tired and content. He might even have slept. Whereas . . .

Whereas provided so innocently with a knife by the steward who served them lunch, he had seized her arm as soon as the man disappeared through the cabin door.

*Snake,* he said, though he wasn't looking at the tattoo of a serpent coiled on her pale wrist. He could choke out words of one syllable quite clearly; more complicated thoughts died in his throat. She forced herself to hold his gaze, to meet the fury in his eyes and *not look down.* If she showed fear, if she tried to wrench her arm free, he would slice the blade across the tattoo and open her veins. She smiled at him instead and agreed.

*Snake.*

The knife trembled a little in his fingers; he could not control them anymore. *Bitch.*

*Bitch,* she agreed warmly.

*Cunt.*

*Slut.*

*Thief.*

*Whore.*

So much abuse in words of one syllable. A lullaby they crooned together. The rage gradually ebbed from his eyes. The steward returned with a pitcher of cold water and Randolph drank greedily, liquid dribbling through his beard. The rage was replaced with a look of sad confusion, and the knife slipped from his fingers to the floor. She stretched out her boot and caught it beneath her heel, her upper body deceptively still.

Just so had she flirted with Charles beneath a score of dining room tables. Her slippered toes skimming wickedly along his calf.

She must not think of Charles. Although he had haunted her, his voice curling between her thoughts, his face rising like a mirage on portholes and train windows. Charles prowled at her elbow, his touch ghostlike on her skin.

Should she have sued for divorce? Gone with him to Brussels? Alva Vanderbilt would not have hesitated.

*We can live anywhere in the world that Austria has an embassy. The United States, even.*

A few weeks before, just outside of Yokohama, Randolph had found a pistol and pressed the shaking barrel against her skull. She waited for the click of the trigger, and when it came, was astonished to find that the gun was unloaded. Randolph's right arm refused to function after that. Paralysis? Or mental reaction to a murderous impulse? Dr. Keith couldn't say.

Japan was at war with China and the harbor at Canton was mined. Jennie had insisted upon going ashore anyway, under cover of darkness and in sampans whose shallow draft would never trigger explosives. Randolph liked the night passage, the moon hanging low over the water. He was easy to manage at first. But when the beacon from a nearby fort sliced across the harbor, he catapulted from his seat and screamed. Shaking his fists at the enemy. She clutched his legs while the sampan rocked and the Chinese guides scolded and swore. She could not forget his silhouette; on bad nights, it came to her in dreams. Randolph falling overboard. A mine whistling. All of them going up in flames.

At least in Canton their scenes had been private. In Hong Kong they had an audience—every English expatriate who wandered through Government House. The Churchills left for Singapore after two days. Jennie trapped in a ship cabin and staterooms again, watching George Keith take notes as her husband's brain rotted.

*You cannot imagine anything more distracting and desperate,* she wrote to her sister Clarita, *than to see him as he is and to think of him as he was.*

Singapore was memorable for the snake tattoo. Keith was absorbed in his work and Randolph was quiet, so she had almost run down the gangway to stretch her legs alone on dry land. She had found the Malay with his ivory and steel knives, his ink intended to brand the skin, set up under an awning near the entrance to the docks, bent over the arm of a British sailor.

Bertie, the Prince of Wales, had a tattoo of five crosses on his forearm. So did his son George. Tattoos were talismans of courage and daring among the Marlborough House Set: a mark of unconventional thinking. Jennie watched the native artist, fascinated, her eyes flicking to the stoic face of the sailor. The man was whistling as his flesh was punctured. Could she bear it?

She took a walk around the town's principal streets, where there was great excitement—the Tenth Lincolnshire Regiment were engaged in some sort of football match and the whole English population was gathered near the pitch—but when she returned to the docks later, refreshed and clearheaded, the tattoo artist was free. He met her gaze unsmilingly as she walked by his tent. She stopped short. Was it an affront to such a man, for a woman to ask for his art?

Impulsively, she held out her left forearm. *Ours would be a left-handed marriage.* "How much?"

He shook his head. "The lady will swoon."

"I have borne two children. I will not swoon."

He hesitated, glanced beyond her as though searching for the man who must have her in his keeping. There was no one behind Jennie. The artist lifted his shoulders slightly.

"These do not wash off. You understand?"

"I understand." She seated herself on his leather stool. "I am embarked on a very long journey. Of the soul, as much as the body. There has been too much pain—*inside* of me, if you understand."

She pressed her fist against her heart; the man nodded his head.

"You wish to feel the pain now in your skin, and free your soul."

"Yes," Jennie replied, with a note of surprise. "A small and delicate drawing, perhaps—on the inside of my wrist." She exposed the pale flesh to his dark eyes. She might cover it, she thought, with a bracelet in moments when the symbol felt too revealing.

She rejected crosses and hearts, flowers and wings. He showed her drawings of snakes, in rings and figure eights, the serpents' mouths devouring their tails. She was both fascinated and repelled. Snakes signified sin, the seduction of the Temptress. The expulsion from the Garden. Did he see Eve in her face?

"Why these?" she asked.

"*Ouroboros,*" he said. "Rebirth, lady."

The idea startled her. A second life? A new journey. A future beyond Randolph's ending. Jennie thought suddenly of Camille, denied all futures. She would allow this man to cut the serpent into her skin. He would scar her with hope. Surely that was worth any price he might name.

She gave him her wrist, and a British pound sterling.

She suffered an alarming few days of infection, her arm red and swollen. The tools could never have been clean; Dr. Keith scolded her recklessness, and painted her skin with iodine and carbolic acid twice each day. But the snake subsided into peace near her palm, repellant and inviting. Her pact with the future.

Jennie looked at Randolph across the lunch table in the midst of the Andaman Sea that afternoon, his knife beneath her heel, and kept up a stream of soothing words. She talked of crocodiles. Rare Asian herons. Strange plants she had seen in her grueling walks through the hills above Hong Kong, and the bonsai trees she had bought in Yokohama. He never answered her but the sound of her voice was important. It beguiled him.

He grew absorbed in his treacle tart, small grunting noises rumbling in his throat. She felt in her dress pocket for her vial of morphine and slipped a dose into his coffee.

When he'd been snoring for at least ten minutes, she bent down and retrieved the knife pinned beneath her shoe. For an instant she studied his ravaged face, her fingertips trembling against the blade. It would take so little to end it all. She could say he had tried to kill her. And that in self-defense . . .

She almost ran through the cabin door.

And from the deck, she saw the bearers. Toiling barefoot with the lead-lined coffin on their backs, intended for her husband's body.

With all her strength, she flung the knife into the oily waters.

"Lady Randolph."

"Dr. Keith."

She turned from her position at the rail. The sun had nearly slipped below the horizon. It must be time to change for dinner. She had no appetite but it was always a relief to see the faces of the other passengers, to move freely among them with Keith at her side. He was at least ten years older than she and *not* one of her admirers, whatever the London gossips might whisper.

"How was he today?"

"Much the same. Listless. Then violent."

"Asleep, when I looked in," Keith said.

"The bearers came," she offered.

"I know. The purser gave me a receipt."

"Ought we to go home?" They had accomplished their object; they had seen Burma. Randolph had been in no condition to understand or appreciate the antiquities of Rangoon or the nature of the people he had forced into Her Majesty's Empire, but he had set foot in the country, at least.

"You miss your boys."

She nodded slightly. Her boys. All of them. *Charles*—

Keith drew a pair of envelopes from his breast pocket. "Then these should make you happy indeed. Our last mail, I'm afraid, until we reach Madras."

One letter was slim—nothing but a telegram. The other was thick and bore her son's hand. She would read it first.

Keith left her alone in the first cool breeze of evening. She tore the gummed flap with her fingernail and began to scan the regular lines. Win's careful handwriting, exuberant with all the small details of his life. A visit to Tattersall's. Polo ponies! A glimpse of Tommie Trafford . . . who had looked alarmingly unwell . . .

Jennie's breath caught raggedly in her throat. *Dear God. No!* She raised her eyes from the sheet of paper, which was trembling now in her hand, and stared wildly at the docks. They wavered before her like a scene glimpsed through a wet train window, half-perceived, unrecognizable. *Winston had gone to Robson Roose.* Randolph's doctor. He had demanded to know *exactly* what nervous complaint his father suffered from . . .

And Roose had told him everything.

Damn the man!

Pain slashed through Jennie's chest. She tasted bile in her throat. Winston had written this—the twenty-year-old boy with the pugnacious mouth, hunched over his desk at Sandhurst. He knew that syphilis could be inherited. And that would terrify him. The sheer precision of his script told Jennie how much fear he was suppressing.

She had kept Randolph's secrets for twenty years. She had never wanted anyone—certainly not his sons—to know the truth. And now Roose—

"The bloody, vicious fool," she muttered.

Her left hand was clenched tightly on the second letter Keith had given her—the telegram. She drew a shaky breath, her vision clearing slightly, and steadied herself. It must be from Roose. Begging her forgiveness for the appalling thing he had done.

But the telegram was from her sister Leonie.

CHARLES KINSKY ENGAGED TO BE MARRIED STOP COME
HOME MY DEAREST STOP HE CANNOT DO WITHOUT
YOU . . .

Jennie closed her eyes. They were hot and wet, suddenly—something to do with the Malaysian weather and the knife that might as well have been plunged in her gut.

He had given up on her. At the worst possible moment—

Hadn't she always known he would?

*He did only what you asked,* a voice protested in her mind. *Exactly as you ordered. You have no one else to blame.*

She crumpled the telegram and dropped it overboard, into the sea.

# CHAPTER FORTY-SIX

More letters awaited Jennie in Madras.

*The girl is twenty to Charles's thirty-six,* Leonie wrote, *and a countess. Her name is Elisabeth Wolff-Metternich zur Gracht, a cousin of the Empress Sisi. Charles told me all about it himself, while briefly in London a few days ago—I think he did not like us to learn the news from strangers. Naturally, she has never been introduced to London Society, and nobody seems to know much about her—but he showed me her miniature. She is blond, with severe features and rather sad eyes, I think. They are to be married in Westphalia, at the schloss belonging to her mother's family, the von Fürstenbergs, just after the New Year.*

*I cannot tell what Charles feels. He guards himself. Even from us.*

Jennie knew Charles in that mood: distant, unreachable, and apparently emotionless. As he had been that first night in Paris, when she had come looking for Randolph and pleaded for his help. And yet, he had helped her freely. Laid down his iron mask. Told her that his love was inviolable.

She tamped down on her anguish and, her fingers shaking, opened another letter.

Fourteen-year-old Jack, writing to Randolph from Harrow with words that his father could no longer read or understand.

*I suppose you have heard that Winston came second in the cavalry contest at Sandhurst. That seems to be important. I have not been happy for nearly six months, ever since you and Mummie left England.*

The next letter was for her. From Winston again, a more cheerful note than his last urging her to keep her spirits up and enjoy life. Jennie laughed out loud. How did he think she had gotten through twenty years of life with his father?

There was nothing from Charles. There would never again be anything from Charles.

She set aside her mail and drew a soft breath. Three-quarters of her soul wanted to cry out. The other quarter looked first for Randolph—and found him lying on his berth, staring insensibly at the cabin wall. Saliva trickled from the corner of his mouth.

Since Rangoon, all fight had gone out of him. He was listless, apathetic, unable now to utter even guttural syllables. He soiled his linen and, like an infant, had to be changed. He could not walk without a strong arm to support him; thank God for George Keith.

*Sinking,* Keith said when he looked at Randolph now, as though not just his patient but the entire ship and all its passengers were about to founder. Keith had sent a telegram to Robson Roose this morning with the latest health report from Madras. Jennie wondered what it said.

She settled herself at the small folding desk the cabin afforded, not far from Randy if he needed her. His eyes were half-closed. She took up her pen.

*I do not blame Charles,* she wrote in answer to Leonie. *I only blame myself for having been such a fool. . . . These four hard, miserable months I have thought incessantly of him and somehow it has kept me going. . . . Leonie, my darling, I am ashamed of myself at my age not to be able to bear a blow with more strength of character. I feel* absolutely mad, *it hurts me so.*

She paused and glanced once more at Randolph. His head had fallen forward on his chest and for an instant she wondered if he was dead. But then he snorted in his dreams and her watchfulness receded.

> *Even now, I cannot bring myself to think ill of him in any way. I know you don't like him—but I loved him. I don't think anyone half good enough for him. . . . He has deserted me in my hardest time, in my hour of need, and I want to forget him— though I wish him every joy and luck and happiness in this life.*
>   *Don't let us speak of it anymore.*

They had intended to stay at Madras's Government House, as usual, but when Jennie emerged from her cabin later that morning in search of Keith, he took her aside to the ship's saloon and sat down with her on a sofa. The only other person in the cabin was an elderly man engrossed in his newspaper. Keith kept his voice low regardless.

"I've heard back from Dr. Roose," he told her. "A telegram in response to my own of this morning."

"And?"

"He agrees with my conclusion—Lord Randolph is in no condition to enjoy these travels; indeed, they may be hastening his deterioration. We are united in the belief that the trip ought to be curtailed, and that our party should start for home immediately."

"Thank God," Jennie breathed. They had intended to tour the entire Subcontinent over the next month—and she could not imagine how Randolph was to be managed on land, with perpetual train and carriage journeys, and endless, painful parades through the lobbies of hotels. "If we are to end it, let's do so quickly."

"That means a train from here to Bombay," Keith said, "and from there, a ship through the Gulf of Aden to the Red Sea. We can reach Port Said through the Suez Canal, enter the Mediterranean, and be in Marseille by the middle of next month."

Jennie nodded. For an instant she felt dizzy, as though all the blood had rushed from her head. *She would be home for Christmas.* "Which of the details must I manage first?"

"That is already done, my lady. I have booked a first-class compartment for each of us, as well as servants' accommodation, on tomorrow's Bombay train. I shall wire ahead to the port there this afternoon and secure passage on a suitable ship. That is enough to be going on with; we may settle our forward plans out of Egypt later." He hesitated. "I would recommend that we carry the lead-lined coffin with us."

Impulsively, Jennie reached for the doctor's hand and clasped it between her own. "You are very good," she whispered.

"It has been a trying time, my lady," he said soothingly. "Why don't you see what you can of Madras this afternoon?"

She gathered her portable easel and watercolors, and took a cab from the piers to Fort St. George. This was the old heart of Britain in Madras—and still housed most of the region's colonial government. From her seat on the fortress walls, Jennie could shade her eyes against the sun and look south to an area known as the Island, set between two rivers, and beyond, the white bulk of Government House's airy verandas. To the east was the rolling stretch of the Bay of Bengal. She gazed out over the port and the water, and made a stab with her brush at ships' funnels and masts.

She ought to have captured the native Tamil dress or the outline of the fort's soldiers in charcoal. Something of the local architecture. The fierce Subcontinental light. A few lighthearted scenes to send back to Winston, so that her son would know she was looking *on the bright side of things*. There had been a time when she had longed to see India. Now all she thought of was home.

Under her fingers, an elusive face took shape. The blade of a nose, two intent blue eyes beneath quirked black brows. Jennie touched the sensitive mouth with her fingertips, her throat tightening. She would leave the shirt collar open, as she loved it best.

———

*Oh, Leonie, darling, do you think it is* too late *to stop it?* she wrote to her sister, before the last call for mail from her ship in Bombay. *Nothing is impossible, you know. . . . For Heaven sake write to him. I am frightened of the future all alone—and Charles is the only person on earth that I could start life afresh with.*

A whistle blasted; the first note signaling visitors to go ashore. She had so little time. *If I have lost him—I am indeed paid out for my treatment of him. . . . Leonie, darling, use all your cleverness and all your strength and urge him to put off this marriage. If only I am given the chance—I will redeem all the past. . . .*

They reached London, at last, on Christmas Eve.

Randolph was carried to shore on a stretcher. Keith walked beside it, his fingers on Randolph's pulse.

On the seventh of January, at Schloss Herdringen in Arnsberg, Charles Kinsky was married.

# CHAPTER FORTY-SEVEN

"Have you got your horses?"

Winston stirred, his eyelids flickering open. He had dropped off without realizing it, the result of the heat from the coal fire and nervous exhaustion. The room was stuffy and dimly lit, the draperies closed against the light reflecting off the January snow. He was sitting by his father's bed in Duchess Fanny's Grosvenor Square house. It was his turn to watch; Mamma was resting. She spent most nights with Papa, although there had been little change in his condition since the New Year—stupor alternated with the most horrifying pain. Only large doses of morphine helped. When drugged, Papa slept for a few hours. When awake, he moaned.

It had been weeks since his father had been able to articulate words. And yet Winston had heard his voice. *Have you got your horses?* He must have been dreaming.

He leaned closer to the bed. A sour odor rose from Papa's skin, which was covered in sores. A gleam of light seeped from between his eyelids, however; he seemed to be turned toward Winston. He could not take Papa's hand—the joints were swollen, deformed, too painful to be touched. He said clearly, "Yes, sir. Three chargers and two polo ponies."

He had returned to Tattersall's after his graduation from Sandhurst, where he had ranked eighth among one hundred and fifty subalterns, the greatest success of his young life. He would not be posted to a regiment for another three months, but Winston was determined it would be the Fourth Hussars. Once Roose had opened his files and explained about the syphilis—once Roose had admitted Papa was dying—he'd known there was no point in waiting for a decision about his future. It was only his to make.

His father grunted. It might have been the word *Good*. His head shifted slightly on the pillow. His eyes closed.

The bedroom door opened, and Duchess Fanny came in. Her face looked dreadful, racked and pale with apprehension. She had no idea why her son was dying, only that there was nothing she could do to stop it. Winston had been sworn to secrecy about the syphilis. He thought it was awfully sporting of his mother to keep Papa's secrets when Duchess Fanny so clearly blamed her for letting him down. "Had you been a more careful helpmeet . . ." was one of the ways she began her conversations with Mummie, and ". . . if only all the world, at home and abroad, had not turned against him" was generally how such conversations ended. Duchess Fanny already wore mourning. Winston assumed she would never wear anything else again.

"Leave us," she ordered him. "Find something to eat."

Number 50 Grosvenor Square, although an unimpeachable Mayfair address, was not a large house. Like so many London places, it was tall and narrow, with a redbrick Georgian front and a single room to either side of its door. The ground floor held the hall and a sort of saloon where guests might wait; the principal rooms for entertaining were on the second floor; three bedrooms were on the third; and the maids slept in the attics. The basement was entirely given over to kitchen, butler's pantry, servants' hall, and offices. A separate building at the rear housed the laundry and two stalls for Duchess Fanny's pair of horses. It was vastly different from the life she had known at Blenheim.

Winston was not staying in the house. There was no room. His father had one bedchamber, his grandmother another, and Jennie the third. He was sleeping at Margot Asquith's girlhood home— her father, Sir Charles, still owned No. 40 Grosvenor Square—but spending most of his time at the Duchess's. He was no stranger to her kitchen, and as it was now several minutes past eleven o'clock in the morning and any formal meal was long since over, he went down the back staircase. Unlike his grandmother, Cook had a soft spot for Master Winnie.

Awareness of the death watch playing out in Grosvenor Square mounted gradually in the public consciousness. Newspapers posted medical bulletins on Lord Randolph Churchill's health. Newsboys hawked headlines on London streets and pasted the doctors' latest statements on sandwich boards, which they walked up and down railway platforms, crying out *Dandy Randy Sinking!* Strangers traded rumors on the top decks of omnibuses and as they waited in queues. In Commons, each day began with a prayer for Lord Randolph's health.

*Even his mother wishes now that he had died the other day,* Jennie wrote to her sister Leonie late one afternoon as she lay on the chaise longue by the embers of her bedroom fire. Outside, the snow had begun to fall again and darkness was absolute, although it was only four o'clock in the afternoon. She could catch the rush of hansom wheels on the wet streets around the square. *Up to now the General Public and even Society does not know the real truth, and after all my sacrifice and the misery of these six months, it would be hard if it got out. It would do incalculable harm to his political reputation and memory and be a dreadful thing for all of us.*

Jennie had been the subject of whispers for much of her life. But she could not bear Jack and Winston to be ridiculed or shunned or even pitied—to their faces, or behind their backs. She wanted an end to Randolph's pain. And peace and silence on his death for the rest of their lives.

She touched the snake encircling her left wrist. In the candlelight, it seemed as though the serpent's eyes flickered. A threat? Or a promise? She could not decide.

———

"Master Winston! Master Winston!"

He jerked instantly out of sleep, one arm throwing back the covers. His batman's face loomed over him, a candle held in one hand; the rest of the room was dark. The fire had gone out.

"What is it?"

"Your father, sir. You're summoned to the Duchess's."

He pulled on his clothes and dragged a comb through his hair. A queer sensation was rising in the pit of his stomach, like a rubber bladder filling with air. It might burst at any moment and leave him in pieces. He breathed in short gasps, aware that his heart was racing.

It was a few minutes after five in the morning. The streetlamps still glowed; the square itself was empty and filled with new snow. He cut across the park, his boots skittering in the drifts, his glove-less hands chill in the predawn darkness. Ever since he'd had pneumonia, it hurt his lungs to breathe freezing air. He felt the stab now and thought of his father struggling for breath. *Let me be in time.* Lights burned in nearly every window of his grandmother's house.

The door knocker had been removed to keep the noise from disturbing Papa. Winston rapped dully on the oak instead. It opened almost immediately. They had been watching for him.

He pelted up the stairs. A woman was weeping quietly—a desperate, hopeless sound. That would be the Duchess. Behind and on top of her sobs wove the thread of stertorous breathing.

*The death rattle,* he thought.

A faint glow seeped from his father's open doorway.

Winston slowed. Stopped short on the edge of *then* and *now.*

"Win."

His mother. She had risen from her chair and come out into the hall. Her black hair was unbound to her waist and she had not changed her dress in two days. Exhaustion made the brilliance of her eyes otherworldly.

"He's unconscious," she whispered as she took Winston's hand. "It's a matter of hours, Keith says."

Winston nodded. He could not speak, but at least he had not cried.

She led him into Papa's room. There was no third chair. He leaned against the wall near the head of his father's bed and stared down at him.

He was still standing there at eight o'clock in the morning, when Randolph died.

# CHAPTER FORTY-EIGHT

The funeral was a state affair in Westminster Abbey, as Randolph had once predicted. Arthur Balfour and George Curzon and Hartington and Lord Rosebery filed into the church in ceremonial robes. Joseph Chamberlain and his sons, Austen and Neville, came. Soldiers attended the coffin to Paddington Station, where Walden, Randolph's valet, followed it mournfully down the platform. The entire Churchill family—Jack from Harrow and Randolph's sisters with their husbands and children, Leonie and her sons, even Jennie's sister Clarita—filled the first-class compartments of the Woodstock train. They did not bury Randolph in the vaults beneath Blenheim's chapel with his father and brother, but in the eleventh-century churchyard of Bladon St. Martin in Woodstock. He had always preferred the open air.

Jennie and Winston were the last to leave the grave. It was such a dreary day, and wet; everything the color of stone.

"I dreamed of friendship," Winston said suddenly, "that never came. Of earning his love, Mummie—and even more, his *respect*. I thought one day I would enter Parliament at his side."

Her heart ached. How brutal for a boy to grow up longing for his father's approval. Yearning for love he never felt. If Leonard Jerome had not cherished Jennie—made certain she knew that her father's belief in her was as solid as the granite shore of Newport—would she have endured and survived so much?

"I didn't know," she attempted. "That you wanted a life in politics. I thought the Army . . . your Fourth Hussars . . ."

"There is no other life worth having," Win said simply. "The cavalry is just a means to an end—a way to make a name for myself. As I must, now Papa is gone."

She studied his profile. Grief and something worse—despair—nipped at his heels like a black dog. "My darling. I understand how you feel. I don't think I have ever spoken to you of my sister Camille?"

His sandy eyebrows furled; his eyes were still fixed on the bleak earth. "Camille?"

"She died when I was a child."

"I never heard that name."

"She was two years younger, my particular little sister. The person I loved most in the world when I was nine."

He looked at her then. "Why have you never told me?"

"Guilt." Jennie's smile wavered. "Because I lived. We were both sick, you see—only I proved stronger. I survived when Camille did not. I would have gone gladly into the grave in her place, Win. But your grandfather told me something then that I ought to tell you now. *Live twice as hard. For the ones who are denied life.* Don't apologize to the world for the days you've been given. *Use* them."

Winston stared at her. "I'm not sure I understand, Mummie. I can't *become* Papa."

"I wouldn't want you to, my darling. You're your own person, and better for it. But you might try, Win, for the things Papa valued—if they truly matter to you as much. Your father set his heart on high office—then threw it away after six months. He was brilliant, Win, but fragile. Too rash and heedless . . . and yes, *weak*. He was driven by ambitions he could never fulfill."

"He was a great man."

"He *might* have been," Jennie replied ruthlessly. "You *could* be. You're tougher than you know. Why not *do* what your Papa only attempted? Fulfill his dreams—as well as your own?"

Winston nodded slowly, considering her words. "Yes. I must at least try. Fight on, for both our sakes. Raise up the fallen standard from the field . . ."

A battle metaphor. It was all he understood at twenty, with his military education, but it was preferable, Jennie thought, to despair. "You know I'll help you all I can."

His fierce gaze returned to the dark mud at their feet. "Tell me something else, Mummie."

"Anything."

"Do you carry his sickness?"

Her heart turned over a second time. He was braced for the worst of all possible news.

"No, my dearest. And neither do you."

He heaved a shuddering sigh. Unable or unwilling, Jennie knew, to ask how she could be so sure.

She pulled Win close. The last time, perhaps, that she would hold him while he cried.

On Wednesday, six days after Randolph's death, Jennie walked Bonaparte along the northern side of Grosvenor Square. She had returned to Duchess Fanny's house with no intention of remaining long; when her body and mind had fully recovered from the terrible strain of the last few months, she would make plans for the future. Winston had gone to stay with friends in the country. Jennie had spent most of the previous day with Randolph's solicitors— his estate was entangled in debts. Almost all of the principal and the remainder of his gold shares would have to be sold to meet them. But she would have the furniture and household goods left in storage while she lived with the Duchess, two thousand pounds a year from the Jerome trust, and five hundred from Randolph. Surely enough for a small house of her own?

Bonaparte barked ecstatically and leapt forward on his leash, jerking her mind from its thoughts. She glanced up and saw Charles Kinsky.

He was standing stock-still in the middle of the paving, staring at her. Bonaparte dragged Jennie forward and rose up on his hind legs to paw Charles's knees. Charles fondled the dog's head, his eyes still fixed on her face. "Steady, old chap."

"Down," Jennie said mechanically, and snapped the leash. "Hello, Charles."

"I saw the news in the Brussels papers—about Randolph."

"Yes," she said. A cold wind buffeted her cheek; she could not stand out on the street for long. It would draw too much comment from the Duchess's neighbors.

"I came as soon as I knew." He reached out, his gloved hand grasping her elbow in the way she loved best. Intimate, protective. Bonaparte danced at their feet.

"Whatever for?"

His eyes widened. "To tell you I was wrong. To beg you to take me back."

"Charles—"

"Six months ago, you talked of *duty*. Jennie, your duty is dead and buried in the ground."

"What about yours? You're married, aren't you?"

He smiled grimly. "Yes. God help me."

She began to walk toward No. 50. "I had hoped you would be happy."

"Without you?"

"You've managed without me before. I did not force your wife upon you, Charles."

"No. I have myself to thank for that piece of blind stupidity." He strode after her. "Leonie wrote to me. She told me all you felt. I know I hurt you deeply, Jennie—I know I drove you to despair— but, oh, my darling, I'm well served for whatever pain I've caused."

She stopped short. "Yes. *You are.* I asked you to wait—"

"I wanted to punish you. I wanted you to feel pain—as I did— when you toyed with Wolverton, and shut me out, and left on your insane voyage. I wanted you to *burn with regret*. But some nights I actually envy Randolph. Death is preferable to living without you."

All his love was written on his face. When he reached out and grasped her shoulders, she could not stop herself—she had wanted him too long. She stepped as though stunned into his arms. She did not care that anyone might see them. *My love, my love, I have wanted you so. . . .*

"Come away with me, Jennie."

She lifted her head. "Where?"

"Paris—New York . . . Constantinople, perhaps. The Archduke Franz will give me any posting I ask."

Again, the cold wind bit her cheek.

"And what of your Countess?"

"I'll have the marriage annulled. Lise will go back to her family. They'll take care of her."

Jennie went still. Then she pushed herself free. "I thought Kinsky men guarded their own."

"They do. I do. *You're* my own, Jennie."

"Is Elisabeth in love with you?"

His lips parted slightly; he did not answer.

"Of course she is," Jennie rasped. Her eyes stung suddenly with unshed tears. "How could she not be? *Her knight of the Holy Roman Empire.* If you leave, Charles, she'll never recover from the blow. She's only a raw girl. I know all about it, you see—because something similar happened to me at her age. *I married a man with secrets.* I learned the truth about him too late."

"Jennie—"

"But to my great good fortune," she persisted, "that man stayed. My marriage would never be the fairy tale I imagined on my wedding day. As you know better than anyone. But I claimed my place in Society and the world. Randolph gave me my *freedom,* Charles, to live as I chose, on my own terms. A life of some purpose." She paused. "That's what it means to guard your own."

Charles drew a ragged breath. Wordless. Stricken.

Jennie gathered Bonaparte's leash in hands that were trembling. Then she rose on tiptoe and kissed Charles deeply, searchingly, on the mouth. Heedless, now, of Duchess Fanny's neighbors.

"I need you like some people need drink or opium," she whispered. "It will cost me dear to cut you out of my life. *But I will wean myself free of you,* Charles. Go back to your Countess."

She had one other visitor late that afternoon, when the lamps were coming on around Grosvenor Square and her bedroom was filled with darkness. She had been sitting alone near the fire without any other light, staring at nothing. She had not wept. There had been too much weeping. But her eyes glittered as sharp and brilliant as cut glass in the dusk.

When Gentry knocked softly on her door, Jennie forced herself to move.

"My lady," her maid said. "A gentleman's come from Government. He wants to see you. Not knowing who he was, I left him in the ground-floor anteroom."

"Did he send up a card?" Jennie asked.

Gentry offered it. *Mr. Malcolm Grey,* it said. *Treasury.*

Jennie smoothed her hair and went down to him.

"Lady Randolph," the man said as she entered the anteroom—it was cold from the air off the street, and no fire had been lit; Mr. Grey still wore his overcoat, although he removed his bowler at her appearance. He was a slight man of possibly thirty, with longish blond hair slicked back from his brow. A pointed chin and small bright eyes that reminded her of a ferret's. One of the new men in Government.

"My sincerest condolences on the loss of your husband."

"Thank you."

Jennie waited for him to explain himself.

"In view of the fact that his lordship can no longer take part in any future Conservative Cabinet, I have been sent to take charge of his official robes."

"His *what?*"

"His robes of office. The ones he wore as Chancellor of the Exchequer."

"Nearly ten years ago?" Jennie struggled to remember. Randolph had been Exchequer so briefly and carelessly that it was hard to conceive anyone cared about his robes or what had become of them. They were black, she knew, like an academic gown, and excessively trimmed with gold brocade that lent a Rembrandt-like opulence. Randy had been lost in their huge folds, but magnificence suited his ducal blood.

"You want them back?" she said, bewildered.

"I am under express orders to request their return, ma'am."

Jennie considered. Then she lifted her chin. "No."

"I beg your pardon?"

"Absolutely not."

"But, Lady Randolph, you can have no possible use for the robes—"

"That is where you're wrong, Mr. Grey." She was thinking not of Randolph now, but of Winston, standing at his father's grave. The brooding purpose on his young face.

"I am saving them for my son."

# AFTERWORD

Charles Kinsky's wife, Elisabeth, died childless in 1909. In 1914, when world war broke out after the assassination of Archduke Franz Ferdinand and his unsuitable morganatic wife, Sophie Chotek, Charles refused to take up arms against England. Recalled to Austria, he kept his London flat in Clarges Street and asked to be deployed against the Russian Empire, on the Eastern Front. He fought there for four years.

In 1915, Jennie encountered Kinsky's butler in London. *Tell him you've seen me,* she said. *Tell him I'm well.* A few accounts of Charles—now Prince Kinsky—came through the lines. How he was set upon by a group of Russians while on horseback alone and routed them all; how he'd been found by a young relative sitting in camp with a British racing form in his hands, talking parliamentary politics. With Austria's defeat, however, Charles's world came to an end. The Austrian Empire was dissolved; his estates and his titles were confiscated or abolished. He died in 1919.

Years earlier, on the occasion of Jennie's second marriage, Charles had sent her a card bordered in black. It consisted of only three words in French: *Toujours en deuil.*

Always in mourning.

# ACKNOWLEDGMENTS

Jennie Jerome Spencer-Churchill was the focus of speculation, adoration, and rabid public interest throughout her life. Her treatment at the hands of some historians after her death merely extended the controversy about her character and worth. Depicted most often as a sparkly afterthought to her extraordinary son, pilloried as a bad mother and a wanton lightweight, Jennie has always figured in my imagination as a profoundly modern woman who lived and died by her own choices, without regrets—a century before that was either forgivable or commonplace.

*That Churchill Woman* is obviously a work of fiction. My storytelling drew from a wealth of biography, autobiography, cultural studies, and personal letters that give Jennie her lifeblood. "But what's *true,* and what did you *make up?*" readers will inevitably ask. And so I offer a note on sources. It is a partial one, a taste of what might be read if the reader is motivated.

The collected letters of Jennie and Randolph, to each other and among various family members, including sons Winston and Jack, are held in the Churchill Archives Centre at Churchill College, Cambridge. (Only a few notes between Jennie and Charles Kinsky survive.) The digital Churchill Archives can be accessed by subscription, and the libraries of many academic institutions hold such subscriptions, which are, by extension, also available to their affiliates. Lord Randolph Churchill's parliamentary speeches are similarly digitized and available online in the archives of *Hansard,* the official parliamentary debate recorder, catalogued by session and date. In some cases, I have edited selections from letters or speeches for the sake of concision. A list of the original letters cited follows these acknowledgments.

Jennie wrote a glancing autobiography—*The Reminiscences of Lady Randolph Churchill* (New York: Century, 1908)—which is notable for its reticence, its gaps, and its blatant fiction. It is also notable, however, for the profound ease and charm of Jennie's voice, which betrays the fluency she had with words, as with so much else—paint, music, people. The literary style of her son Winston is often more didactic, but in at least one of his autobiographical works—*My Early Life: 1874–1904* (New York: Charles Scribner's Sons, 1930)—he sounds like Jennie's doppelgänger. This account of his childhood and school days through Sandhurst is riddled with telling detail, wildly varying emotions, and humor. Winston also wrote the ponderous and encyclopedic two-volume biography of his father, *Lord Randolph Churchill* (London: Macmillan, 1907), although Randolph's friend Archie Primrose—the former prime minister and Fifth Earl of Rosebery—wrote a far less encyclopedic one with an identical title (London: Harper & Brothers, 1906). More recently, Robert Rhodes James offered his assessment, also titled *Lord Randolph Churchill* (London: Weidenfeld and Nicolson, 1995). These biographies focus on the parliamentary and political career and only nod occasionally at the personal life. (Randolph Churchill is long overdue for a completely revisionist look.) The Churchill-authored memoirs offer quotations and family anecdotes that I have embroidered freely.

Jennie's biographers include Ralph G. Martin, whose two-volume work titled *Jennie: The Life of Lady Randolph Churchill* (Englewood Cliffs, N.J.: Prentice-Hall, 1969) remains the seminal work. Martin was able to interview Prince Clary, Charles Kinsky's nephew, for personal reminiscences and family knowledge of his relationship with Jennie. It is also Ralph Martin who recounts Jennie's receipt of Charles's card, from the Austro-Hungarian embassy in St. Petersburg on the occasion of her second marriage, that said only *"Toujours en deuil."* (*Jennie: The Dramatic Years, 1895–1921,* by Ralph G. Martin, Prentice-Hall, 1971, p. 252). Elisabeth Kehoe offered a group picture of the Jerome women in her collective biography of Jennie and her two surviving sisters, *Fortune's Daughters* (London: Atlantic Books, 2004), and more recently, Anne Sebba gave Lady Randolph a fresh look in *American Jennie* (New York: W. W. Norton, 2007). Both Kehoe and Sebba benefited from access to the Tarka King Papers, a family archive of documents held by Jennie's great-great-nephew, including her letters to her sisters. Those documents were also referenced by Anita Leslie, Leonie Jerome Leslie's granddaughter, for her book *Lady Randolph Churchill: The Story of Jennie Jerome* (New York: Charles Scribner's Sons, 1969) and by Peregrine Churchill, Jennie's grandson, for his biography, *Jennie: A Portrait with Letters,* cowritten with Julian Mitchell (New York: St. Martin's Press, 1974). I have cited these secondary sources for my selections from letters Jennie wrote to Leonie concerning Charles Kinsky's engagement in 1894.

Winston Churchill has too many biographers to list, but the fundamental place to start on his life—if not with his own voluminous autobiographical accounts—is William Manchester's *The Last Lion,* particularly *Volume I: Visions of Glory, 1874–1932* (Boston: Little, Brown, 1983). Roy Jenkins's *Churchill* (London: Macmillan, 2001) is also indispensable. But I drew as much pleasure from the slim little volume titled *Painting as a Pastime* (London: Unicorn Press, 2013), in which Winston relates the joy he found in confronting a blank canvas. His mother would have understood. Candice Millard's *Hero of the Empire: The Boer War, a Daring Escape, and the Making of Winston Churchill* (New York: Doubleday, 2016) is a marvelous portrait of Winston-the-Late-Victorian, unleashed on an unwitting empire and living to tell the tale.

Jane Ridley's *The Heir Apparent: A Life of Edward VII, the Playboy Prince* (New York: Random House, 2013) gives us Bertie and Alix in the round; *The Autobiography of Margot Asquith* delivers

Miss Tennant's first meeting with Jennie in No. 2 Connaught Place (Boston: Houghton Mifflin, 1963); and Daphne Fielding's *The Duchess of Jermyn Street* (London: Eyre and Spottiswoode, 1964) describes the life of Jennie Churchill's famous cook, Rosa Lewis. Background on Minnie Stevens Paget and Consuelo Yznaga can be found in *The Transatlantic Marriage Bureau,* by Julie Ferry (London: Aurum Press, 2017). Minnie is invariably referred to as "Lady Arthur Paget," a courtesy title she received after her husband's knighthood in 1906, but during the period addressed in this novel she was simply "Mrs." Marian Fowler's *Blenheim: Biography of a Palace,* details the history of the Marlborough ducal seat through generations (London: Viking Press, 1989).

Greg King's *A Season of Splendor: The Court of Mrs. Astor in Gilded Age New York* (Hoboken: John Wiley & Sons, 2009) is a scintillating portrait of that world. Eric Homberger's *Mrs. Astor's New York: Money and Social Power in a Gilded Age* (New Haven: Yale University Press, 2002) traces the rise of celebrity among the wealthy in the post–Civil War world. Amanda Mackenzie Stuart's *Consuelo and Alva Vanderbilt* offers some detail about the childhood Jennie and her dancing-class partners shared (New York: HarperCollins, 2005). The Preservation Society of Newport County is a gold mine of information about the Gilded Age; the seaside "cottages" its members so lovingly preserve, including Chepstow, built by Edmund Schermerhorn, should be visited by anyone with an interest in this heady epoch in American life. The house the Jeromes inhabited during the summers before their departure for France in 1867, however, is impossible to identify.

One of the best portraits of this period in British history and its principal actors remains Barbara Tuchman's *The Proud Tower* (London: Macmillan, 1966).

In recent years, some have questioned the nature of Lord Randolph's decades-long infection and diagnosis of syphilis, which by varying accounts he contracted and treated when he was an undergraduate at Merton College or later. The alternative, posthumous, and purely speculative diagnosis of brain cancer is offered. I suspect this is a quelling impulse, from those who find it repugnant and unthinkable that Winston Churchill's father should have suffered what they regard as a shameful disease. Syphilis was, however, one of the most virulent and commonplace afflictions known to man before the discovery of antibiotics. Being the son of a duke and the father of a prime minister was inadequate protection against its effects. I am content to note that Randolph's doctors told him he had syphilis; that they told his wife he had syphilis; that they eventually revealed to his son Winston that his father had syphilis; and that Randolph was treated with mercury for the disease. In his final year, his doctors regarded him as suffering from General Paralysis of the Insane—the final stage of advanced syphilis. These judgments and decisions determined the nature of his care and his death; they certainly determined the fierce family secrecy regarding his illness during his lifetime. For those interested in the subject, I would suggest *The Cruel Madness of Love: Sex, Syphilis and Psychiatry in Scotland, 1880–1930,* by Gayle Davis (Wellcome Series in the History of Medicine, Amsterdam: Editions Rodopi, 2008), which details the medical assessment and treatment of those institutionalized for the disease.

These are some of the works I found most useful in attempting to understand the Jeromes and the Churchills, the Gilded Age and the Edwardians, the Marlborough House Set and the Irish Question. I invite readers to suggest cherished sources and comment of their own on my Facebook page: https://www.facebook.com/Stephanie-Barron.

No one has offered more support, inspiration, or encouragement during the nearly four years I spent on this novel than Kate Miciak, Vice President and Editorial Director of Ballantine Bantam Dell. At various points when most editors would either have passed on the book or accepted a manuscript that was just good enough, Kate urged me to dig deeper to find the heart of Jennie's story. It is the greatest privilege I know to work with her; she challenges me to improve my craft every time I sit down to write.

Kelly Chian, Director, Production Editorial, Random House Publishing Group, deserves sainthood for enduring my process.

My thanks go to others at Ballantine as well: unflappable editorial assistants Alyssa Matesic and Jesse Shuman, who answered each of my tedious queries correctly and with lightning speed; copy editor Deborah Dwyer, who sifted the entire manuscript for errors, inconsistencies, and outright bloopers with a thoroughness that saved me considerable embarrassment; publicist Allyson Lord, who heralded Jennie better than I could have myself. My sincere delight and surprise at the beauty of the cover image is due to Laura Klynstra. I love your vision, and your fund of patience with visually challenged authors.

I am one of the few writers I know who has been lucky enough to be represented by one extraordinary literary agent (and dear friend) for my entire career. Without the hard work and canny insights of Rafe Sagalyn, I would long since have been lost. Madeira James and Jen Forbus of xuni.com are the visionaries behind my website; they have my sincere thanks.

And finally—to Mark, Sam, and Steve, who endured endless snippets of Churchill trivia for too many hours to count—all my love. You guys rock.

# LETTERS CITED

The author would like to thank the Churchill Archives Centre, Churchill College, Cambridge, England, and Bloomsbury Publishing, administrator of subscriptions to churchillarchive.com, for access to the digital archives.

Page 35: Letter from Leonard Jerome to Jennie Jerome, discussing her engagement, dated August 8, 1873. http://www .churchillarchive.com/churchill-archive/explore/page?id= CHAR+28%2F1%2F25–26. Accessed 8/1/2018.

Page 59: Letter from Lord Randolph Churchill (Blenheim Palace) to Jennie Jerome, later Lady Randolph Churchill, dated February 4, 1874, in which he discusses his victory in the Woodstock, Oxfordshire, election. http://www.churchillarchive.com/ churchill-archive/explore/page?id=CHAR+28%2F4%2F22–24. Accessed 8/1/2018.

Page 115: Letter from Dr. Robson Roose to Lord Randolph Churchill, dated March 14, 1886, detailing "the approach of the crisis." http://www.churchillarchive.com/churchill-archive/ explore/page?id=CHAR+28%2F47%2F1. Accessed 8/20/2018.

Page 125: Telegram from Dr. Robson Roose to Lord Randolph Churchill, dated March 15, 1886, "The high temperature indicating exhaustion, I applied stimulants . . ." http://www

.churchillarchive.com/churchill-archive/explore/
page?id=CHAR+28%2F47%2F2. Accessed 8/20/2018.

Page 148: *The New York Times,* Saturday, July 4, 1863, p.1. "The
Great Battles." https://www.nytimes.com/1863/07/04/archives/
the-great-battles-our-special-telegrams-from-the-battle-field
-to-10.html. Accessed 8/3/2018.

Page 166: Letter from Dr. Robson Roose to Lord Randolph
Churchill, dated March 15, 1886, informing him that "we are still
fighting the battle for your Boy." http://www.churchillarchive
.com/churchill-archive/explore/page?id=CHAR+28%2F47%2F3.
Accessed 8/1/2018.

Page 168: Letter from Dr. Robson Roose to Lord Randolph
Churchill, dated March 15, 1886, in which he says that they have
had "a very anxious night," http://www.churchillarchive.com/
churchill-archive/explore/page?id=CHAR+28%2F47%2F5.
Accessed 8/1/2018.

Page 182: Letter from Lord Randolph Churchill to Lady Randolph Churchill from Jordal, Norway, dated July 10, 1886
including a description of his journey, his and "Tommy"
(W. H. Trafford's) success at fishing. http://www
.churchillarchive.com/churchill-archive/explore/page?id=
CHAR+28%2F7%2F77–79. Accessed 8/1/2018.

Page 182: Letter from Lord Randolph Churchill Norway to Lady
Randolph Churchill from Jordal, Norway, dated July 13, 1886,
noting that a Cabinet-level salary would be welcome. http://
www.churchillarchive.com/churchill-archive/explore/
page?id=CHAR+28%2F7%2F80–81. Accessed 8/1/2018.

Page 208: Letter from Lord Randolph Churchill to Lady Randolph Churchill describing his disgust at being pursued by
newspaper reporters in Vienna, dated October 12, 1886. http://

www.churchillarchive.com/churchill-archive/explore/
page?id=CHAR+28%2F7%2F85–86. Accessed 8/1/2018.

Page 210: The *Town Topics* entry is cited by Ralph Martin in
*Jennie: The Life of Lady Randolph Churchill, Volume I,* p. 299.

Page 308: Letter from Lord Randolph Churchill, Kissingen, to
Winston Spencer-Churchill, dated August 9, 1893, on Winston's
disappointing performance in the Sandhurst entrance examination and failure to pass well enough to join an infantry regiment.
http://www.churchillarchive.com/churchill-archive/explore/
page?id=CHAR+1%2F2%2F66–68. Accessed 8/1/2018.

Page 355: Letter dated November 18, 1894, from Lady Randolph
Churchill to her sister Clarita Jerome Frewen, cited by great-
niece Anita Leslie in *Lady Randolph Churchill: The Story of Jennie
Jerome,* p. 199.

Pages 361–362: Letter from Lady Randolph Churchill to her sister Leonie Jerome Leslie, dated October 31, 1894, cited by grandson Peregrine Churchill and Julian Mitchell in *Jennie: Lady
Randolph Churchill: A Portrait in Letters,* p. 167.

Page 364: Letter from Lady Randolph Churchill to her sister Leonie Jerome Leslie, dated December 1894, cited by grandson Peregrine Churchill and Julian Mitchell in *Jennie: Lady Randolph
Churchill: A Portrait in Letters,* p. 168.

Page 367: Letter from Lady Randolph Churchill to her sister
Leonie Jerome Leslie, dated January 3, 1895, cited by great-niece
Anita Leslie in *Lady Randolph Churchill: The Story of Jennie
Jerome,* p. 201.

## About the Author

STEPHANIE BARRON is a graduate of Princeton and Stanford, where she was an Andrew W. Mellon Foundation Fellow in the Humanities. She is the author of the stand-alone historical suspense novels *A Flaw in the Blood* and *The White Garden,* as well as the critically acclaimed and nationally bestselling Jane Austen Mystery series. A former intelligence analyst for the CIA, Stephanie—who also writes under the name Francine Mathews—drew on her experience in the field of espionage for such novels as *Jack 1939,* which *The New Yorker* described as "the most deliciously high-concept thriller imaginable." She lives and works in Denver, Colorado.

stephaniebarron.com
Twitter: @SBarronAuthor
Find Stephanie Barron on Facebook and Instagram

## About the Type

This book was set in Granjon, a modern recutting of a typeface produced under the direction of George W. Jones (1860–1942), who based Granjon's design upon the letterforms of Claude Garamond (1480–1561). The name was given to the typeface as a tribute to the typographic designer Robert Granjon (1513–89).